Bridie Jabour is a writer who has worked as a journalist for News Corp, Fairfax and Guardian Australia. *The Way Things Should Be* is her first novel.

The Way Things Should Be

BRIDIE JABOUR

echo

echo

A division of Bonnier Publishing Australia
534 Church Street, Richmond
Victoria Australia 3121
www.echopublishing.com.au

First published 2018

Printed in Australia at Griffin Press.
Only wood grown from sustainable regrowth forests is used in the manufacture of paper found in this book.

Cover design by Alissa Dinallo
Cover image: illucesco/Shuttershock
Page design and typesetting by Shaun Jury
Typeset in Adobe Caslon

A catalogue entry for this book is available from the National Library of Australia
ISBN: 9781760681807 (paperback)
ISBN: 9781760681814 (ebook)
ISBN: 9781760681821 (mobi)

@bonnierpubau
@bonnierpublishingau
@bonnierpublishingau

For poor Matt

CHAPTER 1

Winston was like every other home town in our collective history in that it was incredibly dull but had the power to both enchant and provoke regression in its former inhabitants. It was the beginning of spring so it was a particularly dangerous time to return – the bitumen was warm enough to give off the smell of your childhood when the rain hit and every flower seemed to be in technicolour.

If that was not enough to give a 28-year-old woman whiplash from the nostalgia, Claudia Carter had returned that September to get married. Despite being the perfectly average age to do such a perfectly average thing, Claudia was feeling radical. The idea of marriage still seemed so foreign to her that it was almost subversive.

This was just one of the many ridiculous things that crossed her mind as she sat on a kitchen island in her mother's house, listening to her mother cataloguing her younger sister's flaws.

'And you know, out of all of you, Poppy was the one I

breastfed the longest,' Rachel told Claudia, 'so it's bullshit that it fosters a bond.' Rachel stabbed viciously at the sausages browning in the pan in front of her as she spoke. Rachel subscribed to the idea that cooking dinner was some form of martyrdom.

Rachel's list of grievances was familiar. Her youngest daughter Poppy did not phone her 'Mother'. Poppy never said sorry. Poppy expected everyone to do the things she wanted to do, go to the places she wanted to go for dinner. Poppy always said exactly what she thought. ('That skirt is ugly. Why don't you cut your hair? Your best friend is a monster.')

The truth being that Poppy was – in fact – just like her mother.

At the core of Rachel's gripes, although she would be insulted if it was ever actually suggested to her, was that Poppy did not ask permission to do anything, and even though they were all adults, her children were all expected to ask permission. Claudia did a good job of pretending to ask permission. Poppy, on the other hand, never bothered pretending anything.

'How long did you breastfeed her for?' Claudia asked abruptly.

Her mother looked at her blankly. 'What? Oh, eighteen months.'

Claudia snorted. 'So she could say words and you were still putting your tit in her mouth?' She knew it was somehow wrong to be grossed out, probably something to do with the patriarchy, but it was too juicy. So she filed it away for further mocking at a later date with a more receptive audience.

Poppy was due to arrive tomorrow; their brother was already here, upstairs, avoiding all women, and Claudia's best friend Nora would arrive in just a few days. Claudia worried that this would be the spark to quickly engulf the bone-dry kindling of the family dynamics. Everything a woman feels for her sister –

protectiveness, envy, passion, competition – is magnified twenty-fold when her best friend is around.

And the longer they all hung around Winston the more they would all regress. There would be screaming at each other. Last time they'd met up, Claudia had screamed at Poppy, telling her that (at twenty-five) she had fucked her life up and destroyed Mum and Dad. So Poppy had thrown a wine glass that had shattered all over Claudia's chest. The next morning Poppy had got up and left and they had not spoken since.

And now Claudia was getting married in a week.

Last to arrive would be lovely Dylan, a crucial element for the marriage. His presence would help diffuse any tension between the siblings. That was the kind of man he was: soothing, reassuringly sane.

Claudia was perched at a solid oak island, so close to the gas stove she could reach out and grab her mother if she wanted. The island was too big for the space, of course – it always had been – but Rachel had fallen in love with it, and when she fell in love with something, her steely determination to make it work could only be worn down over painful decades. The kitchen was old but all the utensils were brand new, bought on a glossy-magazine-abetted rampage. She had not bothered to replace the stove, although it was entirely possible it was older than her. But her knives, toaster and kettle all matched and all gleamed.

Claudia had spent her late teenage years living in the house, an inheritance from Rachel's mother, but today she was not comfortable here. Why wasn't she comfortable here? When had this town stopped being her home?

'I thought you would be more excited.' Rachel glanced across the kitchen island and eyed Claudia, who kept her head down. She was fiddling with her ring.

'I am!' Claudia responded brightly.

'Your dress is beautiful. You're going to look beautiful, don't worry about that,' her mother said. 'And you look very slim, you've always been so slim,' Rachel continued, admiringly.

'Yes, well,' Claudia said, picking at her ring again, before looking up and smiling sweetly back at her mum. 'I've always had such motivation.'

Her mother let the comment blow past her: a piece of interloping dust, never to be thought of again. Rachel had endured a lifetime of commentary from her own mother about her weight, who had endured a lifetime of commentary from *her* mother. You might as well feel guilty about the sky being blue if you were going to feel guilty about teaching a girl her size mattered.

Despite being in her sixties, Rachel remained a very attractive woman. She was the only mother at the high school gates who had not conceded her femininity by cutting her hair short; she wore her silver-streaked hair carefully styled with three blow-dries a week. Sometimes, just looking at her mother's figure made Claudia want to sit down, contemplating the sheer amount of effort that went into maintaining it. The daily cycling, the aqua-aerobics classes, the pacing around the house with weights strapped to her ankles, the measuring out of portions. Rachel was the kind of thin that required an immense amount of time and effort; daily self-denials that ensured she remained under sixty kilograms when over sixty years of age. On top of all of that Rachel was just pretty – radiant, even. This hadn't quite been passed on to any of her daughters, who had been polluted by their father's genes, their eyes slightly too far apart and mouths too narrow. Even with youth on their side they did not feel they had a patch on their mother, something they had each made an uneasy peace with towards the end of their teenage years.

Rachel shifted from one bare and pedicured foot to the other. 'I'm still not sure about the bridesmaid dresses you know,' she said.

Claudia exhaled; she had not wanted a bridal party but her mother had called her sobbing about the prospect of her sisters being left out of the wedding. 'It will look so odd if you are standing at the front of the church with nobody around you,' she had wailed down the phone, so Claudia had acquiesced, just as she had by agreeing to a church venue – she had wanted a garden wedding – and to holding it in Winston. She and Dylan had originally wanted to marry in a coastal village halfway between the towns in which they'd grown up.

'If I'm going to have bridesmaids, I definitely do not want to go the full matchy-matchy,' Claudia told her mother firmly.

'Well, just in case you change your mind, I popped down to the dress shop and put a dress like Poppy's on hold in Zoe's size as well. I think when you see them standing next to each other at the dress shop you will see how funny it looks if they are in different dresses to each other.'

'You really shouldn't have done that.' Claudia emphasised the 'shouldn't'. 'I'm not worried about how their dresses are going to look.'

'Well, what are you worried about then?' her mother asked her.

'What do you mean?'

'If you're not worried about how the dresses are going to look, why are you so agitated?'

'I'm not agitated. I'm just sitting here.'

'Well, since you're not agitated and you're not doing anything useful, can you finish these sausages?'

Claudia took the tongs from her mother and watched her walk to the bathroom for what she knew would be the precise length of time it took for dinner to be finished. Rachel might have seen the martyrdom potential in cooking dinner, but that did not mitigate the tediousness of the task.

Claudia started turning the sausages with her left hand so

she could see her glinting engagement ring, picked out and paid for by her at an antique fair, almost on a whim, when she was feeling particularly dreary about her job and prospects. It had been so long since she had felt excitement in her life, but the most drastic thing she could think of was getting engaged. She didn't even bother to hint to Dylan about what she wanted, she just gave the box to him and told him to produce it at a nice time in the next month. Dylan, who was always happy as long as Claudia was happy, obliged a few weeks later.

She did not know why she wore an engagement ring.

She tried to turn over how she felt about the marriage in her mind, as she had done so many times before in her own kitchen, her friends' kitchens (even on one occasion her boss's kitchen), in the shower almost every morning and anytime she was in a supermarket, a task so mundane it regularly sent her into a meditative state. When she had bought the engagement ring she had not really thought much past what time of the day she would announce it on Instagram for maximum likes. Claudia might have thought she and Dylan would just be engaged forever, or even that it was a bit of a joke, or that she would just feel more excited. But it had turned out that she didn't really think she would get married, and she had felt like a spectator through the past year. She loved Dylan, but when she wore the ring she felt like a traitor. Then she felt indulgent for feeling like a traitor. She had never actively wanted to get married. When she was a teenager she'd revelled in brazenly describing it as an 'empty constitution' after once mishearing a teacher who had been asked about its place as a traditional institution.

Claudia had always been the one for whom events just happened: always in the right place at the right time – a geospatial and temporal nook that never required more than a minimum expenditure of effort. She had fallen into a well-paid job for a boutique bank when she was nineteen, she had earned her degree in Economics while hardly showing up for class, and had been promoted almost as soon as the Dean-signed document was in her hands. She had met Dylan and had a blissed-out few years and now she was getting married, having barely made a decision along the way.

And now here she was in her mother's simultaneously posh and decrepit kitchen, dreading the arrival of her sisters and wondering if the next decade of her life was going to look exactly like it did now.

'Hi sweetie, hi doll-face, hi SNOOKUMS.'

Her brother Phinn was doing a pitch-perfect impersonation of their aunt Mary. The aunt who always hugged the girls a little too long and liked to look them up and down while telling them they were looking healthy. Phinn leaned over and bear-hugged Claudia, lifting her off her feet, as if to underline the point.

Once back on earth, she handed the tongs to him. 'Finish these.'

He took them good-naturedly.

'Settling in well? Ready for all your dumb girl craic?' he said cheerfully.

'What exactly do you think is so painfully girlish about this week? Both of us are getting married you know.'

'Yeah yeah, I'm sure the focus on Dylan in all of this has been entirely equal; nobody has made more of a big deal about it for you, I'm sure,' he said, mildly sarcastic.

'If you mock me I will cut myself,' said Claudia, reverting to a joke born years before in the disinfected halls of the local hospital, when she'd been having a particularly tough time. Their oldest sister Zoe had swept into town whispering to Phinn that she'd had great difficulty choosing a wardrobe that said 'concerned but effortlessly elegant sister'. That night she had refused to give Claudia the remote control and, without missing a beat, Claudia delivered the po-faced threat about cutting herself. After a moment of leaden silence, the trio collapsed into laughter. Since then it had become a running joke.

Phinn chose not to react this time and looked over the top of Claudia's head. 'Have you heard the latest?' he said, all the while looking at the doorway for interlopers.

'You finally got laid this year?'

'No. Well, not that, none of your business.'

'You know what you want to do with your life?'

'Unfortunately for you, no.'

'God has called you. You weren't in.'

'No … Seriously … Old mate is back at it again.'

Phinn did not need to explain any further. The recent reconciliation between their father and his girlfriend, Lisa, had always been fragile to say the least.

'This is none of our business,' Claudia finally said.

Phinn gave a grunt of assent. 'But you know who is making it their business.'

Claudia groaned. 'Rachel.'

'Yep, none other than our esteemed mother, and who else?'

Claudia stared at the ceiling, stretching out her arms so she could do a full body groan. 'Poppy.' She hadn't needed to guess; she'd known straight away which of her sisters it would be.

'Award yourself a PhD in Juvenile Behaviour and Failure to Thrive as an Adult and call yourself Doctor Carter because you just scored 100 per cent in the "could our family behave more idiotically?" exam!'

Phinn turned the stove off and moved the pan of slightly too-crisp sausages to the side.

'What are the briefing notes?' Claudia asked.

'Apparently shit-for-brain's car has been seen outside some local footy player's house – and may I put in an aside here, does this woman have any imagination? And Mum thought it wise to let Poppy know, so now Poppy's apparently preparing for the warpath upon arrival.'

'Hmmmm, that's odd. They're meant to be on the same team. Mum was gleefully going through Poppy's shortcomings earlier. She was even referring to me as the "good one".'

Phinn scowled. 'There's more.'

Claudia braced herself with a tight smile.

'Poppy is already here,' Phinn told her.

Claudia propped herself up on her elbows. 'What do you mean? Where?'

'She arrived this afternoon and has set up camp at Dad's house so they can have their crucial favourite parent–favourite child time while we pay our dues here.'

'I knew this was going to be a disaster. Why did I agree to this whole shitfight?'

'Hardly a shitfight, dear,' he responded, grinning. 'I would say this whole situation is utterly fucking predictable.'

Phinn leaned against the doorframe, allowing his shoulders to fill the space in the way of someone who is sizeable enough to have thrown down a few people in his time but not so big that he invariably becomes the target of every dickhead with eight schooners under their belt at any given time. You never want to be the first, the best or the biggest. It's too much pressure.

He was comfortable in his skin. This was partly because of his medium size, which precluded him from having to prove too much in the schoolyard, and partly because of his three sisters. When your youth is spent playing the fourth Spice Girl, you shed anything resembling self-consciousness fairly quickly.

He thought about the week stretching in front of him and immediately felt weary. Not that it would ever show. He kept the same measured disposition whatever the turn of events. He could be relied upon never to lose his temper, but what swam beneath the surface, what was really going on under his dark eyes was never quite understood by the women around him. And there were a lot of women around him.

He gave his mother a kiss as she squeezed past him, and he lazily picked up the knives and forks before he was told. He was already exhausted but at least tonight was just his sister and his mother. Claudia would not fight with Rachel and Rachel knew better than to pick on her. Her excitement at having two children at home at the same time would be enough to make a pleasant evening. It would be another day or even two before Rachel would be driven mad by towels left in the wrong place and yoghurt tubs with missing lids in the fridge.

Phinn had laid down the third plate on the table next to the kitchen when his mother crossly peeked over his shoulder. 'Where's Mary's plate?' Phinn did not sigh. He rarely revealed his exasperation to his mother.

Claudia was not so circumspect. 'I thought it was just us.'

'Your aunt wants to see you – she might be coming around.' Rachel's tone stopped any complaining from Claudia. The ingredients for a successful evening were in place but it still turned on Rachel's whims.

'Well, these sausages are going cold and I have the salad so let's eat.'

The three sat down in the formation that had existed for almost thirty years. Rachel at the head of the table, Claudia at her left, with her brother sitting across from her. If the other two had been there they would have sat in the next seats down, the oldest, Zoe, next to Phinn, and Poppy next to Claudia. Phinn reflected on an article he had seen on how the Queen fed her waiting corgis by seniority, but, as always, thought better of mentioning it.

Rachel bowed her head for a quick prayer, more out of habit than any real devotion, and the three soon were enjoying an easy banter. The camaraderie was built upon an unofficial truce between mother and daughter, enacted years before when they had both decided to stop fighting one another. They had never discussed the reasons, but Rachel assumed that Claudia might have realised that her mother was actually not the most idiotic person she had ever met, and perhaps her mistakes were just as forgivable as anyone else's.

Tonight, unusually, Rachel privately indulged in what was for her a very risky thought: life was easier with just two children. Claudia and Phinn would not fight, almost could not fight. They were not rude to her; they didn't roll their eyes when they thought she wasn't looking. Sometimes she thought they actually liked her. Back when they were all hers, a bunch of still-random cells sitting in the bottom of her belly, causing her breasts and stomach to swell, Rachel had wondered a lot of things. She had wondered if they would be a boy or a girl, if they would have dark hair and light eyes, if they would be smart, if they would make friends easily. But it had never occurred to her that they might not like her. She had never wondered if they would like her. And she missed the bliss of being so naïve.

'Why didn't Dylan come home with you?' Rachel finally asked her daughter.

'Well, I thought it would be nice to hang around without him.'

'You thought it would be nice to hang around without your fiancé?'

Claudia snorted. 'Mum, it's fine to not want to be with someone all the time, to be your own self. You have to keep a bit of yourself for yourself.'

'Why?' Rachel seemed genuinely puzzled. She was one of eight children, she had married young, she'd had four children.

Being a family member had always been full-time work for her; it was an alien concept to be by herself for any extended period of time, let alone to actively seek out seclusion.

'It's good for you. You can't be defined by your partner, you lose yourself a bit. You've always got to be able to survive by yourself.'

'Claudia Carter, are you already setting yourself up for divorce?'

Claudia started laughing. She knew her mother was not angry, but sometimes she could not believe how oblivious she was.

'Don't you think you learned that lesson?' asked Claudia. 'Don't you wish you'd held on to yourself a bit more?'

Rachel thought for a moment. 'I never felt like I lost myself. Certainly in the beginning I would've liked to have been with my husband in the week leading up to the wedding.'

Phinn sniffed. 'Claudia's problem is she wants to be adored and she wants to be left alone: it's profoundly inconsistent.'

Claudia had only a split second to decide whether she should take offence, but found herself laughing instead. 'He'll be here in a few days and you can all calm your farm.'

The tranquillity of the evening was shattered by the sound of the door swinging open. Claudia knew who it was from the rhythm of the footsteps. Poppy appeared in front of them, leaning across Rachel to take the rest of her sausage from her plate and waving hello with her mouth full.

She wore R.M. Williams boots and torn stockings potentially made specifically to annoy Rachel. She was taller than the rest of the women in her family, and wore her dirty-brown chin-length hair brushed out of any real shape. Despite her cowlick she had a fringe and the overall effect was a bush framing a face that always seemed to be tinged pink. Her eyes widened as she stopped chewing, momentarily enjoying the suspense.

'Hello fellow fuckheads!'

'Hello,' Phinn responded, deadpan, but Rachel was already standing up to hug her and deliver the habitual lecture.

'Why do you talk like that? You didn't learn it here.'

Claudia didn't say anything. If there was an upper hand to keep it was importantly maintained by refusing to give her younger sister anything to react to. But then she noticed her bright pink socks dotted with teddy bears.

'Are those my socks?' she asked as Poppy grinned at her over their mother's shoulder.

Rachel's house was old but solid and had been subjected to more than one harebrained renovation. Spread over three storeys, it had rooms that led into other rooms which led into bathrooms which led into dead ends, and there were odd built-in cupboards all over the place, with knobs too high and hidden doors. The siblings had given up on any notion of having their own rooms years before, and now on trips home they slept in whichever room they came across that was still free, sometimes still forced into beds together when Rachel was too enthusiastic with her guest list.

Claudia dragged her feet up one stair at a time, the slow steps a way of bracing herself. Earlier she had staked out a room for her visit, but now when she opened the sliding door she was confronted with Poppy, sprawled across the bed, her boots still on each foot as she lay on top of the doona flipping through Claudia's diary.

Claudia snatched it from her hands, but not with enough righteous vigour: after all, she was well aware that Poppy read the dog-eared notebook she used as a diary every time she saw her.

'You know, if someone read your diary without knowing you, they would think you were single, did not have a brother and completely hated your sisters. It's borderline obsessive about Zoe and me in there.'

'The only thing I care more about than myself and the only thing I hate enough to write about is you two; it is a classic Rachel move to go straight for this you know,' Claudia said, putting the diary back at the bottom of her now empty duffel bag, its other contents spread across the floor following Poppy's arrival.

'Some interesting stuff in there about your wedding.'

'Yeah.'

'Do you have a cigarette?'

'Yeah.'

The sisters changed into bed socks and Claudia stuffed two cigarettes into her bra before they crept downstairs in tandem. Poppy peeked around the corner. 'Clear, Mum's watching *The X Factor*,' she whispered out of the side of her mouth.

In coordinated movements honed over many years in another house when they were much smaller, they silently crept past the living-room doorway and didn't speak again until they had unlatched the back door, closed it behind them and were standing beside the two wheelie bins in the part of the garden that was hidden from sight of either the kitchen or verandah.

Claudia lit each cigarette in her mouth and handed one to her little sister.

'We are the last twenty-somethings in the world still smoking.'

'We are also the last twenty-somethings in the world still scared of our mother.'

'We're not scared of her, we respect her! I've told you!'

Claudia smirked.

'So what's wrong with you?' Poppy finally asked, breathing a steady column of smoke in the general direction of a frangipani tree.

Claudia shrugged. 'I don't know if I want to get married.'

Poppy shuddered with the visible effort of keeping her laughter silent. 'And this is the week you've finally thought you can do something about it?'

'I can't quite put my finger on it. I love Dylan. Well, I am pretty sure I do. But is this it? What if I broke up with him and met a minor royal, some cousin of Wills and Harry, and he was my next boyfriend?'

'Well, you couldn't marry him either.'

'Catholics are allowed to marry into the royal family now,' Claudia told her sister.

'But back to your actual country town wedding, where, at the very least, there will still be a very nice picture of the Queen near the pokies of the pub everyone goes to afterwards.'

'Hmmmmmm. Yes. Classic first-world problem here. I love Dylan. Sometimes I adore him. I like my job. I like feeling powerful.'

'You're not powerful – your boss runs the bank, not you.'

'Thanks for the reminder. I like all of this. Nineteen-year-old Claudia would look at this life and just be fucking ecstatic. I pulled it off, I really did. I shook off the dirt of where I came from, I made a life for myself where this town doesn't matter, our parents do not matter, even you don't matter. I fell in love, and it was all going well until I decided to get married.'

'What? Why?'

'I have become such a magnificent class traitor I can now dwell on this lovely life and really indulge in the superfluous question of whether I am happy. It's triggered a really weird mind-frame for me. Or maybe my crisis triggered my decision to marry Dylan. I keep wondering if this is it; if this is the right path for me or if I am giving up other opportunities, places to travel, even maybe a better relationship. It's like the clichéd Aesop's fable about the dog, who is running off with a stolen bone, who stops and sees his reflection. I have a great, juicy bone – say, marry Dylan – but then what? Is there another bone? So I take the bone that is marrying Dylan and miss out on the bone that is a dream job somewhere because now I have to consider someone else. In the fable, believing that the dog in the reflection has a better bone, he opens his mouth to bark at it and the dumb dog loses his own bone and is left with nothing. The story's moral in Olde English is that "the one who all coveteth, oft he loses all".'

'You mean like in the Devo song?'

'What? "Whip It"? Isn't that about leaving out cream?'

'No, no. "Freedom of Choice",' Poppy started humming. 'You know, about the dog finding two bones in ancient Rome and dropping dead after going in circles between the two.'

Claudia stubbed out her cigarette and turned to creep back into the house. 'So freedom of choice means I drop dead?' she whispered over her shoulder.

Poppy smirked and thrust her hips aggressively. 'Maybe. Or just maybe you're the one who needs a bone.'

CHAPTER 2

Poppy stirred and squinted to find the morning light was hitting her directly in the eyes, at an odd and blinding angle. 'Shit motherfucker bastard,' she muttered. Instead of the old sarongs she usually arranged as a sad ode to curtains she was confronted with lace and blinds. Where was she?

She realised as she turned over. Her mother's house. In her old bedroom. With another body next to her.

She studied her sleeping sister. Her Claudia. She was lying on her side, breathing shallowly, so close that Poppy had copped a mouthful of her cropped hair when she'd rolled over. Claudia murmured and rolled onto her back and Poppy noticed with satisfaction her eyes were smudged with liner she hadn't bothered to wash off last night. So Zoe, their oldest sister, had not completely infiltrated Claudia. Zoe swore by a skincare regime that was complex, rigorous and seemingly 80 per cent unnecessary, and which she was forever trying to foist upon her sisters. She double-cleansed at night, before applying a serum then a night cream, or maybe a night cream and then a serum, Poppy did not quite know or care. Zoe double-cleansed rain, hail or the temporary inner shine caused by sixteen vodkas, and Claudia, when she was on one of her self-improvement kicks would take what Zoe said as gospel before discarding it within a few weeks or months from boredom.

She was joined to their older sister by some invisible, pulsing cord, and when not resisting her, she would try to impress her.

Poppy dug her phone out of the sheets. She physically braced herself and opened her email app.

> Dear Ms Carter,
> Thank you for your interest in interning at the *Mail*. We regret to inform you our program is full for the year but encourage you to gain some experience writing for us and apply again next year.

> Dear Ms Carter,
> We have reached the capacity for this year's intern program at LOTL but thank you for your enthusiasm in the interview. Feel free to send us pitches; in addition to the intern program, we are willing to take three articles a month for the exposure they provide participants.

> Dear Ms Carter,
> We are pleased to offer you a four-week placement in our September intern program of forty-two hours a week at Them Apples.

Poppy lay back in the bed and practised her conscious breathing exercises. She focused on her breath and tried to quieten all around her. Namely, her thumping chest caused by the email and her thumping head courtesy of the night before.

Forty-two hours a week in September. That was the middle of her university semester. She needed to work at least sixteen hours a week at the chain store to make sure she made her $500 a fortnight rent for her room in a six-person share house, and then more hours in one of the mid-market restaurants in the city to buy some groceries. Could she do fifty-eight hours a week and her minimum contact hours? She felt her head slipping beneath the waves. She had been paddling so furiously, paddling so hard for so long, and where had she reached in the seven years since school?

She had a bachelor's degree and was earning $3 more an hour than she had when she was nineteen years old and scanning groceries at the checkout. She was slightly comforted that none of her high-school mates was doing much better than her. Everyone had a shitty job. Some people had a nice husband, some people had a kid. Nobody was a raging success yet. Not so for her first-year university mates. Her market socialist mates – who got nine hours' sleep a night in a bed they did not have to pay for – raged against the privileged at parties filled with Downtown Boys' first album *Full Communism*, never once seeming to notice how rich they were.

Their parents' houses were in the same city as the university.

They only needed spending money.

They didn't need rent money, they didn't need food money, they barely needed transport money. After all, what parental monster would charge their twenty-one year old for their childhood bedroom?

Those freed up from fretting over their bank accounts used the time to cultivate the connections their parents established through friends of friends on the fringes of the industry. That's all you needed.

Poppy allowed herself a moment to reflect on what she was eternally fending off, and let the thought wash over her: Am I going to fail?

When was the time to pack it in and come home? When was the time to accept not everything you had in life was something that you earned, that pretty much none of it was earned, no matter how much or how little work you did, or what your university marks were or how many times you had been published? No matter how much you tried. Poppy longed to be one of the mass oblivious; she longed to be born on third base but still convinced she had hit that home run.

She visually tried to move what she carried around on her chest to her shoulders, to shift it, to make her constant dread wearable for the day. Was she going to work as a typist her entire life; how was she going to pay the rent when she was fifty; where was she going to live when she was too old to work; who was going to look after her parents when they completed their rapid descent into old age; how was her mother going to afford to live; could she die and not be discovered for days? Would Poppy eventually get the phone call that her mother had lain alone quietly for four days? Or worse, had been screaming with nobody to hear her?

Was Poppy going to meet somebody? Did she even want a girlfriend? What if the woman she met was the same as her? What if they both struggled along in crappy jobs and at the end of twenty years had $1300 in savings and a credit card to show for it? Would it be worse if her girlfriend were more successful? Did they want to struggle together, or could she handle being supported? Of course she could handle being supported; she could be pious about it, though: pretend she was conflicted about someone else paying the bills while she wrote but really she wouldn't give a shit. Did some of her family still think she was a freak? Should she listen to Zoe? Now she was getting into ridiculous territory. Of course she shouldn't listen to Zoe.

Poppy steeled herself for kitchen combat and swung her legs out of bed. She wasn't going to spend this week freaking out; she wasn't going to think beyond the next hour for a week, then she could go back to the constant low-level hum of anxiety as the soundtrack to her life.

Downstairs in the kitchen, to her immense relief, she found no sign of her mother. Just her brother rinsing plates at the kitchen sink.

'Mornin'' she said.

'Eat a dick.'

Despite herself, Poppy laughed.

'And what the shit is this?' he continued. 'A man doing the dishes?'

Poppy rolled her eyes and picked up a banana from the counter.

'What are the plans for today?' asked Poppy. 'Is She Who Must Be riding into town?'

Phinn raised an eyebrow.

'Our lovely sister, held in high esteem by many, not just by me her humble sidekick, does indeed arrive today, and you know nobody is going to deduct cool points or Marxist points or whatever points you value on this day of the week if you are nice to her.'

'I'm always nice to her,' Poppy assured her brother. 'I've never been not nice to her,' she went on more adamantly. 'Why would I not be nice to her when there is a ridiculously priced wardrobe and an endless stream of advice on how to better myself without me even having to ask?'

Phinn sighed deeply. 'Just be nice. Or, how about this, be nice to Mum – just be nice to one of them.' He turned to face his sister. 'Zoe's flying here so I'm going to pick her up after lunch, if you can bear it.'

'There was room on the train yesterday,' Poppy replied cheerfully. 'But that wouldn't befit the duchess's image and nine and a half hours rolling through the country with patchy reception may offer too many opportunities for self-reflection.'

'Eat a dick.'

Claudia tried to feign anger but instead let out a giggle that she almost choked on.

'Speaking of self-reflection, how have you found Claudia? She seems, what's the word, pensive? Slightly neurotic? Completely allergic to the idea of getting married in five days?'

Before Poppy could reply there was an almighty crash in the exhibition room.

While their mother referred to it as the dining room, her children gave it its more grandiose moniker due to it being fitted out with what could be best described as an homage to their mother's bloodline: every piece of giant, ornately carved, dark cedar furniture was bestrewn with photos. Photos of their mother, their mother's mother, her sisters; long-forgotten uncles, whose stern faces helped drive out anyone who wandered into the room for a quiet drink. And photos upon photos upon photos of the children: the children as babies, newborns wrapped in blue or pink blankets depending on the assigned gender; toddlers with mud on their faces and gumboots, backs straight in crisp uniforms for the first day of school; eyes glazed as teenagers. There was a deep green couch, luxurious rugs, two dining tables with lace settings and ornaments. So many ornaments. Bronze ballerinas, music boxes, vials of holy water, vases and porcelain children dressed like shabby aristocrats from eighteenth-century England. Sitting in the middle of the floor was Mary, clutching her hand and howling, with shoeboxes of photos not good enough to be framed spread around her.

'Hello Mary,' Phinn and Poppy said in monotone unison.

Mary held up her hand and howled, 'Who puts a mousetrap on top of a shoebox on her shelf?'

'Probably Mum, as this is her house you are snooping around,' Poppy said unsympathetically.

'I thought your mother might have a photo of Mummy that I've been looking for and have lost.'

'And you thought you would take it?'

'I was going to ask.' Mary scowled.

'Why aren't you in your own home? Where's Mum?' Phinn asked.

'Oh I don't know, I let myself in. She is my sister, you know.'

'So you can come in and take photos as you please? I suppose you always do what you like when it comes to Mum,' Poppy said.

Mary stared straight ahead. 'My hand got caught in the mousetrap.'

'Maybe it's not for mice; maybe it's for unwelcome snoopers.'

'You shouldn't talk to your aunt that way,' Mary said, looking Poppy in the eyes.

'You shouldn't go through Mum's things. Offer up the pain to the babies in purgatory,' Poppy replied, refusing to break eye contact.

Mary stood up and made a show of brushing her red dress off. It was ill-fitting and made Mary look slightly witchy with her corkscrew black hair, but everything made Mary seem witchy, including her personality.

Just then Claudia appeared, rubbing her eyes and wearing a striped blue shirt with 'Eat The Rich' written on it.

'Is that my nightdress?' Poppy said automatically.

'She's your sister, she can wear it if she needs,' Mary said gleefully. 'That's what sisters are for.'

'Ah, to take your stuff without asking,' Poppy said as Claudia ignored them both.

'What happened to your hand?' Claudia asked, giving Mary exactly what she wanted, as she dramatically nursed it.

'I got it caught in a mousetrap.'

'You should offer the pain up to the babies in purgatory,' Claudia said as she walked away.

Poppy bent down and began picking up the photos. Mary made louder and louder sighs and sat down on one of the velvet chairs. Most of the photos were black and white and featured an array of sullen children and stoic teenagers. Poppy used to love looking at the photos of her cranky aunts and uncles as children; it had been years since she had seen the pictures.

When two people marry, half of the couple usually find themselves colonised by the other's family. In this case it was Rachel's that demanded complete subjugation. There were weekly dinners with her siblings, her aunts, her uncles, her cousins. Their father's family obligingly faded into the background, only seeking acknowledgement in early December when the Christmas cards began to arrive.

But as the children grew older they began to distance themselves from the drama and grievances that followed Rachel's family wherever they were. The pleas for recognition of their suffering – and by extension their existence – went unanswered. On their myriad feuds the kids remained silent, hoping to snuff out their manufactured needs with lack of oxygen.

The drama continued without them, but the kids slowly learned the lesson guilt-ridden lapsed Catholics can take decades to settle into – if you do not acknowledge it, it may as well not exist.

Their mother, over her sixty-two consecutive years of being part of the family, still had not learned that lesson. It's not that Rachel had an addiction to conflict – the emotional brawls took their toll on her, ignited by bored and unhappy cousins or siblings, pointing their fingers at everyone but themselves for the miserable ways their lives had turned out. If Rachel had an addiction, it was to providing genuine emotional support.

And so she found herself dragged to the middle of whichever tiny opera had been concocted by the various members of her family and, just as they had between the American Civil War and the Second World War, the techniques had evolved with technology.

The favoured strategy at the moment was for whoever was feuding (over slights that happened in 1985, or who had taken a salad bowl the week before, or who Rachel was not showing enough affection to) to play it out through email. Their uncle Peter would email whoever had wronged him and list everything that was wrong with them, calling them idiotic misers or Chelsea Clinton imitators, under the cover of the latest argument. But he would not just send it to the villain of his hour, he would copy in those two or three siblings who he perceived to be his allies. And when they responded, which they always did (to *not* respond was unthinkable), the other sibling would copy in another sister, whoever they thought would be sympathetic to their plight. Eventually the creation would be a chain letter of familial dissent.

Rachel was always one of the first to be put in these rage missives and would find herself on the phone that night for hours, reassuring whoever she happened to pick up the phone to first. Once Poppy and Zoe (in a brief interlude during their teens when they could stand the sight of each other) logged on as their mother and sent a group response: 'You are all behaving like the bastard children you are. I want no part of this pathetic charade of a family'. But they were found out in less than an hour when their mother, upon picking up her mobile during her lunchbreak, saw she had eighty-seven missed calls and thought an aunt had died.

'Did Claudia invite them to the wedding?' Mary asked.

'Who?' Phinn responded as he took each photo from Poppy to take a look himself.

'My brothers and sisters.'

'I think Claudie was generous enough inviting her own brothers and sisters; I don't know that Mum asked about her family,' Poppy said, gently correcting Mary's declaration of ownership over her and Rachel's brothers and sisters.

'Well, she should've,' Mary said petulantly.

'How about you have your own wedding and you can invite whoever you want?' Poppy said, immediately regretting her words.

Mary was not married. She was supposed to be, everyone knew. In Mary's vision of how her life turned out, she was married. Preferably to a man who would pay the bills. The kids were vaguely aware of a couple of men, shadows in their lives when they were young. Mary was really and genuinely supposed to marry one of them, but then one Sunday night he was not at roast dinner and somehow they knew never to ask why or what had happened to him.

The kids intuited that there were reasons but knew not to ask what they were, reasons their mother put up with Mary, her demands, her constant incursions on their lives, her petty tantrums over perceived slights. The explanations were something deeper than 'she is my sister'. But Rachel's children did not want a reason to feel pity, or even kindness, towards their unbearable aunt.

By now Phinn and Poppy had packed away the photos, with Phinn taking care to put them on an even higher shelf, out of Mary's reach. Mary, noting the new hiding place and seeing the purpose behind its selection, abruptly got up and stalked out of the room without saying anything.

Phinn watched her walk out and then retrieved the box of photos and walked to the other end of the room. He pulled a couch away from the wall and opened a small door behind it, long ago used to stash all of his teenage contraband. A faint whiff of marijuana came from it as he stuffed the box inside and quickly closed the door, pushing the couch back into position.

He turned to his sister and grinned. 'I'm going to pick up Zoe.'

'Ding dong,' Poppy responded gravely.

In the kitchen Phinn found Claudia sitting cross-legged on the bench scrolling through her phone while she waited for the kettle to boil.

'Do you follow Rihanna's Insta?' she asked without looking up.

'Do I ever, it's the freshest thing on there; those tits, man, every shot. I think my favourite sports bra of hers is the fluoro pink one. Have you seen she posts Bible verses as well?'

'You know my position on Fitspo, it's a Pentecostal front. First you are devoted to the squats and soon the motivational posts turn to God; 123 years from now there will be PhD theses on how Christianity captured the next generations through burpees and destroyed their knees in the process.'

Claudia didn't look up, still scrolling.

Phinn shifted from one foot to the other.

'So, uh, how are you feeling?' He had always been terrible at broaching emotional terrain and could already tell his timid attempt at wedding inquisition was going to fall flat. Between his mother and sisters he felt there was enough emotional prodding going on, and so was loath to get involved as well as inexperienced at any strategy.

'How am I feeling? I am feeling like I can't even have my

morning ritual of coffee and Instagram without some trespass.'

'Ah.'

At least Phinn was good at knowing when to shut up.

The kettle whistled and he picked it up, pouring it into the plunger, which already had two and a quarter tablespoons sitting in it. As he stirred it with the wooden spoon, Claudia grumbled about the brand of coffee their mother kept in the house.

'And she keeps it in the freezer. That doesn't do shit; it should just be in an airtight jar.'

Every return home was a series of shocks for each former member of the Carter household. Their parents almost affronted that their children had grown into adults with their own tastes and habits. The children taking each change in the household, from the brand of cereal to where the bread was kept, as a personal insult, an attack on the way things should be. Claudia had a theory that their mother kept so many photos of them as children because it kept them frozen in an idealised time when they could be told what their preferences were.

Every home visit was an onslaught of commentary on personal choices. Rachel shocked that Poppy now ate multigrain bread only. Their father becoming paralysed by what brand of beer he should be buying. Claudia now expected personal space, something she had seemed able to do without for her first eighteen years, and which now offended everyone else. Every member of the family secretly thought that – apart from themselves – nobody should change.

Phinn pushed the plunger down and poured Claudia a cup, handing it to her. Her head was still down, offering the occasional comment, for which Phinn had no context without being able to see the photos.

'I can't believe somebody agreed to marry him,' she said finally, looking up.

'Who?' Phinn responded, biting his tongue before he named Dylan.

'Joe Gelder. He was always such a dick; nothing between his ears but the web address for RedTube. He hasn't even realised you don't need to know it anymore, just write the title in the browser search bar and it comes up. You think he knows that? I don't think he does. And someone agreed to marry him, in Fiji; obviously she has no imagination either, but still. So young too.'

'Didn't you go to school with him?'

'Uh-huh.'

'Then isn't he your age?'

'What's your point?'

'You're getting married.'

Claudia sighed and stretched out her legs on the bench in precisely the manner their mother hated in the kitchen.

'I am very young to be getting married,' she said solemnly. 'It's kind of radical.'

'Radical in a Joe Gelder kind of way, I guess,' Phinn said, attempting to sip his coffee.

'Oh, fuck off.'

Phinn quickly changed the subject. Life was too long to take such easy pot shots at his sister.

'I'm going to get Zoe,' he said.

'Good, that'll be fun ...' She paused. 'Don't tell Poppy I said that.'

'I don't know how long you can keep writing in both Poppy and Zoe's birthday cards that each is your favourite without them eventually reading the other's.'

'I also write in the card not to show the other.'

'Creating even more motivation for them to show each other.'

Claudia thought for a moment. 'Well, the first four hours

with Zoe here will be great. I am glad she's coming. She doesn't agitate Rachel like the rest of us can. Are you going to take her to see Dad or just coming straight here?'

Phinn let the question, fat with implication, sit in the air.

'Whatever she wants to do. Pub tonight?'

'I think so.'

Zoe would be a visitor in their galaxy. She had long wrenched herself from the family grip and somehow managed to keep everyone happy without ever revealing much about herself or her life. They knew she worked as a florist in the city. Maybe managed the shop; it was a possibility. From her social media posts they gleaned that she enjoyed going out to dinner and had developed a taste for expensive leather bags. They knew of at least two friends because they would tag her in Instagram photos and, unlike on Facebook, they didn't think Zoe realised that people could see the tagged photos.

None of them was quite sure which suburb Zoe lived in, and she visited their cities frequently enough not to warrant them spending actual money on flying to her and finding any of this out.

Her arrival would be grand, it would take some of the sting out of Rachel's and Poppy's arguments, but beyond that Zoe did not offer much.

Claudia and Phinn knew they were thinking along the same lines but they didn't bother raising any of it.

'Do you want to come to the airport with me?' Phinn asked.

'No, I want to walk around in circles by myself for ninety minutes before I have to spend the rest of the week, which seems like the rest of my life, engaged in conversation and conflict with the rest of you.'

'Fair enough.'

Phinn went over to the drawer next to the pantry and fished through it before pulling out the BMW keys.

'Mum left the Falcon keys on the bench for you,' Claudia said, eyeing her brother.

'Well, if she really didn't want me to take the car I want to drive, she would have slept with these under her pillow.'

Before Claudia could issue any predictions of unnecessary doom he was out the door.

Claudia looked around the empty kitchen and picked up her headphones and phone, slipping her wallet into her pocket. She walked slowly to the front door, a practised, silent movement that signalled to nobody she was about to leave so nobody could ask her where she was going.

She tipped her head to the photo of her mother as she stepped over the threshold, and leaned on the door handle as she closed it so it made no click that could give her away. She bounded down the narrow paved path and, without stopping, shoved her earbuds in her ears for company on the walk. She briefly checked her work email; she had her out-of-office on but she liked to stay in the loop. Of course there was nothing of interest there, there never was. Claudia had not set out to become an economic consultant at a boutique bank; when she'd embarked on her Economics degree she had not really set out to become anything. She was interested in economics and had some inexact ideas about helping developing countries through an NGO, maybe, but instead she had found herself on a very pleasant salary, moving steadily up the ranks of a business which prided itself on the oxymoronic label of being a 'good corporate citizen'. She could build an actual fun life around the hours and her colleagues were decent, and Claudia eventually let go of the fantasy that work was supposed to be meaningful. That was a lofty ambition only the children of the upper-middle class and beyond got to indulge. The rest had to actually earn some money. For most, a job was just a job, and she was thankful that hers was permanent full-time.

There was nowhere in particular she wanted to be or had to go. She just needed to be away from the house and, more importantly, anyone in it. She thought about ringing Nora but what was there to say? 'Hurry up and get here. I don't know if I can do this.'

Claudia took a breath and glanced either side of her at an intersection before crossing the road, a Spotify daily playlist delivering comfort songs from her teenage years. Killing Heidi. Tegan and Sara. Placebo. She giggled as she thought about who she had pined after during that supposedly wretched time. Ryan from *The OC*, mainly. For years she had swung wildly between wanting a boy to save or a boy to save her. She was such an earnest teenager – gullible, too. She believed in the potential thrill of relationships, that they would be tumultuous and take courage and overcome any storm. It had not occurred to her that a relationship could be easy; that it is supposed to be easy.

There was no Ryan carrying her out of Mexico after she passed out in an alleyway. Mostly because when she and Dylan met she could not afford to party for a week on the Gold Coast, let alone Mexico. But also because there was nothing she ever really needed saving from. She was no more tragic or complicated than the next comfortable country girl.

Still.

She thought life could have been a little bit thrilling. That the man she would marry would at least excite her. Nora still jumped out of her seat with glee every time Tom showed up at a restaurant. Claudia could not remember the last time she felt delighted with Dylan. Content, sure. But not delighted. She tried to square this with how she felt about seeing him in a few days. Was there excitement? She did feel a yearning for him, to feel his body close to hers, to be reassured she was not the one being difficult in the face of any family spectacles. But what if he got here and she felt nothing? What if it was confirmation she had only been tolerating him?

She turned into the street that housed her old gym and realised she was inadvertently on the same route she had walked three mornings a year for three years towards the end of high school. There was a quicker way to the gym – where she'd done aerobics – but she had walked these paths regularly because they took her past Charlie Bryson's house. She thought she would become physically ill from the ache of wanting him when she was a teenager, but he had never noticed her, and she'd survived. Claudia smiled and shook her head. The minuscule stakes had seemed so monumental back then.

The first strains of a Verve song filled her ears and Claudia stopped walking. She was going to walk down the aisle to this. She looked down the street, lined with lilly-pilly trees, and waited for an old four-wheel drive to pass her. With the street empty it was time for some visualisation exercises. She pictured herself in the sleeveless sheath dress she had long coveted and wrapped her hands around her imaginary bouquet of Australian native flowers. Her mother had demanded she wear sleeves in the church and somehow her intention to have an A-line skirt had morphed into three petticoats at the bridal shop, but this was Claudia's visualisation and she could wear the dress she wanted. She thought of her sweet Dylan and saw him 15 metres in front of her. This visualisation stuff was a piece of cake. She took a step forward in time to the music, and then another.

And then she saw Rachel leaning forward in the pew, frowning at the crown of flowers Claudia wore on her head instead of a veil. She could see only ugliness reflected in her eyes. She saw her father sitting four pews back instead of at the front, refusing at the last moment to sit anywhere near Mary, who had demanded she be next to Rachel.

Claudia narrowed her focus to the Dylan of her imagination at the end of the aisle. His hair was cut too short. She had told him to get it cut before he came to Winston but she knew he was going to arrive with shaggy hair and end up under the scissors of a 65-year-old woman who had never once done anything but short back and sides.

Everything was off.

Her phone buzzed, snapping her out of the walk down the aisle before she turned and ran in her pretend green heels out of the pretend church.

It was an email confirming an upgrade at the hotel she had booked as a treat for when they went back to the city after the wedding. She had gone into a raffle for the penthouse, but she knew she would get it. Things always turned out fine for her in that enchanted kind of way.

CHAPTER 3

Phinn carefully reversed out of the driveway, keeping watch on the garish pink bougainvillea that grew more like a weed than a hedge at the end. One of his many recurring daily fears was that eventually a child was going to run out from behind one when it was too late to brake. He held his breath for a second as the back tyres went over the footpath. Today he was in the street without having run over a kid. Small achievements and small mercies.

He switched on the radio to hear the first strains of Amy Shark's 'Adore'. He breathed out through his teeth. 'Just five more nights,' he muttered. Just five nights where they didn't have to completely devastate each other.

He raised his finger to Mrs Dowd as she walked down the street, probably towards the newsagent to collect the five newspapers she read each day. Only one newspaper was from this actual town, another was national and the other four were from three different cities, although Phinn had not been able to figure out the connection between them.

Phinn turned left, taking the longer way to avoid the main street where he might as well, publicly check in on Facebook, for how quickly the news would spread he was back in town. He was keeping a low profile. He knew he wanted to delay his old friends and elder cousins from knowing he was back. It would be the same as it was every time.

A flurry of excited text messages, and then he would find himself sitting at the same pub they had been going to since they were eighteen, for one beer at two p.m. The next stop would be twelve hours and twenty-one shouts later and, most likely, smoking his first joint since he had last been back in town. It would be a brief but familiar stumble through what the boys knew as the glory years – trying to recapture how they felt from ages sixteen to twenty-two. Invincible but still open to the possibility their lives could change.

He would see them, just not quite yet.

He followed the road until the houses dropped off and it was just rolling yellowed fields with half-hearted attempts at fences. In another twenty-five minutes he pulled up at the airport and let out a little laugh to himself. There was no designated short-term pick-up; there wasn't even a gate on the car park, let alone anywhere to charge money. Just twenty parks outside of a corrugated iron shed.

Inside was the 'check-in', where a maximum of twenty-eight people would have their bags weighed and tagged before they walked across the tarmac to get on the propeller-driven plane. In a roundabout way it was probably more like how people travelled on private jets than in big airports. No security pat-downs, no racial profiling through random explosive tests, no fluorescently lit food courts selling burgers at a 47 per cent mark-up. Just a pleasant man to take your bag before you boarded the terrifying small plane a 35-metre walk away.

Phinn settled into one of the plastic moulded chairs to wait for Zoe's plane. He thought the younger girls were harsh on Zoe for daring not to be the same person at thirty years old that she had been at seventeen. Poppy, in particular, resented the way Zoe spoke, how she did her hair, how she dressed, the bags she carried. Poppy even felt it as some kind of betrayal that Zoe wore lipstick now. That she was smarter than their parents.

The longer Poppy and Zoe had to spend time together, the angrier Poppy got and the stiffer Zoe became. The last time they had to spend four days together over Easter, Zoe had become so quietly defensive she would eat breakfast in high heels and carry her Chanel bag to the table, a quilted burgundy leather and gold-chained 'fuck you' to greet Poppy first thing in the morning.

Phinn liked Zoe. He liked all his family members but he especially liked Zoe. He didn't care that she had pretentious tendencies, or that she spent stupid amounts of money on getting her hair coiffed. Really, she was just the same as when they had been ten and eight years old and she would smuggle him the Bob Dylan tapes he wasn't allowed to listen to because of a line about the president being naked that Phinn had ruined for their mother by repeating it again and again and again while giggling.

In the distance he spotted the plane, a slightly alarming rusted colour white, coasting towards the airstrip from the west. As he raised his hand to his forehead against the glare, out of the corner of his eye he caught a glance from someone sitting down, just two seats away.

Discreetly, he nodded.

Damn. He knew that he would know them. It was that girl who used to work the checkout with Claudia; she was always too excited to see him. He focused on pretending not to see her.

'Lord, Allah or David Foster Wallace, spare me the small talk,' he muttered under his breath, automatically evoking the structure of the same prayer he had been using since he was a teenager, whose childhood religious curiosity had predictably started shifting to minor rebellion on the literary scale.

The plane dropped closer to the ground so that, satisfyingly, hearing anything else was impossible in the old shed as it landed. Even the overexcited kids who gathered at the fence to be as close as possible to the action resembled mime artists, their squeals of delight lost in the tiny roar of the small plane engines. The propellers slowed down as the engines sporadically coughed into silence, and the stairs to the plane unfolded cautiously, just kissing the tarmac as they were extended out.

Phinn half expected Zoe to step off the plane first, to have her hair blowing just-so and big sunglasses on her face, wearing a crisp white shirt and with leather luggage slung over her shoulder. He didn't know why he expected that image; the reality was that Zoe rarely lived up to what she was trying to project.

Instead an older lady, maybe in her eighties, emerged, and was helped down the stairs, taking them one by one and having a little rest in between each exertion. She truly was a lady, not a woman; she had on a linen skirt suit with beige stockings and a purple silk scarf knotted at her throat. Phinn laughed to himself. This would drive Zoe, the least patient person he knew, nuts. She had been known to interrupt children at McDonald's if she felt they were taking too long to choose between nuggets and a cheeseburger.

Then a man appeared, whose florid, sunstruck face, expanding gut under a pressed chambray shirt and unblemished 'town' R.M.s denoted him as a farmer, who most likely had been down in the city for the day on business. An older woman followed, then a teenage girl, looking surly towards her home town in general, and finally Zoe.

The illusion of easy glamour she was trying for was, as usual, slightly skew-whiff. Her sunglasses fell down her nose and her hair blew into her mouth. Her flared white shirt (Phinn had at least envisioned that detail correctly) was crumpled and her navy skinny cigarette-style pants slightly clashed with her black leather boots and the red carry-all she had slung over her shoulder. She descended the stairs looking down the entire time and began walking towards the shed. Phinn waved through the window and, as she looked up, Zoe grinned. She was happy to see her brother.

The two embraced with the easy joy of siblings who have not seen each other in months and who have all the cross words of a visit ahead of them, but the shared delusion that perhaps it could be different this time.

'Does Mum know you have the BMW?' Zoe asked as they walked into the car park and she eyed the red trophy parked lazily across two spaces.

'Hey, she said I should take the car.' Phinn grinned, dramatically opening the passenger seat door to allow his sister in.

'Hmmm.' Zoe threw her bag in the back seat as she slid in and looked back at the airport. 'If I was a terrorist, this is definitely where I would come. Shave off your beard for Allah, put on a flanno and you'll have control of that plane with enough petrol to get to the nearest tower in no time.'

'Good to see you are still analysing the best ways to kill the maximum number of people with minimum effort.'

'I'm not going to do it myself, I was just observing.'

'Observing how to commit a terrorist act. Yep, uh-huh.'

Phinn slid the car into gear and revved the engine in a display of showmanship before meekly easing the car out of the car park.

'So, how's the first night been? How's my most adored human being? How are our venerated and sane parents?' Zoe settled into the leather seats.

'In a shock to nobody, Mary has been hanging around the house, but Poppy still managed to get her hackles up about it. We found Mary this morning going through Mum's photos in the exhibition room. Poppy really gave it to her.' Phinn chuckled to himself. 'If by adored human being,' he continued, 'you are talking about Poppy, then she is looking forward to seeing you as much as you are looking forward to seeing her. If you are talking about the sister you actually like, then she is fine, but I think maybe having second thoughts about the wedding. Mum is the usual, Dad is fine – from all accounts and text messages.'

'Second thoughts about the wedding? You mean the wedding that is on Saturday? The wedding I am here to perform maid-of-honour duties at?'

'Claudia doesn't have a maid of honour,' Phinn quickly corrected. He had heard Claudia herself say – about 172 times in the past year – that, while there would be a wedding party, there would be no rankings.

'That's just what she tells Poppy; I know I'm her maid of honour,' Zoe said breezily. 'Anyway, second thoughts?'

'Yeah, she just seems, uh, nervous, I guess is how I would put it. She hasn't actually said she doesn't want to get married, but it very much seems that she doesn't want to get married.'

'What do you mean it doesn't seem she wants to get married? And she hasn't said that?'

'Well, not in those exact terms to me, but she seems kind of listless. Like we're talking to her through a glass pane.'

'Talking to Claudia has been like talking through a glass pane since she was four. You still haven't given me any reason you think she might want to call the wedding off.'

'Well, isn't that in the maid-of-honour contract?' Phinn replied, watching Zoe out of the corner of his eye. Checkmate. 'Don't tell her I told you that, by the way; I'm not supposed to be talking about it.'

Zoe glared at him and looked out of the window at the cows in the paddocks with the shoddy fences. She watched a kangaroo bound too close to a cow and then realised there were about fifteen other kangaroos standing very still in the next paddock sniffing the air. The colour of the grass, the smell of eucalyptus and something slightly burnt in the air, of the sun on bitumen for too long, was unconsciously familiar to her, much in the way of one's own limbs. She looked into the distance, realising it had probably been more than half a year since she had seen a proper horizon: one that wasn't the end of a street, or the stars.

'I hate coming home.'

Without having to discuss it, Phinn pulled into their mother's driveway. It was where the girls – only referred to as that between brother and sister – were, and the days of emotional wretchedness would not be worth it if they dared to call in on their father first.

Zoe got out of the car, without bothering to glance back to make sure Phinn would fetch her bag from the seat. She knew he would. As she passed under the kitchen she looked up and saw her aunt's judgemental face peering down at her over the antique kettle, framed by the dark green borders of the window. Zoe thought to herself, Mary could be held up as evidence of

Roald Dahl's theory that if you think ugly thoughts they begin to show on your face. She allowed herself an unenthusiastic wave but knew that Mary wouldn't bother coming to the door to greet her, so she was safe if she circumvented the kitchen – Mary's preferred domain – once inside. She entered through the back door in the long tradition of anybody who comes home again, whether it was against their will or with joy in their heart. The front door was for visitors.

Her mother also left the back door unlocked and Zoe could not be bothered knocking. She paused to breathe in her mother's smell – a mixture of shampoo, body oils and, inexplicably, freshly cut hair – before calling out.

'Muuum.'

'Zoe!'

She listened for the sound of her mother's light step practically running through the house. And then Rachel appeared, hair slicked down with dye underneath cling wrap and wearing a shirt of Claudia's from high school – meaning the shirt itself was probably in its teens – emblazoned with the words 'The Good Times Are Killing Me'. Paired with her knee-length bright orange shorts, the overall effect was unhinged but, Zoe knew, Rachel being Rachel still looked about six times more attractive than Zoe on a good day.

'You're home!'

'Am I?' Zoe said automatically. Her query was more an instinctive response to her mother's factual declaration than deliberate insouciance. However, she forgot that homecomings to insecure maternal figures are no time for flippancy.

'What does that mean?' Rachel said, pulling away sharply. 'Have you seen your father?'

Zoe groaned.

'Nothing, Mum, just a joke ... How are you? What's happening?'

That was enough for Zoe to spend the next fifteen minutes quietly with her thoughts while Rachel rounded off in great detail her friends' latest marital and health ailments, her latest grudge at work, despite being on a three-week break from the cleaning company, as well as something about the garden that nobody had been able to make sense of yet. Zoe made sounds at intervals of sympathy, interest and agreement before finding a gap in the conversation.

'Where's the bride?' she asked brightly, treading carefully so as not to flick the unpredictable switch on her mother's virtual mood settings – from nervously excited to overwrought. The genius had been in using Claudia's role for the week and not the name of Rachel's least favourite child, Poppy. Well, least favourite was probably a bit harsh. Perhaps 'the name of the child she has the most agitated relationship with'.

Rachel waved to the stairs, 'Oh, she's in her room,' allowing herself the language that pretended her children still lived with her, that they still needed her, and only ever resided in their rooms in her house.

'Okay, I have to say hello, you know, as maid of honour.'

'I thought Claudia didn't have a maid of honour; she didn't tell me you were the maid of honour.'

'Well I am,' Zoe said, bounding up the stairs.

'Mary's here by the way,' Rachel called after her.

At the top of the stairs, Zoe turned left and stopped for a moment to survey her sister. Claudia had headphones in and was lying diagonally across a bed that she certainly had not made herself that morning. She was engrossed in whatever she was listening to and had not heard Zoe's steps, despite Zoe being the kind of average-sized woman who still sounded like an elephant in the house. Claudia had her cropped hair pulled off her face by two bright green clips and was wearing what looked like bike pants with a faded green oversized sweatshirt. It was all wrong, but sartorially Claudia was always wrong. Zoe pulled on Claudia's foot, almost copping a kick to the chest for her efforts.

'Don't touch my fucking foot,' Claudia said, swinging around, the fierce arrangement of her facial features completely changing once she saw it was Zoe. 'Hey!'

'Hey yourself; man, could you be more like Rachel with your touchiness about feet?' Zoe grinned back and lay down on the bed next to her sister. 'Are those my socks?' Zoe asked, pointing her head towards Claudia's feet, which were clad in anklets with drawings of pigs flying all over them.

Claudia shrugged.

'I hear you don't want to get married,' Zoe continued.

Claudia shrugged again. 'It's not that – I don't think ...'

'Well, whatever's going on, your maid of honour should be able to help.'

'You're not my maid of honour.'

Zoe nudged her with her elbow. 'Why is Phinn saying you don't want to get married?'

'I told him not to tell anyone I told him that,' Claudia replied.

'Yeah, he told me not to tell you that he was the one who told me. Don't tell anyone, but.'

Claudia began giggling.

'Don't tell anyone, but' was an old shorthand between them. In their family, any news spread more quickly than syphilis during King Henry VIII's reign, and Zoe and Claudia had long mocked it after the quick observation that the most common greeting between relatives was, 'Don't tell anyone, but ...'

'Well don't tell anyone, but I don't know what I think. I can't tell if I am having misgivings about marrying Dylan or if

I am having misgivings about spending this entire week with our family.'

'Well, I would rather marry Dylan than spend the week with our family if I had to choose.'

'Hmmmmmm.'

Zoe decided to drop it. There was no use being too direct with Claudia. Whatever she was feeling would come out at an odd moment, such as when they were discussing what happened to their childhood trampoline, or trying to decide if their favourite colour was purple or blue. It wouldn't be revealed through direct questioning.

'Where's the light of my life, the eternal joy of my soul?' asked Zoe.

'I don't know what yours and Poppy's problem is.'

'I don't have a problem with my baby sister. She's great; I really enjoy her particular brand of petulance mixed with self-righteousness. I find it invigorating.'

'Zoe, not this week,' Claudia pleaded. 'Poppy has actually been looking forward to seeing you.'

'I can't believe my own sister can look me in the eye and lie as if I am a calorie counter in your phone, as if I am a doctor asking if you've ever taken drugs, as if I am our mother.'

'Just be nice.'

'I'm always nice.'

'Don't lie to me – I'm your sister.'

The Imperial was one of the oldest surviving pubs in Winston. It had originally been opened by a Spaniard who sailed to Australia on a promise to his bride-to-be he was going to find a better life for them. He had reached Winston in the middle of summer, a small town high in the tablelands beneath Sydney that had to him the perfect climate. The days reached 28 degrees without ever getting humid. Today's one-hour trip to the beach was back then a day's journey, but the Spaniard was happy enough with that – he had arrived in Australia by boat from Europe, after all. By the time he was shocked by the sub-zero temperatures of winter he had already won some land in a complicated bet with a fellow penniless European.

He worked as a farmhand for five years to save enough money to open the pub in a simple wooden structure to which, over the years, he added a second level, wide verandahs, a heavy oak bar and elaborate doors carved from a eucalypt native to the area. His vision for the pub was a mosaic of influences: from his home town, to the bush surrounding him and the sea he had travelled on, as well as the Indigenous stories he had heard on Gundungurra land. Inspired by their name for a nearby area, Winge Karrabee Karrabee – a place of many wildfires – he painted the bar in flames. Images of mermaids adorned the walls and carved corbels supported the ceiling beams. His mother, weeping for three months after he had announced his intention to come to Australia, had made him two pots that he had carried in a bag on his back and had sat on a shelf near a painting of a heartbroken matador taunting a bull. The Spaniard had done the painting himself, with little to no talent or technical skill, and hung it on the wall in the ancient tradition of doing as you like when you're the boss. After thirteen years he had travelled home to fetch his bride and found she had married his brother and had three daughters.

Brotherhood is like an illness.

Now, all that survived of his lopsided vision were the carved doors. The Imperial had borne witness to the changing fortunes of the town as the bush was bulldozed for farms, small businesses boomed, factories were built and emptied; it had found its niche as a quaint destination for the city bourgeoisie wanting to pretend to escape to the country for the weekend. As agriculture and manufacturing waned, the Imperial had hosted hundreds of leaving parties as the smartest kids fled for larger towns or cities, desperate to be closer to what they thought was the action. Those left behind, the defiant stragglers, soldiered on as the population dwindled, the supermarket and clothing chains replaced their local markets and boutiques. It was the Great Australian Story. The Great American Story. The Great *insert any developed country with a rapidly shrinking middle class* Story.

None of this was on the minds of the Carter kids. A war was brewing. They walked through the doors of the Imperial in the pairs they had established long before they had any concept of battle lines.

Phinn and Zoe entered in lockstep, with Zoe purposefully not making any eye contact with her fellow patrons until she had found a table she liked, beside a window, with four stools scattered around it. She wore a short purple dress with a hot pink cashmere sweater over the top and a denim jacket. Around her neck was a black choker, such a flashpoint trend that it would cause noses to wrinkle in embarrassment in just a month. Pinned to her denim jacket was a small brooch of a koala holding a bunch of roses, and on her feet were Adidas Stan Smiths. If she could have she would've kissed the feet of Victoria Beckham for making the comfortable sneaker okay sartorially, and she was considering asking if she could wear them with her bridesmaid dress but had not quite got the timing right yet. She put her small leather Gucci handbag on the table and dug through her wallet, handing Phinn her credit card. He did not even bother with the pretence of reaching for his own wallet.

'I'll just have a riesling.' Zoe glanced around the bar, taking in the grimy pool table of her teenage years, a few men her age in their tradie gear leaning against the bar with their beers, and the jukebox playing U2. 'Actually, just get me a schooner of whatever you're having,' she said quickly.

'Safest bet.' Phinn nodded.

As he sloped towards the bar, Zoe saw Claudia and Poppy emerge from the bathroom and she stiffened involuntarily. Claudia had parted her cropped blonde hair on the left in a style that should have looked dorky but managed to seem chic on her, offset by a black turtleneck, high-waisted black jeans and shiny pink leather brogues.

What Zoe noticed were her little pink and blue diamanté earrings.

'Are those my earrings?' she asked by way of greeting.

'Is that my brooch?' Poppy said.

'What's everyone drinking?' Claudia said purposefully.

'Hmmmm, white wine?' Poppy responded.

'Really?' Zoe said, turning to Poppy.

'Don't tell me what fucking drink to order, Zoe.'

'I'm not. I just don't think the wine here is going to be very good.'

'I'll have the chardonnay, Claudie,' Poppy said, not moving her eyes from Zoe.

Claudia sighed and turned back to the bar. Zoe looked around desperately for Phinn and saw him leaning casually across the bar, chatting to Steve, who had just poured the drinks.

She scanned the room and her eyes widened as they settled on a man sitting in the corner in a tight black shirt, his chin-length blond hair twisted into miniature dreadlocks. She started laughing and, despite herself, elbowed Poppy in the ribs. Poppy had been working hard on not breaking the silence between them and was almost pushed off her chair for her efforts.

'It's Roy,' Zoe whispered out of the side of her mouth.

Poppy's face stayed completely still but a pinkness began creeping from her shirt collar across her chest and up her throat towards her face. A sight familiar to those intimate with her and barely perceptible to anyone else.

'Has he seen us?' she whispered, refusing to look in the direction in which Zoe was so blatantly staring.

Zoe started giggling. 'No,' she said, shaking her head for emphasis as Claudia arrived back at the table with Phinn, two chardonnays and two beers in tow, carefully setting Poppy's wine down in front of her as she put her head in her hands, groaning.

'Roy's here!' Zoe said joyfully.

'Aw, no way, where is the champ?' Phinn responded, looking around excitedly as Poppy tried to sink lower on her chair.

'Guys, why are we so thrilled about seeing Poppy's boyfriend from a million years ago?' Claudia asked wearily.

'This is a very significant man,' Zoe said between giggles. 'The man she lost her virginity to. The heavy-metal-listening, Being-a-Blairite-is-the-same-as-being-a-Tory, won't-stop-playing-Guitar-Hero wonder boy of Year Twelve for her.'

Poppy carefully raised her wine to her lips and Zoe pretended not to notice when she spat her first mouthful back into the glass. Claudia didn't even bother touching hers; she had wanted a beer all along but sacrificed her preference for diplomatic reasons.

'Heyyyy,' Zoe said, perking up. 'Does he know you're gay?'

Poppy shrugged.

'Imagine if he tries to hit you up for old times' sake. Remember when he wrote that piece for the school newsletter about why all men should be feminists and it got published instead of a piece by an actual girl for International Women's Day? Jesus, what did you see in him?'

'Well, cover, obviously.'

Phinn and Claudia exchanged looks: an almost undetectable raising of their eyebrows. Zoe shut up. Satisfied, Poppy began to loosen up and took a quick sip of her wine, surreptitiously trying to hold her breath at the same time so she didn't have to actually taste it.

Zoe maintained her silence as Poppy finally addressed the table. 'The funny thing about being gay is that there is this perception that you come out and the hard part is over. You wrestle with your sexuality for a few years, you come to terms with it, you come out, it's hard and then it's over. You're eventually in the warm embrace of affection and no secrets. When, actually, you never stop coming out. You have to come out maybe hundreds of times in your life. Does Roy know I'm gay? I don't know. Maybe someone told him, or maybe he will come over and talk to us, and he is a nice guy despite your delightful snobbishness, Zoe; but if he comes over, instead of just chatting I will have to ascertain if he knows I am gay and then find a way of letting him know. Maybe I will reference an ex-girlfriend, an imaginary current girlfriend, or maybe I will find a way to say "actually I am gay", but whatever happens I'll have to think about it and probably come out. Every time I start a new job, see an old friend, make a new friend, I have to come out again. It's funny – nobody really talks about it, and you don't get taught that part in lesbian college.'

Her siblings paused.

'You mean the inner west soccer team,' Zoe said before she could help herself.

Claudia and Phinn waited for Poppy's reaction. Poppy started laughing.

'You're a real bitch.'

'Are you allowed to say that? I thought that wasn't cool anymore. Aren't you gendering me?'

'Oh, shut up.'

Now on a roll, Zoe held up the credit card that Phinn had put on the table.

'Hey Poppy, is this credit card queer? Is it a feminist ally? Don't you have to make sure everything is these days?'

Claudia tensed up; the Sibling Agitator was in precarious territory. But Poppy just kept laughing.

'Not all of us can be satisfied with just being a petty consumer, Zo. Can't all be basics with money.'

'Just let me get you a beer with my mountain of money, dickhead. I told you that wine would be awful.'

Poppy nodded and smiled widely as she pushed her wine away from her; the glass was half full after all.

'Me too please,' Claudia said.

The night was going to be okay.

CHAPTER 4

Claudia: Poppy, where are you?

Zoe: Did you mean to send this to the group chat? Isn't Poppy in bed with you?

Claudia: Shit, ignore me

Phinn: Why. Why must we have a group message? It's just a lot of blundering

Zoe: CLAUDIA, WHERE IS POPPY?

Claudia: If I knew I wouldn't be sending her a message

Phinn: I hate my life

Zoe: Did Poppy come back last night?

Phinn: Lol

Zoe: I don't care! I'm sure she's fine, I'm just asking where she is too

Phinn: OK

Zoe: Did she come home last night; please tell me you didn't leave her at the pub with Leah

Phinn: ROY'S SISTER HAHAHAHAHAHAHA HAHAHAHAHA

Claudia: I'm sure she's fine

Poppy: I am fine. None of you are my real mum. I don't need you checking up on me. What did it take this time? 48 hours and I'm being treated like a fucking baby

Claudia: OK

Zoe: OK

Zoe: If you are a disaster this morning, Poppy, it's not for ever

Phinn: I hate our group chat

CHAPTER 5

Claudia put her phone down and rolled over in bed, looking out the window to the street below. It was not a view she had thought about very much while living here, but since her increasingly longer periods of time away from home, it now appeared ridiculously picturesque.

Massive fig trees, their roots slowly destroying the footpath from below and strangling any native tree that attempted to grow nearby, overlooked groups of unsupervised neighbourhood children as they rode their bikes down the street. Nobody ever had an overgrown lawn. Instead the air seemed to alternate between the constant smell of either freshly mown grass or baking.

Claudia thought of the studio apartment she shared back in the city with Dylan. Of its one bookcase. Of the rack next to the front door so his bike didn't get in the way too much and instead could look kind of decorative as it hung on the wall. Could she come home again? Kanye had rapped more than once about always being able to go back home.

But Kanye didn't have any siblings and his mother was dead.

She sighed and kicked her blankets off. Last night had not been so bad. They had got along, tolerated each other, chosen not to take offence whenever some could have been scraped together – like kindling for a larger blaze to come. It had been fun.

Three more days until the wedding. Dylan arrived tomorrow. Nora arrived today. Claudia wondered how the delicate balance of last night was going to be thrown off by each of them. The good mood Poppy had bestowed upon them last night was an anomaly. It wouldn't last with Zoe, and it certainly wouldn't last with her best friend – Poppy's eternal threat – around either.

Why hadn't Claudia let Dylan come earlier? It had been an act of complicated benevolence. Whatever happened, whoever was there, someone was going to tear someone else to pieces this week – Dylan might as well stay out of it for as long as he could. Claudia had also wanted some time to herself, a thought that made her chuckle out loud involuntarily. She always pictured herself at home, going for runs, walking around the town by herself, calling in for lunch on doting aunts. The reality was that she was either feeling guilty for not being at her dad's while in her mother's kitchen, or wondering if her mother was upset while walking around her father's garden.

The few minutes in the morning were basically all the time she got alone, and that was only because Poppy had scored the night before. She hoped her mother wouldn't be asking too many questions.

Downstairs she found Rachel bent over the counter with Mary by her side, whispering in her ear. Claudia tried to stay silent until she was almost on top of them to see what was in their hands. The floorboard creaked as she was two steps away and the two jumped up. Claudia glanced down at her mother who was quickly shoving her phone in her pocket.

'Hello!' Mary greeted her.

Phinn came into the kitchen yawning. 'What are my favourite witches of the west doing this morning?' he said cheerfully.

'Don't talk to your mother like that,' Claudia said automatically, waiting for Rachel's scolding.

But she just walked over to the kettle and switched it on with all the concentration of a first-time neurosurgeon. Claudia eyed Mary.

'What were you two looking at?'

'Just Facebook, old friends, funny stories. Everyone is ageing but us. It does make one feel better about one's looks, seeing how classmates from forty years ago look today.'

Mary always tried to make her language embarrassingly proper when she was nervous. Embarrassing because it showed what she thought proper language was, her impressions mostly having been picked up from mini-series involving the royal family as soap-opera characters. Phinn suddenly started paying attention.

'Anyone specific you were looking at?'

'Of course not … Anyway, bride-to-be! Three more sleeps! Have you done the tables? I've completely forgotten to give you the name of my plus one.'

'I didn't give you a plus one.'

'Of course you did, you wouldn't be so bad mannered.'

'I didn't even give friends in relationships plus ones, unless Dylan has met them.'

'Those are friends, I am family.'

'What's the saying about which you get to choose again?' Claudia muttered under her breath as the kettle whistled.

Claudia thought about the names cut from her guest list, as Rachel had asked then demanded more and more people be added. In place of thirteen of Dylan and Claudia's friends were Rachel's colleagues, schoolfriends, her cycling buddies and, inexplicably, her yoga instructor.

'Tea?' Rachel said cheerfully. She was dressed in her usual morning attire, which was a dressing-gown with absolutely nothing underneath. She thought she was appropriately and discreetly covered up but the thought of their pants-less mother often left the children stiff with mortification. Claudia never mentioned to Dylan that her mother was basically naked and Dylan hadn't seemed to notice. Claudia pushed the thoughts away as she accepted a mug from her. Nowadays she liked her tea black with no sugar, but when she was a teenager she'd had it milky and sweet, so that was how her mother still made it.

'Your aunt has a plus one now, Claudia,' Rachel said as she handed Phinn a green tea, something he had drunk for four months when he was sixteen when he was briefly in love with a girl named after a star constellation. Now he would consume it forever under his mother's roof instead of revealing he had long ago moved on.

'What?' Claudia said, nose crinkled mid-sip.

'It's manners! Of course your aunt gets a plus one. She is family, she helped raise you.'

Phinn spat his tea back in his cup at this delusional statement, but there was no point arguing with their mother about her awful, awful sister. Where they saw a lifetime of selflessness and generosity from their mother to Mary, all they had witnessed in return from their aunt was her brazen willingness to have her younger sister take care of life's difficulties while she herself sat around moping. But right now Mary's grim visage betrayed a self-satisfied expression from her spot in the corner.

The glance between Phinn and Claudia contained a simple, acknowledged message: 'Thank Christ Poppy isn't here.'

'I've done the invitations, I've given the restaurant the numbers, I've done the tables. This is the first time I am hearing about a plus one.'

'I had assumed I had raised my daughter correctly and I didn't have to ask about Mary's plus one.'

'But you're not even bringing a plus one!'

'Well, only because I don't have one.'

Phinn and Claudia turned to Mary and expressed almost in unison the thought that up until now hadn't occurred to either of them.

'You have someone to bring to the wedding?'

Mary just smiled. 'Maybe. Just put him down anyway, Claudia sweetie.'

Claudia sighed. 'Well, it is Rachel's big day, I guess,' she finally said.

Claudia checked the upstairs bedrooms and found Zoe's bed already made with a note left on it 'Sorry. Not sorry.' Claudia sighed and asked the empty bedroom, 'Why leave tormenting notes when I have a phone?' She could hear Phinn's gait in the hallway, almost loping towards his bedroom, and she stepped out to cut him off.

'Why are you in Zoe's room?' he asked.

'I was just seeing where she was.'

'You don't need to go inside the room to see she is not in there.'

'Jesus Christ, Phinn, I'm not leafing through her diary. You don't need to be on permanent privacy patrol.'

'Well, hashtag just sayin'.'

'How can this millennial family be so bad at millennial mannerisms?' Claudia sighed. 'Anyway, I'm heading out to see Dad – are you coming?'

'If Zoe is gone, and you're going, and Poppy is content somewhere else, then I am definitely going somewhere by myself for seventeen hours. Or maybe two. I'll go kick the footy.'

'You don't want to see Dad?'

'Mate, unlike you I have a clear conscience, zero hang-ups – I don't feel the need to split my time down the middle and divide it completely evenly despite nobody, in particular Mum and Dad, noticing.' Phinn began to walk away. 'I see Dad all the time. We're cool.'

'Thanks for the life advice, solid coming from someone who still holds hands with his mother when crossing the street.'

Phinn didn't turn around or change his trajectory. 'I'm just fucking nice.'

Claudia kind of regretted her jab, but what was a trip home if not a thorough excavation through layers of guilt? As with rock formations created over hundreds of thousands of years, there was a completely random yet effective formulation for each level, holding up the next layer and with the oddest bits of history preserved. The deeper she dug, the more likely she was to come across areas that were still soft. Claudia couldn't just feel guilty about not spending equal time with each parent, she had to also feel guilty about telling her sister she couldn't come to her birthday party when she was five; about the last family event she had not made it home for; about her underwhelming reaction to her brother's thrilling news nine years ago; about calling her sister stupid when she was seven; about whether her low-level mocking was actually hitting a particularly vulnerable spot.

Claudia knew Phinn still held Rachel's hand when crossing the road ('Don't tell anyone, but...' Rachel had confided), but he was just an affectionate boy. Once he had told Zoe that one of his most devastating memories was when Rachel was busy in the kitchen and wouldn't give him his fourth hug of the morning. He told her in a moment of confidence and it had now become a folklore, used at Phinn's expense, just like most of the kids' deepest and darkest insecurities. Nothing was protected from their mirth.

Claudia stood still and listened for any sounds that would signal Phinn's return before ducking back into Zoe's room.

She got out her phone and took a Snapchat of the note on Zoe's bed, typing over it, 'bitch has jumped ship already', and sent it to Poppy. Her phone dinged back straight away with a photo of Poppy lying in bed with her arm covering her eyes. 'I wish I was dead', she had written across the photo. Claudia craned her neck but couldn't see if there was someone in the bed with Poppy.

'You want to come out to Dad's for lunch?' she messaged back.

'Yep,' Poppy wrote back, infuriatingly.

Her message habit was one- to two-word answers, a full stop, and none of the necessary detail unless it was specifically asked for. Claudia bent down from her waist and cradled her arms by the elbows, making a type of frame for her head before gently rocking it back and forth. It was the one useful yoga pose she had learned from the three times she had gone. She waited, let out a breath and then stood back up.

'Great! Where should I pick you up from? Looking to leave in about 45 minutes.' She kept her messages nonchalant after yoga breaths. There was no point in blowing up at Poppy for the way her message was written. That was a good way to get no response at all.

Claudia pulled up by the side of the road two houses down from the address Poppy had given her. She rested her chin on the steering wheel and listened to the last strains of 'I Luv the Valley OH!', humming along before singing in a faux-French accent.

She lifted her phone to let Poppy know she was here, but put it back down in the console and leaned against the seat. A rare moment alone. She had been harbouring the delusion that she would get quality time with her siblings. She wanted to test the waters before her friend or fiancé joined her, gauge the mood of the family, see how she went solo. By this point she knew that she missed him, which on the one hand was surely a good sign, but on the other should be a given. She missed having a reinforcement, someone permanently on her side no matter which family member she was squabbling with and in which circumstances. She missed having someone to do the driving and someone to hug at night. She missed his clarity when she was emotionally charged.

There would be no time with him, really. And, with Nora, she would be busy soothing her sisters' egos, while ensuring her mother felt involved and cherished.

She picked up her phone and messaged Poppy. 'Here.' She picked it up again and added a smiley face. She couldn't help herself.

She leaned back and looked at the house. Like every other one on the street it was two storeys, probably four bedrooms. It was weatherboard and had been painted a dusty pink. Claudia noticed the one next to it had been painted a powder blue. If she stood directly between them across the street, it would make a pretty good Instagram shot. She smiled despite herself. A nice little portrait of home for all the followers. Before she decided whether her little lame joke to herself would actually be a photograph that could garner more than fifty hits on a little heart icon, the car door opened and Poppy slid in next to her. She had on the same denim skirt from last night but over the top was a faded red flannelette top, carelessly buttoned and pushed up at the sleeves.

'Fun night?' Claudia asked.

'It was fine,' Poppy said, staring straight ahead. 'Are those my shorts you're wearing?' she said without even looking at her sister. Claudia glanced down at the loose teal denim shorts she had on with a white T-shirt and gold Birkenstocks.

'I thought they were Zoe's.'

'Hmmmm.'

Claudia started the car before saying, almost under her breath, 'Nice shirt.' Poppy sat perfectly still. Claudia did not bother trying to make any conversation with her on the drive to their father's.

They drove down avenues lined with Moreton Bay figs and soon the similar two-storey weatherboard houses painted in pastels and gloomy neutrals gave way to single-storey brick bungalows. Identical houses all in a row: the front door on the left and the bay-windowed living rooms on the right-hand side.

Claudia pulled into the driveway of one of them, distinct only in that it had pink geraniums planted next to the letterbox. The arrival at their father's house shifted something between the sisters, who – from being single, different entities, drifting apart – suddenly reverted to the unison of their childhood. A time when siblings do not so much copy each other as unconsciously act in tandem.

They opened the car doors at the same time and quickly ran to the house. Inside, their father was waiting by the table where a roast chicken from the supermarket had been cut up. He had never been much of a cook, but what he lacked in culinary skills he made up for in faux grandeur. George drew himself up to his full six feet four inches of height and hugged the sisters at the same time – one in each arm – as they tried to wrap themselves around his enormous stomach.

Claudia rubbed his bald head. 'Hello, Dad.'

'Hello Claudia, hello Poppy,' he said, letting each of them go. 'There's still another fifteen minutes until lunch. You the only ones?' he tried to ask innocently.

Claudia looked at Poppy but she seemed completely unruffled by the suggestion that seemed to be hidden in his question. Claudia was always looking to interpret something as hurt, or anger, or sadness.

'Zoe has gone AWOL and Phinn said he sees you enough and has gone to kick a football by himself.'

George stroked his grey moustache. 'Good for them.' He turned to walk towards the kitchen and automatically Poppy and Claudia fell into step behind him. A habit they must have picked up from when they were children, but whenever they were near him they would follow him around, from room to room, into the garden. Wherever he was, they would be.

'So, Claudia, you're having a little party on Saturday.'

'Hmmmm,' Claudia responded, while picking bits of feta cheese out of the salad he was trying to make.

George looked up from chopping the basil and narrowed his eyes. He seemed to do a quick mental calculation and landed on the side he always did: against pushing the issue. Perhaps for fear that he might actually have to have a conversation concerning emotions, Claudia observed.

'Claudia doesn't want to get married,' Poppy said, reaching across George in a way none of the other kids would have dared and taking a piece of cucumber from right next to his knife.

George responded slowly, forced into the conversation despite himself. He glanced at Claudia. 'Really?'

'No, not really. Poppy has convinced herself I don't want to get married, maybe from a conversation with Mum, or Zoe, or an equally reliable source—'

Poppy interrupted, 'Dylan isn't even here yet, Dad. Claudia does not seem excited at all. It's all very weird.'

Claudia set her jaw and then let it fall back into place, a relaxation trick she used when she couldn't do her odd yoga breaths.

'Dylan's coming in two days because I thought I could spare him some of the inevitable drama. I thought, as I always do when I am quite far away from you all, that I would like some quality time with you.'

'What a silly thought,' George said.

'Anyway, I do want to get married, that's why I am getting married, but I also want to get out of here as soon as possible. So.'

'Well, it's always nice when you pop by,' George said, an edge of sarcasm to his voice. Claudia winced and knew he was referring to the fact she was staying at Rachel's and not his house.

'Did you get the tie I sent you?' She tried to change the subject.

'Yes.' George waved his hand dismissively. 'Does it go with your mother's dress? I hear she is walking you down the aisle.'

Now he was being deliberately obtuse. Claudia made her tone even. 'You're both walking me down the aisle.'

'A special request from your mother?'

'No, actually, I didn't see why it shouldn't be both of you – you both raised me.'

'God forbid she would let you do anything just with me,' George muttered. He reached for the spring onion as Poppy took another piece of cucumber and put the rest in the bowl. 'How *is* your mother?'

'Same. Same same. Mary's still hanging around, draining

her energies, probably her wallet as well. Thank God she didn't have any children. Can you imagine how many people Mum might have had to look after?'

Glad for the break in scrutiny on her upcoming nuptials, Claudia warmed to the much safer subject of their conniving aunt.

'Actually,' Claudia said, 'Mary wants to bring someone to the wedding.'

George's breezy query came as he picked up the salad bowl and walked to the table in the next room, where he had left the chicken: 'Who?'

'I don't know,' Claudia said. 'She didn't seem to know herself.'

She set the ancient pink-bordered plates in front of her father, Poppy and herself as they sat down with George at the head of the table and she and Poppy on either side.

'Oh, I know who,' Poppy said, reaching for the chicken first, even though it was closest to Claudia. She started laughing to herself. 'Mick.'

Claudia, almost dropping the salad bowl, drew in a sharp breath. George speared a piece of chicken breast aggressively with his fork and looked up.

'Mick?'

Poppy nonchalantly finished her mouthful. Nothing either of their parents ever did ruffled her.

'Mick, as in your favourite little brother, yep. How do you think they got together?'

'Mary's usual desire to cause as much wreckage as she can, I'd say,' George said, still holding his poultry-laden fork aloft. Claudia suffered a sudden, inexplicable pang of sympathy for the skewered bird.

'What's wrong with Mick again?' Poppy asked, completely unnecessarily. They all knew the story. Nobody came out of it covered in glory.

'That's enough. Claudia, you said no, didn't you?'

'Yes, Dad,' Claudia said, looking at her plate. 'But I said no before she even told me who the person was. Although I think that Mick would know by now he didn't get an invitation.'

'Good. I can't believe your mother would put you in that situation,' George said.

Claudia just stared at him while he shook his head.

'You mad, bro? You seem mad. You can only be mad, you mad, bro?' Poppy was bouncing up and down in the car seat on the way home. The tenser her sister became, the more opportunities Poppy saw to poke. 'That was a loverrr-ly lunch,' she continued.

'Uh-huh.' Claudia nodded.

'You mad?'

'Nuh-uh.' Claudia shook her head, then turned left without bothering to indicate.

'Are you mad because you don't want to get married?'

Claudia laughed mirthlessly. 'I can't wait for Dylan to get here.'

Poppy stopped bouncing in her seat and studied her sister's profile. Her mouth was set in a grim line with her eyes looking directly ahead.

'What's up?'

Claudia tensed her shoulder muscles, lifting her shoulders up to her ears and then back down again.

'Just: never get married, and if you do, don't tell our family, and if you do that, then don't listen to our family, or be directed by them, or be guilted by them. Although,' she continued, glancing at Poppy, '*you're* never guilted by them. It just washes over you for some reason.'

'I thought they had been good. Mum and Dad seem super-helpful. I haven't heard them complaining.'

'Were we not just at the same lunch?'

'What did Dad complain about?'

Claudia shifted down a gear as she approached a stop sign, looked both ways, and coasted through the intersection. 'I totally paused,' she muttered to herself, smiling. 'Y'know, I actually wanted to invite Mick, but knew it just wasn't worth the hassle.'

'You wanted to give Mary a plus one?'

'No, I wanted to invite Mick before he was Mary's plus one. I've always liked him. He was a good and generous uncle. I don't think Dad has a good reason to hate him so much.'

'Well, he did cheat on Vicky.'

'So? How is that any of Dad's business? Yeah, it's bad, but I don't know why Dad had to get so involved in it. And it's his brother. Anyway, I knew how Dad would carry on so I didn't even bother trying to raise the subject. And then we're sitting at Dad's and he's complaining about the position Mum has put me in, which yeah, is out of line too, but he does it without even a hint of self-awareness. The way those two carry on, no wonder I never want to come home.'

Poppy looked out of the window, suddenly intently focused on the identical freshly mown lawns and the bright day lilies that bloomed all over Winston at this time of year. They were painted on tea towels sold as mementos for stopping in the town and worn in the hair of teen girls who picked them from front yards on the way to school. This year they had bloomed later than usual, something nobody in the town would think to regard as ominous, except perhaps a farmer. Eventually they eased into Rachel's driveway in silence.

CHAPTER 6

Phinn tried to keep a bead on the rotating hexagons spinning rapidly out of sight as the shapes quickly merged into a shrinking white ball still on an upward trajectory as it passed over the grey metal crossbar.

'Dribbly dammit,' he murmured, hands on hips, head tilted. The mistimed kick would mean a walk into the unruly scrub behind the goal net.

He was already tired of walking before he got to the fields, which served as the final border between the town and the bush surrounding it.

Without the car it was a good forty-five minutes on hoof to the browning glorified paddocks, and that wasn't even taking in the 400-metre driveway that the European arrivals to the area were forced to lay down to get to the last decent-sized expanse of land unthreatened by the bushfires during the worryingly more frequent dry seasons.

Still, it gave Phinn time to think on things without the

irritating volleys of perceived offences constantly arcing between his sisters, his mum and his aunt back at the house. At one point he had tried to tune out the chatter and petulant stomping up and down the hallway by reading one of the abandoned history books, before he realised that the background white noise had trapped him in one paragraph on the post-World War II origins of the CIA for forty-five minutes.

He looked back at the looping blue gravel track towards the highway. Phinn had a theory about driveways and the blokes he grew up with.

He noticed that with his invariably wilder mates in town, they would be out of the school gates in a flash and back to their local streets. He watched and waited as they sprinted up the slightly uneven concrete drives to their houses. Once inside they would quickly shed their navy school clothes for different uniforms of Kmart surf-branded T-shirts and hoodies and almost run back into town to yell their expletive-laden greetings to the same wayward schoolmates they had just spent the last eight hours with, in and out of detention. The only difference was that this time the disapproving scowls came from civilian adults outside of shops, not just the exhausted ones in the playground on the Department of Education's meagre payouts.

But when it came to his mates whose houses lay on the other side of the highway, it was a completely different equation. The battered silver bus would stop and drop them next to either a mounted keg or a white-painted stump with a number serving as a postbox. Beyond that, there would be another off-orange trail, sometimes winding a kilometre back to a homestead, usually bordered with barbed wire.

These guys didn't seem to be in any rush at all. They slung their bags over their shoulders and shuffled on, sometimes pausing to launch one of their scuffed sneakers at a fence post.

Phinn marvelled at it. With his pal Zeke, a ruddy-faced son of a dairy farmer, it had been a lazy twenty-four minutes before the pair saw the rusted rotary hoe, the first sign that they were approaching his fourteen-year-old mate's red-brick home. After banging open the screen door leading to the kitchen, Zeke had dumped his grey bag and rummaged in the fridge for the lime cordial as Phinn had watched on, curious. Zeke's movements betrayed no urgency.

'Aren't you going to change out of your uniform?' he'd finally asked.

'What for?' Zeke replied. 'To do what? Make more washing?' He'd lazily pointed at the two-metre-high squat rainwater tank outside. 'That's a flogging, Phineas.'

Embarrassed, Phinn had looked around at the lemon-yellow cabinets. 'Ah, so are we going back to town? To do stuff?'

Zeke turned back to his mate with a withering look. 'What for? We just got here.' He'd suddenly arched an eyebrow and delivered the first of what would eventually be many references to the family's undeclared cash crop. 'I've got to go check on the old man's . . . ah, green patch, out near the pump, just down the road. You can come. If you're not scared of tearing your uniform.'

'Walking?'

'Walking.'

More driveways, Phinn thought now as he rubbed the mud off the Barça-branded sphere and walked back to the bag of other soccer balls in the net. Zeke and all those other blokes outside town. Always shuffling on a driveway to another driveway just to get back in time to another driveway.

He hummed his own remix of Tom Cochrane, making life a driveway instead of a highway.

He lined up another ball on the right-hand corner of the goal box and thought of his other childhood mates in town, like Jase and Brayden, now reduced to faraway Facebook images of sunburnt stubble, Arnette sunnies, tribal tatts on biceps and AR-15s, all set against monochrome backdrops of clay huts and sand horizons.

This time the three steps to the ball lined up perfectly and he felt his left foot take his full weight before his right – one second coiled behind him – came swinging down. The satisfying sound of the strike gave him a full-body sensation. He watched the ball's tiny blur of a logo spin back at him then it disappeared into a strained section of the net at the goal's left edge before suddenly dropping like a shot bird.

'Wonder how many army careers could have been stopped just by longer driveways,' Phinn murmured to himself.

CHAPTER 7

Claudia: I can't wait for you to get here.

Dylan: Uh oh. I hope your family is being nice to you.

Claudia: Not really. I just wish you were here.

Dylan: Not long now my love.

Claudia: Aren't you even going to ask me what's wrong?!

Dylan: Um, I thought you would call.

Claudia: I hate my family.

Dylan: Your mind is like the Earth when men thought it was flat and they could sail off it and didn't go certain places because of dragons. Terrifying.

Claudia: You're meant to be on my side.

Dylan: I am. I will call you in a few hours.

Claudia: Great.

Dylan: Amazing.

Claudia: Fantastic.

Dylan: Super.

Claudia: SPLENDID.

CHAPTER 8

'A broken heart at a wedding is like an ugly baby: everyone will put up with it but keep it out of their face.'

'A broken heart at a wedding is like ice cream for dinner, incredibly indulgent.'

'A broken heart at a wedding is like your nine-to-five job, a fact of life not worth whining about.'

Nora leaned back in her train seat. The scenery had not changed much since she had left the city. She was four hours in with five hours to go.

She looked down at her diary, seeing that the fifteen lines or so beginning, 'A broken heart at a wedding is like ...' seemed rather pathetic once she put the pen down.

She glanced at her watch: like her handwritten diary, it seemed a relic. She assumed her friends kept their diaries in their Google drives, accessible from any device. That is if they kept diaries; she didn't even know if they did. Nora thought it was important to be aware of how much she had forgotten, which she was reminded whenever she read a diary from her teen years and marvelled at the names. She would revisit what at the time of writing had seemed like a life-changing event, but when she tried to conjure an image of it would come up with zilch.

The intricate brass minute-hand on Nora's watch ticked over to midday, a vertical exclamation point on top of its shorter, fatter counterpart. She almost leaped up from her chair in glee. It was a respectable time.

She walked to the dining cart where two young men, probably backpackers, were leaning against the counter watching some kind of sports game on a small screen held closely between them.

Nora smoothed her already crisp jeans. She was wearing a navy soft cotton down T-shirt, but her linen blazer remained draped over her seat in case it got cold later. Her chestnut-coloured hair had been blow-dried two days before so it was that sort of no-effort-ruffled-chic that she so enjoyed.

She watched the two men – adult-sized boys actually, she thought to herself – for another thirty seconds and cleared her throat. They looked up simultaneously, and seeing who was in front of them each tried to serve her at the same time.

'What would you like?'

'How are you today?'

'What can I get you?'

Nora caught the eye of the shorter one, just to save her the hassle of craning her neck slightly more, and smiled without showing any teeth.

'I'll just have a chardonnay, thanks.'

The shorter one beamed. 'Certainly, ma'am.' He turned around and, as he retrieved a miniature bottle from the fridge, Nora felt a wave of relief to see it was 500 millilitres and not one of the tinier ones. He gave her the bottle with a defeated-looking plastic cup on top as she handed over her credit card.

He winked at her. 'See you again soon, no doubt.'

Nora took the bottle and cup and let the comment bother her all the way back to her seat. What did he mean by that? That because she was buying wine at midday she would certainly be back again before the train reached its destination? She could have a glass of wine on the train. It was one of the reasons she had decided on the train: it seemed old-fashioned, kind of exciting. Time for a sit and a long think. A sit, a long think and a drink. They wouldn't offer it on the train if it was a problem, would they?

Nora was having this conversation with herself more and more lately. Did she need to drink wine at every dinner she went to? Could she have a lunch with someone without a bottle of something? Was two nights in a row booze-free enough? Did she need to drink at the cinema? At the China Town food court? At baby showers?

But everywhere she looked at these places, at these events, people were drinking as well. When she googled it a multitude of blogs came up, people who drank socially, were never told they had a problem and they gave up alcohol and then wrote about how it was a problem, an easily disguised problem if you're not drinking at six a.m. and still holding down your full-time job. The bar for being labelled not-a-problem-drinker is in fact very low.

All the blogs said that people who drank 'normally' never thought about drinking. They didn't count their alcohol-free nights and they didn't ask anyone else if they thought they drank normally. But Nora wasn't so sure. She also monitored how much meat she ate, how much sugar she consumed.

As long as she could remember, as a child at the lonely dinner table with just her mother, she ate her dinner faster than anyone she knew and then stared longingly at their full plate, just like she did in adulthood with her glass of wine.

She twisted the cap on her Jacob's Creek chardonnay and poured it into her little glass. She took the first wonderful sip and exhaled. Now was not the time to be thinking about her drinking. Now was the time to enjoy the surge of energy and hopefulness of the first sip, the low and euphoric hum that surged through her veins as she began to shake off all that kept her up at three a.m. She would focus only on the next blissful few hours. Now that she had a little armour, it was time to get out her laptop. Balancing the cup on her knee she slid it out of its simple black case and opened it up on the tray table in front of her. Taking a moment to whir to life, she dutifully typed in her password. MrsTran. It had long been a private joke with herself, a play on other girls' obsessions with what they thought marriage meant and other things she felt intellectually above, as well as a joke about her obsession with her boyfriend. Hamming it up, even when there was no one there to 'get' it.

She hesitated, took a swig of her wine, and opened her email. She clicked on the last email from Tom Tran. It had already been opened but remained without a response. She drained the rest of her glass, glanced sideways at the woman in her fifties beside her who had boarded at one of the larger and affluent coastal towns and was now eyeing her, poured the rest of the bottle into the glass and began to read:

> The fact is, in my heart, I know that I have generally taken you for a figurative ride for four years with little to no intention of marriage or children with you, which has forced me to take a hard look at myself. And I don't like what I see. Especially for you. I think the fact of the matter is you wanted this so badly you looked past the fact I am a pretty small person at the heart of it. And I

know it's a cliché, but I am so sorry and I know that there is someone out there who does deserve you a lot more than I do, especially when I look at what I have done and the fact I pushed these things to the side to be "a good guy". I appreciate now, ironically, that blinding yourself to the fact you love someone, but not enough to give as much of yourself to them that they are giving to you, means that you are NOT A NICE GUY, but an emotionally retarded fuckwit (to paraphrase from Helen Fielding, I guess).

Another thing I don't like about the email exchange is how absolutely cold and impassive this all sounds, when this whole mess has been dragging me into a deep, dark funk for the last ten days. I don't want you to think this isn't devastating for me (leaving aside the whole "poor-me I can't emote, boo-fucking-hoo" confessional at the top there). In the time we've been together, we've done so much, and you have been at my side for so many important things in my life (career change, the six-month healing process of a broken leg, family estrangements, etc.). I can't repay you for that. I wish I could.

And I guess that's the point. I believe this whole situation has seen us become different people. You are growing into your role as one of the country's leading young lawyers. You are also growing into yourself as a young woman, and not the, ah, brash but brilliant teen I first met. And sometimes, like it or not, I feel I am in the way of this because I cannot give you what you want as you grow (and I try desperately to stay in place). Once again, it is not fair to you. And I feel like a terrible person because I have been with you for four years, giving hope to you that something would happen along

> these avenues when it wasn't in me to start with, and is definitely drifting further away now.'

Nora shuddered and let out a low groan. She put down the glass and gently pressed the edge of her palms against her forehead. Reading it physically hurt. She could genuinely feel her heart contract tightly in her chest. She still couldn't quite believe it each time she read it. And she read it much more than she should. She hadn't even told Claudia she had broken it off with Tom. She had done it half as a lark. To try on singledom like slightly different underwear before returning to faithful briefs. Tom was still the man she was supposed to have her babies with, an actual life with. It would have been one last hurrah before settling down. If she was being brutally honest with herself it was also to sleep with one of her colleagues without feeling any guilt. And somehow it had spiralled out into this. An email telling her he had never really loved her. He did say he was devastated and blah blah blah. But that was the essentials of the message. He'd never loved her.

And now she was on her way to her best friend's wedding, unable to talk to the person she was closest to in the world about the break-up because it was happening in the most turbulent week of Claudia's life. Nora assumed it was the most chaotic; she hadn't spoken to Claudia since she had arrived in her home town. But Nora had been friends with her long enough to know what to expect. She was half prepared for an emotional wretch to meet her at the train station. It couldn't be a meeting of two emotional wretches, so Nora really needed to pull herself together.

Just one more read of the email, she told herself.

But first, she thought, standing up, another drink.

CHAPTER 9

Claudia stood on the platform with a bunch of cheap clearance-style roses in her hands. Flowers at airports, at bus and train stations, were a long time in-joke between the two friends. Neither of them could remember what the punchline was anymore ... was it to do with romantic comedies and men never buying flowers in real life? But they carried on. She shifted from one foot to the other and ran her hands through her hair, flicking the band on her wrist and untucking and tucking her pale pink shirt into her high-waisted black cigarette pants. Despite Nora's obvious distaste for them, Claudia was standing in the same black and white trainers she almost always wore, which she thought went with everything and added a bit of funk. Claudia was not nervous about seeing Nora. It did not matter if Nora thought her shoes were dreadful, or if Claudia had not showered this morning, or if she used phrases such as 'more better', which she was prone to do when very relaxed.

A best friend cannot make you nervous: there is too much

of yourself poured into them staring back out at you and it is difficult to find yourself particularly dazzling or intimidating.

What Claudia was worried about was the delicate familial ecosystem that Nora's arrival was about to interrupt. A once-closed natural balance comprising her and her sisters: of ego, of competition over each other's feelings, of insecurities, and some painful memories. The thought that the hurt of some recollections and the dull collective ache they provoked are not just shared with each other exclusively anymore. The realisation that as you get older there are other people you love enough that you can suffer with them too.

It works in reverse too. Secret languages, whatever truly brings you joy, jokes coded for a select few, your most hilarious shames – all once the province of sisters alone – can be shared with an expanded circle as you get older.

Between sisters, their emotions, their feelings for each other, a tricky tenderness, they're all spinning plates – but ornately inscribed, like ancient Chinese artefacts bearing narratives.

Here is the plate that represents you as the person I love most in the world.

Here is the plate showing how suffocated you can make me feel.

Here is the plate holding the memory of us as teenagers, when you told me you pity me and it was the most savage thing anyone has ever said to me and I will never forget it.

Here is the plate that holds a childhood full of fun and mutual adoration.

Here is the plate that only the two of us know about.

Here is the plate holding the constant feeling you are the only adult in the world I have ever wanted to smack in the head.

Simultaneously, your sister is the one with whom you are your most authentic self, who you don't have to watch what you say to, who knows everything you think, but is also the one who can be thrown into a rage at the most oblique reference, the most subtle dig. She knows everything you mean. She knows what everything you say means.

Now Claudia was about to add to this already precarious array of spinning plates, with relationships with people she had grown to love outside the family circle. A husband or wife can mostly provoke ambivalence. They're almost ornaments or accessories in family get-togethers, of complete uninterest to even the most passionate of siblings, who have no quibbles with ignoring the status of their in-laws. Nobody wants to have sex with their sibling, so why would you worry about the person who does?

But a friend. A friend is much more complicated territory.

Claudia could hear the rumble of the train before at last it came into view and she beamed to herself, thrilled at the thought of an arrival whose job essentially was to be in her corner.

The train stopped, shuddering to a final mechanical sigh. Shading her eyes against the sun, she looked down the silver and orange carriages as people began to get off. It was the usual older crowd: chubby older women in tracksuits, with hair that had been set at the hairdresser's just for the trip; young, harried parents with sunken eyes reflecting a ten-hour stint keeping toddlers captive in a ten-metre by four-metre box. Ecstatic children covered in chocolate and sausage-roll crumbs finally tasting freedom. Gloomy middle-aged women and men, who had escaped their home town decades ago and were unsurprised to be back. And Nora.

Nora stepped off a carriage halfway down the platform. She looked her usual cool, calm and collected self, dressed in the uniform of the eternally unruffled and calmer friend. Jeans, unwrinkled shirt, blazer. She wheeled a sleek monogrammed hard black suitcase next to her. Claudia shouted her name, waving enthusiastically, and started bounding towards her friend.

Nora turned towards her, grinning. But as she stepped forward her boot seemed to get mixed up with her suitcase, her foot turned at an odd angle and as she tried to lean on the suitcase for balance it slid out from beneath her, taking her leg with it. Suddenly she was sprawled on the ground.

Claudia hooted as she got to her friend's feet and put out her arm.

'Get it together!' she yelled – an old refrain between the two, but usually reserved for other people's pitfalls.

Nora quickly looked up and down the platform for people who were staring at her. Only a man in his seventies, wearing shorts with knee-high socks, was chuckling and not bothering to pretend it was about anything else but Nora's tumble. Nora took Claudia's hand and jumped to her feet.

'Jesus Christ, spare me,' she mumbled as Claudia pulled her in for a hug.

'You're here!' Claudia, a few inches taller than Nora, nuzzled Nora's neck, inhaling her scent. She stopped and held Nora out at arm's length, studying her face. 'Have you been drinking?'

'Why yes I have, thank you for asking,' Nora responded, laughing. 'What else am I going to do on a godforsaken thousand-year train trip I've taken purely for you?'

Claudia smiled and nodded, picking up Nora's suitcase.

'Let's get you checked into your crappy motel and you can scrub the smell of cheap chardonnay from your skin.'

'This is glamorous in a B-grade movie kind of way. I could see interesting things happening to you while you stay here.' Claudia surveyed the Motor Inn room the pair were forced to push their way into after the water-damaged door jammed.

'Interesting things like sexual assault?' Nora said, looking into the bathroom. The beige tiles were clean-ish. The brown carpet had been vacuumed strenuously, but she could already see that under the beds and down the side of the television cabinet had not had the same treatment. 'Make me a coffee would you?' Nora said, gesturing to the corner where a bar fridge squatted. On top sat a kettle and black sachets of Nescafé Blend 43 and white sugar.

Claudia flicked the white plastic kettle's switch. 'Need to sober up for the dress fitting?'

'Oh, rack off.' Nora was busy in the bathroom, taking out her various potions and gels. Claudia listened to the jet-like sound of the tap running, Nora squirting something onto her hands, the slap of skin on skin and the splashing of the water again.

She reappeared looking five years younger.

'You need to put mascara on and fill in your eyebrows; you look like a teenager,' Claudia said, stretching out on one of the single beds in the room. 'Why did you book a room with single beds?'

'In case you need rescuing,' Nora said deadpan, lying down on the other.

She rolled onto her back and stared at the fake wood panelling across the ceiling.

'How you doin', kid?' she asked the fan. She listened as Claudia let out a low sigh.

'I don't know.'

Nora rolled to her side, facing Claudia.

'You don't know?'

'Yeah, I don't know. I don't feel like I think I should. I should feel excited. I feel dread. Should I be feeling this is the surest thing I've ever done? Because I don't know if I've just allowed myself to be corralled into this and just gone along with it. I don't feel like I've made any actual decisions in this.'

'You feel dread? Is that because of Dylan? Or is it because you have to be here for a week? Is it because you're getting married or because you're at the centre of some weird emotional tug of war between your parents?'

'Well, a five year old could tell I'm not enjoying the guilt trips being laid on me by each of my parents in both their blatant and subtle ways. But maybe I am feeling a bit, I don't know, inconclusive about Dylan? Is this really the man I want to be married to? Do I really even want to be married? It's not very cool.'

Nora snorted.

'I'm not sure what your doubts are. Maybe you are just a walking and talking cliché at the moment and it's cold feet.'

'Hmmm, well maybe the week before their wedding would be exactly the time someone *would* reflect on their life.' Claudia sat up and poured two sachets of sugar into a mug with the instant coffee and picked up the kettle.

'You don't have time to reflect on your life this week.' Nora manoeuvred herself into a sitting position and put out her hand for the mug.

'There's no milk, be careful,' Claudia said, handing it to her. 'You know, I thought you would be more sympathetic, for some reason.'

'I'm here to give you what you need.'

CHAPTER 10

There is plenty to witness when you spend eighteen years living with the same people. Such as, watching them evolve from loving The Wiggles to loving Wilco and thinking that is an extremely individual act, along with approximately three million other teenagers at the time. If you are lucky, your siblings are the only people you ever really belt, that you fight with so ferociously there is hair and bits and skin scattered down hallways for months. Offspring watch their parents eternally commit the sin of being imperfect. Even though their humanness is demonstrated almost daily, the older you get, it still comes as a shock.

When you grow up with people, as opposed to just live with them, when you love them enough to show how enraged you are at their bathroom transgressions, then an unavoidable consequence is knowing them. Really knowing them. A movement of the mouth, the way a hand brushes away a bit of hair, the way their shoulders are set. Undetectable to most, but to those who truly know them, who have grown up with them, the way someone moves their eyebrow can say a hundred different things. I'm mad. I'm sad. I'm bored. I don't like this person. I am attracted to that person. Entire moods can shift within families on the way one of them has moved their hand. There is nowhere to hide from your siblings, from your parents, from your children.

This is how Claudia knew Poppy was going to be a complete cunt at her dress fitting.

Claudia was already standing with Nora in the light-filled upstairs room of the dress shop when her younger sister arrived. The pair were idly flicking through wedding magazines, trying to deduce the differences between the forty-five or so strapless white gowns filling the pages, when the door swung open. Claudia looked up and locked eyes with Poppy and knew. Poppy had her mouth closed, one of the sure signs of her infamous foul moods. It wasn't just closed, it was shut with purpose. She bowed her head slightly as she entered and leaned against a wall after giving her sister and friend a slight wave. She was wearing a short black skirt and a shirt with the logo of a band that had been in their prime when she had been in nappies, but it was her thongs that provided the most extreme visible provocation. She knew Claudia hated thongs. She also knew the final wedding-dress fitting was an event that merited actual shoes. But there she was. She raised her phone and started scrolling through it. Claudia glanced at Nora: beautiful, oblivious Nora. 'Hey Poppy,' she said cheerily. Her enthusiasm was rewarded with silence. Poppy looked Nora up and down, drinking in her ironed white-collared shirt, her espadrilles, her tapered dark jeans, cutting off neatly just above the ankle. She raised an eyebrow but – luckily – she didn't have the kind of cruelty in her to make a seemingly offhand remark that would have the victim thinking about it for three days, that would make someone weep into their pillow at three a.m. while the tormentor forgot what she had said almost immediately. That was Zoe's specialty.

As a silence was settling between them – one Claudia would call uncomfortable, Nora would call innocuous and Poppy wouldn't even notice – a cascade of red tulle entered the room.

It stopped in front of Claudia and the head of a doll emerged from the top of it. It took the trio a moment to realise it was just the woman at the centre of the red tulle dropping her enormous skirt now that she had stopped.

'Claudddiaaaaaaa,' she squealed.

'Amelia,' Claudia responded meekly, while grasping for something else to say. 'Mum isn't here yet.' Claudia stepped back involuntarily. There was just so much of Amelia; she filled the room.

She wore a ball gown. A red ball gown with a full tulle skirt she had to lift so high when she was walking that it obscured her head, bringing to mind visions of a classic seventies crocheted toilet doily, with its dress billowing out just below its plastic bosoms. The bodice was fitted to her waist and there seemed to be at least three petticoats underneath. An intricate, gold-thread diamond pattern was punctured by different jewels. Her dark hair was pulled back in a severe bun and she wore full make-up of red lipstick, foundation that was half a shade too dark, cat-eye eyeliner, bronzer and blush, both in shades slightly too dark and slightly too bright for her skin. The overall effect left one wondering if she was quite mad or if she was so lacking in personality that this was her way of making up for it.

'It's so refreshing to have a bride who doesn't feel the need to diet before her wedding,' Amelia said with a bright smile while looking Claudia up and down.

Amelia was a bitch.

Nora opened her mouth and then quickly closed it again,

the manners so ingrained into her as a child once again short-circuiting her stinging response. Poppy snorted while Claudia, in the absence of any appropriate comeback, just thanked the boutique owner.

'I don't think we should start until Mum gets here,' Claudia added.

Amelia's eyes narrowed slightly. 'This is a very busy shop.'

'We can see that,' Nora said, looking around the space that was entirely empty except for the four women.

'It's okay, Mum would've been out the door but just wanted to put on a load of washing,' Poppy said, speaking for the first time. Claudia looked to her hopefully but Poppy was scrolling on her phone again. Like a menacing stray cat, her crankiness had looked around the room and settled in, making itself comfortable on the green velvet chaise longue. It was here for the morning.

'Are you going to offer us some tea? Maybe some champagne?' Nora asked, inherently scary by the sheer neatness of her clothes and hair. She was trying to fill the room with her 48-kilogram frame, to show Amelia she was committing the most heinous of sins – being a bad host. She wanted Amelia to feel small.

'Oh of course,' Amelia said breezily. 'I just thought since the appointment was for nine thirty a.m. we would have everyone here at nine thirty a.m. and I could offer refreshments at nine thirty-five a.m. Now I think of it, it's been so long that the tea I prepared for you might be cold. Eeeessssiiieeee,' she called.

A plain woman in her fifties appeared, hair cropped, rimless glasses on, holding a tray with five crystal glasses of champagne, a teapot and five mugs.

'Help yourself while we wait,' Amelia said, cocking her head to emphasise the wait. Nora defiantly picked up a champagne glass and found a spot on the chaise longue. Poppy jumped away from the wall, an animation brought to life.

'Hold on! Let's get a photo before we drink them,' she said, reaching her phone out awkwardly in front of her and sitting down so close to Nora she was almost in her lap. She grabbed a champagne glass and beckoned to Claudia.

'I'm not drinking this morning,' her sister said.

'That's okay, just hold the glass for the photo.'

'What is this photo for?'

'Just Snapchat; we don't have a money shot for Insta yet.'

It was on the tip of Claudia's tongue, so close that the way she clamped on it was almost violent. But she didn't say it. She picked up a glass and sat on the other side of Nora, tilting her head just so for the photo.

Poppy returned to her sulk corner as soon as she'd uploaded it. Nora took a swig of her champagne. Claudia's chest tightened as she tried to think of something to say to pull Poppy from her mood. Amelia continued to glare.

Finally, finally, finally, after a century had passed, after the tides had adjusted to a new distance from the moon, after dynasties had risen to power and died out due to infertility, after another planet had been discovered and dismissed from the solar system like an unwanted child, the door opened.

Rachel never apologised for being late. Not because she thought it was not her fault, or because she thought of it as a power play, or because it was so rare. She never apologised because it never occurred to her it was rude to be late – or even that she was tardy at all. She was such a chronically late person it was as if the concept of seconds, minutes and hours did not apply to her: like someone in a pulp sci-fi novel she was exempt from time's terrible, inexorable powers. And if it did somehow apply to her, then nobody else's time would be more valuable than hers anyway.

Trailed by Zoe, she walked in, as excited as Carole Middleton on learning who else would be going to St Andrews.

'She had to hang some washing out before we left,' Zoe said dryly, looking Poppy up and down. Zoe nodded towards Claudia, holding eye contact for a moment and a half. That was the length of time it took to convey, 'Don't blow up at Mum; at least we aren't here an hour late. I see Poppy is in a foul mood so this is going to be a fun morning, but at least I am here for you, don't worry.' If she'd had the time she would have also set her face into delivering an addendum: 'I don't know why you have to bring Nora everywhere when you have me,' but, mercifully, she broke eye contact.

'Hello sweeeeetie,' Rachel said, giving Poppy a hug before the bride, which they all knew meant she had registered Poppy's cloud of scorn as well.

'Aw shit, man, I wish I was dead,' Zoe said, staring Poppy straight in the eyes.

Amelia finally interrupted.

'Let's get in this dress, shall we?' she said sharply.

Nora looked from Amelia to Claudia to Rachel and, after being certain nobody was looking, picked up a second glass of champagne.

Claudia had disappeared, whisked away to a changing room, pulled away by a tide of red tulle. Rachel faced the other women and weighed up her options: she was now bored with Zoe and, after quickly noting Poppy's combative stance, turned to Nora.

'It's so nice you could come, to be here in the days before it really gets manic,' she trilled, unable to help herself. 'Claudia needs all the support she can get.'

Nora, having known Rachel for years, knew that all that was required of her was a nod and smile. Conversation with the matriarch did not need a verbal participant, just some faint sounds of agreement and an adequately interested-looking face.

Zoe cut her eyes at her mother in warning. But Rachel forged on obliviously in her bid to pull her youngest daughter out of her scary funk, while bypassing the well-worn path of confrontation, screams, tears and apologies.

'Have you seen the veil we think will go perfectly with the dress? Poppy made it! She's so clever. Claudia wants flowers in her hair, for some reason. I think it looks so common; you can wear flowers in your hair to your birthday party, why wouldn't you wear a veil on your wedding day? You only get married once – well, that's the ambition. She wasn't letting go of this flower idea and I said why don't you try a veil with a little bit of flower embroidered on it? Well, Amelia said that was impossible to get, that she would order it in for about $220 but Poppy said to leave it with her. Why should tulle be so difficult to sew into? And she did it! She's so clever. Aren't you, Poppy? Just watched a video on the internet, it looks so beautiful, but I haven't seen Claudia try it on yet. It was only $11 to make!'

Rachel used the time she needed to draw breath and look at her two daughters. It was pathetic and desperate the lengths one would go to in an attempt to pull Poppy out of a mood while steadfastly maintaining the pretence that she wasn't in one to start with. It was a complicated process. Often those involved would end up walking around her as if on an unpredictable platform of rotten wooden floorboards, gently testing where they could place their feet with each treacherous step.

Putting aside prior inclinations and private promises, Zoe joined in the pantomime. 'I didn't know Poppy made the veil!'

Which basically translated to: 'Please crack a smile. Don't you want to feel good? Please don't ruin the afternoon. Please don't ruin the week.' It was half-begging, half-praying.

'I just looked it up on YouTube,' Poppy said, glancing up

from her phone. 'Hey, that's a cool photo. You're all at equal distance apart. Stay there.'

Rachel and Zoe didn't move, but there was a certain eagerness to how still they stood. Nora turned towards the camera and Poppy took the requisite eight frames.

Oblivious to the desperate motivations behind the impassioned interplay, Nora actually asked how long it had taken to craft the veil out of genuine curiosity rather than any desire to placate her. Nora didn't even know Poppy had to be placated.

She did not get any response, though. Poppy was already hunched over her phone in a blur of thumbs, ticking sounds and raw intent.

Zoe felt her back pocket buzz with an Instagram notification.

@PoppyBangBang had tagged her in a photo. Zoe read the caption: 'Dress fittings with my Ma and @noranotephron @ZoeYouShould for the most beautiful bride ever #forwhom thebelltulles'. The tips of Zoe's ears went red.

'Wow, that's some real bullshit right there,' she said, looking directly at Poppy while gesturing to the screen. 'Why you gotta do that? Post a photo on social media like you're having an amazing time when you've barely spoken to us the entire time. That's some boring and clichéd bullshit there.'

Poppy raised her eyebrows. 'Well, unlike you I've been to plenty of fittings, so excuse me if I'm not as thrilled by the novelty as you seem to be.'

'You're a real brat, you know that,' Zoe shot back, pointedly ignoring her mother's pleading glances. 'A freakin' class A, Mariah Carey ticket-holding, Prince George mimicking, Bieber entourage member brat.' Zoe's tipping point had been reached somewhere between Rachel's obvious hand-wringing desperation and the delicate sugar-coating that everyone – except Nora – had been trying to apply to a benign discussion on bridal accessories.

'Well, I've actually been here. Some of us don't get to swan in with overpriced handbags, creating an illusion of a personality and then expect everyone to get along with us,' Poppy replied, provoking a sharp intake of breath from Nora, the only reminder she was still in the room.

Zoe responded with the most infuriating thing a sibling can do during a violent crossfire of harsh home truths. She laughed. She didn't think it was funny. It was merely a basic battle strategy, launched for maximum impact on Poppy's fury.

'Girls, girls, stop it, I swear to God, I will tell your father,' Rachel whispered, invoking a long impotent threat that had survived the divorce and remained out of habit.

She was interrupted by the salon door swinging open. In the doorway stood the cheesecloth-clad figure easily capable of restoring Zoe and Poppy's sisterly affection via a well of mutual spite. 'Hellllooo sweeeeties!'

'Helllooo!' Mary bellowed. 'Rachel, I know this was a girls' afternoon, but you told me about the fitting and I thought – well, I'm in the neighbourhood – I might as well pop my head in ... And I'm a girl!'

Poppy's eyes narrowed as Zoe muttered, 'So your purpose for being in the neighbourhood is to crash things you were specifically not invited to?'

Rachel, who came from a long tradition of bestowing her best graces on those least deserving of them, hugged her sister, the previous shouting match now a distant memory. 'Of course you're welcome! Here comes Amelia; I think Claudie has just put on the dress.'

Zoe looked from Mary to the emerging Amelia in horror: she knew Claudia would be just behind her. Amelia did a dramatic bow, took a dainty sidestep and held out her arms for the bride to emerge. Nora idly wondered if the circus-master style that Amelia employed for such grand entrances was not the teeniest bit ironic in the current circumstances.

Claudia stepped out from behind the curtain, a vision resplendent in ivory. She glanced around the room and quickly clocked the distance between Zoe and Poppy, but it was only after she had registered Mary's presence that her face really began to fall.

Poppy turned on her heel and left.

But Claudia was already in tears.

'Why is Mary seeing my dress before Dad does?'

CHAPTER 11

Poppy stormed down the street, fists clenched, chest stretched tight. She could hear her heart. It was compressed and beating madly. Her ears filled with roiling blood. She was muttering under her breath. Nobody walking past could quite catch what she was saying but it was to a steady, basic beat: 'And up two, three, four, five, six, seven, eight, and down two, three, four, five, six, seven, eight, and up two, three, four, five, six, seven, eight.' It was a mantra she had learned when she was teaching barre classes – just one of her fly-by-night jobs that never seemed to involve discussions of contracts, sick pay and holiday leave. It was incredibly easy to convince people you knew about the combination of yoga, Pilates and ballet, and people in the city were willing to pay $25 for the pleasure of being fooled. She would count three sets of eight leg raises to the beat she was reciting, three sets of eight turned-out pulses, three sets of eight making little circles with your arms. She swore she did the counts in her sleep. She also used it to try to calm her anxiety.

She didn't know why she always had to be so awful when there were too many members of her family in one space. She felt there was no room to breathe; she felt herself regressing the minute she was with both of her sisters and mother. The more she told herself before the event that she would behave, that she would be happy, the more the anxiety would move from her stomach to her chest to her limbs – so they wouldn't move – and finally to her mouth, which would inevitably fix in a pout. Something would infuriate her, a flippant remark about her bedroom, a comment on her clothes, a question about her job(s), and all the anxiety, at this point a rapidly whizzing internal combustion of bristling nerve endings, would once again strike the flint of her open heart and become that familiar iron spark before the explosion about to force its way out. Blind rage. Even while she was spitting insults at her sisters, refusing to speak at a lunch table, there would be a small part of her asking, 'Why, why are you doing this?' but a bigger part of her, the part in charge, would be too furious to respond.

She had ruined the dress fitting. She knew that. But her perfect sisters with their perfect lives would get over it. Arseholes.

Poppy continued walking and counting down the beats until the white-hot flare of anger bubbled down and became manageable, a small dark stress ball she could toss from hand to hand until it turned to guilt. Poppy got out her phone and sent a text. Within a minute a message had flashed on her screen. She read it and let out a small sigh, before turning on her heel in the direction of the pub.

Poppy pressed her palm flat to her fringe. She had read somewhere that it was preferable to running your fingers through it because that just made it greasy. She wondered if that was bullshit, like primer before foundation. Probably.

She looked down. She was wearing a long loose black dress with pink patterns of lipstick all over it. After years of dressing in jeans and shirts in an attempt to prove her sexuality – an unconscious plea to those she had come out to: 'See, I am serious about being a lesbian; this shirt is from the men's section!' – she had become more comfortable embracing her *femme* side. She did not know if the dress looked like a shapeless sack or very chic, though. It was slightly irrational given the medium, but if she had known she was going to text Leah today she would've worn something entirely different. Something that accurately conveyed that she was unaffected, and sartorially savvy, but without trying too hard. But anyway. Here she was. She had told Leah she was busy with wedding preparations when she left her house the other morning, so she knew it was her responsibility to make next contact. She just hadn't thought she actually would.

Leah was perched in the corner when Poppy walked in. She sat on a high stool at a small round table – her feet not quite reaching the bar below her – with her spine stiff, sitting ruler straight. Her black shirt read 'Pissed Jeans doesn't care about YOU people' in plain white type. Only because of Dylan did Poppy know this was a reference to yet another band of skinny white men-children with loud guitars. She smiled. Leah hadn't even been halfway through primary school by the time the nineties finished.

Leah looked up, saw Poppy, and they greeted each other with the acute awkwardness of two almost-strangers who have exchanged bodily fluids.

There's the awkwardness of a confessed crush, a drunken kiss with a colleague, or telling an acquaintance they have something in their teeth: awkwardness is a spectrum. On the spectrum, Leah and Poppy were at the fairly niche end where you have sucked their titties and lost your virginity to their brother.

'Tough day?' Leah asked after Poppy's mumbled greeting. They both directed their glances towards vague points of the pub and paused, each waiting for the other to keep talking.

After a beat too long Poppy turned back and pointed to Leah's empty schooner glass. Leah nodded.

Three empty glasses later, a slightly more relaxed Leah was finishing her medium-sized story about how she had decided to run a small-sized business from her parents' house, selling earrings in the shapes of icy poles and book covers.

'Because of copyright, maybe the second worst law after defamation, I can't do iconic book covers, so they are puns on famous book titles. You know, *Grater Expectations* with Pip and a little cheese grater? *Couching Towards Bethlehem*? *One Hundred Beers of Solitude* with an old Spanish guy sitting at a bar?'

Poppy laughed. 'That's clever. You should branch into CD covers next. You can do *Don't Look Back in Hunger* with the Gallagher brothers tucking into a cake or *Nevermime* with the French clown guy in the pool instead of the floating baby.'

Leah laughed and grabbed the table to steady herself on the stool. 'Holy shit, that's good! Maybe you can be my chief strategist. I need to market as well, which basically means I don't know how to use Instagram.'

'Just post a sunset at least once a week and only put up pictures before nine a.m. and after six thirty p.m. Your followers will quadruple.'

'See, you're a natural.' Leah smiled coyly.

'Well, I do have a degree in journalism, which is essentially marketing. And I follow Selena Gomez on Instagram. Really, Selena taught me everything I know.'

'Amen.'

Poppy looked at a corner of the roof of the pub as she addressed Leah.

'It's brave what you've done.'

'What? Starting my own business? The overheads are incredibly low when it is run out of your parents' garage.'

'Hmmm, that and coming back. Knowing when the time was to come back.'

Leah stopped smiling and sagged her shoulders. 'Knowing when to give up, you mean.'

Poppy moved her gaze from the corner to a rag lying on a chair three tables away from them.

'Yes. That's brave too. Knowing when to give up.' She looked at Leah. 'The ground has become sand beneath us. It's falling away. The city isn't made for us anymore, it's a fortress for the wealthy. You want to live in the city now, you have to be born in the city, or come from the kind of wealth that could fill Olympic swimming pools with cash. I haven't quite accepted that yet.'

'How long ago did you graduate?'

'Two years. Two years and seven months. And three weeks. Two years seven months and three weeks and I still don't have a proper job. Just a bunch of gigs. A bunch of gigs in the gig economy.'

Leah nodded empathetically. Truly. She had been there.

'What kind of gigs?'

'Copywriting. A bit of reception work. Delivering pizzas on my bike. I used to Uber but had to sell my car. I'm so tired. I thought I would have a job by now. I am supposed to have a job by now. But I don't even know what the industry is going to look like in five years' time. Where are journalists meant to fit in all of this? You can flog your product direct to the customer online now. I know journalists should exist, sometimes I think they have to exist, but I just have no idea how they are meant to fit into the new model. What is supposed to fund us? Do we just rely on benevolent millionaires? Subscriptions? I honestly can't even see at the moment how something like the press gallery is supposed to exist. I can't see the market demand for it.'

'I just couldn't get a real job. I know people want illustrators; a few years ago you could eke out a living doing it. But now you eke out the same living and rent is five times as much as it was just five years ago.'

'And the planet is being destroyed; the Great Barrier Reef is being bleached. RIP the Great Barrier Reef. We can't have housing and we can't snorkel.'

The conversation had taken the inevitable turn. Their own destruction.

Poppy took a swig of her beer. 'I don't know how we are going to survive. I don't know what the jobs of the future will look like. I don't know how we can save ourselves from being poor.'

'I can't penetrate the future either. I have no idea what we'll look like in five years, what the country will look like.'

'Do you want to know how I comfort myself? Surely America collapses first? We'll get the warning, won't we? We'll have a warning and it will be America. That country will fail first and then we will know what to look out for. Then we will know what's coming.'

Leah sat up straighter. 'I've been doing boxing four times a week – I'm ready for the war.' She grinned and raised her beer to clink Poppy's.

'To being ready for the war,' they chanted.

They were so miserable there was no option but to go home together.

CHAPTER 12

Reasons People Are Wrong, by Claudia Carter, an exercise in being committed to passive aggression and not yelling at my family:

Mum bought blue cheese.

Poppy does not believe in compromise.

Phinn won't stop playing the guitar.

Zoe said I was not interesting when I was talking about the superiority of plunger coffee over Nespresso.

I feel like a moody bitch.

Nobody appreciates it when I'm a decent human being.

The house is already trashed.

It's really windy.

We have a fridge full of beer and the only cold ones are fucking Stella.

Poppy is just a bitch.

I can't think of any more failings for myself. I am just moody.

I thought I saw a dolphin once but it was just wind.

I can't find a candle to light so I can pray Poppy dies next time she goes on an overseas holiday she can supposedly not afford.

Poppy taking my beer despite there being cold Stella in the fridge. She doesn't want anything unless it's mine, then she needs it badly and is obviously entitled to it. Apparently she is not capable of deciding she wants a Bighead and putting one in the freezer herself and waiting for it to be cold. Apparently I should be taking care of her needs at all times. Allowing her to be in my bridal party and choose her own dress is obviously not doing enough for her; I should be making her beer (which she also didn't pay for) cold too.

I pulled Poppy's hair for a not-very-good reason. It's just a beer. Should save the violence for when she commits credit-card fraud in my name for an ugly It Bag or something of the sort.

Phinn took photos of a serious fight.

Dylan is the only decent human being in the family, and that includes me.

I told Poppy I didn't want her here. Which in the moment was true, but in the balance of things isn't.

Poppy will not say sorry for taking my beer.

I am being uncharacteristically passive aggressive but it might be allowed because I am at least funny.

There was no last-minute accommodation in town midweek. That would have showed them.

CHAPTER 13

To say that Dylan was a simple man was to say that the sun is bright. It is true on a very basic level but it's ignoring a hell of a lot of complexity. Dylan possessed those characteristics that are most underrated in human beings. He was funny and intelligent – attributes recited monotonously around the world when people talk about what's important to them. Because it's true but, on the other hand, it's unacceptable to also say, 'I want someone who will ignore my polite requests during sex and just throw me down' or, 'I want someone who will always take my side against my reasonable mother' or, 'I want someone who will accept me as a little bit sexist and racist but fundamentally a decent human being'.

Dylan fulfilled the criteria one usually simply forgot to acknowledge out loud. It was an overlooked quality due to it being slightly out of fashion, a little bit boring and just plain taken-for-granted – he was kind.

When he was seven years old, much to his father's horror, he donned a pair of rabbit ears and hopped up and down his street leaving chocolate eggs on the neighbours' doorsteps.

When he was thirteen he asked the tallest girl in the class to dance after watching her stare at the floor for an hour at the disco.

When he was sixteen he spent six weeks mowing the lawn of a teacher with a broken leg because he knew he had not made any friends in his town yet.

When he was nineteen he would rub his girlfriend's back when she suffered period pain and fetch her a hot-water bottle instead of dismissing it as yucky, whiny women's business like most of his peers.

His kindness wasn't ostentatious, or extravagant, or even worthy of any notable praise, as most of it fell in the category of Decent Thing To Do. But being kind is much more difficult than most of us who have never practised kindness assume it to be.

It was this sweet, kind, slightly awkward man who now walked into the jaws of the Carter family.

Dylan had obligingly made the nine-hour trip by car to Claudia's home town. It was easier if they had their own getaway wheels. In a stupendous mood after uninterrupted hours of listening to Mclusky and Future of the Left, he hummed along to the opening strains of 'She Will Only Bring You Happiness' as he pulled into George's street. The week was going to be fine; difficult at times, but fine, he thought to himself, an unsurprising stance given his perennially sunny disposition.

He turned down the music as he pulled into George's driveway. He was never quite sure if it was the right low brick bungalow he was entering, and liked to turn down any noise for concentration, just like when he turned off the radio to focus on his parallel parking. But this time he knew he was right. The garage door was slightly raised and through the bottom he could see three pairs of bright pink Adidas shoes. Matching anything was a classic Carter giveaway, despite everyone demonstrably being older than five, and was something even the parents joined in on. Dylan allowed himself a sigh. Even from here he could tell they were up to something; they had the whiff of mischief as unity. He wouldn't be walking into a brawl, sulky silences and bruised egos; instead, today, it would be scheming. As he edged the car up the driveway he could see the owners of the pink sneakers had registered his approach. The stances changed and a head appeared at the bottom of the garage door, bending over to get a good look. He saw the ruffled head of his fiancée. Claudia's blonde hair, almost bleached into oblivion, fell over her dark eyebrows and ill-advised grey-rimmed glasses. She saw Dylan and a huge smile broke out as she lay down on the ground and wriggled beneath the garage door.

'Dylan! Love of my life, eternal joy of my soul! You came running back to me!'

She leaped into his arms and wrapped her legs around him.

For a moment there were no doubts. Dylan kissed her nose and placed her on the ground, glancing towards the other two pairs of feet visible in the garage.

'What's going on in there?' he asked.

Claudia cocked her head. 'Family bonding time.'

'Hoo boy.'

Dylan walked over to the roller door and bent to lift it.

'NO!' Claudia stopped him. 'We can't open the door; we can't let anyone see what's going on in there. Wriggle under.'

So it begins, Dylan thought to himself. He briefly considered a protest but he was not wired that way. He lay down on the ground and rolled under the door, coming to rest on his back inside the garage.

'Dylan!'

Poppy and George spoke in unison as their heads appeared in his vision. Despite the weather, Poppy seemed to be wearing a dark polo neck, beanie and sunglasses. George was in a pale blue shirt that read 'This is what a feminist looks like', something he probably found hilarious.

'I don't want to give you the satisfaction of asking,' Dylan said, looking at Poppy as he scrambled to his feet. He shook George's hand as Claudia finished rolling beneath the garage door.

'What are the three of you up to?' Dylan looked around and saw a bright blue Mercedes. 'Whose car is that?'

He walked closer and saw that it seemed lopsided.

'It's kind of a long story,' George said thoughtfully as Dylan walked to the side and noted the two flat tyres.

'Do you think we should deflate all of them, or is two enough?'

'All of them will be a much bigger pain in the arse,' Poppy said, heading to the other side of the car and crouching down. Dylan heard the not-quite whistle of air escaping a tyre.

'This is a nice car,' he said, pressing the edge of his shoe against the rubber, as if he was double-checking it was real.

'It's Lisa's,' Claudia said cheerfully. 'She left Dad.'

'Again,' Poppy interjected.

'She wanted to keep some plates in a different cupboard, and it was just the last straw,' George said, rubbing his jaw.

'So you're letting down the tyres of her car?'

'Well, we paid for it together but it's in her name. I don't want her coming during the night and taking it.'

'What is the likelihood of that?'

'You never know with women; they can turn into real bitches at times like this.'

Dylan looked at Poppy, but she continued to concentrate on the air escaping every tyre. As usual, her staunch feminist credentials evaporated in the presence of the men in her family. Poppy felt Dylan's stare and looked up at him.

'What? She is a bitch.'

George stood up abruptly, brushing down his garish shirt with the palms of his hands. 'You know that you are quite "misfeatured" to Dylan?' he said, looking down at his youngest daughter.

'What?'

'I read it in a book the other day. Zadie Smith, I think. She basically said that the siblings of the people we desire are uglier versions. I thought that was very good. What do you think, Dylan? Do you think Poppy is an uglier, misfeatured version of Claudie?'

Dylan paused. 'I've never looked at Poppy.'

George roared with laughter. 'Pitiful dodge. Come inside and I'll feed you.'

Claudia trailed behind Dylan and George as they made their way to the kitchen, leaving a satisfied Poppy with one last tyre to deflate. Through the side door they went down a hallway lined with eccentric decorative drawings and paintings – not many would stoop to call it art. Mostly they were gifts from his children. Shaky paintings of mountains bought from gypsies in some overly frequented European city that made them feel worldly; sketches from the country, and pictures and pictures and pictures of pelicans, a joke that had long ago run its course, but still they persisted in buying a postcard or painting or drawing of one whenever it was spotted.

The hall opened to the kitchen where a giant bowl of tomatoes sat on an otherwise bare table.

'It's a real treat to have you with me today; I get to cook with one of the most tasty and diverse vegetables there is, but which I was forbidden from even mentioning for twenty-one long years,' George said, picking up three tomatoes and lightly squeezing the skin. 'I'm going to make you strapatsada – a little treat, just for you and me.'

Claudia walked over to her father and peered into the bowl. 'I like tomatoes,' she said.

George looked at her, horrified. 'No you don't.'

'Yes I do.'

'No you don't.'

'Yes I do.'

'Since when?'

'For a few years now.'

'You've never liked them.'

'Well, I didn't when I was a kid, but I have been an adult outside of your house for many years now and I like tomatoes. I feel like I'm hitting you over the head with a metaphor now.'

George stared at his second child for a moment too long.

'I feel bad for you and pity me,' he said finally. 'You can have some strapatsada.'

Strapatsada, for when your child is still breaking your heart twenty-eight years on and you are reasonably sure she is going to break the heart of the lovely young man at your table:

Chop up eight tomatoes and put them in a heavy-based pan that is already hot with a little olive oil. Stir for five minutes and watch as they reduce. Put the toast on and pour into the mixture a tablespoon of tomato puree with some sugar and some salt. Stir.

Crack two eggs into the tomato mixture and stir as if scrambling for another five minutes as the skins of the tomatoes come off. Take off heat. Spread generously across toast and crumble sharp cheddar and basil leaves on top.

Serve.

Try not to look too devastated at the realisation that – for the 482nd time – you are not the expert on your daughter.

George sat down with Claudia and Dylan as they hoed in. Dinner-table manners are one of the first things eschewed as surplus to requirements once the third child comes along, before you start letting go of frivolities such as daily hygiene with the fourth.

'Mary has a new boyfriend,' Claudia said over their chomping.

Dylan raised an eyebrow. 'Hmmmmmm.'

'It could be a big drama for the wedding.'

Dylan finally looked attentive.

'It's Dad's brother.'

Dylan snorted and George stood up. 'It's not a drama. She can see whoever she wants to see.'

'But she wants to bring him to the wedding.'

George waved a hand as if dismissing his court. 'But she's not.'

Claudia looked at Dylan and nodded towards him. 'See, drama.'

George had already sulkily started to scrape his uneaten strapatsada into a bin and was out the door before anyone had the time to start on a second piece of toast.

'As you are well aware, my family is notorious for how reasonably and well they handle the slightest hint of emotional upheaval,' Claudia said, pretending very badly she was not shaken by her father's hasty exit. Dylan reached over and grabbed her hand, tenderly rubbing his thumb over the top of her knuckles.

'What's the deal with Mick?' Dylan asked, hating himself a little bit.

'It's a long and involved and boring story, but basically Mick cheated on his wife in a very visible and humiliating fashion and Dad has never forgiven him. He took her side. She is invited to our wedding; he is not. Dad hasn't spoken to his brother in about five years, I think; won't even be in the same room.'

'What about birthdays? Surely your family has had some birthdays?'

'Oh, you think the fact it is someone else's birthday would get in the way of his grudge?' Claudia laughed her meanest laugh. 'No, it is for the rest of us to work around.'

Dylan picked at the last of his eggs and tomatoes, as he liked to call George's Greek creation. 'Three sleeps until the wedding. Is there anything you would like?'

Claudia brightened. 'A contract!'

'Well, technically I think we are entering a contract.'

'No, like Kurt Vonnegut, he wrote his wife a contract. Basically saying she could only yell at him after he had failed to do something for three days and that he would scrub the bath after every use so it didn't leave a mucky ring.'

'Hmmm, okay, you want a contract?'

'Yes please. Also can you check in with Nora and make sure she is going okay? She is having some Nora time at the moment but she seems a little … odd.'

'Anything else?'

'Yes, come here,' Claudia said, patting the space beside her.

Dylan slid closer. 'I am here.'

CHAPTER 14

Dylan's contract for Claudia, part 1.

So, new contracts. Just the thing. I already promised you one contract and now I am already agreeing to another. I don't know how I feel about that.

Caveat emptor! That's how I feel. Wait, once more with caps: *CAVEAT EMPTOR!!!*

Sounds so authoritative, Latin. I mean, you could probably have built the empire, ornate columns and all, with just the lingo. In much the same way that French gives off that imperceptible balance of sexiness and disdain, I get the feeling that even mentioning cleaning the toilet in Latin loudly enough would somehow conjure up images of Anthony Hopkins sharpening a vintage paring knife in a distant mansion's private library.

PLACERE MUNDATIS LATRINA!!!

Ah, maybe I'm wrong. That should be part of the contractual obligation as well, I guess. Admitting my fault.

I am severely wrong.

(sad face)

EGO SUM SEVERE (pauses, clasps toga over chest, glares at Senate) . . . *INIURIAM!!*

All RIIIGGHT!! Even the stupid Caesarean salad days of this lingo are helping me with what is going to be tough. Law. Contract.

So, in the interest of things being fair at the outset before you move into my leaky, creaky 140-year-old home, I will try and put forward the terms of a contract. Seems like a good excuse to look at the tenets of contract law.

Contract law. Ahem. (Googles quickly.)

Anyhoo. A quick revision of my anti-net stance and some judicious use of ctrl + V shows us that contract law is about regulations directed towards enforcing certain promises.

So, certain promises.

1. I promise (sighs deeeeeply, stares at ceiling) as long as you are in my house I will clean the toilet. *Placere mundatis latrina.* There you go.

   And I will scrub without complaint! Not even in Latin, or its latter-day sleazy unemployed uncle, Italian.

   And I will scrub without looking back on what I have done in that same ivory-coloured locale, not stopping until it is clean and clear and something which a clichéd *Full Metal Jacket* (I know you don't watch war movies, growing up in a household so heavy on the X chromosome) -style drill sergeant would feel good about shouting at some hapless private.
2. I promise I will not say anything about how chores are divided in our household (70 per cent to 30 per cent me to you, just so we have it recorded in writing somewhere other than the census) when you are talking about how women are socialised to be the carer and placate in all their adult

relationships. Because you are right! They are! It's just you were too clever to fall for that.

3. I promise I will always give you a kiss at night when I get home, even if you are asleep, because I know it means something to you that I kiss you at night.

Hmmmmm, this is a lot of promising what I will do, while ignoring what can be equally important – maybe even more important, but possibly less important: what I will NOT do!

1. I will not try to fathom you. Because, as you so often like to declare when you have had five proseccos: *You are not here to be fathomed!!*
2. I will not remind you of melodramatic declarations made when you are drunk. Except for just then.
3. I truly, truly will not use a new towel every single time I have a shower.
4. I will not say 'she seems nice' every time you introduce me to a female friend who I think is batshit insane therefore making you feel like you are also going batshit insane interpreting a banal general comment as a vaguely misogynistic sledge.
5. I will not, ever, stop loving you.

CHAPTER 15

Poppy: I love Dylan.

Claudia: You can marry him then.

Poppy: Aren't you going to ask me why?

Claudia: I know why.

Poppy: Why?

Claudia: You read that crazy fucking contract. A small window into a fantastic and incredibly weird mind.

Poppy: I know he was weird, but my god, what a gift.

Phinn: I have always loved Dylan.

Claudia: All I asked for was a contract!

CHAPTER 16

Zoe leaned over her mother's sink and tilted her head back. She mussed her hair, ran her finger along her chin and, finding exactly what she was looking for, raised the tweezers. Three swift movements later she bent down to survey the bounty against the off-white porcelain of the sink.

She shook her head ruefully. A year ago she had two chin hairs. Now she had four. Dark, curly follicles which resolutely returned to her chin almost the night after being plucked out, emulating the kind of endless punishment doled out to one of the errant gods in her ancient Greek mythology.

Was this the beginning of the long and slow decline? Would she wake up tomorrow and see her mother's startled face staring back at her from the gold-plated mirror frame? Ha! She wished. She would more likely see her father's face staring back at her.

It had almost lulled her into a false sense of security, thinking that the worst thing that could happen to her would be turning into her mother. She idly wondered if there was a psychology field in this called Gilmorephobia or the Lorelai Syndrome.

She sighed and turned from the sink, bending at the waist so her knotty hair would gather over her head to be coaxed more easily into a ponytail. She was sceptical about the value of the beach outing, but Claudia had effusively declared a sibling morning ocean swim would be good for the group, and for the week she was trying to give Claudia whatever she wanted. For the week at least. Zoe had held the refrain 'you get one day' on the tip of her tongue like a clenched fist held tightly within a pocket. She had tried to tell Claudia she was taking unnecessary risks organising any group activity in the week leading up to the wedding, that it was taunting fate to have the siblings spending long chunks of allocated time together, but she had the feeling that the success of the pub outing the other night had made her sister cocky, instilled in her a belief she could pull off a situation where everyone would briefly put down their figurative weapons, like Christmas Day on the Western Front.

She had not asked why Nora was not coming. She assumed it was because she was not invited – one of the many tokens of peace extended towards Poppy for the week.

She jumped at the dull thud against the door before the knot in the pit of her stomach unravelled at Phinn's rising baritone.

'Women and the bathroom. I am so sick of women and the bathroom.'

Zoe yanked the door open and laughed as her brother almost fell onto the chessboard tiles while following through on a third knock.

'There's your precious bathroom,' she said, dropping her shoulder into her off-kilter brother's ribcage. Phinn clutched his side, begrudgingly marvelled at his sibling's footy-style hit-and-spin, and held in his painful groan until Zoe was out of earshot.

He quickly put the body-check behind him and strode to the mirror. He surveyed himself admiringly, in the unselfconscious manner that most women could only dream of in some far-off future where their chin is smaller and their blemishes gone and their eyelashes a bit curlier and their nose not so 'strong' and, and, and . . .

He had not even finished lathering his jaw in shaving cream when the door opened – this time without knock or warning – and his mother was standing beside him in what he instantly knew was nothing but her dressing-gown. Rachel always had been, and remained, the most mortifying on the scale of what people's mothers were like at home – a naked mum. Other people had cake mums, business mums, shy mums, conservative mums, hippy mums, health-nut mums, and a relatively new breed that was also swelling its ranks: Facebook mums.

The Carters had grown up with Naked Mum. The kind who does not close the door when using the toilet and thinks nothing of her children's deep shame when dashing from the shower to the bedroom to get changed after failing to register the empty towel rack beforehand. The ease she had with her body was brought into sharpest contrast when the girls hit the minefield of adolescence and wouldn't even get out of the shower by themselves without first wrapping themselves in a Sheridan-tagged cocoon so as not to do anything as deeply embarrassing as glance at their awkward, rebellious bodies in a mirror.

Regardless, Rachel was Naked Mum when they were children, when they were teenagers, and she definitely saw no reason for that to change now they were adults. They were lucky she threw them the occasional concession of a flimsy nightgown when Dylan was visiting. Small mercies, thought Phinn.

She nudged her son sideways so she took up half of the mirror and reached for her toothbrush and toothpaste.

'Ma!'

'What?'

'Privacy!'

Rachel rolled her eyes and raised the toothbrush to her mouth. 'I wiped your arse for five years; you can shave the pathetic seven hairs on your face with me in the same room.'

Phinn gave a slight shake of his head and, after letting the creeping blush across his cheeks settle, returned the razor to his face.

Zoe checked her phone and allowed herself what she would now consider an uncharacteristic moment of exasperation. It took so many years to lose it, to soothe it, to pretend her incendiary temper was not lurking just below the surface, an impatient shark patrolling a small tank. Years of hard work quickly unravelling as she waited for her brother and her sisters to get in the goddamn fucking car. She leaned over, and in a movement that brought back an entire youth spent sitting behind cracked faux-leather dashboards waiting for her siblings, leaned heavily on the horn.

Somehow, over the blare, she could still hear her mother's voice cut through the front door to her '... and tell that impatient sister of yours not to touch the goddamn horn, there's no goddamn clock at the beach.'

Zoe paused and leaned on the horn again, ignoring the sudden twitch of the white lace curtains of the neighbours' house. She had never learned their names.

She glanced back at the green front door with a small degree of satisfaction as Phinn sprinted out and leaped over the hedge, quickly making up the metres between the yard's edge and the car. He wore bright green shorts patterned with peacock feathers, a blue shirt that looked two sizes too small and, Zoe realised with a mix of horror and bemusement, a red cap that said 'Make Winston Great Again'.

'You know people think they are so clever wearing the Trump parody hats, but all that anyone thinks when they look at you is, "Look, a dickhead Trump supporter",' Zoe said, adjusting her blue singlet to cover more of her chest from the sun.

'Who said I was being ironic?' Her panting brother grinned as he gave himself another once-over in the rear-view mirror. Then it was his turn to study the door. 'Where are your dumb effing sisters?'

'Mate, I'm the one sitting in the car on time,' Zoe responded. 'They were swapping shorts last time I saw them.'

Phinn kept staring at the door, willing his sisters to materialise, while Zoe fiddled with the wires in the car, trying to tune it to her phone so she could play her own music free of inevitable sibling interjection. While her focus was on choosing between the Yeah Yeah Yeahs and the Liars, Phinn looked back and asked as casually as he could, 'Are you, uh, seeing anyone?'

Zoe slid her sunglasses from her head to her face and surveyed her brother. 'Why would you ask that?'

'I'm trying to be a good brother! Interested. In your life.' He nonchalantly pointed towards her. 'All of that.'

Zoe tapped her phone and Nick Zinner's needling guitar line signalled the familiar opening bars of 'Maps'. She cocked her head lightly and squinted as her sisters came barrelling down the front steps, Claudia shoving Poppy a little too hard out of the way.

'Nothing I would tell you about,' Zoe murmured, as the girls reached the car's blazing hot door handles.

Claudia looked hopefully at the front seat where Zoe was perched and shook her head, as if to clear herself of the notion before clambering into the seat behind Phinn.

Poppy instead dawdled to a light jog, before taking exaggeratedly slow-motion steps around the boot to the other side of the vehicle and then finally wrenching open the door and settling down behind her older sister. It had the desired effect. Zoe turned in her seat and looked at Poppy sharply. 'Are we running on Rachel time, or what?'

Phinn sighed and revved the car, reversing slowly onto the road. 'Lovely day at the beach in T -minus forty-seven minutes,' he mumbled.

Poppy, still weighing Zoe's comment, instead looked out of the window.

Rachel loomed so large in their lives that everything was compared to her – a bad mood, an offhand remark, the way they wore their hair; when they were infuriating each other, when they were emotional, even what they chose to eat and how they drank water (three quarters filled, ice-cold). It was 'just like Rachel', they would tell each other in a tone of rote reprimand. They invoked her name on a daily basis, whether it was internally comparing each other to the omnipotent matriarch, or imagining her disapproval in the morning in their respective homes as they guiltily poured their third coffee.

Unable to stomach butter on your toast? Just like Rachel.

Find yourself so moved by the shuffle function on your iTunes that you start crying in the street for a song from thirteen years ago? Just like Rachel.

Late getting to the car to go to the beach? Rachel.

While the invocations of their largely un-silent but definitely long-suffering Madonna figure bore mocking tones, there was no denying she still made up the scaffolding they hung their days and their selves off.

The siblings rode for the first twenty minutes in silence, Claudia preoccupied with marriage, Phinn enjoying the serenity, Zoe trying to think of safe topics of conversation and Poppy thinking about what she looked like staring stonily out the window. Moody? Beyond reach? Melancholy? (She just looked like someone staring stonily out of the window.)

They could smell the salt in the air when the conversational ceasefire was enthusiastically broken by Poppy. 'Hey Zoe,' she thumped the back of the seat in front of her, 'Mary said something funny this morning when we were leaving.'

'Was it that she needed some wart of toad and hair of virgin for the next time she had her cauldron out? Was she thinking of buying a Dyson V6 because her arse is getting too big for her broomstick?'

The four of them allowed themselves a snigger before Poppy continued, 'No, it was something about a postcard.'

Zoe raised her eyebrows as the corners of her mouth pulled up. 'What did she say about postcards?'

Poppy looked searchingly at Claudia for backup. 'She was talking to Mum and she said something about Zoe being good at writing nasty postcards.'

Zoe's smile was wide and genuine. 'Did she now?'

Poppy leaned in. 'Yeah, she did, what was she talking about?'

'Do you remember a few years ago when Mum was having a hard time at work? They kept cutting her hours?'

Her sisters nodded. Everyone remembered. Rachel had tried to start a union at the credit union where she worked as a cleaner, and her boss, a 52-year-old man in a white short-sleeved shirt and pocket pen protector in another town, responded by cutting her hours to the sixteen-hour weekly minimum. A useful lesson in socialism for some of them and the vital importance of personal finance for others. They all remembered a lot of soup and toast for dinner.

Well, Zoe told them, during that time, Rachel actually needed her sister a bit. Mary was living a couple of hours away, rent-free with some poor sucker in one of those hill village-towns full of exhausted middle-aged tree-changers, and Rachel kept calling her. But after the first conversation Mary just ignored the calls. A Rachel in need was a burden indeed, in her sister's mind.

'I was in the area, I forget why, it might have been for work, or I could have just been road-tripping. I don't know why I was in that town; I don't think I've been back since. Anyway, I knew where she was living; I think I had saved the address from when Mum had posted her some things she'd needed a few months before. I was walking past the poky little village news agency and saw postcards for the area. I don't know why but I lost it, I was just so furious, so I bought a postcard and wrote one to Mary. It said something like, "You are a terrible human being, a bottomless emotional abyss with no empathy for the suffering of those closest to you and you need to apologise to my mother."'

The car was silent, apart from Karen O's constant yelp about good things happening in bad towns.

Poppy cackled. 'You *what*?'

'I wrote her a postcard telling her she was a terrible human being. I still don't know why. She has never said anything to me about it. Does Mum know about it?'

It was Claudia's turn to start snorting. 'Oh, she knows about it. She didn't tell me what happened but I remember her telling me you had done something she thought you shouldn't have. Then ... Then she told me a story.'

Claudia paused, long enough to make sure she had everyone's attention, but short enough that their notoriously unreliable attention spans did not wander to a road sign bearing a decades-old double entendre or, even worse, their phones.

'Do you remember that beautiful postcard Mum used to have on the fridge? That she bought in Beirut in the seventies?'

The siblings all remembered the gold-fringed relic from their childhoods. Something they had all gazed at either privately or in concert at least daily, enchanted by the gilded edges, the crystal blue Mediterranean taken from above, a beach club dotted with glamorous young Arabs and sweaty Eastern Euros lazing around in bikinis and dick stickers, glittering chains around their necks and Jackie Onassis-inspired sunglasses on the faces of the women, gold-rimmed Wayfarers on the men. Everyone looked so young and beautiful and impossibly far away.

They had not seen the postcard in years, but none of them could actually recall when it had gone missing. Like so much of their youths – primary school best friends, final-year exams, teenage despair – it had loomed monolithic in their lives until suddenly, inexplicably, it didn't.

Now Claudia had the answer to a question they had never thought to ask.

Roadwork sites and their high-vis sunburnt caretakers whizzed past as she grinned and relayed the tale of her first heartbreak.

She had been nineteen. They all remembered him: a bit lovely, a bit dumb, a bit fundamental. His interests spanned cars, MDMA, never ever letting his feelings show, the gym, and occasionally Claudia. His sister had died in her early teens, which Claudia shamelessly found morbidly attractive. She married this fact with an emotional hinterland for the boy almost entirely confected by herself. In hindsight a lot of imagination hung on his square jaw, tight delts and sad eyes. But he had been her first boyfriend and she had quite an attachment to him. Zoe, Phinn and Poppy all remembered, though even now Claudia would not portray the relationship in such unflinching terms.

He seemed sweet, albeit temporary, until one day he did

something both completely unexpected and terribly predictable, and slept with a woman who was not Claudia. She found out within three days on the trusted Winston bush telegraph, and retired to her bedroom for a week to cry, more out of sheer humiliation and bruised ego than actual heartbreak. One night, drunk on self-pity and one and a half bottles of wine, she confessed to Rachel the reasons for the relationship's demise.

Rachel, who even at the best of times could be magnanimously described as 'smother superior', was blind with fury. In Claudia's retelling she looked wildly through the kitchen drawers, scrabbling through scissors, bobby pins and old vinyl-embossed refidexes. Finally, she turned to the fridge in exasperation and ripped down the azure and white postcard before fiercely hunkering down at the kitchen table to write. Claudia did not see exactly what was written but she had been able to deduce from text messages from the victim days later that it called him a piece of shit, said he was lucky Rachel did not tell the boy's mother – 'a beautiful member of her parish who was unworthy of such heartless offspring' – and said she hoped his beloved bonsai plants died in a huge effing fire involving his car.

Zoe interrupted in disbelief: 'So she actually sent it?'

Claudia giggled even more. 'Of course she sent it! Can you believe it? That beautiful, intricate homage to 1970s Beirut – in its Paris of the Middle East phase – which she had saved for thirty years. And then just to finally send it, turning it into a psycho postcard.'

'I can absolutely believe it,' Phinn said dryly, shifting the gears down as they snaked through the impossibly wide back streets of the beach town to the ocean.

'I wonder what it was like for him. This stunning relic arrives in the post – such a dreamy scene, exotic even – and then he turns it over to read it and it's just pure savagery. A Trojan horse of an absolute bollocking.'

Zoe smiled at the idea of Claudia's vain Adonis going down to another Grecian analogy. 'I think the most savage part of it is that anyone in the house could have read it before he got to it; it was a postcard.'

The siblings burst into new peals of laughter, awed by the most diabolical aspect of their mother's revenge. Phinn tried not to dwell on the fact that Poppy's laugh was the first to cut out seconds later.

'So psycho postcards is a family trait,' he mused as he pulled into a takeaway-wrapper-strewn car park facing an unpatrolled section of mildly undulating surf. The three rusty four-wheel drives with shining roof racks suggested the placid water wasn't providing much incentive for the locals, while a look towards the east revealed just four board riders perched on the water, pointedly looking away from the forty-something paddleboard rider flailing away nearby. Claudia and Zoe opened their doors in time with each other and breathed the air deeply. Poppy was slower, infuriatingly so. Somewhere well after Winston, and almost immediately following the communal joy of psychotic postcards, a heavy mood passed over her – almost as if the quickly changing atmospheric pressure of the sky over the suddenly open water had drawn a coastal cumulonimbus directly down to her.

Straight away her sisters knew they were not going to get more than two syllables from her at a time. As always, Phinn was happy to cheerfully ignore it, but the pall had fallen. The tension was obvious to all four, the chatter died down and the jokes became more forced.

On the beach, Poppy sat on a towel with her silver one-piece swimsuit pointedly beside her. She was not going to put it on.

Phinn sprinted towards the waves and dived under in a graceful arc. Suddenly he was behind the sets and swimming lazy lengths parallel to the beach.

Zoe pulled out her sunscreen and took off her shirt, offering her back to Claudia without bothering to look at her youngest sister. The two fell into an old game, tracing symbols on creamy backs in the hopes they might tan along the same lines. Zoe drew four roses on Claudia's back, while in return she gave Zoe a planet, some stars, and even part of a moon.

'Are you coming in?' Zoe said to the space beside Poppy's shoulder.

'No,' Poppy responded, lifting her sunglasses, Ray-Ban rip-offs, so she could squint at her phone properly.

'The water looks like it's the perfect temperature,' Claudia ventured pathetically.

Poppy held her phone a bit closer to her face so her head shaded the screen from the sun's glare. Zoe shrugged and took off her denim skirt, folding it neatly on top of her sandals to reveal a violently red bikini in a design that tied in a series of knots at her hips and neck. Claudia pulled off her old blue cotton dress and pushed her growing fringe out of her face, giving the effect of a tween boy's body in a black one-piece. She linked one of her arms through Zoe's and walked carefully towards the water's edge, so they could complete the female Carter ritual of entering the water, inch by painful inch, step by tiny step, stopping and grimacing for each freezing wave, no matter how small, to break around their shins, then their thighs, then their stomachs. Finally, when it had reached their armpits, they would duck their heads under, muffling squeals with the foamy tide.

They trod water between sets looking at each other. Claudia glanced anxiously back at the shore.

'Do you think she's all right?' she asked, searching for her sister's horizontal figure on the sand, which she supposed was baking evenly in the sun.

'Oh, she just wants to sit moodily on the beach where we can all see her so we know she's staring moodily at the ocean,' Zoe said, leaning back so she was half floating in the water.

'Do you think I should marry Dylan?'

Zoe swung her legs through the water so she was upright, bobbing like a cork in an Esky of melted ice, and looked at her sister. Claudia was staring straight back at her, eyes glazed.

'I don't have any opinion on who you should marry, Clauds, unless he is hitting you or is a Tory,' Zoe said gently. 'What's going on?'

'Thinking about that break-up when I was younger and Mum's postcard. That was a relationship that looking back was so obviously a disaster, so completely wrong, and I didn't really see it at the time. What if that's happening again?'

Zoe looked out at their brother, the clean strokes of his arm as he calmly freestyled past the impassive surfers towards a rocky outcrop, his head turning every two strokes for one breath.

'I don't think this relationship is the same as that, but I don't know how normal it is to think you don't want to get married a few days before your wedding. What do you think you would miss about him if you did break up?'

'I loved your crooked sleep beside me and never dreamed afraid.' Claudia ducked her head under a wave.

'Huh?' Zoe stared at Claudia as she surfaced, showing her teeth in a forced smile.

'It's a line from a poem about a break-up, called "One Last Poem for Richard", I think. I often think about it when I think about Dylan. The poem talks about how they should have champagne for surviving their break-up, basically.'

'It's only me out here, kid, you don't have to impress anyone with poetry, you can just tell me how you feel.'

'I don't know how I feel.'

Zoe paused to consider Claudia, her relationship, her options. She honestly had no opinion. Claudia attempted to interpret her older sister's silence.

'This is a first-world problem, isn't it?'

Zoe shook her head. 'That's not useful. First-world problems are not enough money for all of the luxuries you covet, slow service at a restaurant, UberEATS not reaching your suburb. Relationships still matter; the people we love matter; our feelings matter. It's true we have more time to think about these things, but do you think the most oppressed people sit around just focused on their oppression? Of course it dictates their lives, but they still have room to fret about the people they love: who's not loving them back, who's loving them the wrong way. This is not a time to check your privilege; you can always go and find someone who needs to check it more and less than you.'

Claudia took in Zoe's words gratefully. 'So what should I do?'

'I don't know, that's up to—'

Zoe's response was cut short as she was suddenly dragged under the water, disappearing with a series of bubbles marking where she had just been.

Claudia tried to scream but rasped instead as she looked around wildly for anyone else in the water. She was just two metres from where Zoe had last been, and instinctively she swam towards the spot before stopping and frantically looking back to the shore, then to her right to the surfers and up at an endless sky.

It seemed there was a wide silence, only punctuated by the slow and regular roll of the waves and the tight uneven spacing of her short, hurried breaths.

Her eyes were suddenly stinging as the sound of a huge break in the water shattered the terrible quiet. When she opened them up again, Zoe was spluttering beside her, joined half a second later by a burly figure laughing hysterically.

'PHINNNNN,' Zoe screamed in fury. She grabbed her brother ineffectively by the shoulders. His body kept rocking in the surf with laughter.

'Got ya,' he said, before turning and cutting through the water towards the shore.

Claudia looked at her sodden sister, still trying to push her wet mop of hair out of her eyes. 'Sweet Jesus that scared the hell out of me.'

Zoe just turned wordlessly and calmly swam in the direction of her brother who was already on dry land, walking towards towels.

By the time Zoe and Claudia reached the towels, Poppy was already yelling.

'Fuck you! What is your problem? Can't you just leave me the fuck alone?'

Phinn bashfully tried to rub his hair dry. Zoe looked at her sister, now shirtless, the straps of her bra pulled down to avoid tan lines on her shoulders. Poppy had both of her fists clenched and was huffing in Phinn's general direction. Still, it took a few seconds for Zoe to notice the spattering of salt water on Poppy's face and hair.

She turned to her brother. 'Did you shake your wet hair over Poppy while she was sunbaking?'

Phinn didn't respond but his enraged sibling snapped back, 'He's such a fucking arsehole.'

'Aw come on, Poppy, what's really the matter? I know he's annoying but you seem to be having a bad time anyway.'

Claudia attempted to sound reassuring. Poppy blinked as her face flushed an endearing pink.

'I'm fine! I just don't think we have to do everything together all of the time. I need some quiet from you guys sometimes; I don't have to come into the water if I don't want to.'

'I know, I know, you just seem really cranky this morning.' Claudia kept her tone neutral, like a zookeeper to a tiger who has had a fright.

Poppy seemed on the verge of tears. 'I'm just not like you guys, I can't be as happy.'

'Oh Jesus, calm down.' Zoe picked up her towel and wrapped it around her. 'It's just a bit of water.'

Poppy let out a scream and, grabbing her bag, stalked off towards a bush track. Claudia looked at Phinn and Zoe, but none of them tried to stop Poppy straight away as her figure shrunk towards the headland.

'What is her problem?' Claudia said, directing her question to nobody in particular.

'She's just a messy bitch who loves drama,' Zoe said. She was already walking towards the car.

What it came down to was this: Poppy was offended by the overwhelming physicality of her siblings. In the real world you were not rough with other adults: you did not grab them, you did not drop your shoulder or elbow into them as you passed by, tickle them or, indeed, pinch them. All of this was supposed to be left in the primary school playground, but it took longer, so much longer, when it came to brothers and sisters. They were still considered young enough to be fair game for a sneakily outstretched ankle while walking around a coffee table, to be shouldered aside while trying to grab a sausage off a barbecue, to be suddenly hoisted, kicking and screaming, in a bruising bear hug from behind.

Don't touch me. Get out of my space. It was hard to assert boundaries, to hold on to yourself when there was so much familiarity. And everyone else seemed to know what familiarity breeds.

The three watched Poppy's retreating figure, her melodramatic stomping, the tension in her balled shoulders as she half ran away.

'Pops! Wait,' Claudia wailed.

She tried to catch up but Poppy raised one hand without turning around to reveal only her middle finger. Claudia reluctantly gave up, knowing better than to try to talk Poppy down from her almighty wrath at these moments. She turned back to the other two who were both casually rubbing themselves raw with their ratty towels.

Zoe leaned forward at the hips to towel her salt-frizzed hair and returned Claudia's pleading gestures with rolled eyes.

'Let Christian Bale over there walk it off. The performance must be *tiring* when so much has to be put into it.'

Phinn shook his head and set his mouth. Not just an ominous sign; the subdued jaw-grind was an unconscious familial call-back to a long-dead grandfather they had never known – a Carter tic that would need a member of the clan's previous generation to verify it. Phinn would not be swayed to sympathy today: that was it, his sisters knew it. They slowly gathered their things and headed to the car, the playful air of the morning fully punctured and now deflating at the regular rate.

In the front seat Zoe checked her phone. 'Well, we have to meet Mum for lunch in forty-five minutes so leave here in twenty. Surely the sulk and dash will be done by then?'

Phinn just sighed deeply, shut his eyes and leaned back in the driver's seat, tapping the steering wheel. Claudia attempted to furtively type out a text in a painfully obvious way, an SOS screed to Dylan, no doubt. Zoe tried to tilt her head to see what was on Claudia's screen, but she was thwarted by the glare so instead she opened her car door again.

'I'm going to try to find her; she can't be far.'

Zoe pulled her top over her head and slid her Birkenstocks back on. On her, the iconic sandals looked the way their namesake designer probably intended when he had created them in 1963 – like giant paddles signalling to onlookers that the wearer had given up on many things in life, but mainly style for comfort. They had seemed more attractive when she bought them, ironic in their ugliness.

She faced the road and looked right, searching down the visible kilometre-straight before the corner rose into coastal scrubland. Several neat brick bungalows lay towards the end of the bitumen, betraying how their owners had little of the laidback beach village attitude associated with such coastal communities in previous decades. To her left was more beach scrub canopy and, she knew, a beaten track that people used for walks to a couple of saltwater lakes, which teenagers used as cover for their pot smoking. Zoe headed to the small thirty-centimetre outline of sand and waffle-tread shoeprints set against the patchy green border.

Phinn opened his door, and for a moment Zoe thought he was going to join her for the grand retrieval mission. But instead he hung one leg over the door and manoeuvred his bulky frame into a more comfortable position to laze in the two p.m. glare.

Claudia stayed on her phone.

Zoe was now slipping on rocks not made for the thick soles of the German sandals, while tentatively calling Poppy's name, in between cursing to herself in exasperation. Dried leaves and sticks crackled beneath her feet, and above her the gum leaves continued to wither and yellow in the dry heat. She watched as the light became more dappled and after 700 metres finally let out a scream.

'*Poppy!*'

The only response was the high-pitched pipe of a stray plover.

Zoe looked at the sky, becoming more sparse through the dense canopy, and down at the moist dirt track. She bent down to examine the ground more closely, looking for recent signs of movement. Apart from her own sandal treads, which were already fading, there were no footprints she could decipher, nor freshly disturbed rocks. She found her focus fading into that all-too-familiar creeping sense of futility. On the other hand, she guessed that she had been gone for ten minutes, so it would mean she had also used up all the time they had left before having to leave to meet their mother.

She picked up her pace, fretting as she finally approached the car.

She thought about how supremely annoying her youngest sister was, while also reluctantly acknowledging how that surface emotion of irritation was grimly anchored by a pit of dread, quietly shared, that was dragging down all the siblings. Deep down she also worried about why Poppy was behaving like this; just how unhappy she could be; how Poppy felt about the form her life was failing to take, like shaping water with her hands; and finally how gruelling this was for Claudia.

When she got back to the car, Phinn was still there, mouth still set in a thin line, listening to New Order. The overall effect was a vaguely menacing counterpoint to Phinn's usual breezy demeanour. Zoe peered into the back seat.

'Where's Claudia?'

'She went looking the other way.' As Phinn finished, Claudia came into view on the other side of the car, her face slightly sheened.

'You didn't find her?' Claudia was slightly puffed.

'No, have you tried calling her?'

Claudia shook her head and Zoe made an exasperated murmur as she pulled the phone from her pocket and scrolled through her Favourites. Despite keeping contact to the bare minimum, she kept her siblings at the top of the starred list in some gesture of loyalty she still did not quite understand.

The phone rang out as she climbed back in the front seat and Claudia took her position behind. Zoe looked over her shoulder. 'I guess we should do a quick drive around to see if we can see her.'

Phinn grunted and slammed his door shut, taking his sweet time to put his seatbelt on before they were trundling down the road. Five minutes later they had completed two laps of the dormant township – both with no sign of their sister.

Zoe could see Claudia's breathing become shallower as her chest tightened. Meanwhile she was trying to suppress the frantic edge to her voice as she raised her phone to her ear every forty seconds to listen to the ringing die out again.

'What should we do?'

Phinn shrugged. 'Fuck her. She's probably got Mum to pick her up and is already at the café. Who cares?'

Claudia and Zoe cared, but they were trying hard not to. This, as always, was the problem.

The trio rode the twenty minutes in silence along the same ochre-bordered bitumen that had delivered them to the coast, but the hysterics they had shared on the eastern run now simply hung in the air as a stark juxtaposition. In unison, both sisters sighed as Phinn rolled to a stop across the road from the café and Zoe finally put her phone in her bag after her last attempted call.

Claudia paused at the bottom of the stairs and shielded her

eyes from the sun as she gestured to the other two. 'How much do you think it would piss Poppy off if we took a selfie here and put it on Phinn's Snapchat story?'

Zoe snorted, while Phinn, refusing to surface from his mood, shook his head and kept walking up the stairs. 'Sounds incredibly productive.'

Inside, their mother was already at a table next to a window, her head held close to Mary's as the two whispered to each other. Phinn quickly clocked the midway-level of the yellowing pinot gris in both women's wine glasses, and was forced to pull his slumped shoulders up and make his choice: half full or half empty?

'Yeah Mum, get on it!' he boomed at Rachel, as his slightly stunned sisters took their seats opposite her.

They made no attempt to hide the absence of Rachel's youngest daughter. That didn't quell their vain hopes it would escape her notice, though.

'Where's Poppy?'

Rachel hadn't even said hello. She addressed Phinn, suddenly deflated. He had never been able to lie and looked imploringly at Zoe.

'She's meeting us here; you haven't seen her?' Zoe replied.

Rachel's eyes narrowed. 'Why is she meeting us here?'

'She wanted to go look for something.' Zoe knew the best strategy for a moderately successful lie was vagueness: scant detail meant what had to be remembered and offered up to Rachel's deductive powers was also minimal. The biggest trick was avoiding any specific destination, object or other person, which their mother could quickly check off through an algorithm of elimination honed from the four children's marathon upbringing. 'I thought maybe she would beat us here.'

'Where did you drop her off?'

'Well, it's not so much that we dropped her off . . .' Claudia tried to back her sister up. 'It's more that she dropped us.'

Mary drained her wine glass and waved her hand at a staff member for a refill. The young waiter looked up from the counter briefly and returned to wiping forks, beside the red-lettered sign urging patrons to ORDER AT THE COUNTER. Mary was too delighted to take much notice.

'You don't know where your sister is, do you?'

The three paused for a moment.

'We know the vicinity . . .'

'We know where we last saw her . . .'

Phinn stared at the glass stem reaching up at the transparent bowl above, distorting his view of Rachel's index finger, impatiently tapping away. Glass fully empty. Fuck it.

'She's a bitch, anyway; we don't need her for lunch.'

'PHINN!' Rachel and her daughters reprimanded him as a choir – the matriarch's high-pitched outrage cutting above the emotional exhaustion of his sisters' duller voices. Mary buzzed with satisfaction.

Eyebrows raised, Rachel reached for her bag and got out her phone. She half-stood up but then sat back down.

'Just before we start lunch, Claudie, where are you staying tonight?'

'I, um, I think we were going to go to Dad's after the beach.'

Rachel sighed. 'Typical. Rushing off to your father's again.'

Zoe cut in. 'We've been at your house the past few nights, Mum! We are having lunch with you right now.'

Rachel raised her hand as she stood up and put her phone to an ear. 'I just feel like an afterthought. You're fitting me in around your father.'

All three siblings lowered their heads. Despite the glaring evidence they had been spending time with their mother, she could still invoke guilt in them. They could clearly hear the dial tone on Rachel's phone and the familiar voice after just two rings.

'Poppy, sweetie.' Their mother walked away.

CHAPTER 17

Dylan: YOU'VE MISSED THIS.

Claudia: NOT AS MUCH AS YOU THINK.

CHAPTER 18

Claudia leaned out of the taxi and furtively looked each way before pushing a $20 note into the driver's hand and darting under the streetlight and into the motel car park. Each hand bore two bottles cocooned in a brown paper bag. Basking in the paranoia, she looked over her shoulder and took the stairs to her right, two at a time.

After ending the ascent with a little jump, she looked down the row of myrtle green doors and found what she was looking for. Holding the four bottles, she kicked the door three times.

A moment later it swung back to reveal a sliver of Nora, in her version of house clothes, before jamming awkwardly with a clunk. The length of chain pulled taut between door and frame at eye level. Nora's face quickly split with a grin as she ducked back behind the green frame. Claudia could hear the chain rattling from its hook before the door opened again properly, giving a full view of Nora barefoot in tan capris and a bamboo cotton T-shirt.

How very like Nora, she thought, glancing at the now limp security chain.

Claudia took one last look behind to make sure nobody knew she was there and stepped over the threshold, raising the brown packages triumphantly. 'I couldn't find anything in this town but prosecco, but look what Mary had squirrelled away for a special occasion.' She pulled open the bags to reveal Veuve Clicquot labels on warm dark green bottles.

Nora squealed. 'It's our secret hen's! Secret hen's, secret hen's,' she hummed the mantra to an obscure tune. Claudia giggled and opened the tiny freezer compartment of the bar fridge, inelegantly jamming one bottle in and leaving two others on the grimy white shelf inside the door and another still warm on top of the fridge.

Claudia gingerly took off her shoes and flopped down on the bed, ignoring the slightest of frowns that crossed Nora's face as she realised her friend was wearing her beloved leggings as pants. Claudia stared at the ceiling and began her run-down of the day, which Nora had already known would somehow centre around Poppy. They fell into the easy repartee built over years of female friendship, gossip, Icelandic politics (always weird how the Euros love to have heads of state who can completely overrule a separate head of government – what is the point?), their pick for the colour of the summer, loneliness, long-ago bosses.

Claudia told her friend how Poppy had slunk into the café after calling a taxi to the small beach town for something in the ballpark of $130.

'Worst of all, I end up being the one who feels guilty,' she said, staring into the moderately expensive champagne in the cheap hotel room tumbler. 'I know she loves me, I can feel how much she wants to be close to me again, and it's almost as if I have run out of patience with her. I can't allow her to be close to me. Every time she has a small fuck-up I shut down from her; there is something about her at the moment I just find so profoundly irritating.'

Nora raised an eyebrow. 'Her personality?'

Claudia ignored the jibe. 'She just wants to love me so much and I can't forgive her for an offence that I can't seem to articulate. I'm sure she wonders what she has done wrong.'

'I can provide her with a list if she needs,' replied Nora, refusing to let it go. 'Maybe she can choose at least one to say sorry for.'

Claudia felt the friction in the air, the tension between friend and family, trying to explain your sister to an only child. She sighed inwardly: you might as well be trying to explain the concept of the ocean to a landlocked desert tribe.

There were plenty of apologies between the sisters; they were just not the kind where you say sorry. In fact they were relationships built on the refusal to say sorry; instead contrition was signalled with a casual text hours later. Had they seen the latest episode of *Broad City*? Or a simple screenshot of a quote; the last between Claudia and Poppy had been: 'It's not enough for me to succeed, my friends have to fail.' A simple 'haha' in response and all was forgiven; it was time to move on without the need to dissect hurt feelings.

The olive branch takes many forms: for the Carter sisters it was communication about entirely mundane subjects that transcended issues invisible to the impartial observer. But none of them ever mentioned the truth that olive trees take a decade to actually bear fruit.

An upbeat declaration that 'I just saw a koala in a tree next to the highway!' invited a response that could mean 'It's all good', 'I'm not going to fight with you anymore', 'I don't feel like holding on to the anger that had me hang up on you last night', 'I'm still talking to you but you're still a dickhead' or even, 'I forgive you'.

Claudia wondered if it was possible for a group of people to put together a complete picture of a person. What would be known about her if Poppy and Zoe and Dylan and Nora walked into a room and laid out everything they each knew about her? All the things they would discover they did not know about someone they considered themselves to be closest to in the world. An imperfect collage.

She was interrupted by Nora clinking her glass. 'You're thinking about your sister again. Can you stop for just one night? I know you say she loves you, but it's really not that difficult to avoid upsetting you so much.'

Claudia smiled and thought about the desert dwellers surrounded by dunes, blissfully ignorant that the wide expanse of sky over their heads could ever run into a shimmering liquid horizon. But she obediently changed the subject. 'What do you think the worst thing about being single was?'

She dipped her head to the champagne, inadvertently missing the brief stoniness around Nora's mouth at the question.

'What is there to miss? It depends on your partner what you miss, I guess. I miss what everyone misses: making my own decisions.'

Claudia nodded. 'Not knowing where the night would take you.'

Nora was careful choosing her words. 'I think that is something where the concept or the memory is looked upon a little too fondly compared to the reality, not knowing where the night would take you. Most of the time it takes you home to bed alone.'

Claudia sat up suddenly. 'Let's download Tinder!'

'What? Why?'

Claudia ran her hand through her hair nervously. Her blonde crop had begun to get greasy at the roots but she was too distracted to care. Her cheeks flushed, filling in the remnants of blush applied a morning ago with brushstrokes gleaned from long-ago YouTube tutorials. She picked up her phone. 'I want to see what's out there.'

The mechanics of creating a Tinder profile were quickly figured out: after a brief hesitation about it possibly being linked to Claudia's Facebook profile they switched her photo to a generic shot and set their net for a 100-kilometre radius – they figured it had to be cast wide in a town like Winston.

It was dumb, but the girls (ahem, the women) had suddenly repossessed the bulletproof recklessness only available for a brief period to those in their twenties fortunate enough to have avoided real tragedy.

They were also a bit drunk.

Claudia flicked through profile after profile of what seemed the same four men smiling from the black rectangle again and again and again and again, variations on a limited number of themes.

A man with his shirt off in one photo, on a boat in another, with a large group of men and beers in hand, sunglasses on for most of them, describing himself as an 'adventure junkie' (read: he has a lot of disposable income and a lack of imagination).

A man with a mystery child in his photo who was obviously not his but a prop being used in what he thought was some kind of ingenious honey-trap.

A man here 'for a good time, not a long time'.

A man who didn't like women with 'to [sic] much make-up' (read: I think the only reason women wear make-up is for men).

There were so many, like children pulling themselves up as high as possible, chest out, for their first school photo. This one grinning in what was obviously his first selfie, or another using a mediocre photo because he thought it was a nice picture. It could be sweet and it could be a bit sad or it could be soul-destroying. Claudia and Nora spent two hours emptying the Veuve bottles and going through the ceaseless options.

'This is a wicked hen's night,' Nora said.

'Wow.' Claudia didn't look up. 'That is some old-school slang I haven't heard in a while – wicked, man.'

'No, I mean this is a wicked thing you are doing, as in Witch-of-the-West-dear-Dorothy thing we are doing. It's kind of evil.'

Claudia looked up, more hurt than she had a right to be. 'Are you trying to be my moral compass?'

Nora sighed and slid off the bed, walking to the fridge for the final champagne bottle. 'I'm not trying to be a moral anything, but what are you playing at? Why are you downloading Tinder and getting married on Saturday?'

Claudia sighed. 'I don't think I'm going to marry Dylan. I'm almost positive I'm not going to.'

It was the closest to a decision she had got. Nora silently popped the cork on the bottle and measured out their glasses, a purposefulness to her quiet as she waited for Claudia to fill it.

'Why shouldn't I have a look at what's out there before I make the jump?'

'Because you're getting married in a few nights. It's kind of tacky. Very tacky.' Nora sat down on the edge of the bed again and shrugged. 'But I can stand tacky more than people realise.'

'You're not going to ask me why I don't want to marry him?'

Nora felt suffocated by the question. She shifted on the bed, steeling herself for a list of reasons why having a man who loved you was somehow not enough. Claudia asked her if she remembered Simon and Gabe. Nora not only remembered them but also the fallout that left her and Claudia in a three-month perpetual hangover.

Two boyfriends, one after the other, who Claudia had let

completely envelop her. Simon had been tall and, with the benefit of hindsight, really hated women. He loved to make promises, from plans to spend the morning at the beach to elaborate weekends away, and then not turn up. Whenever Claudia had dared complain he would say her clinginess was unbecoming. But, she was wildly attracted to him, and any time he texted she would drop whatever she was doing (usually Nora) and go to see him.

She met Gabe when Simon was giving her the silent treatment, and at the time he seemed the polar opposite, but it turned out he was just at the other end of the toxic spectrum. He bought her gifts every time he saw her and bombarded her with messages about how beautiful she was. After a month or so, the messages would become vaguely threatening if she didn't respond within minutes, and then outright threatening. 'But my body wants his body,' Claudia would explain it, as if that was an explanation.

Yes, Nora remembered Gabe and Simon.

'Remember how lovely Dylan seemed in comparison? How sweet? How normal?'

Nora snorted. 'Because he *is* lovely and normal in comparison.'

'Well, what if that's all he is? Just lovely and normal in comparison to these men I had these insane attractions to? I've sort of fallen into this relationship that I think is great because he doesn't harass me or ignore me. He's just nice. Is that all I'm supposed to be grateful for?'

'Yes,' Nora snapped. 'If you feel lucky, it's because you are lucky. It's only going to get more desolate out there. You have someone to hold your hand through it; that's all a lot of people want.'

There was a viciousness in Nora's voice that Claudia was not used to. But Nora was also a bit drunk. Maybe she didn't get it, and that was fine.

Claudia signalled the end of the conversation by returning to her hands, swiping ordinary-looking men on her phone.

'Someone's written to me!'

Nora rolled her eyes. 'They've *messaged* you, they haven't *written* to you.' She took the phone and studied Claudia's inbox.

Hi ☺

If you could choose only three types of cuisine to eat for the rest of your life, what would you choose?

Nora furrowed her brow. 'Well at least he's trying. Kind of.'

Claudia looked up quizzically. 'You don't think he's one of those white slavers, some freak with women in his basement?' She returned to the screen and took a careful sip. 'And a very active Menulog account?'

A few kilometres away from the pair – say, a third of the daily distance of his long-lapsed running regime – Phinn's feet lay over the edge of a single bed at the back of their father's house. It was in a room supposed to be a laundry but, given the option between enough bedrooms for all adult children to visit at once and a garden, George chose the intermittent rewards of loamy flowerbeds and a frustratingly fickle herb garden. The house was empty except for Phinn: George was at the local watching reruns of the previous week's rugby league games, despite having seen them broadcast live, or he was visiting his sister, or he was tom-catting – Phinn did not really care. His phone vibrated to signal a new WhatsApp from a name he associated with high school, hazy pot smoke in bike sheds and other ancient history.

Yr sista single now?

Phinn frowned and scrolled down to the attached photo. It was a screenshot with Claudia's name, her age, and a blurry photo of her taken from a few metres away. Underneath it was a single quote: 'The only thing that might be wrong with you: the human condition.' He rolled his eyes.

It was a screenshot from Tinder.

Phinn moved onto his stomach and studied it again. Then he deleted it and went back to the Sportsbet app, momentarily wondering about joining the old man at the pub for the second half. Amazing how his sisters would all make a huge show out of leaving for big cities, but always seemed to end up in tiny, tiny global villages where everyone knew you all along.

At the motel Nora was invigorated, she was inspired, she was galvanised. What this really meant was, she was lecturing. She had not quite told Claudia what she was doing – how she was behaving – was wrong, but she was getting close. She hadn't told Claudia about Tom either; that was not so close. Claudia was propped up against the dreary headboard of one of the beds, her leggings long ago discarded on the floor along with her bra; her cotton dress now worn like a nightgown. She fanned herself with an issue of *WHO* magazine from twenty-three months before – the same coterie of curvy family members staring reassuringly out from the cover – and sipped her champagne every time she remembered it was in her hand.

Nora was telling her about Kanye and Taylor Swift, making her decide who she wanted to be.

'Look at what drives Taylor: fame. Fame and self-interest, that's it. The friends she has, the lyrics she writes, the clothes she wears, it's all with one goal in mind, to promote herself. To be richer. Taylor and capitalism go together like *Sex and the City* and white feminism. She makes everyone think that's what they want a piece of. I doubt she's made a decision in years that was actually driven by her own taste or preference or even her own happiness. What she has is a fundamentally outwardly directed life; it's self-indulgence at the expense of fulfilment. It's all to feed her self-interest first and foremost.'

Nora rocked back proudly on her heels. She was not usually someone with a spiel, but she had been thinking a lot lately. And listening to *1989*, *Reputation* and *Yeezus* exclusively.

'Kanye, on the other hand – anyone who calls him arrogant is an idiot. You have to think about what drives him, why he acts the way he does, and he's a very funny man, by the way, incredibly self-deprecating. He talks about bringing rap back wearing a backpack with a pink polo shirt! He is making fun of himself!

'But what is he driven by? Love. Love and anger. And his anger isn't just on his own behalf; he's not just angry about what happens to him. He's angry about how other people are treated, he's angry about the poor black victims of Hurricane Katrina and he's angry Beyoncé didn't get the recognition she deserved at the 2009 MTV awards – which she didn't, by the way. Everyone knows that now. He's angry about a lot of injustice for a lot of people and he loves Kim so much. You want your life to have meaning? You need to commit to something. It can be a man, or a woman, or a cause, or a creative output bigger than yourself.'

Nora's speech was starting to drag around the edges. Some of her words were running into each other, her eyeliner was smudged, but Claudia had to concede she had a point. She didn't have much choice.

'Do you want to be driven by love and anger? Or self-interest? Do you want to spend the next few days being a huge brat and agonising over a man who loves you?'

Claudia considered the question like she would consider the question of whether a horse could fly or whether trickle-down economics actually worked. She was completely baffled it was even being asked in the first place. Baffled that she was confiding her deepest fear to her best friend and was being berated in return.

A woman can be forgiven myriad sins and stupid decisions by her friends: hubris, condom-less sex, nights given away to MDMA, extravagant grieving over unreturned calls, devotion to BritPop; but breaking up with a nice guy? That was an incomprehensible act of stupidity. There had to be concrete transgressions, proof the relationship was doomed, knowledge that they had tried. Claudia thought of all the middle-aged couples she knew who were pleasant enough to each other but seemed to have nothing in common. It was courtesy that kept them in loveless relationships for decades. She was beginning to realise how difficult it was to explain the demise of a commitment to a 'good guy'.

'It would be a lot easier for you if Dylan hit me, wouldn't it?'

Nora spat the champagne she had just sipped back into her glass. 'What?'

'You need a reason so badly; I don't know why you are so desperate for me to justify maybe not loving him. You need a list of faults that I can't provide.'

'I'm just trying to understand why you are deciding to dump Dylan the week before your wedding.'

'Well.' Claudia looked down at her empty glass. 'You are acting really strangely; I thought you would be on my team. You're presenting me with a false dilemma: I can be Taylor Swift or Kanye. Maybe the ordinariness of the life I am going to have is not bad, but it's not what you're painting. I'm not Kanye West and Dylan is not Kim Kardashian.'

Nora sighed and attempted a reset. 'I just don't know what

you think you are missing out on, what you think your life will be like single.'

Claudia accepted the shaky attempt at a truce.

'I feel tethered, is all. What if I want to go live in Lisbon?'

'You have never mentioned wanting to even holiday in Lisbon.'

'What if I want to have sex with a woman? I've never done that.'

'I didn't know you wanted to have sex with a woman.'

'I don't! But I could! Isn't that the point? I don't think it would be anything in particular; I think it could be a lot of things. Maybe I would travel to Malta by myself; maybe I would go and do some work in the Philippines. I might go hang out at Quintana Roo. I might sleep with a few more men. I would just be free. More free.'

'You would do precisely none of those things. Oh, maybe you would sleep with some randoms. I thought you were better than romanticising your life. You sound ridiculous; you sound worse than ridiculous, you sound bourgeoise. In the absence of any real problems you have created a pathetic one: your fiancé is too nice.'

Nora's tone was sharp and furious. Claudia was stunned.

'Where is this coming from? Why are you so angry at me?'

'Mate, take your Tinder and your self-pity and take a think for yourself. Even Taylor Swift would be embarrassed by this.'

Nora stood up a little too quickly and for a moment almost finished her rebuke with a wobble. She caught herself and, after making sure both feet were on the ground, she walked towards the door, picking up her wallet from the side table.

'I'm going out for cigarettes.'

Claudia was left with just the champagne bottles for company. Then she noticed her phone flashing.

CHAPTER 19

Sometimes Rachel hated her kids. She thought about this as she picked up a soft pink onesie in size 0000. Just looking at it made her ache. Just below her bully button. The ache she got when she saw one of her children driving by themselves, or paying for underwear, or telling her three weeks after the fact that they were sick and had to stay in bed a few days. It was the ache of not being needed. Of a womb with a permanent vacancy sign.

She would never tell her kids that she hated them, but sometimes it was true. She sometimes thought about the kind of person she would be if she had not been a mother, the way that people married for twenty-three years romanticise the kind of person they would be unattached. Novels written, spontaneous trips to New Zealand, perhaps half a language learned. Of course in reality it would never measure up like this. You would probably still be disappointed in yourself. Maybe a bit unhappier. Rachel did not put much stock in this rationale, though. She liked to think if she had not been a mother she would have a flat stomach. She'd be almost inconceivably rich. All that money spent on sustaining life!

When she was pregnant with Zoe, her sisters, Mary and Wanda, both convinced themselves that Rachel was carrying a child before she even knew. Rachel had yelled at the pair over some long forgotten slight – a completely standard occurrence at the time. But they liked to pretend it was rare to lose control of their tempers. This time they pinned it on hormones. Not just any old hormones; they knew they were so close to Rachel that they could feel her baby. They harassed her for three weeks about whether she had her period before they finally revealed the motive, overshadowing her pregnancy announcement at lunch with explanations of how they just *knew*.

When she was pregnant with Phinn she got fat. Sometimes pregnant women just get pregnant, a volleyball atop firm thighs. Sometimes they gain thirty kilograms with no explanation. Rachel still crossed herself whenever she saw a fat woman. There but for the grace of God.

Carrying Claudia she ate olives every day. That was it.

And Poppy, Poppy she breastfed for almost two years and we all know how that turned out. Also, she slept with another man when she was about six weeks pregnant but nobody ever found out. Sometimes you can be bored, lonely, and make catastrophic decisions. Sometimes your actions have no consequences.

Rachel stood up straight at the thought, as if being called to attention, to account. She looked around and discovered she was still in the shopping centre. Still standing in the children's section, running her hands down size 0000 onesies, which was how she soothed herself when her hatred of her children was particularly intense. She turned to her sister. 'Isn't this darling?'

'As long as you can accept it's darling empty and not full of baby, then yes, it's darling.'

Mary was bored. She had accompanied her sister to the shops with ulterior motives but was finding her routine almost too much to bear.

'Do you really think one of your children is going to give you the satisfaction of a grandchild?' Mary asked, holding up a pack of three bibs for effect.

'Well, I'm sure if they do, it won't be to make me happy. You know how often they think of my happiness.'

Mary nodded thoughtfully, pulling her black handbag over her black shirt, which was tucked into her flowing black skirt. The children liked to compare the colour of her uniform to her soul, it was too easy, but really Mary had just been taken by surprise by what a fifty-year-old body looks like. It wasn't pretty.

'You're always the one making compromises for them,' she continued slowly. Claudia was the one having a wedding 650 kilometres from her preferred venue for Rachel but Mary put the facts to the side.

'They never call you . . .' The longest Rachel had gone without speaking to one of her children on the phone since they left home was five days.

'I just don't know how you do it. They treat you like shit.'

They were in the thrall of their mother in the way most people are. They were connected through the belly buttons. There is a shelf in your soul reserved for your mother, whether she is quite mad, sub-par or cruel. Especially if she is cruel. Rachel was not cruel but she could be quite maddening at times.

She turned to her sister and started weeping. 'I just feel so powerless, so alone. I don't know what more I could do for them.' She discarded the onesie.

'Mick just marvels at you, says you are one of the strongest women he has ever met,' Mary continued, steering her sister by the elbow towards a more interesting section of the shop.

'That's so lovely of Mick. You're lucky to find such a good man, I have always had time for him, even after he …' Rachel wiped her eyes and looked sideways at her sister. '… had all that business with his wife.'

'How are you feeling about Saturday? Your dress is gorgeous; you are going to look gorgeous, even if we haven't seen hide nor tail of any of your daughters since they have been here.' (Claudia had spent four of the past six nights at her mother's house.)

'I'm excited for Claudia, she is a beautiful girl, Dylan is a beautiful man. I won't lie, I could never lie, I do wish there was someone special for me to take along. George will have Lisa; I do miss having someone to celebrate with.'

'Well, you will have me, and wouldn't it be nice to have Mick as well? He speaks so fondly of you; you two have always had a special bond.'

Rachel gave a small nod. 'That would be nice.'

'Everyone else has someone,' Mary reminded her. 'You should have two people.'

Mary had struck the indignant spot. The soft flesh only your sister knows the location of. Where it not only hurts to be struck, but a bruise is left, and nobody else even sees a mark.

'Mary, you're right. I do so much, and ask for so little in return. I think I would like to sit with you and Mick. I'm sure Mick is invited; I'll make sure his seat is next to mine. In fact, Dylan's dad and stepmum arrive tomorrow. Why don't you bring Mick to dinner? I'll let George know.'

Mary nodded and picked up a black dress she had been eyeing off all week. 'You are too kind.'

CHAPTER 20

Petunia's was a restaurant nestled in the middle of the main street of Winston, which – despite the slightly cloying name – was regarded as palatial by the town's standards. But that was simply because it boasted an upstairs *and* a downstairs seating area. It retained a reliable if stodgy menu, one of the last balconies in the town not directly attached to a bowling green that welcomed smokers, and still included an unpredictable microphone in the space's rental cost. It was the natural venue for the wedding reception.

Dylan and Claudia had been paying for it in small instalments for eleven months, with the understanding Petunia's had absolutely no responsibility for how it would look on the night. Claudia could find no wedding decorators, only wedding 'stylists', within a 180-kilometre radius – a distinction that seemed to mean they charged three times as much as decorators would for filling the space with empty jam jars and molasses-scented candles. In yet another boundlessly optimistic act of delegation loosely agreed upon since the initial booking, the seemingly simple job of deciding the final destination of flowers and tablecloth patterns had fallen to Claudia's brother and sisters.

George had arrived that morning at ten in an effort to at least ensure some decorating got done. The move was largely sparked by a chance encounter with one of his old schoolmates, who had stopped his Hilux, laden with his battered tinny, at a service station several days beforehand. After some small talk about Cedric's fishing trip, George glanced into the bow at the plastic bucket holding the mud crabs frantically scuttling over each other in a futile bid for freedom beyond the white curved walls. The sight instantly led George to an ungenerous but probably accurate comparison with his children's organisational capabilities and his realisation that he'd have to step into the interior-decorating role.

He nodded to the owner as he walked past the front counter without saying a word and began his ascent up the curved stairs. He could hear his children before he saw them.

'I'm her sister; I know she will love it.'

'I'm her brother and that means jackshit. When was the last time you saw which flowers were in her house?'

'She said we could do whatever we wanted with the flowers.'

'Yes, but I don't think she envisioned we would try to dye them blue.'

At the top of the stairs, George was confronted with twenty bare tables and what he assumed were twenty pale pink tablecloths thrown carelessly in the corner. He knew they had been dry-cleaned and folded before pick-up. However, one of his offspring who had escaped any kind of relationship with an iron had failed to consider what happened when they were simply emptied out of the plastic bags onto the ground instead of put on the tables. He allowed himself a deep sigh. It was exactly as he expected.

In the middle of the room, Poppy was holding a bunch of daisies as a prop in one hand while gesticulating wildly to Phinn, who was standing forlornly beside a table bearing hundreds of brown paper packages of the same blooms.

'Dad!'

Poppy was excited to see George emerge, assuming he was a natural ally. George gingerly made his way through the tables and hugged his daughter, patting Phinn on the head.

'Hey Dad, welcome to the floral derangements,' Phinn quipped to his darkening old man.

Before George could respond, Poppy had already started on him. 'I've had this amazing idea. Remember when we were kids and we used to dye the flowers blue each week? Wouldn't it be incredible to dye the daisies for Claudia, as a surprise?'

George paused as Phinn shot back at his youngest sister, 'Wouldn't it be incredible if we just did what we were supposed to do?'

Eyebrow arched, George surveyed the room and realised the tables were not in any kind of formation and the sound system remained in the box. Before he could referee the brewing argument, the door from the kitchen swung open and Nora walked in with her head still facing the kitchen entrance.

'Thank you! You're very kind!' she called back to a staff member hurrying out of sight.

In an effort to be as unthreatening as possible, she had made the concession of wearing denim shorts cut off just above her knees. With her leather loafers and ironed cotton T-shirt the overall effect was still more Nice, France, than nice-and-placating, but she was trying. In her hands was a cardboard tray of styrofoam cups, some bearing the small browning stains from the trip up the stairs. She turned her head to the small crew and called out sunnily, 'Good morning! I thought you might like some help. I've brought coffees.'

Phinn rushed over to take the tray from her hands while George broke out into a smile and finally broke his silence. 'Nora, that's very kind!'

'I didn't know what you all drank but I figured a tray of lattes would be safe, and there's sugar in here too.'

It might have been her optimistic survey of the room that led Nora to miss Poppy's deepening scowl. The youngest Carter threw down her handful of daisies and edged around one of the tables.

'I thought Claudia just asked *us* to decorate,' she said in place of a greeting.

'Yes, well, she mentioned to me that you would all be here this morning and I thought maybe I could make it easier.' Nora now weighed up Poppy coldly, with the latter quickly realising that she had heard about the beach the day before. Claudia must have been upset.

Poppy silently picked up a coffee while Phinn sucked his gut in and threw his arm around his sister's friend.

'There's plenty of work for you to do. You can actually settle a, uh, contest of ideas we are having.'

Nora shrugged Phinn's arm off and stepped towards the corner with the tablecloths.

'Are these clean?'

'Do you think we should dye the daisies blue?'

Nora turned back to Phinn, startled. 'The daisies blue? Those daisies? The daisies for the wedding?'

'Yes.'

Poppy had flinched each time Nora uttered the flower's name, her harsh inflection on the first syllable gradually rising.

'How would you dye them blue?'

Poppy rolled her eyes and interrupted. 'It's very simple, you put blue dye in the water of the vases.'

'Why would you dye them blue?'

'Well,' Phinn said, raising his coffee to his lips, 'why indeed.'

Poppy struggled to maintain an even tone. 'Claudia would love it; we used to do it when we were kids – it was so much fun.'

Nora seemed to weigh the response and everything she knew about manners and diplomacy in the seconds that followed, before her eyes brightened at a welcome new distraction heading across the floor.

'Zoe! Rachel! Hello!'

'I'm going to find an iron,' George said, heading towards the kitchen as he scooped up a pile of the tablecloths in his arms. He didn't turn at any point.

Rachel and Zoe picked their way through the chairs from the stairway with the matriarch leading the way in tight white trousers and a hibiscus pink top that made no pretence at her being coy about her figure. By contrast it appeared that Zoe, in a light-blue T-shirt dress, hair tied back from her face and stepping out in Nike joggers, had taken cues from Nora's breezy style, while also trying to dress for the menial tasks of the day. She looked at Nora uneasily and then to Poppy.

'Hiiiiiiii, I didn't know you were decorating too, I thought it was a . . .' She bit her lip. 'A family thing.'

'Well, Claudia told me about the decorating and I thought I could come and just see if you needed help.'

Rachel grabbed a bunch of daisies.

'I see my ex-husband is here as well.'

Poppy finally spoke. 'Our dad is here, yes,'

'These daisies are pretty. They're not the only flowers though, are they?'

The flowers had officially been marked for battle. In one

corner were Nora and Claudia's current tastes; in another corner were Poppy and Claudia's tastes from long before there was ever her friendship, adulthood, distance, independence. And creating another battlefront was Rachel, who simply couldn't see past her own taste to bother considering what Claudia might prefer.

Rachel picked up a few of the daisies and sniffed them. 'Do they seem a bit old to you?'

Phinn volunteered. 'We watched them being picked this morning; they couldn't be fresher.'

'Did anyone think to get some baby's breath? That would be lovely with the daisies. And we need some colour. Do you know what's in season? Gerberas – Claudia loves them.'

Claudia had bought gerberas weekly for her room for an entire spring when she was fifteen. The phase seemed to end with the close of that one solitary season and she had never mentioned or paid for them again, but it didn't matter. She had been doomed to receive bunches of the gaudy flowers every birthday since.

Nora physically stopped herself from gasping. 'I don't think we can have gerberas at a wedding.'

'Actually Mum, I agree on the colour thing. I was just saying we could dye the daisies blue, remember like when we were kids?'

'Yes, I showed you how to do that!'

It was really George who had dyed the flowers with them, but everyone knew better than to correct the record, given the current Cold War dynamic between the parents. Poppy was talking to her mother, who could be relied on for reinforcement when they were not personally warring, but all the time kept her emboldened gaze fixed on Nora, daring this relative outsider to disagree. Daring her to try to prove she knew what was best or who loved Claudia more. No matter how much she was told it wasn't a competition, Poppy was determined to win against her sister's chic shielding interloper.

'I think the baby's breath is a really good idea,' Nora finally responded, sparking a staccato burst from Rachel.

'I'm going to get some blue dye and order some gerberas. Where is the seating plan? I haven't signed off on it. I kept asking Claudia for it but she must have forgotten to show it to me.' Rachel was a bright pink blur speeding towards the kitchen when the doors swung open to reveal Phinn with tablecloths draped carefully over his arms. He leaned towards his mother to kiss her, then started on the first useful task of the morning.

The girls watched in silence as he laid a cloth across a table and moved around it to even out the sides. Nora put her coffee down next to the dreaded daisies and, hoping it was a neutral task, walked over to take one of the cloths for the next table.

'Are you a tablecloth expert now as well?' Poppy almost spat.

Zoe, who had been waiting for the inevitable boil-over as soon as she had seen Nora, quickly moved towards appeasement.

'She's just trying to help; she's here for our sister.'

'She's here because she thinks she's an expert in Claudia and everything else. We're her sisters; this is our job.'

Phinn rolled his eyes. 'You're obsessed with this sisters thing, like it gives you some special magic. *It's just fucking DNA and chromosomes.*'

Zoe and Nora both caught their breaths. Nora, without the aforementioned biological bonds to Poppy, was already fed up. Poppy seemed to share her mother's propensity for intense moods and the dog-like faith that she knew what was best, without it being tempered by Rachel's consideration for others (George notwithstanding). Nora's new strategy was simply to ignore the youngest Carter. She couldn't give a solitary flying ibis if her presence riled her anymore.

'Look, Claudia asked for daisies, shouldn't we just get daisies?' she said mildly.

'We need more tablecloths,' Phinn said emphatically, heading towards the kitchen doors they had all last seen Rachel enter. Momentarily distracted by his self-loathing at getting involved in the women's squabbling, he had actually forgotten he had passed his mother on the way out. So it took him by surprise when he opened the door and heard her voice. Contrary to his usual instinct, instead of noisily making himself known this time, he paused.

Rachel was trying to speak in a low voice but it was beyond her capabilities. Her son's ears pricked up at the sound of his uncle's name.

'He has a right to be there, you know. It's supposed to be a family dinner and he is family, and I haven't seen Mary so happy in so long. And you know what, I couldn't care less what you think; you just have to deal with it. She deserves to bring a partner and he is your brother.'

Phinn could see his father through the stainless-steel shelves on the kitchen island, looking down as he concentrated fiercely on the edges of a tablecloth with his iron.

'He's going to be there, anyway.'

Rachel reached over and patted George on the shoulder, purposefully making him flinch as Phinn stepped forward, letting the door slam noisily behind him.

'I've got to go sort out these flowers now,' Rachel said as way of farewell. 'Hello son.' She breezed past Phinn, who watched his father shake his head slowly, dourly. Without a word, Phinn ducked down to pick up the newly ironed tablecloths but, to his surprise, it was his father who broke the silence.

'What's going on with the flowers?'

'Uh, Claudia wants daisies, Rachel wants gerberas, Poppy wants to dye the daisies blue.'

George had watched his children acquiesce to Rachel's interminable whims and demands for years; he knew come Saturday night which flowers would be on the tables.

'Well, that would be something blue, and it sounds like your aunt Mary is bringing something borrowed,' he said as Phinn hurried out.

In the dining room, the table of daisies sat untouched as Nora and Zoe stood on the other side holding one of the round tables between them. Zoe was gingerly stepping backwards while Nora guided her with what seemed to the Carter girl a very boring version of the 'Time Warp': 'step back and to the left, there's nothing behind you yet, now just wriggle it a little to the right, hmmm maybe to the left again'.

Zoe followed obediently but her uncertain steps still gave the impression of a five year old attempting to waltz with her grandfather. That would be the closest thing to a traditional wedding trope we'll be seeing around here, Phinn thought, as he hauled the tablecloths over.

'Are you sure that table is okay there?' Poppy, arms crossed, leaned against another table so heavily she was almost in a combat crouch.

'Take one more big step back,' Nora said to Zoe as a way of response.

She was happy with her defence mechanism. Nora the Ignorer. Just like cartoon Dora the Explorer's sullen little sister, who cared for neither exploring nor remonstrating with a kleptomaniac fox.

The two women put the table down and Nora turned and surveyed the room. 'We don't want the tables lined up perfectly; it works much better if they are kind of scattered so it doesn't look so regimented.'

Phinn dropped the two ironed cloths on the table. 'Do you want to lay these out now or wait until the tables are arranged?'

Behind him thunder crossed Poppy's face as he waited for Nora's verdict.

'Lay them out now so they stay nice and smooth.' Nora carefully pulled on the cloth to start spreading it across the table and before Phinn could start helping her Poppy had the other side.

'These are rectangular tablecloths; we should make them square so they look even,' she said, lifting the edge.

Nora narrowed her eyes and gave a little tug on the other side.

'The rectangle is fine; as long as it covers the entire table, nobody will notice. If we make them square it will be easier for them to ride up.'

'It's okay,' yelled Phinn. 'This marriage is literally all about round pegs in square holes! All marriages are! It's what makes the speeches interesting.'

Poppy ignored both Nora and her brother and began folding the other side.

'Don't fold that! You will just cause another crease.' Nora pulled back the cloth to try to get the other side out of Poppy's reach, but she had a surprisingly tight hold of it. Poppy gave a violent pull back.

'The square will look better,' she said defiantly.

Suddenly Nora went from Ignorer to Warrior. 'Can you just let us put the fucking tablecloths on the tables without making it a statement about your fucking influence?'

As soon as she had said it she looked taken aback at her own swearing.

If Poppy was shocked she didn't show it. Instead she planted her feet squarely for maximum effectiveness and she yanked back on the cloth fiercely. Nora, ready for it, dipped her shoulders and pulled back at the exact same time, leaving the two held upright only by the tension of the (now-not-just-creased-but-twisted) tablecloth as they both jerked on it.

Phinn's jaw dropped to create an exaggerated 'O' as he stopped and gaped, while Zoe put her hand over her chin, first to stifle her gasps and then her giggles. The wide-eyed brother instantly thought of the shared silence of wildlife documentary makers trying to record a big cat bringing down a buffalo as he stood still next to his sister in a bid to take in the spectacle while desperately hoping not to be the next target.

It wasn't an inaccurate analogy: by now a visibly agitated Poppy had scrunched up the corners at her end into balls so she could get a better grip, while Nora's mouth was set in a determined line as she refused to cede an inch of her side.

'Did ... did she just growl?' Phinn whispered to Zoe.

Zoe grabbed her mouth in a bid to stop her silent giggling fit.

Poppy and Nora refused to break eye contact as they each violently pulled on their side of the tablecloth.

'Just let it go!'

'What is your fuckin' problem?'

'Ooh good swearing,' murmured Phinn.

'Old school, dropping the "g" there,' Zoe replied under her hand. 'Loike it, mate, loike it.'

'I swear to God!' Nora bellowed.

'Why are you even here?' her opponent shrieked back.

A deeper voice joined the fray, booming behind them. 'What are you doing to that tablecloth?'

Nora jumped, momentarily missing a step as her foot landed behind her, but still did not drop the cloth. Poppy didn't even turn to face her dad. Her hands ached.

George stood with four other tablecloths carefully draped across his arms, which were raised to stop the sheets trailing on the ground. He shook his head and asked again.

'*I said*,' he yelled before softening slightly, 'what are you doing to the tablecloth? I just ironed that.'

The girls both let go; Nora, turning the colour of beetroot, tried to delicately smooth the edges on her side.

Phinn finally answered for them. 'It's like a brawl in King Arthur's Camelot, Dad,' he said before comically drawing himself up to full height. 'Welcome to the fights of the round table. For some reason these two think Claudia will care if the tablecloths are folded into squares or a hexagon or something like that.'

His father opened his mouth and then thought better of it and turned back towards the kitchen in preparation for more ironing.

'I guess,' Zoe smirked soberly, 'this is what Ma meant at the engagement party when she got drunk and told us Carter marriages are really a vicious circle.'

CHAPTER 21

Zoe stood outside of the door and raised her fist. Then she put it back down again. A casual observer would see an expensive-looking woman trying to convince herself to knock on a lover's door. Zoe had the right clothes to be sophisticated but something wasn't quite right. She wore Italian brogues, handmade, leather, beautiful. But she wore them because she had seen Amal Clooney wearing a pair in a paparazzi shot and had immediately bought them online despite the fact they were $400.

It was that type of sophistication. Affected. Unnatural. Like criticising hip-hop as shallow without ever having listened to *The College Dropout*. The fundamentals were not there. The taste.

Zoe was not convincing herself to confront a lover; it was worse. A woman she admired was on the other side of the door. A woman she was a little bit in love with in a very specific way heterosexual women can become obsessed with other women.

It has to be a woman you do not know well (how can you truly be devoted to someone you *know*?), but have some personal connection to so you have access to their Instagram, Facebook page and enough personal contact to keep you interested.

You don't want to have sex with them. It's far more intense than that. You want to wear their skin.

Zoe pulled her hair out from its messy bun and scraped through her fingers to create a messy ponytail instead. Then she knocked.

'Who is it?' a voice on the other side immediately called out.

'Zoe,' came the squeak back.

Zoe could tell by the way the door handle was turned that Nora was exasperated. Nonetheless it opened to reveal white linen pants patterned with navy flowers, a crop top that sensibly met the top of the high-waisted pants, only hinting at the toned stomach (Reformer Pilates, Zoe already knew) and Nora's head of damp hair.

'Claudia sent me,' Zoe said briskly.

'Where is she?' Nora remained in the doorway.

'At Dad's. I think she is dodging everyone. She's already heard about the venue.' Zoe stuck a foot in the door. 'Poppy is there too; all is forgiven.'

'What do you mean "all is forgiven"? How can it all be forgiven?'

Zoe started laughing. 'Five minutes passed, that's what happened. You know how willing Claudia is to overlook the fact Poppy is a complete and utter arsehole. Being held to account for one's behaviour is very boring for some people.'

As she spoke, Zoe stepped forward so her foot in the door became two feet in the room and Nora stepped back to avoid coming nose to nose with her friend's sister. Not that Zoe would've minded. She surveyed the room. As suspected it was meticulous. For these straight-girl obsessions to work, the object has to have something out of reach to you, but only slightly. She has to have enough money to fly business class if that's the pinnacle of glamour for you. She has to work as a yoga instructor if you were so bad at sport your grandfather refused to come to your netball games it was 'such a waste of time'. She has to have bouncing curls and an oval face to your lanky thin mane. For Zoe she had to be so particular and organised and clean that she ironed her sheets.

Nora had hung a silk dressing-gown on the hook on the wall for that specific purpose and her silk dresses hung in the wardrobe with three pairs of shoes lined underneath. Next to her pink leather hand luggage was a pink leather structured make-up bag with various lotions and bottles, and next to that was a pink leather pouch with various eyeliners and lipsticks. Heaven for the chronically messy.

Zoe looked up from the two copies of the *New Yorker* sitting perfectly square to the *Gourmet Traveller* and noticed behind Nora in the bathroom was a hairdryer and a bottle of white wine.

'Have you been drinking?'

'Why yes I have, thank you for asking.'

Zoe smirked. 'Righto, what's the occasion?'

'The occasion is being stuck in this town for my best friend's wedding watching her sisters skilfully guide her to the brink of a breakdown. Would you like one?'

Zoe shrugged and sat down on the bed Nora had been sleeping in (she could tell because it had been made with far more care than the other bed, which had obviously just been made up by the professional cleaners).

'Sure, why not?'

Drinking in the daytime. Always a thrill, until the third glass. Zoe had (gladly, gleefully) been dispatched by Claudia to check on Nora. Apparently she had not been quite right since arriving in town, and while Claudia had intuited this she was also very busy with the small question of whether she would in fact marry Dylan or not. Zoe relayed all of this – apart from the gladly gleefully bit – while Nora bent over with a hairdryer that had all the force of a two year old blowing out birthday candles, occasionally staying upright to sip on her chardonnay.

She finally conceded defeat, switching it off with her hair still damp.

'Hmmmmmmmm,' was her considered response.

'We don't have to talk about your feelings, although I have noticed you are not your usual ...' Zoe paused. 'Your usual *sparkling* self.'

There was no way to say that without sounding sarcastic.

'We can talk about things far more interesting than your feelings,' Zoe continued, swigging her drink to arrive at the stage of thought where daytime drinking is an excellent idea leading to resolutions to do it every day. 'We can talk about what's more important in the struggle – race or class. I am white, so I will of course conclude class, but you can argue your side. We can talk about the most overrated mascara we have tried. We can talk about things we have eaten in Paris. We can talk about football. There is literally an infinite list of things we can talk about that are not your feelings so don't feel pressured.'

'Tom and I broke up.'

'Ah.'

Zoe shifted on the bed. She knew what she shouldn't say. She knew the rules of that. Never tell your friend to break up with their partner. Never slag off your friend's ex-partner. Never reveal how much you disliked your friend's ex-partner. Tell your friend how amazing and beautiful and intelligent they are.

But the problem: these were all rules for your friend. There were no such basic guidelines for your sister's friend with whom you are slightly obsessed.

'He wrote me an email.' Nora leaned on the chest of drawers opposite Zoe.

'Ah.'

'Do you want to see?'

'Sure.'

Nora opened the drawer under the television (of course her laptop was in a safe place where she wouldn't sit on it and thieves would not check first!) and passed the computer to Zoe. A small piece of her heart, in her friend's sister's hands, because she was the imperfect understudy at the moment.

Zoe may have been lacking a rule book but she had some experience here. She knew the only way to tell someone that they were the most annoying person in the world. She had been in Sicily when she'd discovered this.

A longed-for holiday. The Mediterranean, her French-speaking boyfriend, balmy nights eating fresh bread and the most perfect steak she had ever tasted. And she couldn't stop being a bitch. There was no real reason; she was just hot and permanently bloated and too comfortable in the relationship. Everything he did annoyed her. She remembered one particular day when he had breathed wrong. The worst! Half a holiday spent with every figurative peace offering slapped from his hands. And for what? No solid reason. He just annoyed her. He annoyed her before she realised part of a relationship is being the most annoyed person in the world. Part of a relationship is looking at someone and accepting, as Ask Polly once put it in a long-forgotten column, 'You are fucking wretched and a huge disappointment in almost every way, and I love you like crazy anyway.'

It was too late when Zoe realised all that. It was too late and she was not sure if she should relay the information to Nora anyway. She did not know if this was the time for relationship revelations or the time for embracing being single. These are the types of things you know if the person spilling their guts to you is actually your friend.

Zoe thought about this while she read the email. She thought about this while being careful to hide the sound of her heart breaking repeatedly for Nora while she read the email. She wanted to tell her everything she knew but she did not know if Nora could be trusted.

Nora, in showing a minute of vulnerability had also inevitably become less attractive to Zoe as some weird and complicated crush.

Zoe was careful. 'It's quite cruel.'

Nora nodded.

'It is quite cruel,' she repeated, almost as an affirmation from a Chinese fortune cookie. 'I obviously haven't told Claudia this. I think this whole crisis,' Nora waved vaguely at her laptop, 'can wait until she is back from the wedding. Then she can devote herself more readily to being my emotional crutch.'

Zoe kindly laughed. 'What are your general thoughts on this? Is this it?'

'You mean are we broken up forever? I can't see us coming back, no.' Nora pointedly didn't elaborate.

'How do you feel about being single?'

'Excited. Lonely. The usual. Being single is more of an identity for me than a reality. I like the idea of it. In practice, I'm not so good at it.'

'Well, almost all of us want to be in a relationship. Whether people admit it or not, it's pretty self-evident. It's nice to have someone who always has to be on your side. It's nice to be known, in your bones known. It's nice to touch another human being. It's not really something to be embarrassed about.'

Zoe talked the talk but at the walk she was pretty pathetic. There was her single status and complete aversion to dating as testament to that. Nora pointed this out, albeit a touch more delicately.

'Oh yeah, but I have the cliché of my parents' marriage breakdown to justify that. I didn't even know the extent of it until my first boyfriend snapped at me over accidentally leaving his oven on and I had a complete emotional shutdown and was inconsolable for hours because I was convinced one disagreement meant we would be screaming the most intimate abuse at each other within twenty minutes.'

That was not something Zoe revealed often and, feeling the warmth of traded intimacies, and half a bottle of wine, she decided to tell Nora about the staircase.

'If happiness is a staircase – if happiness is coupledom, to be specific – then at the top you obviously have happy couples. Those arseholes who have it good, pretty much through no fault of their own. They might be good people, sure, but they basically got lucky. Nonetheless, they're at the top. So where do you think you as a single person – a freshly dumped single person, to be precise – where do you think you are?'

'Ummmmmm, in the depressing nightclub, a thirty-dollar Uber ride away from the airport, which is a four-hour flight away from the palace with the staircase?'

'I'll laugh, but only because I'm feeling charitable. Ha ha! No, my friend, my sister's friend. You're not at the bottom of the staircase, you're three quarters down. At the bottom are unhappy couples. Because they are so far away from a happy partnership. They first have to split up and then work through their issues and figure out what they want and the kind of person they are and then meet someone and then they will get to the top. It's a hell of a journey. You, you have some work to do on yourself, but you're already single. Single people who have sorted their shit out, they're halfway to the top, not at the bottom. So comfort yourself with that. You think a happy relationship is light years away, so far out of reach, but really you're in a better place than people stuck in unhappy relationships that will eventually end. You can at least start looking for a decent relationship soon.'

Nora considered the staircase. 'That's the most pretentious thing I've ever heard.'

Zoe was fine but she was no Claudia. Nora thought she would feel a pressure valve released, or even a vague weight lifted after talking about Tom, but there was still only emptiness. Emptiness and day wine. Zoe was a poor stand-in for her sister; she was a sub-par stand-in for being Nora's actual friend. She needed real consoling, genuine advice, some intimacy in the wake of her devastation. Instead she was stuck listening to self-help pep talks about imaginary staircases.

CHAPTER 22

Claudia lay on her side looking at Dylan's profile. His phone was propped on his chest and his headphones were in, his viewing platform shuddering every few seconds as he laughed at skateboarders falling over in a stunning variety of ways. She put her arm around him and squeezed. Dylan, taking the cue, pulled his earphones out and turned to face her.

She moved closer still. 'Come here,' she muttered.

He wriggled in. 'I am here.'

It was years-old call-and-response between the two, Claudia demanding physical and emotional proximity and Dylan assuring her he couldn't be any closer. He laid his hand flat on her face. 'How are you holding up?'

It sounded simple enough but Claudia knew what he meant.

'I am fine; it's fine.'

She rested her forehead on his and the two lay still against each other. Claudia thought about his question. He always looked out for her. It had been Dylan years before who had first tried to warn her when her moods turned dark and she couldn't get out of bed. Who begged her to see a doctor. Who cooked her endless pots of bastardised pad thai, heavy with soy sauce and lime, the only thing she would pick at. Despite the clichés, it didn't feel like falling into a dark hole, or being followed around by a dog. It felt like nothing. She didn't want to die, but she didn't quite care if she stuck around either; she just wanted to feel something. When she couldn't remember the last time she showered and Dylan found the razor, it was him who made her call her mother, who brought her home to recover.

Every time he asked her how she was 'holding up', she knew what he was really asking. Are you normal upset or going crazy upset? Are we going to go through this again? How could Claudia ever repay him for looking after her, for sticking around? In the furthest corner of herself she questioned her lovability; surely she'd lost a few points of desirability in all of that; who else would want her?

She opened her eyes, her forehead still pressed to Dylan's forehead and his dark eyes doubled to four as she tried to focus while still lying so close. He laughed and kissed her on the forehead, pulling away but grabbing her hand as compensation.

'What are you thinking about?'

It was another one of their private games: the responder got to list three things.

'Ummmm.' Claudia thought better of saying 'the time I went insane and you stayed with me, for some reason'. 'My sisters, how many sleeps it is until we can leave, aannnnddd Maltesers ice cream. What are you thinking about?'

'Corpus Christi, a skater in the 1980s.'

'That's it?'

'That's it. Do you want me to go get you a Maltesers ice cream?'

Claudia sighed and rolled away from him. She shook her

head and instead picked up her phone. He had his, by her standards, ancient skateboarding videos; she had her own personal quest to find Beyoncé's Snapchat.

For three weeks when Claudia was fifteen years old she had decided to go on a diet. Every day she ran 11.5 kilometres and ate only oranges. She dropped a staggering 9 kilograms in that time but then perceived the path she had set out on and changed course, instead becoming obsessive about making sure the sugar content was under 12 per cent in everything she ate.

Such was the power of her addictive personality.

She was careful what she tried, what she decided to do more than once, for fear of fixation. She studiously avoided even a toke of a joint throughout her teenage years and never ate chocolate more than two days in a row because of the destruction she knew would eventually be wrought.

But she had been cavalier, careless; she had stopped paying attention for a minute.

Which is how she found herself barricaded in the bathroom, sitting on the edge of the closed lid of the toilet while Dylan snored softly in the bedroom. Claudia was hunched over her lap so the light of the iPhone illuminated her features, the remnants of mascara lying stubbornly beneath her eyes and her furrowed brow. She was swiping.

Shirtless man, after shirtless man, after man in a suit with sunglasses on his head at the races.

She had been caught off guard by how attractive she found the men on Tinder, an attraction that lay easily beside her guilt. It had been so long since she'd flirted, so long since she had been so viscerally attracted to a body. According to the app in the palm of her hand there were more than plenty of fish in the sea; there were so many opportunities for an easy ego boost, or even an easy lay, they could populate another planet. No matter how many she swiped, there were always more: men visiting from overseas, weirdly defensive men 'not looking for a wife on here', sweet men who put photos of their mum in their profiles, so many men mooning the camera from on top of a mountain, and a lot of men listing their height, for some reason. Claudia found it intoxicating, and she was only swiping, she told herself. There was no harm done in swiping. The men were swiping right back: it had been the rush of notifications in the hour after she'd left Nora's during which she had experienced the first dangerous pulls to open the app again and again. Men swiping right on her, matching with her, signalling they found her attractive. She had not initiated any conversation with them, she told herself. At the moment it was just two adults confirming to each other they would absolutely go there.

But she was feeling something she had not realised was missing until the old familiar tingle had returned. Anticipation.

Her inbox was filling up with hellos and winky faces, but they were easy to ignore; they weren't real messages, just one of the many lines these men were casting out into the night in the hope of a nibble.

Footsteps in the hallway broke the hypnotic hold her phone had on her and she looked up. Someone had just walked past the bathroom and down the stairs. She sighed and glanced at her phone again: 2.45 a.m.

She flushed the toilet and ran the taps for anyone outside who might need convincing her bathroom visit was entirely functional. Someone could be listening in this house at any time. She stepped quietly into the hallway and ducked across to the bedroom where Dylan lay on his stomach, a pillow beneath his head and a pillow beneath his cocked knee. She crawled in next to him and put the phone on the floor, lying on her back and then on her side again. Instinctively, he rolled over and rested his arm across her. She was used to falling asleep in his embrace.

CHAPTER 23

Claudia: Dylan says can you please bring him a tie clip (????) when you come to dinner tonight. Please.

George: I have a tie clip for him. I will bring it for him in the morning. I can't make tonight.

Claudia: Why?

George: Too much to do.

CHAPTER 24

Rachel walked into the living room where her sister was sprawled across a ridiculous green velvet couch. Ridiculous and fantastic. She lowered her book and swung one stockinged leg over the side so she could half sit up.

'I have something to read you,' Mary said as she propped herself up on her elbow and thumbed through the book; Rachel could make out Helen Garner's name on the front. 'Here it is.'

'A crime novelist spoke at a conference about the unsuitability of his usual sardonic tone for the war story he was trying to write, "about young men with their stomachs torn open who cry all night for their mothers and then die". An old man told me, after he had had open-heart surgery, that he and a ward full of other men his age woke in the dark from hideous nightmares, screaming for their mothers. I have never read or heard of a woman in extremis who called for her mother.'

Rachel walked out of the room.

CHAPTER 25

Claudia crouched down in the corner where the kitchen benches met across from the island. She would've preferred to be under the dining table surrounded by tucked-in chairs, but in one of a series of betrayals by her body over the past twenty-eight years she had grown too tall to sit comfortably under there. Instead she crouched in her black boots, staring down at her pale blue socks, a fried egg drawn on each side. She had on a loose white cotton T-shirt with giant roses in yellow, pink and blue drawn all over it, and tucked into her dark denim cut-offs. 'I look good,' she thought to herself as she quietly wept. She heard the footsteps of Phinn coming down the hallway followed by Rachel (you live in a house for eighteen years with the same people and you too would be able to distinguish between the footsteps of the 28-year-old kind male and the 65-year-old frustrated mother). She pulled the top of her shirt over her face so she could not see them for a few more seconds and squeezed her last tears out of her eyes.

'I am going to write a letter to the shopping centre. You can't just put a pole there; they really should pay for it to be fixed.'

'You can't back into a pole and seriously blame the shopping centre for putting it there!'

'There's so much concrete, it's very bright, you can't see properly and there's no reason to put the pole—' Rachel's sentence fell off a cliff. 'Claudia?'

Her second daughter wiped her face while still focusing on her ankles and then looked up.

'What are you doing down there, you dumb doob?' Phinn asked.

Despite her best intentions and efforts up until that point, Claudia sniffed and a fresh burst of tears came on.

'Dad's not coming to the dinner tonight,' she said, putting her face back in her arms.

'Oh sweetie.' Rachel crouched down next to Claudia and rubbed her back, only triggering another cascade of tears. 'Sweetie, why isn't he coming? How do you know?'

'He texted me. He didn't tell me why; he said he had too much to do. I was really looking forward to this. I'm not going to get to hang out with any of you much on Saturday. Tonight was supposed to be the night for a proper family dinner; now he's not even coming.'

Rachel cocked her head. 'Well, you know what he's like. He doesn't mean anything, this is just the way he is.' She traced her fingers up Claudia's spine, a spine she had been tracing since it was an hour old, a spine she had been tracing since before Claudia could even remember.

'You know, sometimes I get the feeling Dad doesn't even like me.'

'Sweetie, of course he loves you, you're his daughter.'

'Of course he loves me, that's not what I said. Sometimes I think he doesn't like me. I know he loves me, but I get the feeling he doesn't like me as a person. I think he finds me high maintenance. Or too foreign to him. Or something. He never seems to feel obligated to make the effort for me. It's like, just because I'm not as oversensitive as my siblings, he can be mean to me.'

'Your siblings are not oversensitive.' As ever Rachel was unbothered by the actual point of the conversation; she only heard descriptors she objected to. You could tell her that your best friend was dead, but if you used a nickname all you would get is scolded for not using the name your best friend's mother had given them.

Rachel stood up, dragging Claudia by the elbow with her. 'Your dad does like you; he's just a grumpy old man sometimes. It's been a big week. You'll still have a great night. We will all be there – don't let it ruin your special night.'

Claudia nodded into her mother's shoulder.

'Now, sweetie, if your father isn't coming, why don't you let Mick come along? It will be nice. You like Mick, he's a lovely man, and it would be nice to have him at one of the celebrations.'

Claudia nodded again. 'Sure, if Dad's not coming, then Mick could at least have dinner with us.'

She did not notice Phinn had not said a word the entire time.

Phinn waited until Claudia had left the kitchen and glared at his mother. 'Why didn't you tell her?'

Rachel pulled eggs and tinned food out of the same shopping bag, shaking her head at the ineptitude of the packing skills of the woman at the checkout. 'She doesn't need to know the car is scratched. She's already stressed.'

Phinn shook his head and followed his sister. His steps slowed as he reached the bedroom door. He was a lifelong student of conflict avoidance. While his sisters had raged around him as children, he had counted how many times he could hit a tennis ball against the water tank with a cricket wicket.

If Phinn had been Queen Victoria, Ireland would have been under Home Rule in 1849, just so she would not have had to undertake an awkward propaganda visit to the country. If he had been in the Iraqi prison Camp Bucca with Abu Bakr al-Baghdadi, the caliphate would never have been declared because he would've distracted the future Islamic State leader with a game of cards rather than get involved in a political discussion.

When Phinn was fifteen and his long-awaited growth spurt was still very much delayed, he had been in the main street with his mother when his mate Tony had yelled at him from across the street. Tony was a year older and three times bigger. He was a surf lifesaver who fancied himself as a bit of a hometown hero but, as he did with most people, Phinn had always got along with him. They were mates. He yelled some insult that was muffled by two cars but Phinn got the general gist. This is how boys communicated; this is how mates spoke to each other. 'You dumb piece of shit!' Tony hollered. Phinn, forgetting he was standing with Rachel for a second, exuberantly yelled back, 'You're ugly!' Tony crossed the street.

Phinn bounced towards him, holding his skateboard under his arm. He held out his hand for their traditional bump of acknowledgement. That's when Tony punched him in the face. Dazed, Phinn staggered forward and dropped his skateboard.

'Mate?'

Tony hit him again, this time in the chest, winding Phinn

for a few seconds. The next punch landed under his right eye. The next one was the one that got him on the ground. Rachel stood on the footpath screaming

'Tony, you son of a bitch, I know your mother, get off him! What are you doing?'

Phinn felt Tony's shoe in his ribs and, from his horizontal vantage point, watched him walk away. He let his eyes sting with tears for a moment but blinked them away before Rachel dragged him up by his elbow and spent the car trip home yelling at him for fighting.

Rachel didn't seem to understand that Phinn had just been beaten up in front of his mother. He hadn't landed a single punch. He didn't care about the physical pain. Nobody gives a shit about that. It was another reminder he was small.

Phinn never found out why Tony suddenly turned on him, and for some reason it was Tony who he thought of as he walked towards his sister's room to detonate a bomb because it was the right thing to do.

He leaned on the doorframe as his sister lay across her bed scrolling through Twitter. Sensing his presence, Claudia rolled over and, without looking up, said, 'Phinn! Listen to this tweet from @dril: "This whole thing smacks of gender," I holler as I overturn my uncle's barbeque grill and turn the 4th of July into the 4th of Shit.' Claudia cackled to herself and finally looked up. 'What's wrong?'

He sighed and sat down on the bed. 'Mum told Dad that Mick was coming to the dinner tonight.'

Claudia shrugged. 'She can tell him whatever she wants; he's the one who isn't coming.'

'No, she told him that before he said he wasn't coming.'

Claudia sat up straight. 'What?'

'When we were at the restaurant decorating it for the reception tomorrow, Mum came up and was talking to Dad. She said she was going to bring Mick since he probably won't be allowed to come to the wedding and it was the right thing to do.'

'What did Dad say?'

'Nothing.'

'Did they see you?'

'I don't know; I had walked into the kitchen but Mum knew I was there when she walked out.'

'So she just watched me cry about how Dad doesn't like me, and she just stood there and pretended she didn't know a thing about it?'

Phinn sighed and moved closer to his sister so he could put an arm around her. 'Yep.'

'Unfuckingbelievable; that woman is unbelievable.' Claudia put her head in her hands. 'So, I am getting married, his daughter is getting married, and there is meant to be a dinner so the parents can all meet each other and we can have a nice time, and really it should just be us and our parents but fucking Mary is coming along because she sees no issue in crashing her niece's special night and she wants to bring Mick, and Dad is so fucking immature that he can't just suck it up for his daughter and be in the same room as someone he doesn't like? Instead he just doesn't show up because he doesn't like somebody; it doesn't matter that it might mean something to me.'

Phinn looked out of the window and on the street envisioned George and Rachel as human beings. As their own individuals, who were not – as the siblings mostly believed – an extension of themselves, whose lives did not surge and recede on the whims of their children. It is not unique to discover your parents are fallible, but it can be savage.

Phinn took a breath.

'Both of our parents are arseholes, yes.'

CHAPTER 26

Nora: Zoe and I can't decide on a wedding topper. How do you feel about one with blue hair?

Claudia: I don't care.

Nora: *Star Wars* themed?

Claudia: I don't care.

Nora: The greater Left project fails unless you choose a wedding cake topper.

Claudia: I don't care.

Nora: Trump just got a second term.

CHAPTER 27

Claudia was forever threatening to do something melodramatic and memorable. And here she finally was, and there was nobody around to witness it.

Claudia walked into a supermarket and started sobbing over the broccoli. She went into a clothes boutique and wept quietly as she looked at shoes. In the Reject Shop she picked up plastic flowers and started laughing because she knew crying while holding on to a $2 fake petunia was too much, even for her.

She sat in the food court and ate a burger and still the tears came.

A part of her was secretly enjoying the image of herself walking around town with tears streaming down her face the day before her wedding. But she did it so discreetly there was nobody to enjoy the performance. It was only a tiny part a performance anyway. Mostly, she was just truly sobbing before her wedding day.

Claudia did not know how she felt about marriage. She felt like a passenger in her own life. She had just let things happen to her so much that now she was getting married. She had always had a vague sense of wanting to wear the dress and have the ring and the day where all the attention was on her. She'd also had the vague sense that marriage was a flawed institution, certainly, and possibly an empty one.

But she loved Dylan. She nodded vigorously as she cried outside a shopfront where people could get their keys cut. She definitely loved him. She also had the creeping suspicion that her happy relationship was weakening her staunch (on paper) feminist beliefs and stunting her moral imagination.

It was hard to be angry at men when you got to kiss Dylan every day.

They had built their relationship, like everyone else, on a thousand small intimacies. They knew each other in their bones.

A year into their relationship his mother had got sick. As vibrant 24-year-olds they had the ringside seats as her cancer caused rapid deterioration. Together they couldn't decide what was worse: the sheer indignity of it all (nobody really talks about that; people are always 'battling' and 'brave', but in reality an adult child ends up spoon-feeding their parent and putting on their clean underwear after a shower), or being robbed of appetite. When someone knows the end is near, when their health has already gone to shit, by rights they should be able to eat and drink whatever they want. Cholesterol and calorie content is irrelevant when death is already assured within months. But instead, cruelly, Dylan's mother was too nauseated even for iced water.

Claudia had watched over Dylan as he fed his mother. She had been beside him when he found out she was dead. They all thought they were prepared for it. They had been in the hospital with her for months. But Dylan told her it was still like a cricket bat over the back of the head.

'Nobody cares if I am cold now,' he had sobbed to Claudia. 'Mum was the only person in the world who gave a shit if I was wearing a jumper or not. There is nobody who cares about me like that.'

It was true, Claudia conceded. She never noticed if he was wearing a jumper or not. She was not going to see a photo of him as a grown man in winter and ask where his coat was. That's not what lovers are for.

She was there when, a week after the funeral, Dylan's sister, Elaine, asked when they would be coming back to visit.

'Why have you got to be such a *cunt!?*' Dylan screamed, kicking Elaine's toddler's toys across the kitchen.

Later Dylan would say Claudia was horrified he called his sister a cunt in front of her two year old. Claudia was actually more concerned about the six year old.

She had once asked him, 'When does it start to feel okay? How long is it unbearable for?'

He hadn't even paused. 'Four years.'

The fourth anniversary of his mother's death had been the month before.

'It's okay, we are in year five now,' he told her cheerfully, turning away.

But it isn't these big moments that make a relationship. They help, kind of, but really it's about all the mundane stuff. Can you go to the shops together for the 480th time? Can you sit on the couch eating stir-fry for the 693rd time? Can you spend 4000 days washing their toothpaste out of the sink?

Can you still make each other laugh after 2894 days?

A few weeks before, a Lexus had pulled out in front of Dylan when he was driving and Claudia began berating him for braking hard. Shifting into second gear, Dylan had snapped at her, 'Maybe when we are married you should take my side against strangers in Lexuses. It isn't in the vows but it's implied.'

Claudia collapsed in laughter every time she thought about it. Including now as she walked past a shoe shop weeping. She thought about Aesop's dog and telling Poppy about it. She thought of bones rotting on the ground around her as she stood paralysed. Maybe eating an apple.

She thought about this as she walked in circles around underwear racks in a shop, eventually picking up green silk briefs. They were nice.

She recited her favourite Philip Larkin poem to herself like a mantra:

In times when nothing stood
But worsened, or grew strange,
There was one constant good:
she did not change.

She made a decision and walked towards the counter. The girl had dark curly hair piled on top of her head, seemingly thousands of bobby pins holding it all together. She wore a denim jacket with a koala brooch on it.

'Hello! How! Are! You! Today!'

She was the last of a rare breed, the enthusiastic shop girl. Claudia smiled despite herself, suddenly self-conscious of her puffy eyes.

'I'm well.'

The girl smiled and folded the underwear. 'These are nice; what are you up to today?'

Claudia shifted from one foot to the other.

'Actually, I'm getting married tomorrow. So just doing some shopping.'

The girl squealed.

'That's SO! Exciting! How are you feeling? The weather looks really good!'

Claudia allowed a smile.

'Good, I feel good. It is exciting.'

CHAPTER 28

Zoe typed her sister's name into her phone and watched as the map slowly updated.

'She's still moping around the main street, more than likely thinking about how romantic and crestfallen she looks.'

Phinn had Zoe's dark satin and polka-dotted skirt spread out in front of him while he frowned and studied the iron. He looked up at his older sister.

'You can tell that from your phone?'

'I've told you we should share locations. Claudia is the only one who will do it with me. I have Dad and Mum's too and about eight of my friends.'

'I'm not sharing my location with you. It's incredibly psycho. Why do you need your sister's location?'

'So when she storms off in a huff on the day before her wedding you and I don't have to waste time looking for her.' Zoe pinched her two fingers together and zoomed in. 'I can tell you the exact shop she is in. It's Shabby Chic. I bet you that she is buying underwear. Crying and buying underwear. I would put a cheeky tenner on it.'

Phinn picked the skirt up by the waist and extended his arms in front of him while shaking it out. He examined it again and inspected the temperature gauge on the iron before pressing it cautiously on the material of the skirt.

'This is an absolute bastard to iron.'

Zoe leaned back on the wall, using it to prop herself up as she stretched her legs out in front of her.

'Thank you, Phinny, I appreciate it. I just can't do it myself – you know ironing is not in my nature.'

The pair fell back into the silence they had learned more than twenty-seven years ago when Phinn first began to talk. It was a silence like an embrace, familiar and comforting and brimming with habit. They knew they were both thinking about their younger sister. Ensconced in their old battle lines, they had stuck with each other when Claudia had slammed the front door, ensuring everyone inside knew she was ignoring them. They were concerned for her from a distance, the way any family member should be. Claudia didn't need their comforting words; she needed to sulk it out. While years ago they might have stealthily taken turns keeping an eye on her from behind street signs and trees, now they had a smartphone and moment of weakness when Claudia shared her location and then promptly forgot about it.

When the kids were nervous they returned to the same conversation topics: recounting blow-by-blow physical brawls from their proper childhood years (the teen brawls were still too emotionally fraught for exploration); how to divide $1 million between them (inevitably someone was cut out of a will); and death. Death was their absolute favourite: who had died, how they had died and the scenarios in which they themselves would die.

The kids loved any hypothetical life-altering situation –

pregnancy, long-lost half-siblings, loss of limb, financial windfall; but the best one, the biggest treat, the one they returned to most often, and had done since they were all in primary school at the same time so could meet at lunchtime for earnest discussions, was death.

'What would you do if Claudia was diagnosed with cancer next year?' Zoe asked, glancing up from watching her sister move, as a blue dot, north from Shabby Chic.

Phinn warmed to the topic immediately. 'Well, you earn the most money in whatever it is you do, so you would have to keep working to send us money. You'd be a useless-as-tits nurse as well. So I would take personal leave, unlimited, maybe even sublet the apartment.'

'I could maybe negotiate nine-day fortnights, or working from home every second week, and then every second weekend I could come down on the Friday until the Sunday while she was resting from the chemo.'

'Yeah, yeah, and it would obviously be best for Claudia to come home. She could come back here and sit up in Mum's house. She would be too weak to shuttle between both so Dad would have to come here to see her. And she would get her treatment – you could pay for any extra drugs she needed – and I would stay with her so Mary didn't drive her insane—'

Zoe interrupted, 'Mary wouldn't matter. Claudia would be dying, civility would be dead. No need to be civil, civility is absolutely the worst hangover from the twentieth century. Civility would be dead; we could just sit around and watch Claudia be rude to Mary all day every day.'

'Right! Mary would be irrelevant. She fades away, not even a footnote in this story. I bet she would try to throw herself over Claudia, really work up some emotional capital. There'd always be one of us with Claudia, though. We'd do shifts, make sure she wasn't by herself.'

Zoe skipped ahead to the most wrenching part, the best part. 'And *the funeral.* It would be unbearable, little Claudie's funeral. I almost would not want to go.'

Phinn picked the skirt up and ruffled it around the ironing board to expose the unironed back, looking at it mournfully.

'It would be so hard. Almost unbearable, but we would have to go.'

'For Mum and Dad,' Zoe agreed.

'We might even have to do a reading,' Phinn continued. 'I would want to wear black. A black shirt, a black tie – silk – with my black suit, maybe about five days' worth of facial growth.'

'I would wear pink, something really joyful, to celebrate our Clauds. I would read something eloquent about how nothing would be the same again. Something like W. H. Auden but not as well known.'

Phinn nodded. 'It is a great poem, but every man and his dog has it read at their funeral. We'd be shattered. What music would she want?'

Zoe cocked her head. 'Well, she liked tools of manipulation, so at the beginning something really over the top, something that just has the entire congregation sobbing. "Into My Arms" is a good one. "Into My Arms", or maybe, maybe "Little Dreamer".'

'"Little Dreamer"?'

'I've been listening to it every night, by Future Islands; it's very haunting; it goes "I found you dreaming, I'm dreaming of you always".' Zoe began humming. '"And as we say goodnight, I hold you close and tight, No more raging suns, only waning ones, Like the waxing scar where my lonely heart, Once bloomed before I met you".'

Phinn winced. 'Ooft, that's good. Please stop destroying it by trying to sing.'

Their intimate silence returned as they both thought about their lives minus Claudia. Poor, weak Claudia. A wisp in the wind after her brave endurance of cancer – not a battle, never a battle. One just endures. And then she would be gone and they would be three. Inconceivable.

One of the most addictive bits of hypothetical deaths was how much you could emotionally wring yourself out, get to places barely conceived of in your soul, be enveloped in sadness. Almost convince yourself the death had happened and get to stand thrillingly on the edge of the abyss of grief before returning safely to the land of the living and healthy.

What they both refused to factor into this comforting and twisted game of yore was that it would not be them at the centre of the funeral. It would not matter if they wore black or pink, really. They wouldn't be at the forefront as they once would've been. They wouldn't get to pick the music. They wouldn't even get a couple of thousand dollars from Claudia's superannuation.

Phinn and Zoe both looked at each other sadly.

It would be Dylan making the decisions.

Phinn pulled out the skirt and clipped it to a hanger before handing it to Zoe.

'If you die I am leaving the family. Sorry Mum, you're on your own; you have to deal with the girls and Dad for the rest of your life.'

CHAPTER 29

Rachel and Mary were giggling. Whole body-sobbing, can't-breathe, borderline-hysterical giggling. Perched on the end of Rachel's bed, they were holding each other as they gasped for air, laughing.

It was not clear what was so funny, but a bottle of Moët sat between them, the beacon of the lower middle-class looking for posh signifiers.

'I was on my knees!' Rachel screamed. 'I thought: Jesus, Mary and Joseph, Our Lady is appearing before me, I'm having a vision, she's here.'

Mary held on to her arm as she half slid off the bed, laughing. 'You thought Our Lady was appearing!'

'I swear to God, I was even scared, I couldn't believe it.'

Mary pointed across the room to a small globe emblazoned with the word 'Medjugorje', a holy site in Bosnia-Herzegovina. Inside the globe was a plastic white figurine in the shape of the Virgin Mary. A gift from Zoe, beneath it was a switch, which triggered a flashing light that changed from pink to blue to purple to green as it lit up the figurine.

The night before, Rachel had got out of bed at two a.m. to find it flashing in the hallway and dropped to her knees in prayer while thinking about the pilgrims who would arrive at her house over the next 1000 years seeking the healing powers of the Mother of God who had appeared to Rachel, the patron saint of lost causes, taking the mantle from Jude. It was a holy moment, and her first prayer was for her children, but she was also forecasting her future glory.

Forty seconds on the ground and she realised it was just a flashing light. Her sainthood was revoked; she returned to life as an ordinary mother of ungrateful adults. Now she sat on her bed, slightly drunk, clutching her sister while she relayed the tale. Her halo well and truly diminished.

Rachel laughed harder.

'You, you are a wild bit of gear,' Mary said through giggles. She opened her mouth to say something but thought better of it and closed it again. Her laughing had ceased. She stood up, wobbled a moment, and looked down at her feet to get her grip, realising the bottle of champagne on the floor was empty.

The movement evoked Rachel's children to her. Her children when they were learning to walk. Her children when she thought of them as tiny morons, marvelled at how useless a human child was for so long. Her children when they used to chase her around the house squealing, 'Mummy, are you walking away from me?' but in a language only she could interpret. Their toddler English.

'You know the minute your children finally are interesting is the same minute they don't want to hang out with you anymore,' Rachel said in the general direction of her sister who was now rummaging through the wardrobe. Mary winced and turned to face the bed.

'Don't be like that. Your children may be brats but tonight is one for fun. Your daughter is getting married. It's not just her day! It's your day as well.'

'My children are not brats,' Rachel snapped. 'This is what's supposed to happen – you grow them in your belly with minimal effort from their father and then you keep them alive for years ... They don't just want to take money from you. They don't even care about destroying your body, even though they eventually do. They don't want to take your life as you knew it, but they take that as well.' Rachel jabbed her chest. 'They want to take a piece of you away from you.'

Mary was silent as she took in the ramifications of her sister's compulsion to breed. It had never occurred to her to try to love someone more than she loved herself, or that she should.

She started laughing.

Rachel knew she should be wounded by the reaction but, as with most things these days, it was too much effort. She joined her sister laughing, leaning over to clutch her heart as her guffaws took over her body.

'You're right: it's my weekend too, none of this would have happened without me, they owe me their lives.' She walked over to the wardrobe. 'Sometimes, Mary, sometimes I dare to think you are jealous of my children for taking me away from you.'

Mary snorted but did not look at Rachel. 'I know you would throw me from a window in a second to stop one of them cutting their big toe.' She pretended not to seethe. 'What are you going to wear?'

Rachel held up a flowing white dress, carefully embroidered with roses. A slip underneath fell to the mid-shins and the overlay had sleeves falling to the elbows. Rachel had spent about 82 per cent of her waking hours over her lifetime ensuring she maintained the weight she was at twenty-five and the dress nipped in to show the years of denial on her waist.

She held the dress to her body, covering the Leicester City jersey she wore to bed. Mary whistled. 'That's beautiful. Is Claudia going to be okay with you in that dress?'

'Why wouldn't she be? It doesn't matter what I wear, I look fifty-two.'

'You're sixty-five.'

'I feel thirty. Sometimes I walk past a mirror and think, "Ma! You're here!" and realise it is my face staring back at me.'

Mary laughed. 'Well, I'll be your mirror, darling, you're beautiful. I'll get us another bottle of champagne.'

Leah rolled off the top of Poppy. 'I'm sorry, I can't.' Poppy groaned and rolled over on the bed, covering her stomach as Leah stood up.

'I can hear your mum giggling downstairs.'

'So?'

'I can't focus on this,' she said, waving her hand over Poppy's body, 'with your mum sounding like she's laughing at us in the room.'

Poppy propped herself up on her elbows. 'She's just going through her special event ritual; she's getting sloshed with my evil aunt. She can't hear anything.'

'But I can hear her!'

Poppy reached across the bed for her Britney Spears T-shirt. Was it ironic or was it just lame? Poppy couldn't decide. But she did like Britney. She pulled it over her head and sat up.

'Fine, we won't have sex to the sound of my mother giggling. I'm out of here in two nights, though, and tomorrow will be all about the wedding.'

Leah cocked her head; she was only wearing her cotton underwear but did not seem to have any of the shame about her body required of women. She had one perfect breast, a perfectly round spongy mango; the other one was a bit lopsided, almost half a cup of water smaller. It wasn't immediately obvious; you had to have spent as much time as Poppy studying them. 'I know, time to bid each other adieu. Maybe I will see you next time?'

Poppy groaned again. 'What about the cliché, Leah? We have been hanging out for five days; lesbian law says we are basically married – we should have a cat by now, grand plans, everything.'

The cliché had become a tired joke already between the pair, but they kept running with it in place of any actual shared history, the kind one needed to build personal jokes, exchange sly glances that sent the other into stitches, true affinity. Leah picked up her jeans and riffled through the pockets, pulling out a piece of paper. 'I actually found the ultimate example of this: the lesbian calling card. I wrote it down to remind you of me. It is almost embarrassing, and a prime example of why everyone thinks lesbians are too emotional. Patricia Highsmith wrote it to the one woman I think she ever had actual feelings for.'

Leah tossed the note on the bed and pulled her jeans on and then her blue singlet.

'Have fun at the dinner tonight, and tomorrow. Call me when you give up and move back here.' She leaned over and kissed Poppy on the mouth and winked. Then she left.

Poppy reached over the side of the bed and picked up her phone, opening her email app hopefully. Groupon, the *New Yorker*, Goop – all the emails she intended to open but never got around to. Nothing from her future employer. They were still out there.

She jumped off the bed and closed the door then picked up the torn piece of paper, examining the back of it. It wasn't from a notepad; Poppy suspected it was the back of a novel. 'Desecrated,' she muttered to herself.

She flipped it over and read it. Pausing. Then read it again. Her shoulders started shaking and soon her giggles were intertwined in the house with her mother's drunken exclamations from downstairs.

'My green and red goddess, my jade and garnet, my moss and hollyberry, my sea and sun, my marrow and my blood, my stop and go baby, I adore you, I worship you, I kiss you, I cherish you, I defend you, I defy you ever not to love me, I caress your nipples with my tongue.'

CHAPTER 30

George leaned back in the chair he had pilfered from his uncle's house due to his mortality. He pressed the remote and the television flicked on just as the first kick of the game sailed through the air. His timing was a fine art. He poured his mid-strength beer into a glass.

A blissful Friday night, he thought to himself.

CHAPTER 31

Nora had spent a lot of her time lately lying on the floor listening to Kendrick Lamar. Well, she thought she'd spent a lot of her time lying on the floor listening to Kendrick, but really it was just a lot of time in the past week.

Like Claudia she had the knack of viewing her life from a helicopter perspective – she liked to be melodramatic even when alone, to picture how she looked lying on the floor in her dressing-gown staring at the ceiling and listening to 'Love' by Kendrick Lamar.

Nora muttered to herself 'just love me', then sat straight up. 'Okay, maybe that was a little pathetic,' she said to the room. Speaking out loud to herself was a longstanding habit; it started in the spring of being twenty-five years old when she'd moved in by herself for what she thought would be two years at the most. She fully intended to meet her husband. Her ovaries were aching even back then. She had moved in by herself and begun building her lovely life. Livin' lovely. Then she met Tom and everything was on track and now it was six years later and she had mangled her chance at happiness and was still talking to herself.

She stood up and tightened her robe, pulling her towel from her damp hair and patting it. Dinner was in two and a half hours. She walked over the beige carpet, the exact faded colour of lost hope, and opened the tiny fridge. It was too small for her Tasmanian bubbly to stand up in, so the bottle lay diagonally across a shelf. It was a celebration, right? 'Right!' she answered herself, pouring out a glass. She walked over to the iPod and switched it to 'You've Earned It', her latest favoured podcast. She cycled through various podcasts that were made by and for alcoholics in the forgotten corners of the world. They made her feel better about herself. Smug, almost. This one was the best find by far. It was three women somewhere in the Midwest in America, housewives who had found each other online and rambled to each other every week with barely a nod to structure or form. They spoke about being wine mums and giving up drinking. There was a pornographic quality to it; you heard things you felt you should not be hearing.

This week they were talking about rock bottom. They actually spoke about rock bottom fairly regularly but they usually called it different things: 'realising stuff', 'my turning point', 'when I knew I had a problem', 'when I hated myself the most' – myriad ways of plumbing the depths. They seemed to have had a series of rock bottoms because it was a different story each time.

Nora loved hearing about the wine hidden in laundry baskets, the drunk school runs, the nip of whisky while pretending to brush their teeth. She didn't do any of that. She just liked celebrating. And commiserating. And puncturing boredom.

Nora listened to Margaret telling the story of when she crossed the line. It was when she drove her daughters and their two friends home after a bottle of wine at the school play. She had driven her own daughters after a bottle of wine a few times, but now she was risking other people's children. Nora snorted.

'You were only drink-driving your own daughters so it was fine!' she berated Margaret. She shook her head and took a sip of the sparkling wine. She only ever drank nice stuff; that was the other thing. Of course it was fine. People who have problems don't care what they drink. Nora did.

She pulled out her eye-shadow palette and started smudging her lid with pink the way she had been taught when she was twenty-two on the David Jones floor by a Chanel assistant. Maybe it was time to learn a new technique. She had read somewhere that you can tell at what age a woman was most happy by the way she does her make-up. Women with frosted pink lipstick had a good time in the 1980s and women with brown lipstick felt their most beautiful in the 1990s. Women with black-lined eyelids were watching the Duchess of Cambridge too closely in 2011. Nora had her doubts about the happiness theory. It was more likely it signalled the age when they learned how to do their make-up properly and they had not bothered to update it since. It probably signalled when they were childless and had the most time to think about themselves.

Nora just knew pinks and coppers suited her brown eyes and lipstick would be rubbed off by whatever she ate tonight. And drank. She downed the rest of her glass and poured another one. She rubbed primer on her face. She did not actually know what it did but had been advised to use it by numerous magazine articles and so obeyed.

Margaret's voice floated into the bathroom. 'I would watch the clock at barbecues waiting for a respectable time to pull out the bubbles.'

Nora frowned as Margaret continued. 'Then I couldn't wait to get home so I could drink properly. I should've known then, that's not normal, wanting to leave family and friends so you can drink properly.' Nora smiled and returned to feeling smug.

She thought about picking up her phone for another peek at her email. She didn't really need to look again. She had read it so many times it was memorised . . . 'because I cannot give you what you want as you grow (and I try desperately to stay in place).'

'Don't think about Tom,' she told the mirror. Instead, she thought about Claudia.

Would Claudia be doing this for her? Renting a sub-par motel room, buying her cake toppers, trying to get along with her siblings. Of course Claudia would do it for her. But, would she actually end up doing it? Had Nora built her life too much for herself? Her question for the ages. What if she didn't meet someone? Was she okay with that? Intellectually she should be. Intellectually she kind of was. A life of RSVP-ing for one to weddings. Of sleeping on the couch in family holiday houses because it was deemed she did not need her own room. A lifetime of going to events with the faint hope she would meet someone.

She finished dusting her blusher across her cheeks and smiled at her reflection. 'It's not time to be put out to pasture just yet,' she told the mirror. As she spoke, 'The Final Countdown' boomed through her speaker in place of Margaret's confession about putting her daughter in front of the TV in the morning because she was too hungover to deal with her.

Nora walked over to the phone and saw Tom's name on the screen. Tom was calling her. 'Arrrrrrgh,' Nora said to the screen. 'Whhhhhyyyy?' She cleared her throat and mashed the screen to accept the call, raising the phone to her ear.

'Hello?'

'Uh, Nora, hello.' She heard his voice and sat on the edge

of the bed, cradling her forehead with one hand. She looked around and spotted her wine glass next to the bathroom sink amongst her make-up brushes. She stayed silent and stood up to fetch it.

She took a slug and finally replied. 'Hey Tom.' She let the silence between them hang in the air. 'What do you want?' she finally said.

'You haven't replied to my email.' Tom stated the fact as if it was a question.

'What am I supposed to say to it?'

'Jesus, Nora, whatever you think. What your response is. Are you just going to be finished with this?'

Nora exhaled and opened the fridge (again) to pour out another glass (again).

'You want to write your way through it, that's fine. I don't see why it has to be a correspondence, though.'

'You finished this, Nora, and that's fine. But you're also the one who rang me asking if you had made the right decision.' Nora winced; she only had the vaguest recollection of that late-night phone call. Tom continued. 'Why can't you show any emotion in a break-up?'

Nora clenched her fist in time with her teeth.

'I don't owe you emotion. I actually don't owe you anything. You can write anything you want; the winner can always write history. Comprehending it is an entirely different thing, and I don't owe you any comprehension.'

Tom snorted. 'Listen to you – you think you sound so poetic in the face of real emotion. The winner may write history but, remember, in some cases the loser ends up sapped, trapped and never moving forward.'

'Did you just call me a loser?'

'You called yourself the loser.'

'Tom, why are you calling me?'

Nora heard his breathing become slightly shallower.

'I just miss you, is all.'

Nora allowed herself an emotion, a safe one, but an emotion nonetheless. Fury.

'You miss me so it's okay to torment me? Do you ever think of anyone but yourself? Do you know what a sad cliché you are? Moping around over the break-up you made ninety times worse with a savage email and then calling me to make you feel better, calling me to demand correspondence?'

'Nora, we're grown up, surely we can talk?'

'Tom, we are grown-ups with no children together, no pets together – we don't even have a lease together. There is no reason we have to talk after we break up.'

She heard Tom wince at the other end of the line.

'I wrote you something else.'

'Jesus Christ, Tom, I have to get ready for a pre-wedding dinner. Remember? The wedding of my best friend? That I'm here at alone? I don't have time for this bullshit.'

Nora hung up. She might be history's loser but she felt the phone call's winner. Satisfied. She hesitated and then opened her email app. 'I am *affronted*,' she yelled at the room.

There was an email from Tom. She couldn't help herself. He obviously couldn't help himself.

From: Tom Tran
To: ANoraAble
Subject: Fury

So yeah, your fury. I can understand it to an extent. I don't know why I feel the need to justify myself but I also think I owe you some kind of response after our last conversation, and all those years.

It's ironic, one of the reasons I always felt kind of uneasy in the relationship was the way you and your friends took on sharing emotions as a kind of group sport. There's no denying there is a huge amount of love in that particular unit. Huge.

But given the amount of people and the demands that this level of affection accorded, it was just as much a force of nature with the power to cause huge rifts as much as forge bonds. It was overwhelming.

I came in and seemingly faked entry to this group WHICH SPENDS SO MUCH ENERGY TRYING TO LOVE OUT THE COLD by remaining in a relationship I don't really know I was into.

And the fact is, I know what I have done, even if I can't face up to the motivations or what stray neurons were bounding through my mind, and it is the worst kind of thing to do to any kind of love between two people. It is. To turn something into a big lie – whether or not it was – is probably the coldest thing I have done. Am doing.

Nora slammed her laptop shut. Arsehole. Arsehole arsehole arsehole. She wanted to write back and she knew that she should not. She would not. She tossed the computer onto the bed and ran her fingers through her hair. 'You won't write back,' she said to the mirror. She looked at the green printed dress she had carefully hung in the bathroom so the steam from her shower would get the creases out. She needed to get out of this motel room.

CHAPTER 32

Dylan grabbed at the zip at the base of Claudia's spine and pulled it up, leaning over and briefly kissing her on her back as he did. She turned to him with half of her hair curled and the other half still frizzy and kissed him on the mouth.

'Is there still time to run away?' she asked.

Dylan grinned. 'We don't have to get married here if you don't want. We could've stuck with the original plan; I know you just wanted to make your family happy.'

'Wellll, it wasn't just about making my family happy.'

'It was a lot about making your family happy.'

Claudia put her hands on each of Dylan's shoulders – she only came up to his chest when she was in her bare feet – and rested her head on his shirt. He put his hand to the back of her head and smoothed it along her hair.

'You look so pretty, you are so pretty, we're going to have fun, I promise.'

Claudia exhaled.

'I know but I just wish Dad was coming. He would come if it was Poppy's wedding dinner. He just doesn't care enough about me.'

Dylan pulled Claudia closer so it wasn't just her head pressed against his chest.

'That's not true, your dad loves you so much, he's just being a bit strange. Don't let it get to you like that; you can still have a good time.'

Claudia finally stepped back and picked up her curling wand, turning away so she was facing the mirror again and could continue burning her hair in an effort to make it look bouncy. Dylan moved closer to her again and kissed her in the same spot on her back that he had before.

'Don't let it wear you down; it's going to be great. Dad and Yvonne are here, so that will make the dinner easier tonight. You worry so much about the rest of your family – just enjoy it. Have you eaten this afternoon? Do you want me to go make you some toast before you put on your lipstick?'

Claudia looked at Dylan's reflection and smiled guiltily.

'Can I have an apple and slices of cheese?'

'Of course, my love!' Dylan walked out of the room but before he was halfway down the hallway Claudia called out his name again and his head reappeared at the doorway. 'Yes, my love.'

Claudia studied his face for a second, drinking in the details of his slightly crooked nose and deep-set eyes. 'Can you cut up the apple for me?'

CHAPTER 33

'Things You Should Be Afraid Of', an extensive but not exhaustive list by Poppy Blanche Carter:

That there is hypocrisy in lobbying against victim blaming but refusing to walk home at night by yourself

Susan Miller dying

Gen X becoming like boomers

Nuclear war

A robot taking your job

If the priest has washed his hands before giving communion

Never getting to the stage where you don't mentally add up your grocery basket before going to the checkout

Being homeless in your sixties

The pension not existing when you're in your sixties

The moon – it is not trustworthy

People finding out you secretly think cultural appropriation is not a real problem

That you're inherently unlovable

Your parents getting old. Truly old
Having to move home when home is fifteen hours from anything interesting
Being left behind
Being irrelevant
Never properly understanding political theory
Brioche buns

Things you shouldn't be afraid of:
Looking fat at your sister's wedding
Ruining your sister's wedding
Ruining everything

Poppy looked up from her phone and sighed. She had always been averse to recording her thoughts, but some long-ago article in what would euphemistically be called a 'women's' magazine had suggested lists. At least once a month she found herself typing two fingered, into the notes section of her iPhone, lists that were loosely based on what had distressed her lately. She knew she had come home at a stressful time: her work was in flux, her renting situation was in flux, it would be generous to say that the state of her finances was in flux. And now she had an almost severe allergic reaction to Claudia's wedding. She found herself relegated to the role of sooky youngest child and bizarrely played along accordingly.

The brute force of her changes in mood shocked even her at times. But she also felt helpless in the face of them. If she examined her situation closely she guessed she would find shame at the root of it. The week with Claudia had seemed a parade of everything she was failing at. Poppy wanted to be happy for her sister but felt her faith broken in a queer way by how easy it was for her. She had the partner, she had the job, she had the city life. There was so much Poppy would've done for an ounce of the security and yet Claudia was so blasé about it. She was blasé about it and also seemed further and further from Poppy with each year. When they were teenagers, Claudia would have been more loyal; she would not have brought a friend into what was supposed to be a family week.

Poppy had always had problems with rage, but she had shocked even herself with what had been brought to the fore this week. Before she had only been dimly aware of the fury that was evidently running through her veins. After each outburst she felt guilty, but then Nora would show up, rubbing in their faces her bond with their sister. Or Claudia would appear, apparently manufacturing emotional problems the week before her wedding while Poppy had her own real problems. She was still dismissed as a baby; every suggestion she made was talked down; she couldn't even raise the prospect of doing something different with the daisies without feeling as though she was being derided. She was just an extra at any supposedly important family event, basically ignored at the dress fitting, entire conversations going on as if she didn't exist on the beach day. If that wasn't enough, she'd watched Nora being deferred to the whole week, with Claudia sneaking off to the motel room thinking she was so clever and that nobody would know where she was spending those hours.

Coming home had only confirmed to Poppy how alone she was.

CHAPTER 34

Claudia was the first to arrive at the restaurant, wearing a sweeping strapless purple dress. It was almost a gown, but her lack of jewellery made it a dress. She was trying to go for Kim K simplicity but her hair was not sleek enough and the dress needed tailoring. The overall effect was one of cluelessness. It would show up well in photos against the restaurant's wall of hanging plants, so, small mercies. She had managed to slip past her exuberant mother and aunt with her dress and shoes and make her way to Dylan's hotel, which he had managed to rent just for the afternoon under the guise of an odd kind of romance. Any excuse to be away from Claudia's family.

Claudia had silently got ready while Dylan played her songs from niche bands in the nineties (Mclusky, Guided by Voices, Pissed Jeans). It was nice but Claudia was gloomy. She walked through the doors of the restaurant reeking of apprehension; it shrouded her as she made her way directly to the long table without bothering to ask the waiter about the reservation.

Nobody else was bothering to sit eleven people in the middle of September.

A girl of about nineteen approached her wearing black pants that were slightly too long and leather shoes that she obviously used to wear to school the year before. She smiled widely as she pulled a notebook from the pocket of her white shirt.

'The Carter table?'

Claudia nodded. 'I'm evidently first to arrive.'

'Are you getting married?' the girl asked, holding her pen over her notepad as if interviewing Claudia, not preparing to take her order.

Claudia nodded again but didn't say anything.

'That's so exciting! How long did it take to find your dress?'

Claudia smiled weakly. 'A couple of tries.'

The girl cocked her head and let out a sound, something like a blissful groan and a clucking. 'You're nervous! It's so cute! I can't wait to get married. Is your sister Zoe?'

Claudia looked around the restaurant, willing one of her family members to appear. The country town politeness did not return easily to her when she was home and she hated small talk. She didn't even want to make eye contact when telling someone to get her a wine. Nobody materialised; there was nobody to save her.

'Yes she is; can I have a glass of pinot grigio?'

'I love her flower business!'

'Her flower business?' Claudia finally looked at the girl properly. Her greasy fringe was trying hard to cover a breakout and her eyes were the same colour as the plants behind her.

'Yeah, I follow it on Instagram; it's very cool what she's doing.'

More to add to the list of things Claudia did not know about her sister. She'd been mysterious when she was getting dressed to go to parties when Claudia was thirteen. Back then Zoe seemed like a person who was only fully formed when away from her relations. Everyone suspected there were entire aspects of her hidden from the family and only coming into full view once they were not there to witness it. Claudia remembered being shocked when she saw her sister order a passionfruit juice. They had never known she liked passionfruit. It went further than material tastes. It seemed that, away from her family, Zoe read different books, watched different television shows, had an entire set of political beliefs they were not allowed in on.

She had not only somehow managed to maintain the emotional distance as an adult, but also created a new physical one. The family barely knew what she did for a living and Claudia would bet $500 nobody even knew exactly what her degree was in.

And now Claudia was being told she ran some kind of business. They vaguely knew she was a florist but that was the extent of it. Of course they had asked her about her work, but the family were used to Zoe's easy dismissals. A question about how she was going always seemed to turn into a discussion about what was for dinner that night or some recently released movie. It's easy to get away with in a large family, being deliberately obtuse. When there are so many people vying for a place in the conversation, distraction is a daily occurrence. And that was before the chronic self-obsession was factored in. She was like one of those riddles that gets more complex the closer you look at it, that opens up double the amount of unsolvable aspects once one part has been figured out.

The girl interrupted Claudia's thoughts. 'We don't have any pinot grigio.'

'Of course, I'll just have chardonnay,' Claudia said, pulling out her phone. 'What did you say the Instagram was?' The waitress told her the pun in the hushed tone of someone who was saying a password out loud for the first time.

Claudia had just brought the page up and was scrolling

through photos of roses dip-dyed in food colouring to turn the tips shades of blue, green and red when she heard her name shrilly called out across the restaurant. She winced. Without looking up she knew it was her aunt and that her aunt had been drinking.

Claudia had taken a seat in the middle of the table out of a sense of duty, since the dinner was supposed to be for her and Dylan, and from her vantage point had a direct line of sight to the front door of the restaurant, as well as through a window to part of the car park.

Mary made her way across the maroon carpet with Rachel clutching her elbow. They were both wearing high heels they were clearly unused to and Mary had even put on a push-up bra to give the effect of two slightly milky orbs spilling out of a black sleeveless top, which was tucked into a mid-length skirt of the same colour. Next to her, Rachel watched her feet as they took each step; she was wearing bright red patent leather heels that had seemed such a good idea in the shop.

Without hesitating, the two sat down in the middle of the table in the prime position directly across from Claudia. 'Of course,' she whispered to herself.

'Hello darling.' Mary's cheeks were flushed and an unsure hand had applied liner to her lids. 'We're first here!'

'Yes, so far everyone is four minutes late,' Claudia responded as the waitress gently put down her wine in front of her.

'Can we get a bottle of prosecco, sweetie?' Rachel said, looking up at the girl. The girl nodded, carefully writing the order in her notepad and scurrying away.

Over her aunt's head Claudia saw Zoe and Phinn walk in together with Poppy slightly behind them. She looked at her mother as she spoke to her aunt. 'No funny business tonight.'

Claudia enjoyed the spectacle of watching her siblings when they didn't know they were being observed. It was like seeing yourself on film: familiar but not quite like you imagined. Perhaps a bit more clumsy. She saw Zoe squeeze Phinn's upper arm as she turned to say something to Poppy, and from Poppy's reaction she knew it was an inappropriate comment, most likely about Mary. Zoe was making peace with Poppy; she had obviously not been in a good mood in the lead-up to the night and Zoe was trying to diffuse her before the dinner. Claudia could tell all of this from the few steps they had taken, just before Zoe met her eyes and waved enthusiastically. This was the tribe for which she knew all the codes, the secret signals, the language. That you cannot choose your family is such a pathetically obvious statement, but it is often forgotten what else you can't choose. You can't choose to fully and wholly extract yourself – you can sometimes, if you're lucky, choose to learn the language and signals of another group, but you'll never be properly fluent. Not only does the language have to be learned from birth, but you have to help create it as well.

Zoe, Phinn and Poppy formed a line as they arrived at the table, swarming on three seats across from Claudia. 'You can't sit there. It's reserved.'

Zoe raised an eyebrow. 'Reserved for someone more important than the bride's sister? The maid of honour?'

'I don't have a maid of honour,' Claudia said, without having to even form the words in her brain before they were out of her mouth.

'As a matter of fact, yes,' Mary said, ignoring Claudia. 'It's for my plus one.'

Zoe laughed cruelly and nodded to Claudia before moving down a seat, not-so-secretly pleased to be saved from an evening next to Mary.

Claudia narrowed her eyes. 'Are those my earrings?'

Zoe touched the toucans studded in her ears. 'I found them

at Mum's.' She turned to Phinn and they began what looked like a serious, hushed conversation that Claudia assumed was just about which drinks to order. She tried to think of the last time she saw her older sister with a bunch of flowers but couldn't come up with anything. She thought, perhaps, maybe it was Zoe who had sanctioned her decision that daisies would be the easiest, prettiest and most understated flower to have at her wedding.

Poppy sat at the end of the trio, fiddling with her phone and whispering, as an aside, that she would drink whatever. Claudia thought just a few years back to being Poppy's age and what it was like: the uncertainty, the hope. The realisation that you don't have all the time in the world, that it does matter if you leave things for a few days or a few months. Every word you don't write, or sing, or film is in fact a backwards step, a black mark against your supposed fate. She remembered it dawning on her that perhaps her life would in fact be ordinary, that maybe she was not destined for specialness. She remembered it was hard letting go of the hypothetical futures with friends: 'when you're a graphic designer for *Vogue* and I'm a famous writer we will . . .' 'when I'm in charge of the company and you are based in Los Angeles . . .' It was harsh realising some things were irrevocable, that sometimes they had messed up, but she didn't remember being as mean about it as Poppy was. Perhaps because, secretly, in the bowels of her soul, Claudia was not shocked.

'Are you, Claudia?' Mary drew the attention of others at the table back to the bride to be.

'Hmmmm?' she responded noncommittally, trying to convey flippancy.

'Are you changing your name?'

Claudia laughed. 'No, I'm not, I'll still be Claudia Carter.'

'Such a good feminist,' Poppy called sarcastically down the

table. 'You're still getting married but it's okay, it's tantamount to the third wave, because you're not changing your name.'

Zoe winced and Claudia's nostrils flared. 'Excuse me?'

'What? I'm just saying, you must be proud you're not changing your name. It must make you feel like a good feminist. Even though you're still getting married.'

'What do you mean "even though"?'

'Well, it's still an oppressive institution, any way you look at it. It's oppressive for women; you can't erase its long history. And you're choosing to take part in something that deliberately excluded queer people for so long, so I don't really find it tenable that you could pretend you're not taking part in something archaic and harmful. But hey, love is a compromise and feminism now is just a series of personal choices that conveniently benefit the individual.'

Zoe tried to intervene. 'Come on now, I don't think Claudia's marriage is a political act.'

'But that would mean the personal isn't political,' Poppy responded, staring at Claudia.

Claudia responded by snorting, 'A lot of people don't have time for the "personal is political" because they're focusing on things that matter, like legislating on reproductive rights and marching for fair conditions for the working class. I know it must feel so nice to think at this point in history your identity is unimpeachable and righteous but, Poppy, let me tell you, some people have real problems and your unblemished soapbox is an illusion.'

Phinn visibly bit the inside of his cheek trying not to laugh as he turned his head from his youngest sister so she couldn't see. But with his eyes he said to Claudia: 'Owned.' Claudia quickly looked down at her hands so as not to provoke her sister further with her satisfaction while Rachel slammed both of her hands on the table.

'Enough!' she yelled, but her children were silenced anyway by the arrival of chinking glasses and a promising bottle. The young waitress looked at Zoe adoringly as she poured red wine that seemed to be within the price range of 'I know I'm not paying for this'. Zoe nodded to her in thanks while Phinn leaned back to allow his glass to be poured and pulled Poppy's next to it. Poppy ducked her head to look at their mother, who still had the secret power of ending arguments when she truly wanted to invoke it – the wedding eve dinner of her daughter being such an occasion.

Before she could launch into a mini-lecture, though, two male hands landed on Rachel's shoulders, causing the entire table to jump in their seats. 'RA-CH-EL,' the voice that belonged to the hands boomed. 'I see nothing has changed.'

Wearing an ill-advised and ill-fitting powder-blue suit with an Akubra on his head, it was their uncle Mick. He leaned down and kissed Rachel on the cheek as she laughed, and then turned to Mary and kissed her on the mouth, as an almost undetectable groan rippled down the table. Mary blushed and pulled her beaten handbag off the table. 'Here's your chair, darling.'

'And here's the beautiful bride!' he responded, leaning across the table to give Claudia a kiss as she patted his back in reply. 'Hello Mick.'

He let out a satisfied sigh as he sat down and bellowed to nobody in particular, 'A schooner of Guinness, please,' then turned to the Carter siblings on his left. 'How the hell are you? I haven't seen you since the official shunning!'

'Well,' Phinn said, breaking the silence, 'I missed the official bit.' The girls, who had suddenly found the patterned walls so fascinating, waited for Mick's permission to laugh before they joined in his chortling.

Claudia relaxed. Maybe the worst was over.

Through a mix of shame and champagne, Mick's presence righted the topsy-turvy balance caused by people at a table who are far too intimate to be polite to each other and have spent enough time together in a week for age-old resentments to be at precise boiling point. The Carter siblings and Rachel were all too embarrassed by their treatment of Mick over the past few years, and shy from the lack of contact, to truly be themselves with him around. Mary was giddy to the point of being sick and did not seem to have the capacity for her usual barbs and varied hypocrisies.

So it was to an unusually subdued group that Dylan's father and stepmother were introduced when they at last entered the restaurant thirty minutes later. Claudia's furious text messages with a running commentary on the time had been studiously avoided by Dylan, and Claudia couldn't even manage a pissed-off glance in front of his parents.

Yvonne and Jerome had arrived in Winston that afternoon and spent a blissful few hours gossiping with their son before the dreaded formal proceedings. They had not been given fair warning on what to expect but the Carter charm could be deployed on a whim and they would not have to face the reality of the family that evening. Instead they got a sparkling and entertaining alternative.

Rachel was the first to rise from her seat and embrace the couple. 'It is so lovely to finally meet you. Claudia talks about you all the time. I am so sorry her father can't be here to see you as well. How was your trip?' she enquired as she squeezed each of them, and Dylan gave Claudia a peck on the forehead. The couple could barely mutter a greeting as the rest of the Carters descended upon them, a rampage of hugs and compliments. Dylan pulled out the two chairs that had been left empty next to his own and ushered his dad and step-mum into them, at which point an expectant silence fell.

Yvonne smiled finally. 'Lovely to be here.'

Mick cleared his throat. 'I was just telling the rest of them, I devote about 35 per cent of my day to not being Catholic, to not blessing myself, to not offering a compromise with God for anything, whether it be for my daughter to survive or for the light to change to green quicker. I want to thank God for everything: for Mary, for my sisters, for my father, for my job, for my city. It takes enormous concentration to remain ambivalent on the subject of religion.'

Jerome smiled weakly. 'My father thinks we might be part Jewish,' he responded.

Mick seized upon it. 'Aha! Then you would understand perfectly the daily battle of the cultural Catholic to steer clear of any actual God.'

Jerome signalled for the waitress and ordered more red wine for the table. He was sitting next to his son and directly across from Zoe, for which Claudia privately thanked God, Allah and Oprah. Zoe could chat at any level: rich boomers loved her, country people loved her, Nationals voters loved her, socialists loved her, teenagers loved her – everyone could chat to her. She leaned across the table and asked Jerome how he and Yvonne had spent the afternoon, securing at least twenty-five minutes of the couple feeling comfortable.

Claudia checked her phone. It was now fifty-seven minutes since the supposed start of dinner and still there were empty chairs. She suddenly grabbed Dylan's wrist underneath the tablecloth and leaned over. She whispered sharply, 'Nora isn't here.' Confused, Dylan looked over at the bar of the restaurant where the waitress was fetching the fifth bottle of wine for the evening and back to Claudia, repeating her statement to her as a question.

'Nora isn't here?'

'Nora isn't here.'

Claudia tried not to sound betrayed and focused more on the alarm. Nora had taken on the role of bridesmaid over the past few months. She had taken Claudia out to a champagne lunch and made her feel excited and special when all she felt was clichéd and put upon. She had picked her shoes and booked facials. She had told her, 'It's one day,' when Claudia had tried on the bridal persona of melodrama, and now Claudia sat facing her mother and wretched aunt and her siblings, with Dylan and his parents on one side but nobody on hers. Nora was supposed to be on her side. Now she was an hour late and counting.

Claudia stood up with her phone. As she excused herself to go and make the call she looked through the windows to the car park and saw Nora. Nora sprinting across gravel in black-and-white heels so high that Claudia could almost hear the crack of her ankle if there was one misstep. She saw her stop outside the door and look down at her gold dress. It was not the green dress for the festivities Nora had showed her earlier and it was not very Nora. It was not very appropriate. From the table it looked like it was made of gold lamé and it scooped down across her chest before joining at the back where it scooped even lower, stopping just above her hips. The dress ended mid-thigh and, beneath, her hastily self-tanned legs glistened. She tugged at the hem and touched her long hair, which in stark contrast to the dress was blown out in understated loose curls. Nora seemed to take a deep breath and pushed the door open, entering with a smile already plastered across her face. Claudia waved mutely from the table and sat back down as Nora picked her way carefully through the tables. She stopped just behind Mary and waved. 'Sorry I'm late, everyone, I have no decent excuse, I must buy a bottle of champagne to apologise.' She leaned down and kissed Rachel. 'You could be the younger sister of the bride!' she offered as penance, and then gave Mary a quick peck and squeezed the Carter siblings' shoulders before making her way round for introductions with Dylan's parents. Finally she sank down next to Claudia. Her lipstick, a deeply uncharacteristic shade of pink, was already smudged around her lips, as if it had been applied by a delighted four year old.

'I'm sorry, I'm sorry, I'm sorry,' she whispered. Claudia leaned in and smelled something sour on her breath: toothpaste from five hours ago and bubbles upon bubbles upon bubbles.

'What are you wearing?' Claudia hissed.

Nora looked down and seemed surprised by what she saw. 'I hated the green dress. I decided it was so boring.' She giggled and ushered the waitress over. 'Have we started on the champagne yet? It is a celebration. Can you bring me a bottle of champagne?'

The waitress's eyes widened and she picked up a menu from the table. 'What kind?'

Nora glanced at the list and giggled again. 'None of this is actually champagne, you know?' Claudia elbowed Nora but she seemed oblivious, studying the list more carefully. 'This is actually quite good, mostly Tasmanian sparkling – hard to find on a decent list actually.' She looked at the waitress and gave her a crooked smile. Claudia noticed her mascara had fallen beneath her eyes and was smudging along with the eyeliner. If Claudia had been in the mood, she would've enjoyed the spectacle of her uptight friend in such disarray. 'We'll have the Arras, thank you,' Nora finally decided. Before Claudia could grab Nora again she had leaned across the table. 'Rachel, you look ravishing. That is exactly your colour.'

And Rachel, easily flattered, was soon deep in conversation about what shoes she would be wearing the next day. Claudia sighed and looked down the table. Mary and Mick had their heads close together, a beast mutated from a family but sharing no actual genes themselves. Poppy was steadfastly ignoring any attempt by Phinn to broker peace for the evening, between Zoe and Poppy or just in general. Claudia watched as she downed a glass and swiftly refilled it. Claudia hated the way her younger sister drank: it was quick and stupid and if anyone dared comment she showed her defiance by aggressively speeding it up. To Claudia's right Dylan was chatting with his mother while Zoe occasionally interjected. It was a moment in the evening when the family was behaving in a way that Claudia assumed almost every other family behaved. Civilly.

The young waitress, a constant presence, hovered at their elbows, eager to take the first order. Claudia counted the bottles on the table and looked at her watch. It was an hour and twenty-seven minutes since their booking had begun, there were seven bottles on the table and they hadn't even ordered dinner. She nodded to the waitress and interrupted the conversations flowing around her. 'Time for dinner?' It was posed as a question but everyone knew it was a command.

The waitress returned from the kitchen with two bottles of Mumm and delivered them to Dylan, who took one and loosened the cork, letting it go off with a *POP* that silenced the chattering table. Claudia raised an eyebrow as Dylan poured her an almost-overflowing glass and handed the bottle to the waitress to finish pouring the rest of the table. He must have arranged for the bottles to be brought to the restaurant earlier in the day; they were not usually served. Her family and his parents looked at him expectantly as he took a long sip.

'I want to say a few words,' he said, wiping his mouth with

the back of his hand and looking down at his fiancée. 'Claudia and I agreed there would be no speeches tomorrow, but I couldn't let the occasion go without briefly saying something about Claudia. Mostly, that I love her. I think it's an easy enough thing to say; it's important to show as well. I hope that by marrying her she can see it as my most public declaration and demonstration of what she means to me. When I met Claudia I was a very lonely man. I did not really know that. It was not something I gave much thought to, but having her in my life has revealed so many things to me. How fun life can be; how stupid it is to be too cool. Not that she isn't cool, but she never feels too cool to show how she feels – to be joyous, to be furious, to be sad. It may be clichéd but I did not even know I had the capacity for so much demonstration of love – let alone the love I feel for her – before she showed me how to show it. The joy of saying "I love you" every day; the joy of showing you are excited to see someone just because they're walking through the door at the end of the day. I didn't even know the proper joy – to my great shame – of hugging someone so much.'

Dylan looked down and gently touched Claudia's face.

'We are each other's subtexts. All of my unspoken thoughts and motives, what I really think and believe, it is in you. Life without you would be like walking along without my arm, you are such an essential part of me now.

'I love you.' Dylan glanced around the table before looking at Claudia again. 'Despite everything, I love you.'

The two kept looking at each other, smiling, until Mick finally finished Dylan's speech for him.

'To Dylan and Claudia,' he said, raising his glass. Everyone at the table obediently raised their champagne flutes.

'Cheers,' Claudia said, clinking with Dylan's glass and leaning in to whisper in his ear.

The rest of the table could not hear what she said.

The food came out, stodgy and warm with piping hot plates. Overdone steaks and steamed vegetables were a staple of the venue. But nobody complained and most people seemed to be forcing something into their stomachs without being rude or inappropriate. Dylan and Mick's parents created a stricter atmosphere: whenever there are witnesses, everyone has to be on their best behaviour.

They would've made it through dessert too if Rachel had just eaten her lasagne.

CHAPTER 35

The Carters had withstood some epic battles over three decades. Rachel had once become so drunk she had screamed at Claudia in front of a restaurant that she should've home-schooled her to make her a better daughter. When they were younger, Zoe and Phinn had a physical fight so brutal it became legendary for the huge tuft of hair that Phinn ripped from Zoe's head and his subsequent broken nose. After one Christmas Zoe and Poppy had not spoken for five months because they had both drunk too much champagne and Zoe had told her younger sister she was spoiled and selfish. Poppy had once left both George and Claudia crying in a pub when she'd told them that she had been emotionally and physically abandoned as a teenager by both of them when everyone had left home. Even Phinn, as a twenty-one year old, had made Zoe cry in a rental car when he said they all couldn't wait for her to leave a holiday so they could finally relax and have a good time. Three years before, Rachel had to put herself between her two youngest daughters when – while still only on the entrées – they had begun punching each other for reasons nobody ever quite untangled. The cruellest lines, the most heartless remarks, the most devoted insults – they had all been said out loud to each other at one point or another, and more often than was believable they had descended into the physical even when they were much, much, much too old for that shit.

But it all paled in comparison to Claudia's wedding.

Rachel had pushed her vegetable lasagne around her plate for most of the meal before declaring she could've made a better version. At the end of the table Poppy smirked. 'When?'

Rachel's eyes flashed. 'What is that supposed to mean?'

Poppy's back straightened. 'Did I stutter? When have you ever made lasagne?'

Phinn made himself smaller in his seat while Zoe tried to stop the iceberg they were heading for. It seemed small now, innocuous even, but there was a hell of a lot going on underneath. A much bigger fight loomed than a casual observer at the table could possibly foresee.

'Mum's made lasagne before – you know her food is good,' Zoe said, trying to catch Rachel's eye. 'My steak was quite good, actually. How was your dinner?' she said desperately to Dylan's stepmother sitting across from her. If she could cut the conversation off at the head then Poppy could simmer by herself for a while longer. But Yvonne didn't see the signals and just nodded.

'Mum,' said Poppy, 'have you ever eaten a meal at a restaurant that you haven't complained about? You have such high and mighty tastes for someone who didn't even make sandwiches for lunch when we were kids.'

Claudia heard someone inhale sharply and realised it was her. Slowly, she exhaled, thinking she should intervene but finding it impossible to raise the energy. Next to her Nora let out a small squeak and Claudia knew she was trying not to laugh. Although, what exactly was funny had not revealed itself.

'Oh, here you go again, I'm just the worst, your father is a saint, never wronged anyone in his life, and as usual I have to be the enemy.' Rachel's voice cracked. 'I don't understand what I have done to you to deserve this. For you to think this was all my fault.'

Poppy finished her glass of wine. She was drunk and petulant. As usual. 'You're so selfish; everything is about you – you're not the victim here.'

Between Rachel and Poppy, Phinn snorted. Beautiful, calm, take-no-sides Phinn. Phinn, who was legendary for vacating the premises so thoroughly during one argument between Rachel and George that they had found him in a garden two houses away, cowering under a bush, hours after the fight was over. Phinn snorted, then laughed.

'Do you ever listen to yourself, Poppy? You have zero capacity for self-reflection. You're the heavyweight fucking champion of self-absorption. What do you mean Mum always has to be the victim? You're the one picking a screaming match at Claudia's wedding dinner after spending the entire thing pouting into your wine glass while you become more obnoxious – if possible – with each passing hour. Grow the fuck up.'

'Hey, hey,' Mick said helplessly. 'It's okay, kids, we can leave it at that.' Mary put a hand on his knee to quieten him. Not only was it hopeless, but also she was delighted, enjoying the spectacle of her sister's children at their most hideous and vulnerable. There was nothing like her sister's perceived parental failings to cheer her so. Having no children herself, she of course didn't know that you don't get to choose how they turn out. Parenting is almost a myth – so many come into the world with their personalities seemingly fully formed, and from there any parenting efforts are constantly interrupted and derailed by friends, shopkeepers, aunts, nanas, even siblings. Particularly siblings. People's precious babies are open and susceptible to corruption from outside sources almost from the minute the midwife hands the baby to the panting and exhausted mother.

Poppy, who had temporarily been stunned into silence by her docile brother's intervention, was standing at the end of the table.

'Finally you speak, after all these years? All these years of being too pathetic to take a side? Do you want Mum to come and hold your hand now? You've always been such a mum's boy. You think it makes up for being the stupidest out of all of us and the most boring. Well, you're still not Mum's favourite and – even if you were – it would not make up for the severe lack of personality.'

Phinn just looked away, while Mick was the only one who made any attempt at remedy. 'Poppy, come on now,' he whispered.

'Just let her ruin dinner; it wouldn't be dinner if she didn't ruin it,' Dylan finally spat. If Phinn was a wild card in the dinner table argument, then a particle microscope would have been needed to pick out the probability of Dylan getting involved. And yet, here he was. Claudia turned to Nora, elbowing her pleadingly in the side. She desperately needed her to do something, to remind the family they were not just around family, to remind them there were reasons to be on their best behaviour, but Nora was nodding along to whichever music was playing dimly over the speakers while the waitress stood three feet away in awe.

Dylan's words had been delivered like a slap. Even Mary didn't seem to get any thrill out of them; instead shame settled on her face, making itself at home with the other Carter siblings.

Dylan stood up. 'Your sister is only here because of you. She's only doing all of this because of you. She never wanted any of this: not the wedding, not to be here, not the party, and certainly not the guilt trips. Can't you just settle down for one weekend? Just looking at you makes her tits itch at the moment, and she's still here.'

Dylan was telling the truth, but aged wounds are not made to withstand the truth. The sneaking suspicion your family is making fun of you behind your back; the nagging feeling that perhaps your father actually thinks you're quite boring as a person; your secret acknowledgement your sister is more entertaining, cleverer than you, doesn't actually need you; the fear that the only people who know you in your guts don't actually like you. All of these conflicts arise from wounds carefully cultivated throughout your childhood. Throwaway remarks nobody remembers. The time when you were thirteen and played kiss, marry, kill with your siblings and each of them chose to kiss or marry each other while one by one saying you would be the one they would kill. It all remains. It's buried deep but always within yourself you carry every eye roll, every whispered criticism, every bit of the fuel for your secret and total belief that you are not good enough.

It never goes away. Usually the only people able to rake over this are the people who were there for the damage in the first place, but occasionally somebody who should know better finds the bit that aches.

Poppy looked from Dylan to Phinn to Zoe, who had managed to escape most of the wrath by refusing to surrender to the desperate pull of her siblings. Poppy threw her glass down and, shaking, turned on her heel and stomped out of the restaurant. Dylan looked down at Claudia who was leaning across her plate, staring at the table, while only the shake of her shoulders gave away her sobs. Torn between the daughter who didn't deserve this and the daughter who was devastated, Rachel chose the latter and pushed her chair out to chase after Poppy.

Dylan's father watched Rachel's retreating figure, a mild look of appreciation across his face. 'I think,' he said finally, 'I think I will have a Scotch on the rocks and perhaps toast the fact I didn't have any daughters.'

Zoe got up slowly, wary of any sudden movements, even after Poppy had left. Nora hiccupped.

'Hey, Zoe's going to leave just as stuff gets too much again.' Nora smiled sunnily in Zoe's direction as Claudia grabbed her leg under the table and squeezed it as violently as she could without being obvious. Nora just brushed the hand from her leg. 'Oh, you're always complaining about your family anyway, Claudia. How many times have you told me you're not coming back here again?'

Zoe paused as she was starting to turn away. She opened her mouth but decided against it and walked towards the doors through which her mother had exited a few minutes earlier. Phinn looked across at his sister with hurt but, returning to form, didn't say anything.

Claudia hesitated, but so briefly it was detectable only to Dylan. Standing up, she put her hand on Nora and Dylan's shoulders. 'Stay here,' she said firmly, while looking directly at Mary. She walked around the table and nodded at Phinn.

'Oh man,' he muttered, throwing his napkin on the table. He stood up and followed his sister through the doors.

Claudia and Phinn heard Poppy before they saw her. Around the corner of the entrance, in the car park, her voice floated back to them. Or rather screeched back to them.

'You've always been selfish; you only ever thought of yourself and then Claudia and then maybe the rest of us. It has always been about you.'

Poppy's words were slightly slurred. Claudia had not realised how much wine she had drunk. Then it occurred to her that the same went for her mother as her voice rushed around the corner too.

'*I'm* selfish! I gave up everything for you! You think I wanted to be in this town, ever? You think I wanted to do the job I did? You think you know everything that happened to me? You're a selfish little bitch who I spoiled too much.'

Phinn and Claudia sped up their steps and turned the corner to see Zoe rubbing Rachel's arm, almost pleading. 'Come on, Mum, I can take her home, just go back inside.' Rachel snatched her arm away as Poppy started yelling again.

'You have no idea what is going on in my life because you have never thought to ask, and I come home and have to keep being treated as some kind of invalid, as stupider than a baby. I don't need your permission for anything; the only time you ever notice me is when you think I should be asking for permission.'

Rachel pushed Zoe to the side and grabbed her youngest daughter by the shoulders, squeezing them hard as she finally screamed.

'I REGRET EVER HAVING YOU.'

The siblings froze as the words reverberated between them. One can always suspect, or even just half suspect, that perhaps their existence isn't the greatest thing to ever happen to their mother. Perhaps she could have been smarter, richer, prettier, happier if you'd never existed. But the home is designed – for the lucky ones – to quash any of those notions. Popular culture is designed to put motherhood on an impossible pedestal and there is little to no evidence anywhere that women ever regret having children.

But, they must. Sometimes, they must. Something as simple

as the law of averages says they must. Children may suspect it, but it is rare as snow on the Great Barrier Reef to actually hear it. Especially from a mother who still loves you.

Phinn looked at Claudia who looked at Zoe, who was the only one who could bear to look at Poppy. Poppy stood defeated in her ill-fitting dress. Her shoulders slumped; she held her head in her hands desperately. Rachel stood panting and staring at her daughter, who finally met her eyes. Poppy's eyes went cold as she screamed and rushed at Rachel with her hands outstretched. For a moment Zoe thought Poppy was going to hug their mother, then she thought she was going to hit her. Poppy rushed at Rachel and with the full force of her body shoved her. Family legend would speculate on the reason for the shove. There could be thirty-four different viable reasons for the shove: she could have been shoving her out of the way to run away, she could have just had a physical reaction, she could have just wanted to touch her mother but hate her at the same time. Poppy never said why she pushed their mother.

All four of Rachel's offspring – the womb-mates, the babies she had nursed in her insides between her bladder and liver, and torn herself open again and again and again and again to bring them into the big wide world – watched in horror as Rachel stumbled backwards and in her stupid shoes lost her footing, her ankle falling away while the rest of her followed backwards. It was likely a combination of shock and hurt and wine that made Rachel fall the way she did, and a combination of wine and hurt and shock that stopped any of her children from reaching out to try to catch her.

She fell slowly and then all at once and the silence was broken by the crack of her head against the corner of the gutter.

Rachel went limp.

Claudia was the first to scream. Then Zoe screamed. Then Phinn screamed. And they were all screaming. Poppy, the drunkest, was also the one who had done a first-aid course as part of the requirements for one of her legion of jobs.

'Don't touch her! Don't touch her!'

'What the fuck, Poppy?' Claudia yelled, kneeling on the ground. '*You* don't touch her!'

'No! I mean it. If she's hurt her neck you shouldn't touch her.'

Claudia rocked back on her heels and sat on the ground, looking to her older sister for guidance. Zoe was still standing with her hands over her mouth, gaping at their mother. She looked at Phinn and then Poppy.

'I don't know but it makes sense – who has their phone? We need an ambulance.'

Phinn touched his back pockets while Poppy patted her sides. They had all left their phones inside. 'I'll get them,' Phinn said, gratefully stepping back.

'No.'

Phinn stopped mid-step and looked back to see who had spoken. His sisters were now crouched around their mother and he saw Rachel's hand grabbing Claudia's.

'No,' she said again, her voice raspy and thin. Phinn stepped off the footpath and stood next to Rachel's shoulder. Her hair was fanned around her head, and her lips – along with the rest of her face – were drained of colour but her eyes were open.

'Ma! What do we do?' he said.

'Water,' she whispered. 'Don't tell anyone.' All of her effort went into the last three words while Claudia stroked her head and rolled her eyes at the command.

'What people think is incredibly important right now.' Zoe couldn't help herself.

Phinn nodded at his mother. 'I won't tell anyone.' And he turned and ran inside.

'Sorry Mum, sorry Mum, sorry Mum,' Poppy was muttering

on the other side of Rachel while Zoe and Claudia glared at her. Rachel grabbed her hand and tried to sit up but immediately realised it was too ambitious and lay down again.

'Don't try anything, Mum,' Zoe murmured, 'it's a concussion.'

Claudia kept anxiously stroking Rachel's head. 'How do you know it's a concussion?' she asked her older sister.

Zoe allowed herself a smile. 'It's pretty basic; what else would it be? She can move, she can talk, she's completely out of it, she hit her head – she's concussed.'

Claudia felt her sides for her phone but realised again it wasn't with her.

'Don't google it. It'll say she's going into seizure and has cancer,' Zoe said, trying to sound reassuring. Poppy rocked on her heels and eased back so she was sitting on the other side of Rachel, the movement reasserting her briefly forgotten presence with her sisters.

'You should get out of here. You need to leave. Look what you did to Mum,' Claudia said sharply.

'She's my mum too,' Poppy said, seemingly groping for a way to somehow defend herself.

'Go away,' Claudia said again.

'Don't,' Rachel whispered, 'it's not her fault.'

Zoe snorted. 'It's absolutely her fault.' But she nudged Claudia; her eyes were pleading.

'Be nice to your sister,' Rachel croaked as Phinn reappeared with a bottle of water. He briefly relayed the scene inside, explaining how he'd managed to give the impression they were in some kind of family conference and shouldn't be disturbed. Tenderly, he lifted Rachel's head from the ground and held the water to her mouth so she could drink. She managed a sip and then turned her head away, signalling enough.

Somehow the four of them were going to have to get her home without anyone knowing her youngest daughter had ever so briefly knocked her out. The siblings huddled closer to her and in the shadows of the streetlight attempted to devise a plan. The oldest three did most of the devising, the youngest having been unofficially banned from any attempt at contribution.

'We could borrow Mick's car, or maybe Dylan's parents'.'

'Who here is under the alcohol limit?'

'Nobody.'

'We could let Mick in on this and get him to drive us.'

Rachel grunted in protest.

'We could Uber.'

'Mate, this town has not entered 2003 yet, let alone 2017.'

'We could taxi.'

'Mum knows all the taxi drivers; she won't let us.'

'This is one curly evening.'

'We could ask Leah.'

Poppy had waited until her siblings could see all avenues were exhausted before she broke her self-imposed embargo (silly for her brother and sisters to even entertain the thought they had imposed it). Claudia began to shut it down but was stopped by the fact it was the closest thing to a legitimate course of action any of them had. Phinn looked down at Rachel, who did not register any protest.

'Should we be calling an ambulance instead?' he ventured.

Rachel gingerly shook her head. 'I'm fine. God isn't letting me die tonight – I've said too many prayers,' she whispered.

Claudia sighed from deep in her bones and asked her mother again if there was not a single person inside they could ask to take her home. But Rachel was resolute. And almost everyone inside was drunk. Poppy grabbed Rachel's wrist and examined her watch. 'We've been out here for forty minutes.'

'Everyone was ordering dessert when I got the water,' Phinn offered.

Despite herself, Claudia laughed. Their guests ate dessert

while outside they had come to terms with their mother's death and resurrection and then her pride. Standing up, Poppy made the decision for everyone and left them crouched in the gutter while she went to get her phone and call Leah. 'As usual, the only goddamn one who can make a decision,' she said as she walked away. That it was her fault their mother was lying in a car park with a head injury didn't seem to occur to her.

Dylan was trying to decide whether he would make it worse or better if he went outside. On the one hand all of the siblings had been gone forty minutes with their mother; on the other it was Rachel out there with all of her children.

He smiled tightly at his father, trying to pre-warn him against any jokes about in-laws and outlaws. But if Jerome was finding any of the behaviour odd, being on his best behaviour was preventing him from saying anything.

Nora turned to him and smiled lopsidedly. 'Maybe they're all just entranced by Tinder!'

Dylan frowned. 'What?'

Nora, who had already consumed about eight more 'one mores' than she should've, did not quite grasp the enormity of what she had just said. She giggled.

'Well, you know, it can be quite addictive.' She looked around the table at the polite conversations everyone else was trying to immerse themselves in. 'We only had a look the other night and it turned into two hours.'

Dylan's face went stern. 'Who's we?'

Nora's brain finally caught up to her and, after a few seconds' delay, her eyes widened and she clapped her hand over her mouth.

'Nora. Who. Is. We?'

'It was just a lark, me and Claudia, having a lark. It was nothing – I was just showing her the app dating world.'

Dylan looked down at the seat between them. On it sat Claudia's bright green purse, decorated with ostentatious flower brooches in purples and reds. He glanced back at Nora who still sat with her hand over her mouth, but her wide-eyed stare had turned to terror as she clocked Claudia's purse at the same time. Dylan flipped it open and reached in, bringing out Claudia's diamanté-covered phone. He typed in the numbers of Rachel's birthday and flicked across the screens until he realised he didn't actually know what the Tinder icon looked like. He scowled and opened the search bar; the app appeared before he had even typed in the N.

Dylan did not even consider if he wanted to open it: driven by a quiet rage that usually lay dormant, he stumbled through the app until he found the inbox.

Nora was quietly pleading with him, 'Don't open it, it really was nothing, we were just looking at it, there's nothing on there, it doesn't mean anything,' her begging interrupted when she finally saw that Dylan wasn't merely swiping through. He was reading. Reading when there was not supposed to be anything to read. She leaned over for a better look at the screen but Dylan pulled back so that only he could see it.

There were at least seventy messages. Most of them were unopened and were simple one- or two-word introductions from the men, but he could see at least a couple that were more than that.

He opened one from a David. His last message was unanswered from Claudia and simply said, 'I'll show you mine if you show me yours', but before that was a stream of mundane questions, answered loquaciously by Claudia.

The first concert she had ever been to.

The last Coen brothers movie she'd watched.

The best Spice Girl.

It was the dullness of the exchanges that made it even more offensive. Dylan could feel something deep inside him crack open. He had an impulse to do something violent and memorable: he wanted to punch a wall; he wanted to punch someone's face. He felt all that made him happy in the world falling away, an entire future rearranged beyond recognition.

Dylan was brought back to the room by Mary's roar; he looked up to find Mary, Mick, Jerome and Yvonne smiling at him expectantly.

'Sorry, what . . .?' A long-vanquished stutter almost returning.

'I was just saying, you proved the old proverb right about bad beginnings making good endings – remember when you refused to eat anything but carrots and chocolate eggs for two years?' his father said.

Dylan looked down at Claudia's phone again and locked it, shoving it back into her purse without looking. He took a deep breath and smiled.

'And then I changed so much I had trained myself to eat olives and chillies by the time I was twelve!'

CHAPTER 36

The most terrifying things in the world mostly revolve around your children and your parents. There's nowhere to hide from your children. If you have them you have to accept you leave yourself completely exposed. Even with a partner you can obscure the most unsavoury aspects of yourself; sometimes the other just won't notice them, or other times they are simply too consumed by their love for you, their luck at finding you, to really care.

But children rarely feel lucky that you are their parent. There are no alternatives to consider. Not only do they see you clear-eyed, but also there is no way you can hide from them. Every hypocrisy, the way you talk to waitresses, how much work you actually do in the home, how often you are angry, how often you repeat the same joke, the fact you use packet mix for gravy, how you choose to spend a spare hour, how long you lay in bed in the morning, the worst smell you leave in the bathroom, how you treat the friends you complain about the most in private, how long you spend on Facebook – your children see it all. You cannot present a more glittering, a more palatable, a more *together* version of yourself to your children.

Alternatively, the most terrifying thing that can happen to you is seeing a parent weakened. Being essential to them. After relying on them for so long, never questioning their existence, having a central tenet of faith that not only will they always be there, but that they will always care.

Zoe and Claudia were both considering this – unbeknownst to each other – as they carried Rachel to Leah's waiting car. Rachel was doing a half imitation of walking, but her stagger relied on a daughter on each side holding her up as they guided her to the red Nissan Pulsar, sitting with its lights dimmed, like a drug dealer waiting for a client, just around the corner from the bright entrance to the restaurant.

Poppy walked ahead of them and leaned through the passenger window to exchange hushed words with Leah. It looked intense but the conversation could be boiled down to: 'Hey. Hey. Thanks for doing this. What happened? Never mind. I will tell you later.'

Poppy opened the back door and her sisters eased their mother into the back seat before each sat on either side of her. 'Hello Leah!' Claudia said brightly. She couldn't help herself; even in times of chaos she tried to put on her best face for strangers.

Poppy hesitated and opened the passenger door, manoeuvring into the front seat. She looked up to see her brother standing at the door, relieved. 'No room for me,' he said. 'I'll go back inside.' The awkwardness of providing an explanation for a tipsy and prying audience was infinitely preferable to a car trip with his concussed mother, angry sisters and a possible lover.

The group sat in silence as Leah put the car into first gear and carefully pulled onto the road. 'Thanks, sweetie,' Rachel muttered, resting her head on Zoe.

They moved through the night past the chicken shop Claudia had once thrown up in when underage and drunk; the café where Phinn had made terrible coffee on Saturdays during high school; the tree they used to sit in smoking on Friday nights.

Claudia thought about her wedding, the next day. She thought about the future mapped out for her; the love of a good man; how exhausting excitement actually was.

Poppy thought about how close Leah was sitting next to her.

Rachel thought about her headache.

Zoe thought she shouldn't have come home.

Their considerations were punctured by Leah delicately turning into Rachel's driveway, her duty done. It took longer to get Rachel out of the car than the entire drive had taken, but finally Zoe and Claudia had their mother balanced between them.

'Should we be putting you to bed?' Claudia asked anxiously as she shuffled forward.

'I told you,' Rachel was barely audible, 'I'm not dying tonight.'

Poppy watched them move towards the front door, and turned to Leah. She leaned over and quickly kissed her.

'Thank you. I'll see you later.'

She opened the door and self-consciously followed her sisters and their mother inside without looking back. Once the door was closed she heard Leah's wheels reverse out of the driveway and the motor fade down the street.

Without speaking, the sisters undressed their mother like a doll, lifting her arms for her while they pulled her dress over her head and rolling her stockings down her legs. Startled, they all noticed her bikini line had been waxed. They had grown up with a mother who had embarrassing dark tufts exploding outside of either side of her swimwear. Maybe we don't know everything about our mothers. But they didn't say anything to each other. They lay Rachel on her back and kissed her forehead. Just as they were turning to leave the room, she beckoned. Claudia, Zoe and Poppy looked at each other and bent over their mother.

'Be nice to your sister,' she whispered.

They weren't completely sure which one she meant.

Later, after the sisters had gone to different rooms with no explanation, too tired to lay any more blame for the night, Poppy crept into her mother's room wearing the same faded pink LCD Soundsystem fan club T-shirt she had worn to bed when she was fifteen. She walked around the bed and climbed under the blanket next to Rachel.

She lay in the dark and listened to her mother breathing.

CHAPTER 37

Claudia was already asleep when Zoe flung her door open.

'Claudie! Claudia!' she shout-whispered. She took two steps in and saw the lump that was her sister underneath the doona, even her head obscured. She put her hand on the lump and shook it. 'Claudia! You need to wake up.'

Claudia groaned and rustled under the doona, revealing her face but still refusing to open her eyes.

'Claudia, it's Nora.'

Claudia sat bolt upright. 'Nora? What?'

Zoe held up her phone. 'Dylan just rang. Nora is really sick at the restaurant; the others had gone home and he found her vomiting near some bushes.'

'She what?'

'Don't tell anyone but … her and Tom broke up.'

'Wait, what? Nora is throwing up and Tom and her broke up?'

'She didn't want you to find out during this week but her

and Tom broke up just before she came here. Don't tell her I told you that, though – nobody is supposed to know.'

Claudia stood up and grabbed a pair of shorts to put on under her makeshift pyjama top. She pulled her phone from the charger and was greeted with a blank screen, no notifications. She wondered why Nora hadn't tried to call for help.

She did not wonder why Dylan had called Zoe.

Shoving her feet into her Nikes, she grabbed Zoe's arms to steady herself and then stood up properly to meet her eye. Something was not right. She felt the mechanics of an emotional demotion as she grasped the meaning of it being Zoe who had burst into her room and not her ringtone direct from the scene.

'Why did Nora tell you about the break-up and not me?'

Zoe shrugged Claudia's hand off her in irritation. 'Let's stick to things that actually matter.'

The sisters didn't bother to put up a pretence of quietness as they rushed out of the house. Rachel would not be waking up for a while, and neither of them cared if Poppy was disturbed. In fact, it would have given them both an ounce of pleasure to disturb her.

Zoe drove as Claudia texted Dylan to say they were on their way and to ask for a condition update.

'Still breathing. Still vomiting,' came the reply.

As Zoe pulled into the restaurant's street she could see Dylan's shoulders outlined by a streetlight as he bent over, seemingly to pat a petrified dog. Zoe swung the car to the left and then reversed back so they were parked next to the two figures. As Claudia got out of the car she could hear Dylan muttering in soothing tones.

'You're okay, it's okay, nobody thinks anything.'

His sentences were punctuated by sobs as Nora, on all fours, heaved her shoulders back and retched. Claudia kneeled down beside her and started rubbing her back as she looked up at

Dylan, who eased his hand from between her shoulders where he had been patting her.

'She's pretty sick,' he finally said.

Claudia instinctively leaned over and kissed Nora above her ear. 'It's okay, I'm here.'

Nora sobbed again. 'I can't do this.'

'Can't do what?'

Dylan answered for her. 'She's been saying that for half an hour; I think she means she can't keep feeling this sick.'

'Jesus,' Zoe interjected. 'She hasn't stopped vomiting for half an hour? How long was she out here before you found her?'

Nora's gold dress had ridden up at the back, revealing her tummy-tightening underwear, and her hair was matted with vomit. Zoe pulled a hair tie from her own head and clumsily gathered Nora's hair in her hands, pulling it back from her face to secure it. Dylan crouched on his haunches. 'We left pretty soon after you guys had gone. Dad picked up the bill. I think Nora was there at the end; she knocked over a full glass of champagne and then asked for another one.' He hesitated and looked at Nora with pity. 'They wouldn't let her have one.'

Nora heaved again but this time nothing came up and she simply spat. Claudia kept rubbing her back while Zoe tried to objectively assess the situation. 'I don't think we need to take her to the hospital.'

Claudia snorted. 'This is the second time tonight we are considering such action.'

Dylan looked confused but Zoe ignored both of them.

'She's still conscious, the vomiting seems to have slowed, I think we can get her to bed, and if she can keep down water then she can just recover at the hotel.'

Nora attempted to contribute to the plan but could only muster another sob. Claudia leaned forward to look her in the face. Nora's lipstick was smudged across her lips and her eyeliner had almost been wiped away, leaving black splotches from her cheeks to her hairline. She met Claudia's gaze and closed her eyes before hanging her head, conceding that the effort was just too great to keep it upright. Claudia put her lips to her ear again.

'It's okay, I'll look after you.'

True to her word it was Claudia who stayed in the hotel room with Nora. Dylan was out of the question, and the embarrassment at waking up to Zoe in her space would've been too traumatic for Nora. After Dylan and Zoe had helped her to get Nora into the room and left, Claudia had spent minutes that felt like days tugging at the tight dress, coaxing Nora to keep her arms over her head as she eased it off. She put Nora under the shower and filled up a glass of water for her to drink out of while she sat on the floor, unable even to stand while trying to wash away the night.

Claudia turned off the water and gathered Nora in a towel, helping her to the bed without bothering to find new underwear or a nightgown. Once she was lying down, Claudia pulled up the blanket and sat on the floor to keep watch over her friend. Nora opened her eyes.

'I told Dylan,' she whispered, her throat hoarse and raw from the evening's turn of events.

'Told Dylan what?'

Nora groaned. 'Tinder.'

Then she rolled over and softly began to snore.

'Jesus Christ, between this and telling Zoe about Tom, it's a confidentiality spree,' she said, more to herself than her semi-unconscious friend. Then the panic started to rise. Dylan knew about Tinder. What exactly did he know about Tinder?

Just that she'd downloaded it? She had left her phone next to him all night.

Nora would not only be wrought with the hangover of nausea and aches in the morning, she was definitely heading for The Fear. The physical hangover is small time compared to The Fear, a cringe-fest of emotional paralysis as all the actions from the night before are slowly recalled.

Claudia already knew this was not the end of the friendship but the thought would surely be with Nora once she sobered up. If Claudia was going to rage at anyone, it was going to have to be herself. She'd had a lifetime of lessons in forgiving and not-quite-forgetting, courtesy of her sisters.

CHAPTER 38

Claudia rolled over, raising her arm before it landed with a thud on the empty space next to her. She sat bolt upright. The empty space next to her? In a moment she got her bearings. She wasn't at home. Any of her homes. She was on the floor of a beige motel room with Nora in a bed snoring next to her. She had had no intention of falling asleep. She stood up and walked out of the motel room. It would take her thirty-five minutes to walk to Rachel's house but she needed the time. She was in no rush to break Dylan's heart.

The sky was indigo as light from the imminent sunrise began to creep through the shadows.

'I'm supposed to get married today,' she said to a few tree branches full of leaves as she started down the street. 'All I need is a husband.'

She was still wearing her pyjama T-shirt and shorts from the night before and she could feel her make-up caked on, streaked with the oil from her skin. She rubbed her eyes and inspected the impressive amount of eye shadow that had stayed put through the drama.

She wouldn't have minded if the walk had taken a couple of days. Weeks, months even.

Instead she was at the front door long before she wanted to be.

She felt along the ridge above it and took down the spare key, opening the door just enough that she could sneak in but not so far so that it squeaked. She squeezed through the gap and a sound as familiar as her fingernails greeted her. Dylan's breathing.

In the living room she found him shirtless and still in his trousers from the dinner, sleeping softly in a barely contained position on the couch. Claudia kneeled beside him and rested her forehead on his shoulder, kissing it gently as he stirred awake.

Dylan looked at her groggily and rolled onto his side, reaching his arm out towards her. She winced as he gently started stroking her hair.

'I really wanted to marry you,' he finally said.

'I know.'

Dylan began to quietly weep. Claudia averted her eyes, but beyond the guilt found herself strangely unmoved.

'Don't you kind of want this too? Haven't you felt something missing?' she finally offered.

'No.'

'I'll pay back my half of the money we put in.'

'No you won't.'

'I guess it's a good thing we didn't have enough money to book a honeymoon.'

'For you, yes.'

'You'll be okay.'

'I hope you will be.'

ACKNOWLEDGEMENTS

Thank you Séamus, Anna and Alice for being born. All characters are fictional.

Thank you to all of my friends who have inspired and motivated me over the years with sparkling and tough conversations, including but not limited to Ricky Morton, Candice Gallimore, Kylie Dunn, Shannon Molloy, Katherine Feeney, Tulsi Combe and Maria Lewis. Thank you in particular to my early readers Georgia Waters and Veronica Foulkes. I also owe a deep gratitude to Australia's premier group chat.

To Christopher and Philomena Jabour – nobody says it enough – you are wonderful parents.

My agent Jeanne Ryckmans seemed to make magic happen, and Angela Meyer took my draft and made it a book. I am also indebted to Clive Hebard and Penny Isaac who were the midwives at the end; and the talented Alissa Dinallo for her striking cover design.

Helen Garner allowed a few of her devastating sentences to be used in this book, for which I am deeply grateful.

And finally, to my husband, who was the first person I gave this book to and still hasn't finished reading it but who makes me cleverer and funnier every day; and to my son, who did absolutely nothing, but whom I feel the need to acknowledge nonetheless.

90539301R00208

Made in the USA
Middletown, DE
24 September 2018

talking of my friends downstairs. I do hear one thing, and that is as clear a crystal; somebody speaks to me. I don't see her and I don't recognize accent.

'My life is exactly as it should be.' She says to me.

I believe her.

Despite the fact that I still looked better than Brigitte Bardot in her prime, unbelievably I reached the age of forty. Lisa arranged a truly marvellous birthday party for me on the Royal Iris ferry back in Liverpool. Lisa had always arranged my birthday parties and they were always brilliant. When we were back together we were the same best friends that used to be when we were sneaking out of school to smoke cigarettes in the green bus shelter with the broken windows.

Unfortunately neither of my boys could make it. Bruce did not really want to come, he said he was too busy preparing to start University. Dylan, my eldest would have liked to have come but he had an important gig with his band that same night that he couldn't get out of, he was very good. He would not have enjoyed this party too much though, Lisa had arranged for the music to be almost entirely YES. Five hours of almost nothing but YES music – heaven!

Half way through the night I realized I hadn't seen either Steve or Lisa for a while. The DJ put The Beatles' '*Happy Birthday*' on as Lisa re-appeared pushing in the biggest cream cake I had ever seen. It was about six feet high and almost as wide. I didn't have a chance to think about what I was meant to do with it because the thing suddenly came to life. It was Steve, whom Lisa had covered in about a hundred tins of squirty cream and trifle sponges. Before he had a chance to jump on me, I leapt on him causing the cream to splatter everywhere onto everyone. Steve had the foresight to wear shorts for this stunt but I spent the rest of the evening in a totally ruined Chanel dress but I didn't care. I had only bought it especially for this night!

I go upstairs to let the warm breeze dry me off. Finding the front-most position of the boat, I climb up onto the shiny black railings that meander around the boat deck and look down into the river churning away below me, staring into the darkness. The wind blows straight in to my face, whistling past my ears. It's so loud I can't hear anything. It blocks out the music and the

hated Steve and was planning to go back to Paris. I had always trusted Lisa; we had always been totally honest with each other about everything so I could not and still cannot understand why she said that. She almost destroyed my marriage.

One of us was lying or at least unaware of the truth. I knew Lisa wouldn't deliberately lie to me but if she hadn't then it meant that I was wrong. She said that until the day when I got lost in the rain, the day I imagined that I had made Jean-Marie jump off a church tower to his death I had been treating Steve like something I had stood in. She was amazed that he had stayed with me for so long, it must have been torture for him living with someone he loved but who despised him.

None of this sounded familiar to me at the time. I told her she was lying. I said to Lisa that I didn't understand because I had really made up my mind that I would leave Jean-Marie that Christmas of 1969 and I did. Lisa was then wondered why I was talking about things that happened nearly three years ago. She agreed that my marriage was fine for a while, actually it was more than fine but she said that about six months ago, about the time that those Jean-Paul Sartre plays I liked were being shown on BBC2, I started talking about Jean-Marie again. She said I had been writing to him. I remembered those plays, they were BBC 2's big thing for 1972 but I definitely don't remember these things that Lisa told me I had said.

She said that ever since the nightmare in front of that church I was different. What I thought was a nightmare turned out to be a blessing. Whatever it was, it changed not just my life but also Steve's, Dylan's and Bruce's for the better. Lisa thought she had the perfect explanation. She thought that my vision where I killed my lover was symbolic. She said I had suddenly realized that I loved Steve not Jean-Marie so my mind had to construct the image of myself symbolically making him kill himself so that I could accept it.

didn't matter, I came to realize that there is no such thing as perfection. Nothing can ever live up to one's expectations although some things can come pretty close.

Steve insisted on keeping the same hairstyle he had in the sixties far too long. He seemed intent on giving all our money away to the boys, he was even more pretentious than I was but worst of all thought Genesis were actually better after Peter Gabriel left. That was quite unforgivable. Some people said that I became even more selfish, irresponsible and vain but being so beautiful it was my right! Neither of us were perfect but together we were a fantastic couple. Our two boys turned out pretty good too which was extra satisfying because it wiped Evil Bitch's eye, as we used to say back in Liverpool.

The seventies turned into the eighties and Steve and I were still together and still in love. It wasn't the same love we had for each other when we first met but it was right for us. Despite Mrs Thatcher's attempts to recreate the austerity of post-war Britain, everything seemed to go marvellously for us. Steve started a successful computer business with our old friend, Mr Spitfire and was happy. My little charity went from helping a few Bangladeshi villagers to a chain of trendy boutiques selling ethnic goods to horrendous yuppies at ridiculous prices that all went back to Bangladesh; I was a sort of Robin Hood in shoulder pads. After a break of a few years I even started writing again which was such fun. My best friend Lisa, I am glad to say is still my best friend.

I remember back in 1972 asking her whether she had actually said those horrible lies to Steve about me wanting to leave him and go back to France. I was astounded to hear her say yes. Not just yes, I seem to recall it was something like, 'Of course I did, you dozy cow.' Thirteen years later, it still hurts. She was utterly convinced that I had been telling her for months that I couldn't stand living with him anymore. She said I was always going on about how much I

CHAPTER TWENTY=THREE

Summer 1985

Steve says that he remembers that picnic we had in the rain as the start of our new life. He says that I had changed, I was almost a different person. I know what he meant, I felt like I had been given something precious, a gift, the perfect life.

It was like starting from fresh with him, I actually had to seduce him. It wasn't easy but it was exciting and thrilling. We both managed to forget the wilderness years as we ended up calling them between the time I came back from Paris and our picnic in the storm (our story became more exaggerated as time went on to eventually including a bit about the boat nearly sinking as waves crashed into us). We went on dates again, we had parties, some of them almost respectable, we went on holidays, he dragged me to see Pink Floyd and I dragged him to YES; we were a happy couple.

Me telling him over and over again that I loved him became a bit of a joke but it seemed to do the trick. Over the next few months he began to realize that I really did and always had done.

Steve was not the perfect husband and I certainly was not the perfect wife. Also, as his evil bitch mother liked to keep telling me, I was definitely not the perfect mother either. This

much better mood than when we left. He rowed us back to the other side of the pond and I washed my muddy shoes by letting them trail behind me in the water. They were soaked but clean enough to wear again so I put them on and squelched towards the bus stop.

I don't think I ever stopped telling him how much I loved him all the way home on that bus. I was making up for all the times recently when I had ignored him, been beastly to him and given him every reason to doubt me. It was unpleasant to accept but I began to realize what a supreme bitch I had been.

Steve didn't say much on that journey home but he didn't get much of an opportunity. I was working on the premise that if I told him I loved him over and over again he would eventually know it was true. The other passengers on must have thought I was a drug crazed fan and Steve was some sort of a rock star. It felt a little like that, he was my idol.

hopeless. It was just over two years since Paris, I can't imagine what madness made me do all that but that was all in the past now. For the last two years I really thought I had been helping Steve get back his life back together. I was used to these irrational outbursts, they were perfectly understandable because I had betrayed his trust so badly. At times like this when he was so far away from me I felt so lost.

I tried to remember a dream I had tried to forget. In this dream Steve was right, I did leave him but life with Jean-Marie was simply awful. It was terrible because in this dream I think Steve died or maybe I killed him. It was dark and horrible but it was just a dream. I suppose it was because he had been saying this so many times it must have worked its way into my subconscious.

We finished our pork pies, our cheese sandwiches and wine but left of course the tinned ham sandwiches because tinned ham is simply vile (and I don't know anyone who can actually eat that repugnant filth.) We threw them to the ducks, they didn't seem to mind.

'Our relationship is a bit like that daft song, "*MacArthur Park*" – you know, someone left the cake out in the rain.' Steve said as he prized the soggy sandwich bags out of the mud and squeezed them into another bag. 'You know, one minute there's love and happiness in a sunny park, then washed away by the rain of reality.' He had clearly been thinking about what I'd been saying.

I couldn't help myself, I just had to sing! He joined in with me to sing the last line: '*Oh No-o-o-o!*' I made him laugh – that was wonderful.

The rain was now falling so hard it was actually hurting us. After about twenty minutes we gave up on the picnic and dashed back to the bank where Steve had to tip up the boat to empty it of water. Despite being so wet that we feared we were about to dissolve Steve was in a

I couldn't say: 'Steve, your mind is playing tricks on you again.' could I? I cared too much for him. I tried not to look upset, I remember at the height of his illness he used to hate sympathy.

I tried my best to tell him that I loved him but he looked very uncomfortable. I might as well have been telling him that I had just signed us up to join the Conservative Party. Steve didn't believe a word I was saying. I don't know which of us had the most confused and astounded expression on our faces. His poor mixed up mind was telling him that I couldn't stand him anymore. He assumed that telling him I loved him was some nasty trick I was playing on him. It was breaking my heart.

'Darling, why can't we be like we were the other afternoon when we had that lovely picnic when it wasn't raining. You remember, it was really sunny, we got stoned and thought you could see goldfish with monkey's faces?'

'You see – you're doing it again. I know that you are talking about one those blokes you like to invite back to our house when I'm not around. Why do you say these things?'

It was pointless even replying to this. He began stuffing the rest of the pork pie in to his mouth until I slapped it out of his hand. I was about to slap his stupid face but I just about managed to stop myself. I was incensed and as vain as it sounds I heard myself screaming at him.

'You've got to love me you stupid fucking arsehole! I am Julia and you do love me.'

'Just fuck off Julia, of course you know I still love you.' he spluttered with a mouthful of pie.

This should have made me glad, it should have been what I wanted to hear but the words made my heart ache. He loved me and I loved him but he was so far away that it seemed

relieved. He was strangely resigned to the fact that he was right, that I was planning to leave him. I was absolutely furious with him. Didn't he realize how hurtful he was being? I couldn't imagine why he could even entertain such an absurd idea. Lisa was my best friend, surely she wouldn't have said that. I didn't know what to do so resorted to throwing my arms around him. For the second time that day he pushed me away.

'What are you playing at today Julia? Why do you keep trying to touch me? He snatched a wet pork pie and took a chunk out of it.

'Well?' he asked, trying to prompt me to a reply. I turned and stared intensely at him trying to take in this ridiculous situation. Where was my director now?

He didn't give me a chance to reply. 'You're going to come out one of your clever sarcastic put-downs now aren't you?'

My arms dropped from him in disbelief. 'Steve, you bloody idiot, I'm not going to leave you. You mean Jean-Marie? I've not thought about him for...' I thought it best not to mention yesterday's daydream just now, 'haven't thought about him years. Why would I? I love you, you arsehole.' I wasn't sure he heard me, I said it again, 'I love you Steve. I am not going to leave you. Who else could show a girl such a good time as an afternoon in the pissing rain, eating soggy pork pies having just ruined one of my best pairs of shoes? You know I love you don't you!'

He folded his arms and gave me a very suspicious look. 'Cut it out. Just once can't you stop laughing at me? I'm trying to give you the chance of acting like a civilized adult, the chance to walk away from this joke of a marriage with some shred of dignity.'

over the lake. We couldn't see the band because there were just so many people. It was different today, because it was raining we were the only people mad enough to be there. Even the ducks were conspicuous by their absence.

Climbing out of the little boat onto what was now quite a muddy bank I got one of my shoes stuck in the mud. Getting my hands disgustingly dirty I had to take them off, I left them in the boat. I would decide what to do with them when we returned. Walking barefoot through cold wet mud was not really how I had imagined my lunch date to be. As the rain really started to pour down the thought of a boring restaurant seemed somewhat more appealing at this time.

From the bag he had with him, Steve threw a blanket onto a patch of ground beneath a tree that was almost sheltering us. Ignoring the fact that the paper napkins were becoming decidedly soggy, he proceeded to lay out the food and drink he had brought. He apologised that it was probably not going to be the most impressive picnic we would have but he only remembered to get the food last night so had to buy everything at our little corner shop. The selection of pork pies, sandwiches of cheese or tinned ham plus a packet of fairy cakes looked quite good. He also managed to get a bottle of white wine, which because of the weather was nicely chilled.

'I spoke to your friend Lisa a couple of days ago.' Steve said sipping some wine. 'She told me that you're thinking about going back to that guy in Paris. Is it true?' I realized now what had been on his mind. That question had been gnawing at him all day, if not longer.

I could tell that he had been desperate to talk about this and as soon as he had done so he appeared to breathe properly again. Because the wind was now driving the rain directly at us and his face was completely covered in his hair he looked a little like the Dulux dog or one of those hairy gonk toys. Although I could as much see his face as he could see mine I think he looked

be able to speak to him, I needed to talk to someone about yesterday. I couldn't keep this vision or whatever it was inside me.

I had not noticed earlier but my husband did not look particularly well today. Sometimes things really got him down and he wasn't himself. Today was one of those days I told myself and having to go on strike against his will didn't help. I thought it would be for the best to let him sort out whatever was on his mind without bothering him with my pathetic problems.

As that day progressed what happened to me the day before began to drift further and further away into the past like a dream. By about midday I had sobered up after my Russian breakfast. With the rationality returned, I was wondering why I had been so bothered about it. It was just a bad acid trip, nothing more. I was perfectly fine now. I was back in character and this was how I was meant to be.

Today was Steve's unplanned day off so I wanted to make something of it – he was going to take me for lunch. Rather than being predictable and taking me to a pleasant restaurant in town, Steve took me to the park for a picnic; in the rain. I told Steve on the bus there how much I was looking forward to this. He didn't seem to believe me and when we arrived his mood was a very quiet one. Considering that this was his crazy idea I thought that he might have been a little more enthusiastic. It looked like he wasn't going to be much fun but he sometimes had days like this, I didn't mind. The very gentle drizzle that was dampening the air when we left the house was starting to get a little more solid now but as Steve said we've planned to have a picnic and a little rain is not going to stop us.

He hired a rowing boat and we headed for the island in the middle of the small artificial lake. It reminded me of the time we went to see Eric Clapton's band, Blind Faith in Hyde Park before any of that Paris stuff happened. We hired a boat then and listened to the music drifting

I didn't know why he said that. He was acting so out of character, he was behaving as though we had just had a row, I couldn't remember fighting but he was clearly upset with me. It was ghastly of him to repay my excited expectation with that scornful frown. I so wanted to talk to him about my experience I had had yesterday if only to find out if he could shed any light on where I was. Had we been to some awful party and I took something I shouldn't have done? Had I done something really bad? Had we had a massive argument? Why I was upset and wandering around the streets lost in the rain? I wish I knew what had happened because it felt like I had wandered into a play half way through without a script and without knowing what scenes had just been played out.

Steve was treating me like he hated me; no, that wasn't it. He was treating me as though I hated him. If I kept smiling at him; he would know everything was alright I told myself. I went towards him to give him a hug but he pushed me away like a stray cat. I wish I could remember what I had done to annoy him. It can't have been that serious because he was still washing up the frying pan I had just used.

I was regretting drinking all that vodka more than ever now, I needed a clear head. I wanted to know what I had done, where that place was and why I didn't have a coat on. I suspected that whatever part of town that was, there was a wild party still going on with one less gypsy.

Steve wasn't working that day. Much to his annoyance it was another official strike day. When he told me this, I suggested that we'd go out for lunch on this enforced day off. I hoped we could talk then. The idea seemed to cheer him up a bit, he had an idea of where we could go. I asked where we were going. He was deliberately ignoring me. Today of all days I needed to

In the morning I woke up early and went outside to sit on the little wall in the back garden. The sun was hot and it was scorching my face, it felt nice. I didn't usually drink at that time of the day but I felt I needed something after yesterday. I poured myself a glass of vodka and drank it down in one. It tasted like fire-water but it certainly woke me up. Here in the daylight, in the bright sunshine of this normal morning I could make my nightmare that was yesterday to be just that; a nightmare.

I wanted Steve to wake up so that I could tell him all about my weird experience but he seemed to just like lying in bed. The doctors had said he needed his sleep these days but I was desperate to speak to him. I suddenly realized that maybe I shouldn't tell him. How he would take the news that I was having hallucinations about Jean-Marie, that boy who nearly broke us up? I had another drink of vodka to help me think and instantly regretted it: why was I drinking this horrible stuff?

All that alcohol certainly didn't make the functioning of my mind any more efficient, all it seemed to do was to make me exceptionally hungry. I poured the rest of the glass down the sink and decided to make myself a fried egg sandwich. I don't think I'd had one of these before; it was rather 'transport café' but it was delicious. I made a phenomenal mess in the kitchen but was too tired to clear up myself that morning and anyway, we had to leave something for Doris to do. After all, that's why we paid her. But then Steve came down and started moaning to himself about the mess in the kitchen but nevertheless cleared it all up himself. I was just so happy to see him all I could do was smile at him.

'What are you grinning at me like that for?' he asked.

'Because, you dear thing, I love you.' I replied without a moment's hesitation.

'For God's sake.' he huffed.

I wondered what could have made me think about him now. I don't think I've thought about him for years. There was that letter he wrote to me a few months ago but I didn't even open that. I recognized his handwriting so it went straight into the bin along with the rest of those memories. It was strange thinking about him again: for a few seconds it was like he had never been out of my thoughts. Considering how completely obsessed I used to be with Jean-Marie, it was extraordinary that I couldn't even remember what he looked like anymore. I tried to remember him again but I simply couldn't see him. Considering I'd just nearly scared myself to death a few minutes earlier with a vivid image of him smiling at me as he plunged to his death it made no sense that I couldn't remember what he looked like.

All I wanted now was to get home. I wanted to be back in my own house snuggled up safely in my own bed. I started walking, I didn't know where I was heading but I thought that eventually I would recognise something.

It took a long time to get home but when I saw my house even with all the lights switched off it was the most heart-warming sight ever. Steve had already gone up for the night when I finally closed the door behind me with a satisfying thud. I loved the warm and welcoming scent our house had; tonight there was a hint of peppermint too. It felt so good to be back, I had no idea how long I had been gone for. I felt like kissing the furniture.

Quietly I tip-toed upstairs and took off that silly dress and slid into our bed. He didn't wake up when I climbed in, sleeping he pulled the blanket over himself. I wanted to snuggle up with him, I wanted to tell him all about what had happened. I wanted to tell him how glad I was to see him. He didn't seem to want to wake up. I was sure he noticed me but was pretending to be asleep. It had only been a couple of years since his breakdown; he was still a little fragile so it was best not to disturb him.

calmed me down a little but I was still too scared to walk on. I wasn't even sure where I had been walking to so I resolved to stay there a few minutes longer.

I looked at the church in utter disbelief of what I thought had just happened. It was a hideously ugly building, how on earth I could have imagined that this was Notre Dame? It couldn't less like that beautiful cathedral if it had tried. I had never seen it before, I didn't recognise it at all and I realized that I had no idea whatsoever where I was, other than definitely not in Paris.

I just wanted to go home, I was scared and I was cold and I was lost. Also, I had no idea why I was wearing a skimpy thin gypsy dress in this rain; no wonder I was so cold. The insane nightmare about the hunchback of Notre Dame was freaking me out. It took all my composure just to keep standing still and not be screaming and pulling at my hair. I knew all about Syd Barret of Pink Floyd who lost his mind because he took too many drugs so I prayed to God that I wasn't losing my mind as well. I really did, I looked to the church and prayed to God. I hoped he wouldn't notice the joint - I was holding behind my back when I was speaking to him.

My mind had played tricks on me before but never quite to this extent. They had never involved me before. I usually just imagined weird things or had premonitions about other people. This was so vivid, so horrifyingly real.

He looked at me directly in the eyes. Somehow, he was telling me that he knew he had to die. He was staring at me and smiling, really smiling. He looked relieved. He wasn't just stoned; he didn't believe that he was really Quasimodo, he knew exactly what he was doing; killing himself, sacrificing himself. He was looking at me, the girl who loved him, the girl who tricked him into jumping but he was smiling.

...Part Four

CHAPTER TWENTY-TWO

I thought I was going to faint. Everything was hazy, everything was swirling around and I was dizzy. Suddenly it was growing darker but I was determined that I was not going to let myself pass out. I tried to stand up straight. I tried to figure out where I was. Had I just watched someone leap to their death from Notre Dame Cathedral? Had I just shouted up to him and told him to jump? Had I just caused *his* death? He was there, right in front of me but there was nothing there now. I couldn't have imagined it, it seemed too realistic, the colour was too vivid and the blood was too red.

It was simply too ridiculous but for a moment, for just a fraction of a split second I imagined I saw him looking back at me, questioning me from the blood-stained flagstones. It could not have been him, not my beautiful foreign student, why would it be?

Maybe I did pass out for a second or two but then I felt something burning my fingers. I hadn't even realized that I was smoking; I threw it to the floor. That proved at least that I wasn't dreaming. Finding another made-up joint in my bag was a relief: I needed that. I leant against the shiny black railings that meandered around the courtyard of this church and lit it. I didn't care that I was smoking pot in front of a church, Jesus would not mind on this occasion. It

‘Quasimodo!’ she shouted back gesturing like Lesley Ann Down in the film. ‘Help me my love. Only you can save my life. Swoop down and save me.’

The hunchback could not let the evil Frollo kill his beloved gypsy dancer so he climbed onto the ledge and shouted down to her.

'Esmerelda!'

'Save me my darling! Swoop down on the rope like you do in the film and rescue me.'

He grasped the rope which was not there and leapt from the top of the high tower to save her life.

End of Part Three…

She was saying goodbye to something for the last time. She did not know what, but something was coming to an end. There was both something beautiful but also something false that she had to finish. It had to be ended it properly this time.

As the moon and the lights along the river reflected on the silvery Seine she was saying goodbye to her magical world. It was the time to go; now before the perfection started to tarnish. She had made up my mind and it had to be done. It was the most important decision of her life and nothing could stop her. If she did not leave now she would be trapped there forever. Her life and her future depended on it.

For a few moments longer she stood there, trying to permanently etch this fabulous view in to her mind. She never wanted to forget this place, it had been her home and her life. Paris has been the place of her dreams for years and now she was giving it all up. From her bag she took a joint but hesitated before lighting it; was it right to smoke pot on top of a cathedral? She put it back and watched the waters of the Seine become blurred as they mixed with the tears in her eyes.

Night had fallen, the man she loved was beside her again. After his second tab of LSD she could tell by the expression on his face that he was really tripping. She wasn't sure whether he noticed but she gave him the gentlest kiss on his cheek. He carried on staring out at a city that was hundreds of miles away from where she was. She slipped off the little wall and dashed unnoticed down the stairs and back through the church. Then she was outside on the flagstones in front of the great church. Above her she could see him still, he had not moved.

'Quasimodo!' she shouted up.

He snapped out of his dreamy state and shouted back in character, 'Esmeralda!'

the little wall that went around the balcony and dangled her legs over the edge. The realization that there was nothing between her feet and a very large drop stopped her fit of giggles. Nick climbed up and joined her. They put their arms around each other and felt safe. As the sun began to set over the mountains Nick took out the remaining tab of LSD; he offered to Giuliana but she said he could have it so he did. She just smoked another joint and watched the ash she flicked fall ever so slowly all the way down to the ground.

They sat there together as the sky changed from blue to red with their arms around each other like lovers should. They didn't speak, they didn't need to, this was so precious, nothing needed saying.

Then as the stars began to fill the clear summer sky above them, something happened to Giuliana. She was at the top of Notre Dame. The stone tiles under her feet felt strangely soft but she was not hallucinating, she wasn't the one who had taken the acid but she knew she was there. She wasn't Esmeralda, she was still herself but she was there looking down on Paris. To the left of her was a stone gargoyle. She wondered if she was able to touch it; she was and it felt cold. Everything felt cold, it was not summer anymore. There were signs that it had been snowing. Traffic was starting to build up on the Pont Neuf as commuters began their journeys home. The last of today's Bateaux-Mouches were giving their tourists one final view of the Isle de France before night fell.

She was in Paris - of course she was, where else would she be? For a fraction of a moment she wondered why she had been thinking that it was odd to be there. She needed to think, she needed to be sure that what she was going to do was the right thing. She had been in Paris for months. She had experienced the most amazing time of her life, she had been happier than she could ever have dreamt of.

‘We’ve got another tab – do you want to try it?’

Giuliana smiled, ‘Not in the mood just yet Pussycat – why don’t you have it?’

He didn’t register her reply. In his mind he was looking at the great cathedral of Notre Dame and Giuliana in her Gypsy dress was Esmeralda.

Nick wanted to go inside so they sneaked past the workmen who were having a smoke outside in the sunshine. It was beautiful and sunny outside and daylight was percolating through the stained and dirty windows making the air inside foggy. Their footsteps echoed on the cold stone floor as they tiptoed out of sight from the workmen. Normally the stairs to the bell tower would be off limits to the public but there was nothing to stop them now. They dashed up the well-worn steps to the top: Esmeralda pursued by Quasimodo.

The winding staircase ended with a tiny doorway leading to a tiny walled balcony in front of the clock-face. They shielded their eyes as they emerged back into the blinding sunlight. It was windy up there, Giuliana's hair was blowing everywhere – it made her laugh like a little girl. He hugged her and she kissed him.

From their vantage point on the tower they looked out over their city with the Pennines in the distance. 'This church is called St Judas - it's unusual to find a church called that.' she said having misread the sign outside which actually said, St Jude's.

'Judas?' quizzed Nick, 'Yes, that's an odd name for a church.'

'Yes, but it shouldn't be.' she explained. 'Julia said that Judas was part of God’s plan. God chose him, someone weak and pathetic to sacrifice Jesus so the guy could be re-born.’

‘The guy!’ Nick laughed, ‘You can’t call Jesus “the guy”!’

Giuliana started laughing so much that she could hardly stand. She tried to compose herself but every time she looked at Nick’s face she burst out laughing again. She climbed onto

The LSD was playing with his mind which had moved on from just being to giving him a sense of awareness of something else around him. It seemed to be Julia who was now speaking to him. She was telling him he wasn't real, that he was her French lover from years ago, that if he left Giuliana's life, Giuliana would become Julia but Julia in the past. He knew that Julia wasn't really there but he no longer argued. Whether she was there or not, the LSD made her story seem perfectly logical. She genuinely cared about his beautiful Giuliana as much as he did and he needed to make everything perfect for his perfect girlfriend.

Giuliana watched Nick sit quietly by the water with his eyes sparkling. They were flitting rapidly from one thing to another. His head was flicking cat trying to catch a fly but his eyes always ended up smiling at her. He described the monkey faced goldfish leaping like salmon up the stream in front of them.

Although refraining from taking LSD, Giuliana had smoked a joint so was feeling mellow. She leaned over to Nick and kissed him. 'I love you, I always will.'

Eventually they had to make their way back home. They walked arm in arm through town saying that they would have to do this again next weekend. As high as they were, somehow they both knew that would never happen. Every so often they had to stop for a kiss, it didn't matter where they were or who was watching - when they needed to kiss they simply had to kiss.

Workmen from the City Council were loading tools and scaffolding back into a couple of scruffy vans. They had been doing some work to a rather unspectacular but large church. These vans were parked across the sidewalk so Nick and Giuliana had to walk in to the road to get past. Standing in the middle of the road Nick stopped and said it looked like Notre Dame.

'It looks more like a fire station.' Giuliana replied. 'Why does such a beautiful country have such ugly churches? Notre Dame – wow, that must be some powerful acid you've got.'

'Keith would be proud of you.' Giuliana said as she wolfed down her second. They tasted absolutely delicious. Neither of them thought that they had eaten for days. They hadn't eaten at the barbecue and they couldn't remember yesterday; they did not want to think too much about recent past. Today they were going to be happy, today was a new start; they both knew that.

It was another lovely summer's day and Nick had a suggestion. 'What about a picnic in the park?'

Giuliana liked that idea, she had images of cucumber sandwiches, red and white checked table cloths on the banks of the river Cam as 1920s students punted past wearing straw hats, drinking champagne. She wanted to dress up that day, it was a special day so she put her pretty gypsy dress on.

'You look fantastic,' Nick said, 'You look like Esmeralda.'

'You look like Quasimodo.'

When they got to the park, they unpacked their two Sainsbury's carrier bags which were masquerading as picnic hampers. They sat and kissed under an acorn tree, they fed the ducks with their left over crusts and smoked a couple of joints by the side of a pretty stream.

Nick had a couple of tabs of acid with him, after they had packed their rubbish back into one of the carrier bags he took one. It made things brighter and more colourful. Grass wasn't just green, it was really green, almost as if it had just been painted. Nick felt like he was in a dream but one where he still knew he was dreaming. Those thoughts that his brain had tried to repress and memories he thought he had smothered were freed. He looked at the beautiful stream beside him and listened to it rippling past. It still looked the same and sounded the same but it was as though there was something more, something beneath, beyond and before what he was seeing. The LSD made him wonder whether if he looked harder he might be able to see it.

Everything made sense to both of them when they woke up the following morning, they still felt cut off from the real world but they also felt free. They had been trapped in some distorted mirror image and now they had escaped. Despite the state Giuliana in particular was in last night, they both woke up fresh. Giuliana saw a half empty bottle of vodka at the bottom of her bed. The thought of drinking at this time in the morning repulsed her now. Today she no longer wanted to be that girl. Nick had already gone downstairs make some coffee. She lay on the bed smiling listening to the unfamiliar sound of him clearing up. From somewhere she could also hear YES but could not identify where it was coming from. She knew now that she and Nick had been living in a pretend world, a fragile perfect world that was about to shatter. They were both moths about to be consumed in the invisible flame of another's consciousness. The flame was blinding them, they could feel it burning them but neither could see it.

That morning Nick had woken before Giuliana and finding the video of' *The Hunchback of Notre Dame*' still in the machine, he switched it on. It was the version starring their pin-up, Lesley-Ann Down as Esmeralda. Giuliana had been forced to watch this so many times that she almost knew it off by heart. Hearing Nick's involuntary dreadful Quasimodo impressions coming from downstairs she could tell what stage the film was at.

Both Nick and Dylan both openly admitted that they thought this was a truly dreadful version but their adoration of Lesley Ann Down bore no bounds. Not wanting to have to endure this again she had a long refreshing bath then went down to see Nick after the film had ended.

'Giulia,' he asked, 'how about a fried egg sandwich?'

'Si, sono molto affamati.'

'The spirit of Keith lives on.' he said and he skipped into the kitchen hoping to find some eggs that were less than a month old.

CHAPTER TWENTY-ONE

September 1985

Neither of them needed to say anything. They did not need tell each other because they both knew. Neither of them understood why they knew, they just knew. When they spoke about the Julia that had just visited them, they talked about her as though she was someone who no longer existed. Julia, the real and permanent vibrant and incredible Julia was someone else. That almost dishevelled and demoralized woman had gone, they knew that their real Julia was somehow re-born. They knew that it was because of them but again, they could not explain it.

Today Giuliana was really happy. She was happy for Julia although she could not describe why. She was happy for Nick whom she realized she loved more than ever before. She was happy for herself because she had reached the Heart of the Sunrise. Today however was also the saddest day of her life.

Repressed memories and emotions broke through the crumbling mental barriers flooding through her mind. Liverpool, Julia, wandering lost in the city, loneliness, weeks of debauchery and sense of total emptiness. Giuliana could see herself listening to someone like Julia telling her how their lives were interlinked and how she had to leave Nick. Those hallucinations were so intense that she knew they had to be real.

She gave him a playful dig and he kissed her again. She wanted so much to love him, to be content with him. Something was telling her that she would, this life wasn't boring, this wasn't dull, this was what she wanted. Like her suitcase, the lure of Paris had been kicked under the table for now. Like the mad relative locked away in a forgotten room of her memory, Jean-Marie was still that secret stupid dream she knew was pointless and destructive but was difficult to wake up from. Now however she could feel herself waking up. She began to think that she finally knew who was controlling her life, writing her script and pulling her strings and it scared her: it was herself.

garden path. She didn't hesitate anymore; she opened her front door and heard that The Beatles' *White Album* was on the record player.

Steve was standing up listening to '*Julia*', he knew the words to this song backwards but he was reading them off the lyric sheet as the song played. The last time she had heard this song was in Paris, the day she had been to Versailles. Jean-Marie had put in on when he heard her coming up the stairs. Steve wasn't playing this song for her; he was playing it for himself. That was what was different about those two men. She was surprised he was at home today but even his Japanese electronics company had to close on the days the government said so in order to conserve the country's power.

Steve hadn't noticed Julia come in. He thought she was still in bed upstairs, he hadn't noticed her go out. As John Lennon finished the last verse Julia walked up behind him and hugged him. Without speaking she leant over, picked the needle up before it went to the run-off and put it back to the track that preceded '*Julia.*' They both loved this song and Paul McCartney's lyric seemed to have been written for them. He was singing just about them, he knew how they felt about each other more than even they had themselves. They looked into each others' eyes and mouthed the words of the song.

She was content with life and found it hard to believe that only an hour beforehand she had fished her small suitcase out from big cupboard, filled it with some clothes and had set off to the station to catch the boat train for Paris. Steve smiled at her. For the first time in years Julia was where she wanted to be. She surreptitiously kicked the suitcase under a table.

'At least you're not playing Pink Floyd's *Julia Dream* to remind you of me'

'I don't need reminding of you – you know I'm always thinking of you.'

care anymore? Why didn't people have jobs? How had the Tories got back in? Why did the miners need to strike? What had happened? Where has everyone gone?

Everything was supposed to get better, everything was supposed to change. Things did start to change or at least she thought they did. Was she so completely and utterly wrong? The flower of the sixties dream bloomed but then rotted on the branch leaving behind a world just as bad as the one before.

'One bloody loaf per customer! They never had any bread anyway' she screamed inwardly. A couple of young women went up to the supermarket door to go in but found it locked. Great, her local Fine Fair had run out of food again. The women were grumbling about the bloody miners bringing the country to its knees, bloody food shortages, about the bloody three-day week, about the bloody power-cuts.

Why are we getting used to this now Julia asked herself. Why aren't we shouting and protesting anymore? Julia felt like shouting at them: don't just moan about it – do something. …and another thing you dozy fuckers, you're as thick as shit if you don't realize it's Ted fucking Heath who is causing all these problems not the miners! People like this annoyed her. The women turned around to look at her and in a moment of supreme embarrassment Julia realized why they were staring at her. She had felt like shouting at them, she felt like swearing at them but she hadn't actually intended to say it out loud. She realized that she actually had shouted at them. 'Sorry,' she said very quietly but then burst out laughing, she could hardly stop. She had almost forgotten what her own laugh sounded like.

She was still smiling about the incident at the supermarket when she reached her house. She looked down the garden path and paused. She didn't quite know why she was standing there. She had intended to be very far away by now not cautiously tip-toeing back down her own

stuck to the brickwork: 'Benefit tonight in aid of the striking miners.' She thought that deep down, she should be one of those people actually doing the fly-posting but now she couldn't even be bothered to finish reading it. Once upon a time she thought there was a time when she could be bothered to be bothered.

Julia walked on into Thatcher's brave new economic world. She walked past the houses still full of mums and dads who were always at home now because they had no work to go to. She walked past the pubs where former steel workers, car makers, miners and dockers sat nursing their one pint that was now all they could afford. She walked past the queues of the hopeless outside the ironically entitled building called the job centre. Why didn't she care anymore? This was not how she should be but this was the way she was.

The street spread itself out to the horizon, but it had no sense of urgency about it. It led her along its dirty grey tarmac and cracked paving flags which she could feel beneath her feet. She kept walking, walking away from the house, away from her life. She kept walking until her feet started to hurt but she was willing herself to keep walking. She was not walking because the street was making her, it was her choice.

'Support for miners' families?' asked a woman who must have been at least eighty thrusting a collection bucket in front of Julia who dropped in ten pence. Julia wanted to feel sorry for her but couldn't. Why couldn't she care anymore, she used to be passionate about everything when she was younger but she had forgotten how that used to feel. She couldn't feel anything; she just kept walking until she came to a supermarket. There was the usual sign outside the Fine Fair: '*only one loaf of bread per customer.*' What a shit country this had turned out to be! What a shit life this was! All those dreams of a better world, all those ideals of moulding a new world based on peace and love, all the hope of the sixties. Why didn't anyone

became merged. Everything became part of itself. Giuliana's own future was now mapped out, it indistinguishable from Julia's future.

Giuliana could not let this happen. Julia was meant be someone wonderful and beautiful. She was Woodstock, she was stardust, she was golden. She should be wild, carefree, and reckless. She should still be the amazing girl that Giuliana had read about over and over again when she was a teenager. She should be a fantastic eccentric forty year old teenager. Julia deserved a fairy tale life. Her story had to have a happy ending and that is exactly what Giuliana had to ensure she was to get.

'What can I do to help you?' Giuliana asked.

'I think,' Julia said quietly, 'Since our lives are mirroring each other if you change your life now, it might change mine. Since that life of mine that you could affect has already happened, it would mean that if you changed your life today, mine would change fifteen years ago.'

'None of those horrible things that happened to you would have happened. I can give you a new life.' It all seemed so logical. 'I get rid of Nick and Jean-Marie will have gone from your life. Jean-Marie would not have gone to London, your husband will still be alive.'

Julia and Giuliana hugged each other. They both knew something but were not too sure what it was. Ignoring Nick, Julia then walked out of the door. Nick threw his cigarette onto the floor and grinding it into the carpet stared out of the window with Giuliana watching Julia shuffle down the path. Giuliana thought she could detect a slight smile on the woman's face; a smile that told her that Julia knew she was going to fix things.

Julia walked unsteadily into the street. Her emotions were shattered. She took a deep breath of air as she gripped the wall for support. Standing back, she noticed there was a poster

'You're not in love with Giulia, she isn't real anyway; she is me. That's all she is, just a reflection of me. She's even got my name for Christ's sake. Don't you think that's more than a coincidence?'

Despite the absurdity of Julia's story, Nick was now far from amused: 'I want you to go. Go back to Liverpool or London or wherever you bloody come from. Just go.'

'Come on Nick, think about it. Why would a beautiful Italian model, a TV star fall in love with a bloody history student at Sheffield University? No disrespect to history students but ask yourself: why would someone like Giuliana, a film star, a pin up abandon her career, move from Rome and move in with you in student digs in Sheffield? It just wouldn't happen would it? Think about it, none of this is real, is it.'

'Look,' he said firmly, 'just stop this please. Just fucking stop it!'

Julia looked lost for words. Giuliana answered the question for her. 'I need to fix things. It's why I'm here. It explains everything.'

Giuliana said those words but she didn't know what they meant. She knew that Nick wouldn't know either; she was very scared. She was here in England, living in this student house for a reason. She didn't understand yet but she knew it was something she would have no choice about. It was not going to be easy, it was not going to be comfortable but it was vital.

Somehow the corrosive power of that relationship Julia and Jean-Marie which finished all those years ago was still alive. It had been preserved like a parasitic insect in amber waiting to burst back into life. Giuliana had become infected, she was a carrier. She had fed and it became even more potent. As it grew it consumed more and more of her life. It was consuming her present, it was consuming her future, it was even consuming Julia's past. Everything it devoured

‘That cannot happen. This cannot happen!’ Giuliana cried to reassure her.

‘You don’t understand.’ Julia said. ‘It has already happened, my life is ruined but for you it’s not too late. Don’t let this happen to you.’

‘Giulia, what the bloody hell are you both talking about?’ asked Nick puffing impatiently on a cigarette. She ignored him and carried on looking into Julia’s eyes for answers.

‘Please Giuliana,’ Julia implored, ‘leave Nick.’

Giuliana looked at Nick’s ashen face. He was speechless, he looked like he was about to scream at the woman but his innate politeness stopped him. What had they been talking about?

He stood in front of her, face to face: ‘Excuse me, why are you telling her that?’

‘Because I know who you really are.’ she said. ‘You are Jean-Marie. I knew I recognized you from the moment I met you. I always thought you looked familiar.’

‘OK, so according to you I’m some crazy French hippie and according to you,’ he said, glancing briefly to Giuliana, ‘You’re not Julia and I’m supposed to be having an affair or something with you! Do you two realize how insane you both sound?’ Nick felt like screaming when she then tried to explain to him that she herself was in fact Giuliana but another version like some sort of Hindu avatar.

She carried on, ‘Have you ever felt you weren’t in control of your life Nick? You ever feel like things just happen and you’re a passenger, unable to do anything about it? I know why. You’re not real, you’re my Jean-Marie. Giulia is me. You’re just a ghost from my past. I bet you didn’t even exist before I met you? Can you remember anything that happened to you before last year? Answer me! Prove to me that you’ve had a life before then! You can’t can you.’

He didn’t even think it deserved thinking about: he was a ghost! This woman needs help. The only response Nick could muster was to laugh at how absurd this was but she carried on.

'Yes, it was too good to be true.' Julia echoed.

She could hear her! She knew she was there! She had answered. Julia did not need to say anything else. Giuliana knew precisely who this was. She was Julia, the only Julia. She was the Julia who allowed her life to be wrecked by obsession. This was the real Julia, this was the Julia that she had made.

The woman now looked at Nick and spoke. 'Maybe it was love to start with but love with such a burning passion can never last. The explosive passion of love should evolve, it needs to change; it doesn't die out, it becomes something different, something deeper, something stronger. Love has to grow. Remember when you first met her? Do you remember how you felt?'

Nick did not reply but Giuliana answered for him: 'Exactly the same way as I do now.'

'Exactly the same as it will always be; at least that's what you'll believe. People are made from failure and sadness as well as success and happiness you know.'

Giuliana wanted to rush in and shout 'I know you're talking to me. Please tell me what to do!' but she was scared. Things like this didn't happen to her, things like this didn't happen to anyone. She quietly walked into the living room.

'I couldn't let go of Jean-Marie, even when there wasn't anything left of him. All that there was in the end was what I had made myself. He wasn't even Jean-Marie anymore, he was almost just a blank page I was projecting a memory on to, a memory frozen in time.'

Nick was getting angry, he didn't want to hear any of this.

'I used to feel like someone else was controlling me, like each day was a page in a book someone else had written. It was easy just to drift along with whatever happened but I lost Steve. Steve was murdered. I made this happen, I killed Steve.'

‘No I’m not talking about Dylan,’ she said looking straight at Nick. ‘It’s you. You think you and Giuliana love each other so much don’t you?’

Nick looked bemused.

She carried on talking: ‘Sometimes you can love being in love so much that you no longer love the person anymore. You can just be too in love with being in love. You do not love Giuliana.’

Nick felt he had to answer. It was one thing being nice to someone whose son had been injured and whose girlfriend screamed and swore at but what gave her the right to poke her nose in to his personal life? ‘Excuse me, do you mind not saying this please.’

‘You must know that you and Giuliana are not really in love?’

Nick was getting irritated with her now, she wasn’t listening to him, he felt she wasn’t even looking at him. ‘I’m sorry but why are you saying this? I know Dylan’s hurt and you’re not thinking straight but I’m sorry but you’re wrong. Totally wrong.’

Frozen like a statue, Giuliana stared through the crack. She didn’t care what was happening to Nick; that was nothing compared with what she was going through. She simply wanted him to be quiet. For the first time since meeting this woman, she wanted to hear what she had to say. Giuliana was transfixed, she needed know what she was thinking. She was desperate to shout, ‘What are you saying? Tell me!’ But she was too scared to move and the words were still born in her mouth. All she could hear was Nick being loud getting more angry and upset.

Dylan’s mother carried on speaking, looking directly into Nick’s eyes but Giuliana knew whom she was really looking at. ‘Paris wasn’t real was it? Paris was a fantasy.’

‘But it was wonderful,’ Giuliana whispered to herself, ‘it was too good to be true.’

she imagined she thought she was but couldn't. A few hours ago she felt that Julia should have been somebody else but now that seemed like the weirdest acid trip she had ever had. Of course that was Dylan's mother; that was the way she had always been.

She looked through the crack in the door and listened. Nick could tell that her son's accident, the long drive and then Giuliana's insane verbal abuse had all taken their toll on Julia. She always looked tired but today she looked as though she hadn't slept for weeks. Her long straight hair that was normally tied neatly into a pony tail was loose, her grey hair hanging like that made her look much older than she was. Maybe it was a nervous thing but she kept fidgeting and searching for something she never quite knew what in her voluminous old handbag. For some inexplicable reason, this really annoyed Nick.

Giuliana knew that they didn't know she was there but when Dylan's mother spoke to Nick, it was as if she was speaking to her instead.

'It shouldn't be like this.' Julia Fairfax began to sob instantly making Nick extraordinarily uncomfortable.

Nick tried his best to stop this unaccustomed show of emotion: 'It's alright. Dylan will be absolutely fine. Probably won't even see any scars. Doctors are so clever these days.'

'No,' she said. 'THIS! THIS shouldn't be like this.'

'I know, I know.' Nick said.

Lurking silently behind the door like a shadow herself, Giuliana knew that this stranger, this inexplicably distorted reflection of a friend she could no longer remember was actually talking to her.

Nick tried to smile at her. 'It will give Dylan something to impress the girls with: cars bounce off me like Superman!'

It was such a sad story. Dylan had clearly been wanting to confide in someone for a long time, she was glad to be there for him. Everything his mother had believed in she rejected. She didn't want to see any of her old friends and she didn't want to listen to any of the music she used to love. She hated and detested the old Julia and was determined to reinvent herself into something respectable. Being blessed with natural intelligence she had no problem in enrolling at University and gaining a doctorate in the history of art. She liked the security of life inside the closed thick walled academic world. She was safe and hidden from the real world. Not unlike escaping the mundane world of the sixties into the psychedelic hippy counter culture, escaping into the academia away from Thatcher's brutal image driven world was another hiding place. As unlikely as it seemed to her old friends who occasionally bumped into her, Julia became the archetypal dusty academic.

'That's how she got to present that TV show then?' Giuliana said.

'What! Are you having a laugh? My mother on TV. Where on earth did you hear that!'

Giuliana wondered why she even thought that.

Today she looked even more bedraggled than usual having been at the hospital with Dylan most of the night. She had wanted to see me and Nick, it was important to her. Nick was watching Dylan's video of 'The Hunchback of Notre Dame' which Dylan had left behind. This was not the famous 1939 version but a made for TV film which the boys preferred because Lesley-Anne Down was in it.

Still sitting on her bed, Giuliana could hear the film. She was scared to go downstairs, she thought the vodka was still affecting her. She smoked a very thin joint to calm her nerves then sneaked to the bottom of the stairs and looked through the slightly open door. She listened to them talking. The woman was obviously Dylan's mother. She tried hard to remember who

Giuliana had learned from talking with Dylan that his mother's life took its ruinous course about fifteen years ago. He told her that it all started when his mother had an affair with a French student. For a few months she lived with him in Paris. She had lived inside a fairy story. She had escaped to somewhere even better than reality. It was crazy because it was not a life that needed escaping from. Her life in London had been fantastic but Paris was magical. Then it ended, it ran its natural course and fizzled out but.

Dylan said his mother came back to England on a Christmas day. He said he and his brother couldn't have wished for a better present but it was not to last. Shortly afterwards, their lives were devastated.

'The French guy couldn't accept that she had left him for my dad. He wasn't right in the head and this tipped him over the edge. He found our house and killed me dad. That was the worst day in the world. To try and take her mind off everything she got more involved with a charity in Bangladesh. She took me and Bruce over there. Bruce caught some horrible disease over there and died in a couple of days. That was it for her. She gave up life, she gave up the charity and just vegetated but do you know why?'

Giuliana asked him to carry on.

'Because she was still obsessed with that maniac who killed my dad. After what that insane bastard did, she still loved him. She used to say how much she despised him and wished she could go back in time and never meet him but it was obvious that she still had feelings for him. She even started visiting him in jail. As long as he was alive, she told me once, she would still love him. That was it for me. I couldn't live with her any longer and I ended up moving in with my Gran/ I haven't really seen much of her since.'

CHAPTER TWENTY

September 1985

Voices downstairs woke Giuliana up, one of them being Dylan's mother. She certainly couldn't face going downstairs with now having made such an embarrassing spectacle of herself at the hospital. None of that made any sense to her. She had been looking forward so much to seeing Nick again and felt so contemptible for completely spoiling their reunion. She had made such a complete idiot of herself.

Giuliana didn't care too much what Dylan's mother thought of her, since she first met that woman she had never liked her. Dylan's mother was an incredible disappointment to her. Giuliana didn't just know all about her, she was one of her heroes but now having met her, every one of her illusions were shattered. Her idol did not just have feet of clay, the woman was as vibrant as mud. Being obsessed with the sixties, flower power and London, the image of Julia Fairfax, the wild child of the swinging sixties had taken on near god-like status in Giuliana's mind. She imagined she led the life Giuliana would have adored to have had; wearing flowers in her hair, listening to rock music and believing one hundred percent that that peace and love would change the world. When young she had been a real visionary but now she was just Dylan's mother, nothing else.

towards her. He was holding a towel to clear up the vomit on the floor. She could see that he was in the room talking to her but at the same time she could clearly see him downstairs with Julia. They were writhing and slithering over each other like slimy bloated snakes. She couldn't stop seeing these two images, she wanted this to be a dream, she wanted still to be asleep. She could not believe that what she saw last month really happened; she couldn't believe that she had completely obliterated this from her mind for the last month.

Nick was at the side of her. He was mopping up the sick next to her bed. He was saying something to her, he seemed angry but she wasn't listening. Eventually he went and her memories of today came back. Nick having sex with Julia no longer hurt as much as much as Julia having never existed. Then she remembered what she knew; Julia was in charge. There was nothing to worry about because her Julia was in charge. Now with a smile on her face, she fell asleep again.

It's my fault, she told herself. I've turned Julia into that woman. I'm going to turn myself into that woman. Julia's ramblings were her only explanation but even these could not explain what had happened. Why have I made that woman my own future? It's because I've stayed with Nick. I'm going to end up like that, end up a nobody, a pointless pathetic withering wallflower.

She somehow managed to convince herself that Julia, her Julia was doing this. Julia tried to warn her but she ignored her so Julia had to resort to shock tactics. Julia was so clever. Giuliana knew that if she just believed in Julia she could get her back and save herself. She just had to have total and complete faith in her friend and accept that nothing that appeared to be real today actually was.

She went home by herself. She looked at their new TV and remembered why they needed this new one. She opened a new bottle of vodka but collapsed on her bed before she could finish it. After a short while she realized that if she didn't get up straight away she was going to be sick in the bed. Her head however was throbbing and any movement whatsoever was definitely likely to induce vomiting. Giuliana decided to stay exactly where she was and subsequently threw up on the floor. She felt much too ill to clear that up so just faced the other way. Nick would clean this up. Even though it was her own fault she was in such a state, she knew Nick wouldn't mind. She hoped he would come and do it soon because the smell was making her nauseous again.

A terrifying sound of clanking chains woke her from her sleep. Ropes strained and groaned as they twisted around some hideous medieval contraption hidden in the darkness behind her bed. These invisible ropes were attached to her arms and shoulders and pulled her jerkily up from the pillow. Her eyes were stinging with what felt like smoke. This pain was the only reassurance she had that she was actually awake. Through this fog she saw Nick walking

woman who she loved was no longer Julia? Somebody was trying to make her think that Julia, the real Julia never existed. Shouldn't she be terrified that she was either going mad or a victim of some conspiracy that even her boyfriend was part of? She should be crying in utter desperation. She was completely alone in a foreign country with no family, no friends and could not even trust in her own memories.

She didn't care, it was just happening. She had to put her faith in the explanation that it was the alcohol or the drugs just playing with her mind. She had heard stories about how LSD can cause effects even years after it had been taken. This just had to be some really bad trip but it felt so real.

Nick watched her through the window smoking another cigarette. He could not be bothered chasing after her. He couldn't face her after what she had just said. He had never known her behave like that and use such language before; it was horrible to see. He wanted his old Giuliana back. He watched her light another cigarette and wondered what was going through her mind. She looked calmer, he thought about going to see her and putting his arms around her but was afraid that she might run from him again. It was better not to try, just in case.

The nicotine helped her concentrate. Thoughts were trying to flood her mind but she was damming them up behind a wall of disbelief; it was the only way she could stop herself screaming.

She allowed one thought through: Julia, her Julia. Clear and logical thoughts that made so more sense of what was happening today began to ransack her mind. What she used to say about them sharing the same life did not seem as crazy as this horrible parallel universe that Giuliana thought she must have entered. Julia had said that Giuliana would become her one day but now that Julia is now that other woman did this mean that she would now become her?

Nick raised his hand as if he was going to strike her but stopped himself before making contact. Dylan's mother broke free of Giuliana's grasp and cowered in the corner of the room. Despite his injuries, Dylan jumped up yelling and screaming at Giuliana. 'If you can't hit that stupid drunken bitch Nick, I bloody well can.' He lunged at her but his broken ribs forced him to re-think his actions and he collapsed back onto the bed shouting in pain. Nick looked shocked. He couldn't believe his girlfriend had said anything like that and using language like that. What was the matter with her? He was starting to hate the effects the drink was having on her. He ignored what she said; it wasn't her, it was the drink. He tried to talk rationally to her but she got worse. He could not stop her from screaming and shouting. Dylan and his mother simply looked on in disbelief. Whatever was going on in her mind, Nick felt unable to help.

She marched up to the reception desk and demanded the nurse tell her who 'that fucking woman' was. Then as calmly as she could, she tried to explain to the nurse that that woman was an imposter. She was pretending to be Dylan's mother. Whilst pressing the emergency security call button under the desk, the nurse stoically explained that the lady was called Julia Fairfax, the mother of the young man who got hit by a car last night.

Giuliana was subsequently escorted outside by a couple of security guards. By the time she was in the car park she had stopped screaming. Nick tried to follow her to see how she was but when she saw him she hid behind a car. He didn't try too hard to find her, after a cursory glance around he went back inside. After Giuliana's verbal assault on Dylan's mother, he needed to check that she was o.k.

Giuliana felt calmer, she had no reason to be but she had stopped panicking. That she wasn't panicking then began to worry her. Shouldn't she still be running around the hospital screaming? Shouldn't she be at least concerned that the woman she had known for months, the

No, because Nick wouldn't be in on it too. Nobody would be playing a trick on me now: not at a time like this. Maybe someone's hypnotised me? No that's ridiculous so is this woman pretending to be Julia and why does Nick believe her?

'Affanculo!' she yelled. 'Cazzo di droga.' and stormed outside. The hospital looked the same as it did when she arrived earlier. She must still be drunk, it was the only explanation. She smoked a cigarette; she had never smoked so zealously in her life before. She was willing that when she went back the real Julia would be there. Her wonderful, beautiful Julia but no, not the Julia she saw last month thrashing around on the floor with Nick. Maybe she was seeing things to try to blank out the truth? night. She didn't know what she wanted. In her mind she was forcing the real Julia to be there but when she returned to the ward she wasn't. That same dowdy middle-aged woman was still sitting next to her boyfriend and was now comforting Dylan who was calling her Mum.

'Nick,' she said taking him to one side. 'That is not Dylan's mother. You must know that. Dylan must know that. She just isn't his mother. You know Dylan's mother, we both know her mother and that's not her. For fuck's sake Nick, what the fuck is going on?'

'What the hell are you talking about? And keep your voice down and stop swearing.'

'Ci sono cose nella vita si riolvono solo con un vaffanculo! Porco dio, don't tell me what to do. I think I know who my friends are! Julia's my friend, she's lovely, bubbly and glamorous; Jesus Christ, you fucked her a few weeks ago!'

Dylan's mother turned around, more than shocked.

Giuliana grabbed her hair and thrust her face right in front of Nick's. 'Would you fuck this? Really Nick, would you fuck this?'

Giuliana did not answer: who was this woman? What was going on?

'Oh, I'm sorry, I am nosy; I'm being a teacher again, sorry.'

That proved it, she said to herself: Julia Fairfax isn't a bloody teacher, she's an art critic. Maybe this is his step-mother. Yes, maybe his father remarried. This must be his step-mother. That did not explain why the woman thought she knew her. Still trying to think of an explanation she kept silent. It must be the drink: I must still be drunk. She looked at Nick, she needed him now.

'Who the hell is that woman?'

'What do you mean?' he said, questioning her grasp of English.

'That is not Dylan's mother. Julia is Dylan's mother'

'What do you mean? Of course that's Dylan's mother. That's Julia, you've met her before.

Of course she had met her before, Julia was her friend. She knew her better than she knew Nick. She wanted her here now. She looked at the woman, this was ridiculous. Of course she wasn't Dylan's mother. She did look a bit like her around the eyes, there was some similarity but without any of that mischievous sparkle. The shape of the face was the same but without the grace. She just wasn't Julia but she could have been related; an older sister maybe. She made him clarify again who she was. Julia Fairfax, Dylan's mother, the woman she had met before.

Nick gave her the coffee and was talking to her about Dylan. He was talking to her about her son, Dylan. Giuliana knew she wasn't drunk, she wasn't tripping, she wasn't mad and she knew that wasn't Julia. It had to be some sort of trick; it was like when they changed Miss Ellie in Dallas: everyone acted as though she had always been Miss Ellie but that was just a TV programme. This was actually happening - things like this just don't happen. It had to be a trick.

It wasn't working; Nick was still chatting with that old woman but Giuliana wanted whoever she was just to go so she could speak to Nick alone. After all these drunken, drugged up weeks, after living in this fantasy, she now needed to talk to him about that night. She wanted to hear him tell her she was imagining it.

Nick said he was going to get the woman a cup of coffee and told Giuliana to keep Dylan's mother company whilst he was gone.

Giuliana's heart missed a beat. Hearing her name on his lips made her insides churn: how could he so calmly just say that? How could he stand there looking like nothing had happened? How could Julia ....she could not even continue that train of thought. It was absolutely impossible for her mind to even consider that Julia, her Julia could have betrayed her. She could not have done that; not with Nick, not with her boyfriend. Her head was hurting: no, it couldn't have happened. She needed to stop thinking, she needed to answer Nick.

'Is she here?' she asked timidly.

Nick looked bemused: 'who?'

'Dylan's mother.'

'You're talking to her.' Nick said thinking that perhaps this was not the best time for Giuliana to be fooling about.

Giuliana did not reply. She didn't even wonder why he had said that. This obviously was not Dylan's mother. This wasn't Julia. She wasn't interested in why Nick was joking with her now, was he trying to lighten the mood? Was he trying to ignore what happened last month? Did Nick know how she felt about Julia? Was he saying this was Julia just to be cruel? She didn't know what to say, she waited for this woman to speak.

'I hear you've been doing some acting again? Is it one of the classics?'

dullest cardigan in the whole shop and held it up to Nick to see if he approved. He nodded that it was fine but she still wasn't sure; she would have a think about it.

Giuliana was walking past and when the woman saw her she put her hands out gesturing her to come close so she did. The woman put her arms around her and gave her a big hug. Giuliana had no idea who she was but the woman seemed to know her. 'Have you seen Dylan?' she asked.

'Yes. He's doing fine.' Giuliana answered cautiously.

'He might be out tomorrow but he looks in so much pain. I always used to tell him to be careful crossing the road.' Her voice sounded familiar but she didn't know who she reminded her of. She thought she was probably someone she met on the Royal Iris, a friend of Julia maybe.

Giuliana was fully awake and the effects of the alcohol had worn off. This was the first time she had been sober for a long time. Out of the safety cage of the house something was making her think about the night Nick attacked her, she was thinking that that didn't really happen, she was thinking that Nick had sex with Julia. Inside the unreal atmosphere of the hospital, she was finding it increasingly difficult to detach herself from what happened that night. Did that really happen? It did happen. She watched him and Julia do that in front of her. She ran away from him but he found her and she went back with him. Why? It was impossible to believe. It had been easier to ignore it but now, it seemed like she had just woken up from a dream and ended up in a nightmare.

Since they saw Dylan, Nick's manner had changed; now he seemed to be the one acting as though nothing had happened. She could not understand how he was living with himself but she still didn't want to say anything. If she ignored it she might be able to pretend it didn't happen.

had happened. Unplanned events made Nick and Giuliana uneasy. Until this had happened, they were safe, sheltered and secure living only in their own eyes. In such a world, there were no worries. They did not have to contribute to life, to put in any effort because other people had already written a script for every scenario beforehand. This was new, this was happening now. They were there on that bus as themselves and it scared them. Nick knew it was Julia. Julia, the author had changed everything, she had re-written his character but not finished the storyline.

He tried not to think about this, he tried to focus on how gorgeous Giuliana looked instead. She did look gorgeous but she looked like Julia. He wanted to smash her image out of his head. Even when he looked at his beautiful Giuliana, inevitably under-dressed for bus travel, he was thinking about Julia. He was so glad when they reached the hospital, seeing his best friend in pain was preferable to thinking about how he was betraying Giuliana.

Dylan was not as badly hurt as they had expected. His arm was in plaster but other than that he was fine. The doctors had sedated him making him sleepy so being visited, even by his friend and a beautiful Italian actress was not something he could manage. Both his visitors could see that he was in no fit state to receive visitors but neither of them wanted to leave him. They did not want to be alone with each other again. They had to be asked to leave by a nurse.

Leaving the ward, they both went in opposite directions down the corridor. At one of the little charity shops in the hospital foyer Nick recognised somebody and said hello to her. She looked up from her rummaging in the second-hand clothes bin and gave a cautious smile to Nick. Her unkempt tangle of long grey hair had clearly not been brushed that morning no doubt as a result of her rushing here to the hospital. She appeared to be in her late forties and looked remarkably at home searching through second hand clothes. She pulled out the plainest, greyest,

CHAPTER NINETEEN

September 1985

They both crawled out of their bed at what normal people would call lunch time. Giuliana found an unopened bottle of vodka so that was her breakfast sorted. She couldn't remember whether it was Rahul or Rizwan but one of Penny's doctor friends was knocking on their door. At first neither of them wanted to answer it but curiosity got the better of Nick and he went to see what he wanted. Rizwan looked extremely uncomfortable when he saw Giuliana walk into the room. She was still wearing the shirt which Penny gave her yesterday although now it was stained with vomit.

Rizwan had come over to tell them some news. 'He is not seriously hurt, well he is a bit but it's nothing bad but Dylan had been in an accident. Yesterday, just after you left the party, he decided it would be a good idea to go for a walk down the middle of the road. He then got hit by a car. He was unconscious but Penny and me and Rahul made sure he was alright. We got an ambulance and had him taken to The Royal Hallamshire. Penny who is working there, is with him now. Penny suggested that I called around and let you two know.'

Nick and Giuliana decided to go straight over there and visit him. 'Stupid sod,' Nick said exasperated. 'What sort of idiot get's themselves run over?'

They found some cleanish clothes and caught the bus to the hospital. It wasn't necessarily that they were worried about their old friend, it was because something unexpected

REWRITING HER STORY: Mark Bowman

was worth it simply to hold her. Nick didn't notice that something was troubling her. It didn't matter, she just looked sexy, that was all that mattered.

It was still early evening when they went to bed. Nick knew she was really tired, she was barely awake but he still managed to make love with her. A short while later she realized that if she didn't get up straight away she was going to be sick in the bed. She wondered if Nick had just had sex with her – she wasn't sure. Her head however was throbbing and any movement whatsoever was going to induce vomiting. Giuliana decided to stay exactly where she was and subsequently threw up. She felt much too ill to clear that up so just faced the other way and went to sleep. Nick would clean this up, he wouldn't mind – she was right.

A terrifying sound of clanking chains woke her from her sleep. Ropes strained and groaned as they twisted around some hideous medieval contraption hidden in the darkness behind her bed. These invisible ropes were attached to her arms and shoulders and pulled her jerkily up from the pillow. Her eyes were stinging with what felt like smoke. This pain was the only reassurance she had that she was actually awake. He face had been stuck to the pillow with last night's vomit and pulling away made her face smart. She watched something putrid and yellow drip slowly down a strand of hair that was hanging down in front of her burning eyes. It stopped halfway like a spider going down its web then it fell onto her legs.

There was a noise to the side of her. She looked onto the floor. Nick was there cleaning where she had had another accident last night. She didn't have the energy to speak and even if she could she doubted that she would be able to open her mouth. Her lips felt as if they were bonded together with cement.

He knelt up and smiled at her: 'you look lovely, you're so perfect.' he said then kissed her on her dry crusty lips then she fell asleep again.

turned to Nick to see what expression his face was conveying. Nick smiled at him so the young trainee doctor cautiously but excitedly put his arms around the half-naked Italian and kissed her back.

Both Penny and Dylan felt horribly embarrassed for Giuliana. Penny suggested several times to Nick that he should have a talk with her and get her to calm down. She didn't want her own friends to get the wrong impression of Giuliana. She didn't want them to think that her friend was some sort of slut, a drunk, someone who behaves like this. The sorry truth however was that this was exactly how Giuliana was, she had been this girl ever since she came back to Nick. She was his idealized girlfriend, she was his fantasy. Nick told Penny not to worry, Giuliana was just enjoying herself.

Penny could not take any more, genuinely upset, she told Nick that they had to go. Nick was stunned, he could not understand what was wrong. Giuliana could hardly walk as she went around everyone, still topless, giving them a goodbye hug. Rizwan decided that he was now in love.

Penny was more than relieved when they both finally left, she hated seeing someone she cared about being like that. It was even more distressing for her to see Nick behaving this way. Even after what he did to her a few weeks ago, she thought he was better than that but no, he was enjoying watching other people leering at is girlfriend and letting them grope her. It was not the Nick she knew, it was the Nick Dylan said he was.

To provide her with some modicum of dignity, Penny insisted on giving her friend a long shirt to wear on the way home although Nick thought looked better with just two of the buttons done up. It was still hot and virtually carrying her most of the way home exhausted Nick but it

light the barbecue. Dylan tossed a couple of cans of beer over to Nick and Giuliana when he noticed them arrive.

Penny had wanted to see Giuliana. She was very worried about her. It didn't make any sense to her that after Nick assaulted her, she was still living with him. Penny needed to get her on her won and talk some sense to her. When Penny saw the state Giuliana was in when she arrived, she knew that she wasn't going to be able to get through to her. Penny was disappointed with Giuliana, she thought she had more about her than just being some lout's sex object.

Although she knew she was not going to get anywhere with her, she tried to ask if she was happy.

'We're going to run a chain of trendy cafes.' was Giuliana's unexpected nonsensical response. Dylan was not interested in what she was saying. He was looking at Giuliana then trying not to look at Giuliana, then looking at Penny not looking at him looking at Giuliana. As though Giuliana had been at the party for hours and Rahul and Rizwan were friends she had known since childhood she was instantly singing and dancing to *Roxanne* with them. She drank the can Dylan gave her then drank some more and sang and danced some more. Penny's party, the free concert, the drink and drugs made this afternoon her Woodstock. It was her 1969; it was her time to be me.

When Annie Lennox came on the TV doing one of her mournful dirges, Giuliana decided it was time to get a tan. Nick watched from the other side of the garden in disbelief as she took off her bikini top in order to sunbathe topless. He was so in love. A few songs later he engaged in some meaningless talk with Rahul as he watched his girlfriend who had long since abandoned her bikini top get up and dance to U2. By himself, he sat on the step smoking and watching his girlfriend drunkenly stagger and fall on to a surprised Rizwan whom she tried to kiss. Rizwan

Nick tried very hard to listen to Giuliana enthuse about the blending of textures of the smooth yoghurt and the crispy biscuit but found it impossible. How could he listen to this when she looked like this?

It took about half an hour to walk to Penny's house, it was all uphill and it was uncomfortably hot but neither of them cared. Hand in hand they slithered along the sun washed street of Victorian terraces which grew hotter with each step. The heat made the gradient much steeper than usual but it was the best walk either of them had ever had.

Giuliana felt the tips of Nick's fingers stroking her bottom through her bikini pants, she liked that. 'I really think it could be successful – it would be the latest trend – we're going to be the inventors of a new craze.'

It wasn't because of the heat but Nick could feel his legs physically shaking, he thought he was about to collapse. Nick felt as though he was burning. He didn't know what he was feeling, he knew it was love but it was not the same love that he felt a year ago. His mouth was dry like the air which tasted dry, dry and saturated with nothingness.

'These yoghurt and shortbread cafes really could be the next big thing. He replied, still with his hand evidently super-glued to her pants.

'We need a good name.' She said wincing as she sensed him touching her. 'Yes, something to attract the yuppies.'

Nearing Penny's house, parked cars like scorched bones of animals abandoned in the desert radiated their own heat hazes distorting the air. They added to the dry white empty heat, they added to the nothingness.

Sting was on TV by the time they arrived doing some old Police songs. Penny, Rahul and Rizwan, Penny's housemates had moved the TV into the garden and were currently attempting to

thought it delicious. Unable to think of what to say, they both threw their arms around each other and kissed. They had only walked about ten metres from the house and now both of them desperately wanted to go back and make love again. After a while they composed themselves, Giuliana asked if they really had to go.

'We've said we'd go – shouldn't really let Penny down.' Nick begrudgingly said.

For Nick, watching her walk along Crookesmoor Road in just that bikini was almost as good as making love to her. Attracting disapproving looks from properly dressed people and lewd comments from a bunch of lads walking past on the other side was such a thrill. She could feel his hand trembling with excitement and could hear his breathing getting faster and faster, she relished the effect she was having on him.

After ten minutes of walking in silence Giuliana stopped and looked as though she thought of something very profound. 'I know what is brilliant idea!' she said, apparently to herself.

'What?' he asked.

'Me and you run a bar but not selling drinks. No selling yoghurt and... what do you call those thick Scottish biscuits?'

'Shortbread?'

'Yes, Shortbread. We run a bar selling yoghurt and shortbread.'

Nick caressed her bottom and asked her to explain.

'This morning I dipped some shortbread into a tub of yoghurt – my senses had an orgy it was very, very delicious – in fact, it was the best thing I have tasted ever.'

virtually lost their ability to socially interact. They liked their life of self imposed isolation because to them, that was what being in love meant.

Like every morning, Giuliana started that day with a vodka breakfast. To prepare herself for the party she finished off the bottle, Nick didn't notice these days. He thought it endearing how she giggled after she slurred her words or bumped into the furniture then cursed in Italian. As forecast, the 13th of July was a very hot day – this meant it was a sunbathing day for Giuliana, a bikini day. She chose a bright yellow one which she knew was Nick's favourite because it was the smallest one she had. It was quite possibly the smallest one anyone had.

Nick went downstairs to wait for her but she was already there fastening her shoes. She had a little bag over her shoulder but was wearing nothing other than the tiny yellow bikini; Nick expected that at least she would have a wrap-around skirt but no, she was going to walk up to Penny's house wearing nothing else but this ridiculously small bikini. He had to remind himself to start breathing again: Se was actually going to go out like this.

Nick thought that they probably had already made love that morning but the sight of her just about to go outside looking like that gave him no choice. Live Aid had probably started anyway so what did another ten minutes matter? Out of breath and grinning like Cheshire cats, they both lay together on the litter-strewn living room floor staring at the ceiling wondering how life had got so wonderful.

'O.K,' she said when she could speak again, 'let's go.'

She took Nick by the hand and pulled him up too then immediately dragged him out of the house as he was still pulling his shorts back up. Like most self-respecting Italians, sunglasses appeared from nowhere and she smiled into the hot summer sunshine letting it tingle on her face. Nick's eyes were permanently fixed on her bikini pants. She saw him looking and

had replaced the TV. Dylan did not really feel inclined to pass on Penny's invitation but thought he ought to do as she asked him.

'Do you and Giulia fancy coming over to ours tomorrow to watch this Live Aid thing? We're having a…'

He stopped and put his hand over his face. 'For God's sake mate, it's distracting you standing there like that – tie that bloody dressing gown together.'

Nick looked at himself and shrugged his shoulders. It was his house, he wasn't going to be told what to do.

Dylan continued, 'As I was saying we're having a barbecue. Penny's got a few of her doctor friends coming - they're the only students left in Sheffield now. Unless you come I won't have anyone stupid to talk down to.'

'I'll see what Giulia thinks.' He said without any emotion in his voice.

Dylan did not want to stay. The sight of his friend's private parts dangling in front of him was more than disturbing and the state of the house – his old house was really depressing.

'I need to get back now – Penny's run out of milk so she can't have her morning brew until I get back - so do you reckon you'll be able to make it?'

Nick said he would think about it. He was not sure, why would he want to share Giuliana with anyone else? Dylan was glad that Nick closed the door quickly after him; walking away from a house with a semi-naked man waving at him was not an experience he thought he would wish to share with the neighbours.

Giuliana thought it sounded a cool idea to see Dylan and Penny again. If she thought it was a good idea then so did Nick. When the actual day arrived neither of them were that enthused about it. They were not used to company now, in just a couple of weeks they had

Half an hour away but in a different world, Dylan and Penny had been discussing Nick and Giuliana. My son would have been content if he never saw Nick again but Penny persuaded him that he ought to go and see him. They had been so close and she believed friendship was important. Her boyfriend should not just abandon him because of a phase Nick was going through. Everybody was talking about the forthcoming live Aid concert and since it was expected to be a sunny day, Penny was planning a barbecue to coincide with the concert on the TV this coming Saturday.

The knock on the door surprised Nick. His first thought was to quickly empty the ash trays containing used joints and check that there was no evidence of drug use anywhere else in the room. Sheepishly he peeped through the window and was relieved and a little startled that it was just his old friend.

'Bloody hell mate!' Dylan exclaimed as Nick opened the door, 'Cover yourself up – It's not normal to open the door to someone stark bollock naked!'

Without showing any expression whatsoever on his face he just said, 'Oh, it's only you.'

He eventually put a fairly filthy looking dressing gown on and Dylan walked from room to room gazing with horror at the state of the house. Dylan hardly recognized his own home. He had only been away for a few weeks but it was nothing like it used to be. He was glad to see that at least Lesley Ann Down was still there. He made a mental not to take that back with him. A wall of marijuana and stale alcohol fell on him as he walked inside. It looked like the place had been taken over by squatters, it was horrible. Nobody seemed to have washed up or cleaned the floor since he lived there. Plates of half-eaten food lay everywhere, glasses, cups and even cereal bowls were strewn across the floor containing remnants of alcohol and cigarette ends. At least he

her. There was something horribly wrong with Nick, something she did not want to see but knew was there. It was like seeing those bomb sites that still littered Liverpool like gashes across the face of the city which nobody seemed to notice. When she looked at her perfect man, for just a fraction of a moment, she saw something terrifying. Looking at Nick was like looking at a shell, a perfect shell gilded with the purest gold leaf onto a fragile spider's web.

She sensed that writhing and churning beneath that fragile frame was a nest of vipers of pure hatred. Not just hatred, beneath that veneer of perfection was nothing but absolute self-hatred. She could not believe that anyone could really despise themselves as much as this. It was beyond her reason and she did not want to know why. Finding out would break the spell and she could not let that happen. Within him, an all-consuming fire seemed to have destroyed everything but that gossamer thin shell that she had made herself; that she had made herself love.

'Why do I love your arse so much?' Giuliana slurred as she tried to grab him but missed and felt herself fall off the sofa.

Laughing, Nick pulled her up from the floor.

'I am being serious,' she said stroking his bottom. 'What is so great about this? 'It is only a bottom, it is only pelle e muscolo - skin and muscle so why is it so nice? Why do girls like boy's bums? Logically it really isn't anything special.'

'Genetic programming I guess, Nick mused. 'Something inside our heads to make boys fancy girls and girls fancy boys.'

That was enough dope induced philosophy for now. On her hands and knees Giuliana crawled over to Nick and wrapped herself around him. Nick could not imagine that life could be better than this.

blurred into one fuzzy long Friday night. Apart from the times when they had to trudge down to the corner shop or the off-licence neither of them left the house. They didn't see anyone, they didn't do anything, they didn’t even bother to get dressed most of the time. They were like a pair of caged animals oblivious and ignorant of the outside world, unaware of the existence of anything beyond these four walls. Neither of them wanted to believe that the real world was out there, that there was anything outside the house. Here they were both safe, they had everything they could ever want and convinced themselves that they were happy. Their life was just themselves.

They only existed in a drugged and drunken state of almost semi-consciousness. They were just about capable of being able to eat and drink and make love - and they did make love a lot. Making love, or more accurately, having sex seemed just to happen, it was always happening all of the time, all over the house. Sex happened without them even thinking about it or even realizing they were actually doing it. Had they been sober they would have realized that this could not go on forever but for them there was no future or past, there was only the now.

Nick was drunk every day but Giuliana was very drunk every day. The drink blanked out everything bad and that bad thing was me. I had to be erased from their lives, what happened, or might have happened that night a few weeks ago could never be remembered. Giuliana was just one thing, she was his unchanging sexual fantasy and Nick was the prince charming in this inebriated swirling dream.

Once upon a time Nick used to bound around as enthusiastically as a puppy but now he just sluggishly sloped from room to room around dragging his slippers across the filthy, un-vacuumed carpet. He even stopped objecting to Giuliana playing YES when he was around. The alcohol and the drugs made it easy for Giuliana to ignore what her brain was struggling to tell

CHAPTER EIGHTEEN

August 1985

Ironically, if Nick had continued with his studies, he would have written a dissertation about how people during the Reformation completely changed the way they thought and behaved. He would have been analysing how people could behave in a manner that they previously would have considered utterly abhorrent to them but would now seem normal. Neither Nick nor Giulia could see anything wrong of different in how they spent their next few weeks. The next few weeks were horrible but neither of them noticed. In their own private world they were both in love and everything was wonderful.

Nick's course, like those of Dylan and Keith were over, they were no longer students. Keith had gone home and Nick would never see him again. He would not have seen Dylan either had it not been for Penny having a clinical placement at the cardiology department of the Royal Hallamshire over the summer. Dylan had nothing better to do so decided to stay in Sheffield a few weeks longer before moving to Oxford to begin his MA.

For Nick and Giuliana, it was as though time had stalled. They didn't want it to move on so nothing changed. The days and nights of those weeks stagnated. Time stopped moving and

in to a life with the girl he loved. He didn't know what to do, there were no comfortable and well-rehearsed scenes to relax in now. This was new, this was happening now.

Nick clenched his eyes tighter, he needed to think harder but it was no good. He was seeing me. I was standing in that doorway at my flat in Liverpool with the towel around my feet. dropping her towel. Why was this all he could see?

Neither of them felt self-conscious of how they looked, all that mattered to them was that they had found each other.

Sporting a scruffy beard and filthy clothes, it was clear that Nick had not washed for days. His clothes were torn and dirty and splattered with blood from the cuts and bruises on his face which he had gained on his odyssey. Giuliana also did not look like she had washed or indeed been sober for days either. Layers of make-up were crudely plastered upon more layers of smudged greying thick make-up. Her once pretty, floaty dress which once was sexy now was stained, torn and made he look rather pathetic. Saying very little on the journey back, they arrived in Sheffield. Together, the comfortable familiarity of the house welcomed them back. They locked the door behind themselves and quietly climbed the stairs where they fell exhausted onto the bed. Everything would be normal now.

He did not think about how he was going to explain to everyone else why this girl whom he had had so horribly mistreated and physically abused was back with him, living in his bedroom. He couldn't explain it but he didn't care anyway. Falling asleep next to her back in his room, he was happy again but far from easy. There was so much that didn't make any sense.

Something inside him kept trying to tell him the truth. The truth about what he did to me that night downstairs in this very house just a couple of weeks ago. The inevitable truth that if he loved her, she needed to be free of him. Nick truly wanted to save her but how could he - he was the lowest of the low? He was too selfish to do what he knew he should do.

'You have saved me.' She had said to him. He wondered how on earth could someone like him be anyone's salvation. He had betrayed her, how could someone like him give her life back?

He closed his eyes and tried to think. He tried to escape back into his cool, happy-go-lucky student persona but that person didn't belong with him anymore. He was trapped, locked

bouncers but he continued to find more and more clubs to barge into searching and checking whether every girl he saw was her or not.

Being chased by a policeman was not part of Nick's plan but after apparently 'scaring the customers' one of the nightclubs called the police to get rid of the 'homeless nutter' that had broken into their establishment. The lack of food, water and sleep made Nick very unsteady on his feet but he did manage to get away from the pursuing officer by hurling himself off a first floor balcony on to the road below. With his body running solely on adrenaline he didn't know whether he had hurt himself, he just knew he had to keep on looking. He had not finished searching this club before he was chased out – he decided he needed to go back in. He ran around to the front of the building but the security men were certainly not going to let him in. They were on their walkie-talkies asking someone to let the policeman know that the crazy tramp was at the front door.

Nick knew that the policeman would be appearing any moment now but he could not run – he needed to go back inside – he needed to find her.

It was fate, Giuliana thought when he grabbed her shoulder as she was walking out of that club two minutes later.

'Nick, you found me. You saved me.' She was more drunk that he had ever seen her before. Despite the stupidity of it, despite that this defied all logic, she flung her arms around her undeserving saviour and kissed him. They did not say much, he was too exhausted and she was far too drunk to really know what was happening or even where she was. Somehow they managed to drag themselves to Lime Street Station where they both slept on the floor for a couple of hours until the trains started again and then they caught the first train back to Sheffield.

A moment later he was walking away then he was running away. He didn't know what had just happened, he didn't want to know. He was away from me, that's all that mattered. He didn't even want to know why I had done that. I didn't want to know either. It was not my proudest moment. Did I do it to try to turn him away from Giuliana? To make him see that he didn't really love her? Could I show him that if he really loved Giuliana, he wouldn't have these feelings for me? Why couldn't he see that he should leave her alone? Nick was trying his utmost to imagine that what had just happened didn't but he was unable to quell that eruption of teenage lust and desire which I learned he had for me. Maybe I had fanned the flames just enough to burn away his delusion of a relationship?

He knew for definite that Giuliana was somewhere in Liverpool. He didn't have a plan, he didn't know where to look he just went. He would go to every bar and every wine bar in every street in Liverpool if he needed to.

I slammed the door after he had walked off. I screamed – it wasn't working: he's still in love with Giuliana, he was going to find her and nothing was going to change. What I had just done was stupid, I was disappointed that I had resorted to such a cheap trick. I also felt quite embarrassed about exposing myself to my son's best friend.

Nick was used to the strange looks he now attracted as he stormed in and out of every pub he could find. He didn't care anymore. He couldn't remember when he started doing this, he couldn't remember when he last ate or had a sleep or even had a wash.

By the early hours of that Liverpool morning, he was looking very ragged and smelling rather unpleasant. He headed straight to where the nightlife was; Giuliana had to be there somewhere. His dishevelled appearance was now making it more difficult for him to get past the

Both our faces betrayed the utter disappointment that neither of us were whom we were expecting. In Nick's case, the shock of seeing me again that made his mouth dry up. He had tried to wipe my very existence from his memory but I could sense that seeing me in place of Giuliana made the air in his lungs turn to stone. The last time we had seen each other was that night in his house; that night when we had that sex. My mind couldn't accept that I had sex with this boy. That night it wasn't him, it was Jean-Marie. I knew it couldn't have really been Jean-Marie but how could it have been this sad, pathetic boy? It was impossible. I hated him for not being Jean-Marie. It didn't happen, I did not have sex with this boy. This boy raped my friend Giuliana, he was scum.

Exhausted and unable to reconcile what had happened and with what was happening now Nick allowed his mind to switch off, he just stood there without speaking. I was admonishing him for hitting and raping Giuliana. He knew that if anyone should know the truth it should be me but was not able to question what I was saying. I could not let him, I would not let him believe anything else. The truth was mine to make. I knew he was scared. I hoped he could not see how scared I was. I needed to do something. It was totally stupid but it was all I could think of.

'Boy!' I said after a long silence.

He took a step back wondering what I was going to say. I didn't speak. I raised my hand to the top of the towel, loosened it then dropped it to the floor. It was an act of desperation, I knew it was wrong. Nick was unable to move. I stood, framed in the doorway completely naked. Nick could do nothing other than look at me.

'Like what you see, Nick?'

find her, the girl who can change my life, change my own past. Tomorrow, after a good night's sleep, I was going to find her.

Early the next morning, I was back in the city, I knew where she would be. Heels as high as these, I learned were not conducive to running like a maniac along cobbles of the dock road but they could not deter my progress. I got to the flat where she stayed few weeks ago. She had to be here. Since I owned this flat I let myself in. Fantastic! Inside, there were signs that someone had been there recently. Glasses and cups remained unwashed, there was some soup congealing in a pan, it was still runny so could not have been standing there long. There was milk in the fridge, I smelt it - it was fresh. She had been there very recently. I would wait, she would be back soon.

Tossing my hair out of my face in order to look at myself in a full-length mirror, I had left my parents' place so quickly this morning that I looked a bloody mess. If Giuliana was coming back soon I did not want to be found looking like this. I couldn't be seen looking anything less than immaculate could I? There was hot water so I decided to have a quick shower. Just as I turned the water off I noticed that someone was banging on the door. I wondered how long it had been going on. It sounded urgent. I knew exactly who it was – it was definitely Giuliana, this was our lives repeating themselves itself again. Grabbing a towel and quickly throwing it around myself I ran the door and flung it open.

My heart sank. 'Well you've got a bloody cheek.' I exclaimed when I Nick standing there. Nick, ignoring the fact that he must know that Giuliana was so much better off without him had had decided he had to find her.

'How dare you! After what you did to that poor girl, how dare you come here looking for her.'

‘Did the fact that Jean-Marie murdered my husband stop me longing for him?’

‘Good point Julia, Good point.’

I had to give my old friend a hug. I told him I didn't know any of these answers, all I knew was that I had to finish this for myself and for Giuliana

‘When did you get this revelation?’

I thought for a moment: 'Actually... just now!'

'Wow man!' exclaimed the ageing hippie, 'I've helped you see through this tapestry of illusion and see who we really are again.’

After this revelation, we had coffee and Mr Spitfire hugged me and kissed me goodnight. His hearing was not as good as it used to be so didn't hear me whisper in his ear: Good bye, I will miss you so much my darling old friend.'

Even without being able to hear my words I think he still sensed that this goodbye was one he should remember.

I jumped in a taxi back to my parent’s house just out of town. The trouble with arriving at such a palatial residence in Liverpool was that taxi driver always expect a huge tip, assuming I am Lady Muck. My father told me that when I had been out he had taken a message from Julian from the film company. Apparently he had seen Giuliana in Liverpool. He had asked me to contact the studio urgently if she made contact. This news caused me to jump up and down with uncharacteristic inelegance. Despite knowing me, or rather being acquainted with me for all of my life, my father, to whom exhibiting any sign of emotion was an alien concept, this outburst caused him to quietly exit the drawing room. I was so excited. What I’d done the night after that damned fancy dress ball a few weeks ago or how I had devastated the lives of Giulia and Nick now seemed of minor importance. This was such wonderful news: Giuliana was here, I needed to

‘You’ve always been divine Darling but I’ve never known you thought yourself as God before.’ Mr Spitfire quipped before summarizing again. ‘You take Nick out of Giuliana’s life and she will be happy whilst at the same time Nick being out of her life will mean that Jean-Marie will not be haunting the mind of you in the 1970s which caused much shit to go down.’

'Mr Spitfire,' I said nodding. 'that is a perfect summing up of what is happening.'

'Far out!' which seemed slightly weird coming from a seventy year old.

'Come on man,' I pressed him, 'there must be some questions – you surely can't believe all of this can you?'

Mr Spitfire leaned back and smiled; he could oblige.

'The groovy thing is to get this Nick guy away from her, yea?' he asked. 'Tell me that you didn't shag him in front of the girl just to show her that he was an absolute bounder?'

Thinking how only Mr Spitfire could get the words groovy and bounder into one sentence I smiled. 'I couldn't have arranged anything more devastating for Giulia that would turn her permanently away from Nick that that could I? It worked out perfectly – it was brilliant wasn't it?

Mr Spitfire grinned and nodded knowingly.

'The problem is my darling friend is that I didn't plan it at all. I honestly did not do this thing on purpose. What happened was that I was with Jean-Marie. Nick was Jean-Marie, not just in my mind. He was real, that was really was Jean-Marie.

I belied this, therefore so did Mr Spitfire but Mr Spitfire's mind was questioning what would happen after that. ‘Will you still be like you are now? Will you have done the same things, been to the same places, know the same people? Will you have actually had this conversation we're having now?.... but lastly, haven’t you already got rid of Nick from the girl’s life though by sh boyfriend in front of her? Nothing’s changed has it?’

Mr Spitfire thought he had heard the last of my mad ideas years ago but telling him what happened on that awful evening made his wait worthwhile. I could be completely honest with Mr Spitfire. He listened to me without any criticism or judgement.

'So, if you can change the course of Giuliana's life, it will not lead her to the tragic events you've had. I dig that – kind of makes sense – kind of destinies colliding but not sure about the other thing.'

'You mean how changing her life will change mine?'

'Yes, tell me again; are you saying that when her life changes from its current route, yours will have somehow be changed – it will have already been changed back from the time when you yourself were at that stage in this girl's life.'

'So you get transported back to 1970 knowing everything you do now?'

'No, I will still be here, it will still be now but my past will have changed – none of that shit that happened to me will have happened – Steve will still be alive – We'll both be forty years old. Forty years old and together.'

Mr Spitfire looked quizzical. 'How baby? If your past is going to get changed then this conversation we're having now ain't going to happen. You might not still know me in this alternative universe. Hey, I might be dead!'

'Look,' I said, 'I don't understand it either but I know this is true. And why can't events in the future influence events in the past? Because time is linear you're going to say but if God exists outside of time where everything; the past, the present and the future is all happening at once, why can't we?'

I realized what I'd said and started to laugh.

Part Three…

CHAPTER SEVENTEEN

August 1985

It was why Mr Spitfire was born – to listen to my mad, far-out, drugged-up stories and crazy dreams. I loved the way that however insane my ideas were, he would always believe them. I had grown up with him. In a sense, he made me what I am today. Since meeting him again at my party a few weeks ago I knew that Mr spitfire was the one person in the world who would believe anything I told him so I called him. Mr Spitfire decided to treat me to dinner. He knew a rather splendid South Indian in Liverpool and booked us a table. I arrived there first and saw Mr Spitfire walk in a few minutes later. I waved to him but he didn't recognise me at first. I had decided to go back to being a blonde again so I looked quite different to the last time we met.

Eventually he realised it was me. 'Oh my God. Am I having dinner with Brigitte Bardot tonight?'

'I hope not because I'm bloody starving. And furthermore, my old friend, she's about ten years older than me so I hope I look better than she does.' I did look better than Brigitte Bardot these days, I was never given to false modesty! The food was delicious and we chatted about our respective visits to India, we loved India.

...End of part Two

been wanting to break up with Nick for a while but I was too nice to hurt his feelings over the phone. Dylan, Keith and Penny had all seen that in those weeks before I went to Liverpool I didn't really want to be with Nick anymore. They had seen me drinking more and more, going out by myself more and more and just sensed that there was something wrong. Looking back, they were surprised the relationship lasted so long – it was so one sided. They spoke amongst each other about how upset I seemed when I arrived yesterday. How I clearly didn't want to be with him and how there must have been something very wrong because when I got there I spent most of my time with Nick's mother.

Dylan tried to explain how Nick must have felt. His sexual tension and frustration must have been bubbling up for weeks so would have been exasperated and angry. After all those weeks I was finally in his house but hiding from him, he obviously couldn't control himself and simply had to have her. He was a monster.

Believing what everyone else believed was easier for us both to believe than the truth. That Nick actually had sex with Dylan's mother in the living room with me watching was a million times worse. It simply did not seem like it was possible.

As much as Nick tried to regret what happened he could not. He knew deep down that he had taken advantage of a vulnerable woman but he knew that it was the most incredible thing that had ever happened to him. Given the chance he knew he would do it again. He hated himself. How could he have done that? With Dylan's mother? How could he have done this to Giuliana? Nick knew he was poison. He knew he couldn't allow himself to continue to pollute the life of the girl he loved. He was a virus eating away at what he cared about most in all the world. Like Judas, he knew he didn't deserve love.

Nick just carried on staring vacantly into space which made Dylan even angrier.

'Where's Giuliana?' he yelled. 'Is she alright?'

Still Nick just sat there silent and unmoving as though Dylan wasn't even there. He squinted at the house silhouetted against the sun; everything looked normal. In the daylight, in the bright sunshine of this normal morning the nightmare constantly showing inside his head of what happened last night seemed like a ridiculous bad dream. Dylan's yelling at him was the least of his importance. I was watching from the bedroom window, I finally knew the truth, I knew what he was like, he was not the person I thought he was.

Dylan went back inside. He started calling my name. I didn't want to speak to him but when he started banging on my locked door I had to let him in. He looked horrified. I had forgotten that my face was covered with blood, it must have been a shock for him. He asked me what happened. I couldn't speak. I couldn't really remember what happed, I didn't want to remember. I was not going to allow myself to remember. Dylan kept asking me what had happened. All I said was, 'Nick.'

By the time Keith came back I was gone. Nick knew the real truth about what had happened but the other truth that everyone else now believed was so much more believable to him that it was easier for him to believe that too. He had to get out that house. Dylan and Keith told him that I wouldn't be coming back and who could blame me. His housemates were disgusted with him, disgusted that last night although I had locked myself away in the room, I must have come down for a glass of water or something and that's when it must have happened. He grabbed me, he attacked me and forced himself on me. Dylan had seen the blood and bruises. His opinion of Nick had changed in a second, no longer was Nick his quiet friend, Nick was someone who raped met. It was obvious to Dylan and Keith when they thought about it that I had

All I wanted to do was get back to my room before I woke up or sobered up then maybe none of this would have happened. Why was my face covered with blood, I didn't know? Retracing my steps, I slowly and quietly walked backwards out of the room and threw up at the bottom of the stairs.

Julia had managed to climb on to the sofa and started to giggle. She threw her head back and began to laugh loudly. Nick was cowering on the floor in the corner of the room. He wondered what had just happened. Had it really happened? He closed his eyes so tight that it hurt but the world was still the same. He could hear Julia. She was still laughing but she had got up now and was dancing around the room clapping her hands – she looked insane. Nick did not move. I looked in disbelief wanting to gorge my eyes out as he stared at this naked woman, old enough to be his mother, drenched in his own sweat dancing naked in front of him. I could see that more than anything else in the world, even though he knew I was sitting watching this, he wanted to have sex with her again.

###

Dylan arrived back at the house from wherever he had been at about six in the morning. He found Nick sitting on a low wall in the back garden staring into the sky. Although it was early in the morning, too early for most people to be awake, the sun was hot. He was facing the sun with his eyes tightly closed letting his face scorch in the full force of its glare. Dylan grunted to him but got no response. Dylan was not awake enough to care so trudged past him into the house. About a minute later, he was very much awake. With a considerable amount of foul language, he stormed out of the house demanding to know what the hell had happened to the house. Why was everything smashed? Why was there vomit all over the carpet? Why was the TV smashed?

In the now darkness of the living room their silhouettes were like a couple of wild animals devouring each other. Wiping the hair from her mouth and face Julia looked up. Nick was still tossing her up and down and side to side, grabbing at pieces of her. She was writhing and kicking her feet wildly in the air as Nick drove relentlessly into her. Although she tried to keep her head still she was being flung about so violently that it looked like it might snap off. She tried harder then realized she needed to speak.

Taking a big breath she managed to speak. ‘Giuliana, Pussycat, Darling, this can't be happening. It's you isn't it. And...'

Julia tried to focus on Nick's face looking slightly bewildered.

It took Nick a little longer to realise that I was actually standing in the room. It took him longer still to notice the blood dripping from my face. It took even longer for his body to realise that it needed to stop having sex with Julia. As his eyes focussed on me and adjusted to the reality of the situation, his movements into Julia became slower and slower until finally coming to a halt. Nick didn’t even try to think of what to do or what to say. There was clearly no solution so he did nothing. He didn’t even bother to move.

I wasn’t moving either. My boyfriend, my perfect wonderful boyfriend was having sex with Julia. I wanted to think that I was so drunk that this wasn’t actually happening. Out of breath and covered in sweat, Julia slithered from beneath Nick and crawled towards me on her hands and knees. She was too exhausted to stand up so reached her hand up to me for help but I couldn’t move.

She was still gasping for air and could barely speak. With the back of her hand she wiped her lips, those lips that hours earlier I thought tasted so delicious. 'Sorry Darling,' she managed to gasp out, ‘that was a little selfish wasn’t it?’

Maybe she was just completely stoned and had no idea what she was doing. He didn't care. Maybe she was right, maybe he was Jean-Marie, it didn’t really matter right now. What mattered was that she was kissing him with a passion he had never imagined could exist. A year’s worth of repressed lust was now released in a deafening, blinding mind numbing burst.

Fifteen years of absence, fifteen years of longing for Jena-Marie were now distilled into this one moment, this inexplicable reunion. Nick didn’t care at all whether she knew what she was doing. He didn’t care whether he was taking advantage of a woman too stoned to realize what was happening or whether he was just being used to satisfy her sexual desires. He just kept repeating that yes, he was Jean-Marie and yes, he loved her. If he was to be Jean-Marie for this moment to exist then he would willingly sacrifice himself to be Jean-Marie; there was nothing else in the world other than this.

They were rolling over each other, clawing and thrashing together on the sofa. They didn’t notice when they fell off, they just carried on gouging into each other, dangerous and completely out of control. Nick hadn’t switched the television set off so when they knocked into it, it crashed to the floor exploding like a bomb. They didn’t notice the shards of glass shooting across the room. They didn’t hear the bang that couldn’t drown out their screams and the pounding of their heats. They didn’t notice something clawing at them trying to pull them apart, they just pushed it away as though it was a fly. That was me. I was thrown against the table which nearly knocked me out. Neither of them would allow anything to stop this moment. Their love making became ever more intense, louder, frighteningly faster fuelled by distilled passion and repressed desire. Love making was the wrong word, this did not look like love, it looked like sex.

began to walk towards the house the Venus of the barricades appeared to be unsteady on her feet. She stumbled and had to cling on to the wall to keep herself upright. With a new resolve she strode towards the house looking even more like Liberty Leading the People. I had to go downstairs to see her. I didn't want her to be alone with Nick.

Nick opened the door to her and had to take a couple of steps back. He had never experienced such an intense stare before; it took him by surprise. He felt her eyes burning right through him. Her beautiful eyes that Nick had so many times tried to gaze surreptitiously into now petrified him. They froze him; he could not move, could not speak and could not think. If watching her getting out of the taxi was surreal, this was like being in a dream. She walked up to him and clasped his hands in her own. She smiled.

'Bonjour Jean-Marie. Il a été, depuis longtemps, n'est-ce pas?'

He had no idea what she was saying, no idea why she was holding his hands, no idea why she was looking like that into his eyes.

'Je sais qui vous êtes. Tu savez qui vous êtes. Tu es Jean-Marie; mon Jean-Marie.'

Gradually Nick began to understand what she was saying. Either she had started speaking in English or he began to understand French, he couldn't tell, it didn't really matter right now. She was telling him that he was Jean-Marie, telling him that he was her lover, telling him that she had always loved him. It didn't sound stupid to Nick, things feel normal in dreams. He was in a fantasy, riding a ghost train and just taking it all in without any questions.

He didn't know whether Julia was pretending, whether this was some sort of joke she was playing or whether she really did believe he was Jean-Marie. He knew he didn't believe it but didn't care; if she told him he was Jean-Marie then he would be Jean-Marie.

dare he! She was not like that. She was a sophisticated, elegant and fascinating human being not some cheap tart.

At two in the morning, Channel four's red triangle film which Nick had been watching came to an end. Dylan said to him that he would be staying out tonight so he and I could have the house all to ourselves for our romantic reunion. Nick was so stupid, he had absolutely no idea why I hated him. He could not accept that anything was less than perfect.

I heard a taxi pull up outside which was an unusual for a student area. Looking through the net curtains I saw it was Julia. I thought she said she would be staying at the hotel but I couldn't think properly so didn't know.

She was still in her costume but as expected had abandoned the flag that had previously provided some semblance of decency. It was just too surreal a vision for me to take in, it wasn't real. My Julia was outside in the street, stumbling out of a taxi completely topless. I watched her leaning against the cab searching for money in her purse with her breasts dangling in front of the driver's face. Watching this physically hurt me, I was filled with the most acute anxiety. I desperately wanted to stop what I was seeing. I wanted that taxi driver to stop looking yet at the same time I wanted to watch it forever. That the taxi driver would not understand her, he didn't know what she was like, he didn't know she was an artist. He was thinking that she was some drunken slut who flashing her tits. He might even be thinking that she was a prostitute; it was the middle of the night after all.

'Please God, no!' I heard myself shouting. 'Why is she letting this happen?'

The taxi drove very slowly off. The driver took his time so as to have one last look in his mirrors. This would certainly be a something to tell his friends although he doubted any of them would believe him. In the artificial glare of the street lamp Julia did look like a painting. As she

headache just thinking that word. I didn't want to think of her as sexy, she meant more to me than that.

I looked to Nick hoping he hadn't noticed and was shocked to see him blatantly leering at her. I could understand him appreciating her appearance but he was making no disguise of the fact that he was staring at her with utter lust, it was absolutely horrible. It was devastating. He was meant to have been longing to see me again and he was leering at my friend. It was disgraceful. I couldn't believe it. I sat opposite him fuming.

After her taxi took her away I told him and Dylan that I had a headache and went upstairs, taking a bottle of malt whisky with me for company. On my way up, I heard Dylan saying to Nick: ridiculous bloody woman. You know that as soon as he gets there she's going to take that flag off and sit with everyone with her tits hanging out.

I was furious with Julia, she was not meant to be like that, she was not meant to be thought about like that. I was furious with myself for my stupid thoughts but I was even more furious with Nick because I know he was imagining her arriving at that party and casting off the Tricolor to the amazed gasps of the other party-goers. I didn't want to think about the effect she would have when she walked into the ballroom dressed like that but I knew Nick, the filthy pig would be. I slammed Nick's bedroom door behind me and locked it. He was not welcome here, I hated him.

Where the hell had that bottle of whisky gone? I couldn't have drunk it all could I? This night had definitely not gone to plan. I was sitting alone, horribly drunk and horribly sad in Nick's locked bedroom and downstairs he was watching the TV on his own. I couldn't bear to see him. I couldn't believe how he was ogling Julia. Looking at her like a piece of meat. How

‘Well I’m sure you like the appreciate the symbolism don’t you Nick? I’m sure you like what you see?’

Nick felt the ground beneath him cave in when she said that. What was she saying? Nick did understand the symbolism. The bare breasts represented innocent natural beauty, symbolic of the age before Eve ate the apple, symbolic of beauty through strength. Nick was staring intensely at Julia’s breasts as though he had never seen such things before. I walked over to Nick and asked him what he thought. I wanted him to snap out of that slightly peculiar trance and stop staring at her breasts, he was being rather rude.

‘Well I think you look simply too divine for words.’ I told her. ‘Like a goddess.’

She held her hands and whispered in her ear, ‘You are my goddess.’

That made me smile and she put her arms around me and gave me another kiss, that second kiss I had so long been wanting. Whether it was because of that or the half bottle of vodka I am not sure but my legs gave way and I collapsed onto the sofa. Nobody noticed, I didn’t want Nick to notice and I certainly didn’t want Julia to notice. I didn't know what to do next, or even whether I should do anything next. I wanted to throw herself back into her arms and let her kiss me again but when I looked up Julia had moved away as though nothing had just happened. Nick was too transfixed with Julia's artistic statement to have noticed and Dylan was still too shocked.

After a lot more shouting between Dylan and his mother, with a considerable amount of bad language, a compromise was reached. Julia eventually agreed to drape the flag around her shoulders to preserve some of her modesty. When she eventually covered herself, I felt such so relieved. I started to breathe normally again and the banding of my heat stopped hurting. I was angry with myself for having such ridiculous feelings. Why did I find her so sexy? It gave me a

down the stairs to show the result of our efforts to Dylan and Nick. I thought about walking in first to give a sort of explanation but I thought Julia's costume would speak for itself.

'Jesus Christ Almighty! You're not seriously planning to going out like that!' exclaimed Dylan, coughing up his coffee over the table when he saw what his mother was wearing.

'Don't blaspheme Darling. You'll burn in hell.'

'O.K.... for fuck's sake, you're not seriously planning to go out like that! Tell me please that you're not fucking seriously fucking planning to fucking go out like that!'

'Language. language Dylan, there are ladies present.' She admonished him.
Dylan was used to his mother embarrassing him. He used to think she did it on purpose but gradually he realized she just liked to shock. Tonight she had possibly topped all her previous efforts. Tonight, she declared, 'I am Marianne, the symbol of the French revolution from Delacroix's famous painting, 'Liberty Leading the People.' I am the bare breasted goddess, determined, proud and free striding over the bodies of the fallen carrying the Tricolor to victory.'

Dylan was not sure whether his mother actually believed what she was saying but she told him he was simply too uncouth to appreciate art and gave him a history of the painting and how close she resembled the original down to the torn red Phrygian cap.

'But Mother - bare tits! You cannot go out like that.'

'Surely you understand the Delacroix's symbolism?'

'Mother; fuck Delacroix - you can't walk around Sheffield, past Debenhams with your tits hanging out! It's not bloody normal. Seriously, I'm not joking, please, just please think about it. This is fucking Sheffield not some Paris commune in the sixties. You'll get arrested. Jesus Christ Mother, can't you see you're....for fucks sake just no!'

thought was very rude. I was sure that he used to be quite find of Julia but now he seemed to hate her, it was very odd. Dylan sensed that there was a strange atmosphere developing but Dylan being Dylan, did his best to ignore it.

After our coffee, Julia noticed that she was running horribly late and she wondered whether she could get ready for her party here. Dylan mentioned that Nick’s room was surprisingly clean and maybe she could get changed up there. Nick was almost breathing fire as he agreed. When I offered to go up with her and help with her costume, I am sure flames began to shoot out of his nostrils. I can’t think why he was annoyed, he was going to be there all evening, Julia was going in about an hour.

'Oh Darling, you are so sweet. Nick?' Julia said, 'you don't mind me stealing Giuliana from you for a little while do you?'

After all those lonely weeks apart and such a fairy tale reunion, Nick was not expecting his girlfriend to simply abandon him to help his friend's mother get ready for her fancy dress ball. He tried, rather unconvincingly not to show how annoyed he was, but I confess, I didn’t really care. I was the one who had driven across this county to see him, so he could just wait until I was ready for him. I went to the car with Julia and helped her bring in her huge suitcase from the back seat, I also found a fresh bottle of vodka which I took with me upstairs.

When Julia told me about what she would be wearing tonight it had sounded so fabulous, so different and so daring. The idea was fantastic but I don’t think I fully appreciated how this would look in reality. Julia would have to look amazing. Julia could never look dull but when she was finally ready, for the first time I was actually shocked. I wasn’t sure that it was actually ok to go out in this outfit or to actually sit down to dinner like this. But she was Julia, she could do anything and she looked amazing. We were both rather pleased with ourselves and we dashed

that and I knew Nick would like it. I didn't want that to be the dress I wore for Julia, I wanted it to be the one I wore for Nick.

Julia knew she should look away but didn't, she kept staring at us kissing. I think I know why, she wanted it to be her standing there being kissed like that. She wanted that student to be Jean-Marie. She wanted that pretty young girl in the little red dress to be her. Julia knew this was wrong and I knew then just how much she hated herself. I saw her out of the corner of my eye and her eyes looked so sad. I felt terrible for her.

I felt terrible for ruining Nick's plans. He had been looking forward to tonight for ages, this very moment was all he had been thinking about for weeks and I was ruining it for him but I couldn't help it. I couldn't stand for Julia to be so upset. I wish she hadn't kissed me just half an hour ago, even with Nick kissing me so passionately, that one quick but gentle kiss kept barging into my head.

It was obvious that Nick wanted Julia to leave as soon as possible, I knew that for some reason he really disliked her these days but I was so glad when Dylan made an appearance and offered her a cup of coffee. Dylan had diplomatically stayed up in his room for a bit to give us both a few moments of privacy but he spoilt his uncharacteristic moment of thoughtfulness by stomping into the room and with a knowing wink, laughing to Julia: Bloody hell Mother, you can tell he's never had a girlfriend before can't you!'

Nick had made such a special effort for this evening to be just perfect. He had cleaned the house for me, to prepare us a special dinner, made his room immaculate and even change his bedsheets, which he must have had to go to the library and find a book on, since that was not something which came naturally to him! He desperately wanted for us to be alone right now and his body language towards Julia was not very nice to Julia. He didn't even speak to her which I

were in love, maybe this was exactly how it looked – two people made for each other, desperately in love? The more she thought about it, the more nonsensical her theory seemed.

Nick was nothing like Jean-Marie, he was pleasant, reasonably good-looking but he was no Jean-Marie. Jean-Marie was amazing. She just had to close her eyes and she could see that body; he was like a Greek god. She could still smell him, she could taste him she could even feel the heat coming from his flawlessly tanned skin. He was so clever, brighter than anyone she had ever met since. He was a beautiful man, not just handsome, not just suave and sophisticated, he was a real man, muscular and masculine and yet so caring and sensitive. He was perfect. He was nothing like Nick.

She felt a strangling inside her stomach as she realized she was day-dreaming about the man who killed Steve. Why, after all these years, after knowing that man brutally hacked her lovely husband to death was she was still in love with him. This was the reason she hated herself. This was why after all the good she had done she felt her life was totally worthless. How could she possibly even think about that man without her every cell exploding with hatred? How could anyone other than a monster possibly love that monster?

She wished she could turn back time to the time before she ever met Jean-Marie, to the time before she first went to Paris when she and Steve were inseparable.

My arms were clenched around Nick. Nick was crying with happiness. The scene so reminded Julia of herself and Jean-Marie. She could hardly bear to look – she was seeing Jean-Marie, she wanted to see Steve but she couldn't. She watched Nick's hands climbing up the backs of my legs inside my dress. I was wearing the same little red dress I wore at that club in Liverpool the other night when we pretended to be stars from Dallas. I knew I looked good in

Was she going to say anything? Was she going to kiss me again? I remained completely motionless just in case but no, Julia switched the engine back on and pulled out onto the road as though nothing had happened. The taste Julia of lipstick was still on my lips, it was beautiful. Sheffield was just half an hour away now.

That day I arrived back Nick was sitting by his window. He was looking forward to something wonderful. Now, a week later he was sitting by his window again but trying to work out why that had happened.

Eventually the 2CV drove into the street. Julia considered pleading one more time for me to finish with Nick but didn't have the opportunity. I had already opened the door, got out and was virtually up the path even before the car had stopped. I had missed being with Nick so much that I almost crushed him as I threw my arms around him. We smothered each other in kisses; it was exactly what I needed. Everything felt right, everything was as it should be. All those doubts that Julia had put into my head and what just happened in the car half an hour ago now seemed even more utterly ridiculous and manipulative. I could never leave him.

Julia felt a cold chill run through her as she watched Nick and me kissing. This display of what appeared to be happiness was making her cry inside. She wished she could convince me of the truth but didn't know how to. She remembered what she was like with Jean-Marie, nobody but herself could ever have convinced her of anything about her feelings for him. That's what confused her a little. When it was her and her French student, by this time in the relationship she had started to get tired: Giuliana showed no signs of this.

A wave of doubt suddenly hit her. What if she was wrong? What if her theory was as insane as she knew it sounded? Maybe these two young people embracing in front of her really

‘Of course I’m not unsure; I’ve been looking forward to seeing him for weeks. I thought you knew me well Julia, you must know that.’

‘Please Pussycat, think about whether there might be something in what I’ve been saying. I know you think I'm as mad as a hatter but I am right, I can see things that you cannot. Please believe me, you and Nick must break up.’

My mind was made up; I wasn’t going to bother to reply. To lighten the mood, Julia put a tape on. That did the trick. With U2's '*New Year's Day*' playing at full volume on the car’s stereo and the roof rolled back, I leant back, let the wind blow through my hair and both sang along.

'You sing worse than me.' Julia laughed.

I laughed back and looked up into the blue summer sky at the interestingly shapes. They looked like animals, faces and shapes, I tried to point them out to Julia. She smiled at me, leant over and held my hand. I closed my eyes and smiled; it felt lovely.

Seeing a lay-by approaching, much to the surprise of the car directly behind who was blasting its horn, Julia swerved her car into it and screeched to a halt. Grateful that I was wearing my seatbelt, with eyes now very open, I asked if there was a problem with the car.

‘No, there’s nothing wrong.’ Julia answered. ‘Just close your eyes again.’

I kept my eyes shut expecting her to give me a cigarette and opened my lips slightly in anticipation. Instead, I felt Julia’s lips very softly kissing mine. It can only have lasted less than a second but I kept my eyes closed and tried to make it last longer. Eventually opening my eyes I saw Julia leaning over me. I wondered what the expression was on her face, it was kindness, pure kindness. Julia couldn’t bear for me to be sad and yet she knew with absolute certainty that this was what would happen to me. Julia couldn’t bear for me to be sad and yet she knew with absolute certainty that this was what would happen to me. I could see this so clearly in her eyes.

I was not the same girl who left Sheffield those few months ago. Julia had changed me but even more so, Liverpool had changed me. Liverpool had ended my love affair with England or at least my idea of England. The gloom of the recession there had cast a heavy pall of despondency over everyone and everything. It trapped them, pressing down on them and suffocating as though it was pegged down with rusting spikes made from the hopes, dreams and futures of everyone who lived there long since abandoned in the river.

Still however there was the humour, the laughs the cocky attitude pretending that there was nothing wrong. People were living in poverty; this was a city in one of the richest countries in the world and people were living in poverty. What amazed me was that there were still bomb sites from forty years ago peppered throughout the whole town that still hadn't been cleared. I thought that was quite symbolic of something but was usually too drunk to give it too much thought. I couldn't understand how everyone including Julia simply ignored this dereliction and deprivation. There was a falseness there, the city believed it was something it wasn't, This was something which I could understand. It had got used to ignoring the obvious and pretended to be something else. Like myself, its image was nothing like the reality.

I was desperate to get back to Sheffield not just to see Nick but to get back to that life I thought I wanted. In Liverpool I was starting to become someone different, someone I didn't want to be. I realized that I had stayed away from Nick for so long on purpose. I needed to get back to Sheffield, I needed to see Nick again and sort things out. I woke up early that morning, I couldn't sleep. This was not because I was anxious, not because I might be making a huge mistake in going back to him, I just didn't sleep too well.

Crossing the Pennines felt like passing the point of no return. Julia sensed my unease.

'If you're not sure I don't mind turning around and taking you back.'

They were all watching a music show on Channel 4 as Nick walked into the room. Penny was complaining about who she was looking at.

'Without wishing to sound snobbish, why is it that that this person is considered talented just because he's got a cockney accent?' she asked. 'Being common shouldn't be something to be proud of. Is being an uneducated yob some sign of talent these days? Maybe I should give up medicine and become a glue-sniffer – get more respect! Move to a council estate, live in a free house, remembering to put oily engine parts in the garden and piss on the carpets oh yes and do nothing all day except hang around shopping centres, mugging the occasional old lady. Yes, that's what society appreciates these days.'

'Don't you just love her!' exclaimed Dylan, giving her a kiss.

Nick smiled then she surprised him. She stood up, walked over to him and gave him a little hug. He was not expecting that, she was nice. Nick made himself a cup of tea but appreciative that he must not outstay his welcome, he took it back to his room. He sat looking out at the street again, Penny's little hug meant a lot to him. It meant that even knowing what she believed, she didn't hate him. Keith had been less understanding. As far as Keith was concerned, Nick was a monster.

How quickly someone's life can change. Just one week ago everything was so different. Just one week ago Nick was still standing at that window but grinning from ear to ear because he knew that any minute I was coming back from Liverpool. He was going to see me sat in that silly little car waving at him.

On that day Nick assumed that I was just as excited as he was. In just a few hours we were going to be together again. Despite Julia's reservations, she was going to take me over because she needed to be in Sheffield that weekend anyway. She had organized a fancy dress charity ball so needed to be there.

like that Lesley Ann Down picture, never changing. As time progressed however Nick almost had to acknowledge another reason it was sometimes it was better when I didn't phone. With increasing regularity, when I phoned him I had been drinking. Sometimes I was so drunk that he could barely understand me. Why wouldn't he realize something was wrong? What did I need to do? Why did he never wonder why I was always drunk when I spoke to him? Those inebriated conversations never lasted too long and as soon as I had hung up, in Nick's mind I was the same as always, his perfect loving girlfriend. All that had mattered to him was that we were in love and nothing could ever change that.

As Dylan had said, Penny did come over the following evening. Doing medicine she was considerably busier than her on/off boyfriend was so her visits had become much less frequent recently. This was Dylan's excuse for Debbie, his extra-curricular girlfriend.

'I'm only human.' he once said, quoting The Merchant of Venice, 'If you prick me, do I not bleed?'

'You certainly will bleed when Penny finds out' was Keith's retort.

Her visit that evening was her first since the incident with Giuliana that weekend but of course she knew all about it, everybody did. Nick had not really moved out of his room since that day but did pop down to say hello to Penny. He thought he should have felt more nervous about seeing her knowing what she now thought of him., knowing what she believed he did.

Penny was an inexplicable contradiction; she had such unsympathetic and heartless political views but she was also one of the sweetest and most compassionate people they knew. Everyone liked Penny and although Nick didn't really care what anyone else thought of him at the moment, she was one person whom he did not want to despise him.

Music began playing from another room in the house; probably Dylan's. For a moment, Nick considered going to see him but he wasn't in the mood for company. He knew he wasn't himself and didn't want others to see him this way. The music stopped, he heard footsteps approaching. Dylan came in, sat down and lit a cigarette. He offered one to Nick.

'Thanks mate.' Nick replied, cautiously taking one out of the pack. They sat in a noticeably awkward silence until Dylan, mentioned that Penny was coming over again tomorrow. He knew that Nick liked her company but wasn't sure whether he might be rubbing it in that he still had a girlfriend whereas Nick didn't. Dylan finished his cigarette, said he'd see him in the morning and went. Dylan was probably Nick's best friend, he was somebody he could trust but he was certainly one person who could never know the truth. Dylan accepted people's failings, he knew everyone made mistakes. Nick was his friend so he tried but he wasn't sure however if he could ever forgive Nick for what he did. Nick knew this but would rather have him believe the lies about himself, about why I left him rather than know what really happened.

I may have gone from his life but to him I was still everywhere. Staring out his window for hours I was there, I was the sunlight between the trees, the flames that painted the night, the candlelight that flickered in every window. He could not believe that I was gone.

When I first moved to Liverpool I used to phone him every day, sometimes two or three times. It was like the time when I was filming in London last year. But as the weeks went on the phone calls became less frequent. It didn't really make any difference to Nick; I was in his thoughts all the time and whether he spoke to me on the phone or not he could always hear my voice.

He did not mind me not phoning; there was nothing wrong, it just made him look forward even more to the next time we spoke. He was different to me. I had changed but to him I was just

CHAPTER SIXTEEN

July 1985

Nick had a large easy chair near the window of his room from which the city skyline provided a constant picture postcard. By day the city filled every space, it was solid, strong and loud. Nick felt part of this scene, part of the city he was watching. For hours, he gazed with glazed eyes at the life outside and soaked it up. He could feel the clouds of lazy smoke coming from the few factories still working in the east of the city, he could smell it, he could taste it. The gradual coming of nightfall had a calming effect on him. The hazy red glow of a town at night had been giving him a reassuring warmth ever since he could remember. This night, he needed some familiar comforting as he sat watching the lights.

It had become late, were it not for a nearby streetlamp he would be sitting in darkness. It was the middle of summer but nevertheless Nick pulled the duvet from his bed over himself. His eyes passively soaked in the night. Gazing at the windows opposite he wondered what might be happening behind those closed curtains. Cars drove past; where were they all going, who were they going to see? He looked to his bed and remembered that only a few weeks ago his girlfriend was laying there. He noticed a hair on his pillow, was it hers? He leant over and picked it up, twirled it in his fingers then dropped it on the floor.

Why would Julia not want to have lived that life? It is the exactly the life I want. At that moment in the middle of the night, still with my head spinning with the effects of alcohol I knew I would do exactly as Julia had asked; leave Nick. How could I not?

Lying in bed, thinking about her, it was inexplicable that Julia could be hiding such sadness. Julia had led the most amazing, fulfilling life. I thought about the stories I'd heard about her in the 1970s. 1971 was a big year for her, inspired by George Harrison's benefit concert for the devastating floods that had killed half a million people a year earlier she went over to Bangladesh herself to help. Initially she found a charity organization to work for but as she saw more and more of the problem she began to realize that East Pakistan needed more than just charity. She had what at the time was the rather unique idea of helping indigenous artisans and village businesses sell their goods in London. Trendy London boutiques would love hand-crafted pieces of art made by village craftsmen. Spoilt stupid Londoners with more money than sense would be the saviours of these poverty stricken people. It was a wonderful idea and it worked. The money raised in the shops all went back to Bangladesh where it was reinvested in these village businesses.

Within a few years Julia Fairfax had reinvented herself as the woman who saved the lives of hundreds with her trendy boutique selling ethnic art in Chelsea. By the mid-seventies villages not just in Bangladesh were making goods for her shop. India, Kenya, even Sudan were soon benefiting directly from Julia's commitment to curing the world.

She began to campaign for human rights in these countries, she began to campaign for women's rights and in the UK she even set up her own socialist pressure group to help the downtrodden in her own society. She was no longer just the glamorous groovy hippie who wrote a few books. To those who knew her and those she helped, Julia Fairfax was almost a saint. She was someone who really had changed the world, someone who had made it better. If I could make just a fraction of the difference to the world that Julia had done, I could feel that my life had a purpose.

knew: the beautiful, cool, chic, the sophisticated woman with the designer clothes with hoards of eager young men swarming around her.

Looking directly into my eyes, Julia gently put her finger on my mouth, 'Shush. Of course, you know this. You know more about me than I do myself. You are more me than I am.'

I did not know what to say, it was getting far too strange, it was getting disturbing. A few minutes ago everything was wonderful but now I was scared. I couldn't bear to see Julia's face become so sad. Julia tried to maintain her composure but a tear began to evolve in her right eye.

Her eyes became more watery until the tear slowly trickled down her face. It stopped on her cheek and glimmered. I thought she could see my reflection in it; I kissed it away. It tasted both of sweetness and sadness. Another tear felt on her other cheek. Knowing what I was going to do, Julia gave me a little smile and kissed that one away too. Julia put her arms around me. That felt nice, it was alright now.

It was a very hot night. The air was heavy and sticky. Were I back in Italy I would have the air conditioning on but here in Liverpool that was an unknown luxury. I lay on top of my bed, alone in the dark knowing that I was not going to fall asleep before the sun rose. The sun would be up again in a few hours, I wished it would come sooner. I lay there thinking about Julia. Remembering the feel of Julia's bare legs on mine when we were sitting on that bench. I remembered the touch of her hands on my skin. I remembered Julia unzipping that dress then sitting on this bed completely naked. I moved my hand to the edge of the bed to where she had sat naked, smoking her cigarette. I wished she was there now.

I wished the sun would hurry up and rise. In the morning these thoughts, these wrong, wrong thoughts would never have happened, it was alright to have them now because soon they would never have existed.

new bright young things like herself were finally given a voice. I knew all about this, I had read about it but it was wonderful to hear this being related by Julia who was actually there.

Julia stopped talking and stared into space. I thought she was going to get up so I needed to say something to keep her sitting on my legs.

'Hey, since we're in Liverpool, let's go to the Magic Clock.'

'That's long gone Pussycat - How do you know about The Magic Clock?'

'That's where you first met Steve. It was the night Brian Epstein came in with his posters promoting The Beatles' first single. You fell in love with him instantly although you were a little worried that from the way he looked, he might be a homosexual.'

'How do you know - how can you possibly know this?'

I didn't know, I honestly couldn't answer. There was one explanation; Julia's explanation but that was ridiculous. Nevertheless I didn't just know what happened that night in this city thirty years ago, I could remember it exactly. I could remember how Julia felt. Then my mind was suddenly flooded with intense sadness. I was feeling; what Julia was feeling.

'You love Steve as much today as you did when you first met him don't you? More than you ever admitted, even to him. You never wake up any single day without your first thought being that overwhelming, crippling sense of shame and sorrow about what you did to him. You can't live with yourself can you?'

I was horrified to hear those words come out of my mouth. Julia told me to stop. She didn't want to hear this. I didn't want to hear this. She was still sitting on my lap and I felt her skin turn colder. What have I said? What have I done? I did not want to know about this other Julia, this unhappy and fragile Julia. Julia was secure and content behind the mask everyone

I winked back at her and flicked up her dress too. Hilarious. I was so much enjoying being part of Julia's life. I was enjoying just being with her. Sophistication. class and elegance radiated from her yet at the same time, as hard as I tried, I couldn't stop thinking that she looked sort of slutty which I liked.

My mind was spinning, I didn't know what I was meant to think when I looked at her. I had given up trying to understand what was happening, I was totally captivated, willingly enslaved. I had been swept into the swirling water and was caught in the current. being dragged along but didn't care. Julia knew that I was no longer in control but it took her a while before she stopped caring that she wasn't in control either. We were both moths about be consumed in the invisible flame of another's consciousness.

After a couple of hours, we staggered out of Romeoz and emerged into the humid night air. Neither of us intended to but we had both got very drunk. It was because we were those mysterious celebrities, drinks just kept being given to use. After tottering in our high heels towards the town hall, which took quite a bit of skill considering the distance and how drunk we were, we found ourselves standing by a bench that Derek Hatton had conveniently put there for us. I collapsed onto it first and then Julia sat on my lap. The feel of her bare legs on mine felt nice. I wanted to stay like this a little while. I didn't want this to end.

I wanted to know more and more about this wonderful lady. I loved her books, I loved her books before even knowing who Julia Fairfax was. Putting my arms around her, I asked her why she became a writer. Forgetting to drop the Texan accent she had used in the club Julia said that she became inspired to write after going to the famous poetry reading at the Royal Albert Hall in 1965. She talked about Alan Ginsberg and the Beat Generation poets who were there. She said it was the catalyst for the London Free School. The energy and creativity of London's

bragging about how successful they were and air headed pretty-pretties with nothing more important to them than how they looked and getting off with the richest yuppie to fill their vacuous lives.

From the moment their tips of our shiny shoes touched the illuminated gaudy coloured floor we knew we were stealing every particle of the attention. Despite the deafening maelstrom coming from the speakers, the taps of our polished heels on the varnished wood clipped cleanly through the air forcing every eye in the club to gaze at us. Clearly we were dressed to impress but I don't think that's why people were staring at use, or as I should say, Julia. Her presence, her attitude, the way she walked or even just stood simply outshone everyone and everything else. I hate these sort of places but it was great in there, everyone was looking at us.

Who are they? Are they off the TV? They must be famous, I'm sure I know them. They're from 'Dallas'? No, they're from 'Dynasty.' I'm sure that's Joan Collins!

We felt like real film starts so had to live up to these assumptions so we immediately began speaking in American accents; Julia tried her best to do a Texas accent deciding that she would rather be from the Dallas show rather than be mistaken for Joan Collins who was about ten years older than her.

We had a great time and even bumping into Justin or Julian, I couldn't remember which was which, didn't spoil our fun. Whichever brother it was mentioned their concern about my quality of acting. I don't think my defence. 'I am a shit actress, I can't act.' Did much for my cause but he wasn't listening, he was desperate to keep me in his film because of something he couldn't explain. As the brother, or possibly both of them told me how great I was, Julia decided that now was the ideal time to flick my dress up.

scrambled into the dress. It was still warm, that felt nice. I looked at myself in ther full length mirror; do I look cool or what!

Strutting around like Mick Jagger I suddenly became aware that Julia was sitting on the edge of my bed completely naked. I tried not to look shocked - Julia was acting as though this was perfectly normal. I was annoyed with myself for feeling unsettled; this was just so Julia: stop being so 'English!'

When Julia had finished her cigarette, begrudgingly I had to take it off and gave it her back. I picked the towel up off the floor and wrapped it back around myself. I lit myself a cigarette to steady myself. We were just two friends getting ready for a night out, absolutely normal. It was nothing to Julia and should have meant nothing to me but seeing her naked in my room, I felt my heart pounding, giving away something I did not want to admit.

'Looked an absolute dream on you Pussycat.' She had said but when Julia put it back on, I could see how perfect it was back on its rightful owner. Only Julia would dare to wear something as short as that; she was so confident, such a sexy woman. If she was brave enough to wear that, I was going to dig out that tiny red dress I'd always been too embarrassed to wear before. Julia joked that I looked like a tart, I think I agreed but why not? After we'd got ready, we then both went out giggling like naughty schoolgirls. Outside in the street they we just couldn't stop laughing. I don't remember which of us started it first but a challenge was set for us to flick up the bottom of each other's skirt at the most inappropriate moment.

'Are you trying to get me arrested?'

Romeoz was predictable. As soon as we went in we remembered why neither of us frequented these sorts of places. Horrible thumping dance music and full of exactly the types of people neither of us would ever want to be associated with. Loud, self-obsessed yuppies

'Spelling it with a 'z' of course makes it wild, wacky and rebellious.' I added, now standing in a little puddle made from the water dripping off my hair.

'Yes, it just shows that any establishment with such a flagrant disregard for the rules of English must surely be one operating outside the confines of a civilised and moral society where casting aside the rules of spelling are just the tip of the insidious iceberg in this wanton hedonistic land where anything goes no matter how sordid and sexually depraved.'

Julia eventually went inside and did a Generation Game twirl to show what she was wearing. Her friend was taken aback – it was so short. She was wearing one of her old dresses from the late sixties; a very short white mini dress with orange and pink ovals printed on it. Giuliana thought it looked absolutely fantastic on her.

'Groovy' said Giuliana.

'Yes, it's fab.'

'Far-out.'

'Gear'

Eventually running out of sixties superlatives she began just to marvel at the dress.

'Ghastly man-made fabric; hideously sweaty and as scratchy as hell.' Julia said quietly as if not to disappoint her.

I wasn't really listening, I was stroking the dress with the due reverence it deserved: not only was this from the late sixties, not only was this Julia's dress but she had probably worn this whilst getting stoned with some rock band in Notting Hill or somewhere. Then she suggested I should try it on. Oh my God, I could try it on! Julia casually unzipped it, peeled it off and tossed it over. I was like a child on Christmas morning, my towel got thrown to the floor and I

Over the next few weeks Julia became a fairly regular visitor to my little flat. When she came over we would listen to YES for a while then usually go into town. Nobody would believe that Julia was nearly twice my age as we became regulars at the city's trendy night spots. They didn't usually get too drunk, we just smoked a few joins and talked. Julia's voice and that cut-glass English accent were so utterly charming, I could have listened to her speak for hours. We liked to sit on the grass by the riverfront, snuggle up to each other and Julia would tell me about her adventures and her wondrous stories.

In just a few short weeks there was no doubt that these two exiles from the real world were best friends. There were no secrets between us, there were no hidden feelings. We knew each other better than we knew ourselves. There were however a few subjects that we would try not to talk about. I would not speak about Steve and Julia would try, very badly, not to talk about her wild theory of us sharing the same life.

One Saturday when I was wishing I had managed to get back to Sheffield, Julia called unexpectedly. I was having a shower when I heard the doorbell ringing incessantly. It sounded like an emergency so I leapt out and quickly threw a towel around myself and opened the door.

'Tonight we are going clubbing!' Julia announced even before I'd finished opening the door. I had been feeling miserable, I was really missing Nick and going to a night club was the last thing I wanted to do but as soon as Julia said it, it became a wonderful idea.

'Good idea, I hate those bastard seal cubs.' I said which she thought was quite witty for a foreigner. 'Some of the girls at the studio had been to a new club called "Romeoz" that they thought was pretty cool, we could try that if you like?'

'Romeoz....spelt with a "z" Julia said like a disparaging Victorian school teacher.

By the time I came into the studio Sir Charles had left which was probably a good thing because I had been drinking quite a lot. Julian and Justin however were not concerned, they knew they had a new star, they told me about the change in direction. I listened to their enthusiastic new ideas without really paying too much attention. When they finished I smiled and said glibly, 'yes, whatever, that sounds fine.'

Julia called around to my flat that evening excitedly waving a magazine in the air. She grinned showing me the magazine she had brought from Italy that I had featured in. Not only was my face on the front cover but there were six whole pages featuring me inside.

‘Would I be right in thinking that the readers of this particular periodical are teenage illiterate boys?’ Julia asked, referring to the fact that the article featured very little writing just photographs of me, mostly topless.

‘No,’ I joked, ‘some of the greatest novelists and journalists began their careers describing girls’ bottoms.’ To my relief, Julia laughed, it was nice to see her laugh. Looking at those photos with Julia, I had a sudden longing for the old days. I hadn’t done many of these features but nevertheless I used to love photo-shots like those, they were such fun. It felt wrong to think about how fun and exciting that former life was. It was life before Nick, life before my perfect relationship. It was such an unusual feeling, it hurt like a real physical pain. When Julia left that evening, she gave me an even tighter hug than usual. I felt good about that: Julia really did understand me.

As Julia drove off, I poured myself another whisky and idly leafed through that old magazine. It was like looking at someone else flicking though the pages of that pretty girl posing provocatively. I missed that girl.

people I've ever met, I know she has taken Miss Moltisani under her wing but Julia only ever sees the good in people and I'd hate to see her throw her money into a bottomless pit.'

The others reassured Sir Charles that they could handle this; none of them wanted to lose Giuliana.

Sir Charles trusted his sons' judgement but said there was something else to consider. He placed a newspaper cutting on the table. The headline read: 'Playboy Murdered. Links to Mafia denied.'

'You know what this is about?' he asked his bemused colleagues. They all looked blank. He read the article then summarized it suggesting that The Mafia had allegedly funded the abandoned re-make of Wuthering Heights on which Miss Moltisani had worked. He postulated that bearing in mind that the girl cannot act that she may have obtained her role in that production due to the fact that her family have been linked to organised crime families in Italy.

'Essentially, Sir Charles said, 'this guy was in the role that I find myself in now. He was murdered. Murdered probably by Miss Moltisani's.... family, I think is the name the use.'

The others quickly pointed out that all the Mafia links were made up by the newspapers; it was co-produced by the BBC for goodness sakes! The murder of the man with the red bow tie by gangsters had become something of an urban myth throughout the industry in just a few weeks.

'Nobody ever found out who killed this man but think guys!' Julian said, 'Giuliana may have known this guy but hey, she is obviously nothing to do with the Mafia. Furthermore guys, assuming she was, simply because she's Italian is extremely lazy stereotyping and actually quite racist.'

Sir Charles was easily convinced, he trusted his sons' opinions.

Venue: *Liverpool Dockside Films Productions Office*

Present: *Julian Beswick (Producer), Justin Beswick (Producer), Sir Charles Beswick (Chairman of DFP), Danny McKenzie (Director), Sharon Murphy (F.D.)*

Agenda Item: *Acting inability of Giuliana Moltisani.*

'So, what are we going to do about her?' Julian asked. 'It is quite clear that the girl can't act to save her life.'

The others nodded their heads in disappointed agreement. Justin, who was Julian's brother suggested a re-write of the screenplay to accommodate her. 'I know this is a radical suggestion but although Miss Moltisani is probably the worst actress any of us have ever worked with, we've got to admit that just her presence on film is quite electric. There's something about her that's impossible to explain that just makes people want to watch her.'

Sharon, the person who looked after the company's finances agreed. 'If you think you can do it I actually agree. It's not just because the girl is so gorgeous, and even I can see that, her on-screen presence is hypnotic.' she paused to finish her coffee and said, 'This film needs her – people will want to watch her – people will want to pay money to watch her.'

Sir Charles, the father of Julian and Justin lighting his cigar added a note of caution. 'Has anyone worked out how much this is going to cost? I've not met Miss Moltisani yet but unless you've discovered a new Brigitte Bardot we are going to lose a bloody fortune. Even though Julia Fairfax is putting up most of the money for your little project, Julia is one my oldest and dearest friends and I feel obliged to protect her investment.' He took a long drag on the cigar and with his face subsequently obscured by smoke he continued. 'Julia is one of the loveliest

I have to confess that my performance became worse and worse but I didn't care. To my amazement, for no reason I could possibly imagine, they kept forgiving my lateness, my sometimes appalling acting and my fiery Italian temperament which I exaggerated and exploited rather a lot. I could do no wrong, I felt at times like I was actually living in their piece of worthless fiction, in a world where there were no consequences. I wished that someone would stop treating me like I was so bloody perfect.

Sometimes I wouldn't turn up until midday and was so drunk that I could hardly stand up never mind read the script but even then they would still tell me how was great I was. How pissed do I have to get before they tell me to fuck off?

On evenings, I would either go for a walk by the river or when in a less romantic mood, along the dock road past the disused shadowy warehouses. Liverpool was so right for me now, I liked its mood, it felt like me. I liked being alone because then I could be myself. Alone, I had no image, no ideal to live up to.

Obviously, I didn't believe Julia's story about having to leave Nick, about not being in love with him but nevertheless I thought it was a brilliant story. I did however have to admit that I did rather enjoy being away from Nick. It was liberating not to be his perfect girlfriend. Away from Nick I was free to be whoever I wanted and to behave however I liked. This was guilty happiness and this guilt grew worse when I realized more and more that I didn't want to see him all the time. I still knew however that we did have the perfect love together, I could think of nothing more magical than the feeling inside when I was with him or even just when I thought about him. It was all too confusing.

EMERGENCY PRODUCTION MEETING

something that had once been so real and vibrant but was now just a reflection of what it had once been.

Despite the faults or maybe because of them I really liked Liverpool. It was falling apart but bizarrely there was building work all over the city too. Derek Hatton and his socialists were in charge and Julia believed they were going to do wonders. Julia even had a signed photograph of Cllr. Hatton. That was just odd. It was hilarious that a politician was giving out signed photographs – very showbiz! I felt good, I was happy with my new job, it felt good to be doing something again. It was different from what I'd been used to; quite Bohemian or as Keith would no doubt have said: arty farty bollocks. What was so refreshing after stagnating with Nick for all those months was having something to get up for each day, except for days when I had a hangover!

I had intended to go back to stay with Nick every weekend but the filming schedules were such disorganised shambles I found that they were still taking Thursday's shoots on Saturday mornings. The producers teased with me that this level of disorganisation must remind me of working in Italy. That was quite insulting but sadly accurate. As the project dragged on, the days began to drag even more, schedules became abandoned and the time between takes lasted longer and longer. So much free time allowed me to catch up on my reading but it also allowed my account at the off-licence to get bigger and bigger each day. Sometimes there was so much time between scenes that I could drink a whole bottle of vodka. I discovered that I liked vodka, it didn't leave any smell on my breath; a nice clean drink.

The producers didn't like vodka. Vodka made their star forget her lines but did give them a reason to explain why their shooting schedule had become so disorganised which was better than admitting they were so totally unprofessional.

words I simply accepting them. I knew it was nonsense, I knew I didn't simply just want to humour Julia and yet, everything she was saying I thought I made perfect sense.

'It's essential my darling, you've got to leave the boy. Unless you get rid of him, you will destroy yourself like I did.' Julia warned very sternly. 'That is why destiny or maybe God himself has put me into your life.'

Did she just say that God himself put her into my life? Only Julia would think that she was God's own messenger!

After I phoned Nick that same evening after this conversation, what Julia had been saying sounded too unreal to have actually happened. I didn't want to think about mystical signs, dumping Nick and I certainly didn't want to believe that me and Nick were not in love. I felt rather foolish about humouring Julia that afternoon.

Filming over-ran so I was unable to go back to Sheffield that first weekend. Instead, on a sunny Saturday afternoon, Julia and I found ourselves sitting on the steps the bombed-out church in Liverpool, traffic fumes and cigarette smoke were battling for position in our lungs. At the end of the road, the big shops of Church Street were breathing out and sucking in mindless swarms of shoppers but where we sat and to the side of us, the shops were either empty or boarded up.

Julia said that when she was at art college there, this used to be one of the main shopping streets and was once a very prosperous area. Evidence of this pernicious decay was everywhere; we walked down to Probe Records which although was just two minutes from Church Street was like being in a different city; a dark, dilapidated and forgotten piece of history. Nothing in Liverpool was what it seemed. It pretended to be brash, glitzy and confident but underneath it was falling apart and desperately sad. We both felt an almost personal grief for the loss of

she kept speaking, she was telling me to be myself, be Giulia Moltisani, to stop trying to be Nick's idea of perfection, not to be anyone else. For me however it was impossible to stop wanting to be like Julia Fairfax especially when Julia Fairfax herself was telling me that I am reliving her life.

I adored Julia, I loved the whole sixties psychedelic philosophies of love but this was too much for me. I knew there could be nothing supernatural happening but nevertheless it was a gloriously insane theory, it was gloriously Julia! I had read about Julia, I knew things about her time in Paris. Like me, she had had been in love with a foreign student. It happens, there was nothing paranormal in that.

It was my turn to comfort Julia now. I put my arms around her: 'Do you really think I am you, fifteen years ago? Do you think I am you when you were having your affair in Paris?'

'God yes. I think you are and you've got to change. I wouldn't wish my life on anyone.'

I was stunned, 'But your life has been incredible. It's been amazing.' I gripped her hand and looked into her eyes.

'No Pussycat, this life of mine that you see isn't real. It's as much an illusion as the love between you and Nick.'

Part of me wanted to shout, 'Bullshit' but I knew I never could. I was in love, everyone knew that but this woman had told me I wasn't.

'So,' said Julia, 'are you leading my life or am I leading your life.'

Just because it was Julia saying this, in a way I wished I could believe her. 'We've been brought together so that I can learn from you? I have got to dump Nick?' Hearing those crazy words coming out of my mouth sounded like the most stupid thing I had ever said in my whole life but for someone like me who didn't just drift into situations, as I heard herself saying those

that you've found it. Nick's pleasant enough but he's really just a nobody who can't believe his luck getting you as a girlfriend. Come on how many students in Sheffield are living with a real Italian model? You're a somebody. It's not the way it is meant to be.'

Julia expected me to scream at her or to throw my boiling coffee into her face. She had seen me lose my temper before so braced herself for a reaction but for some reason I did nothing. I said nothing and thought nothing. I just looked at her and without moving began to cry.

I think I had been smiling constantly for six months. I had not allowed one negative thought or sad emotion to enter my head since moving to my idealised England with my idealised boyfriend.

'Why are you with Nick?' Julia asked, unable to stop herself now. I still could not speak, I just kept crying but for the first time in months it felt good. Those tears were real tears, I felt them burning into face with real pain, real emotion. Real emotion felt so good – it felt refreshing.

'I know exactly why you are with Nick,' Julia said putting her arm around me. 'It's because I was with Jean-Marie and your life is a reflection of mine. Don't know whether it's supernatural, coincidence or, without sounding a little big-headed, you're just copying me but it's not actually you that wants to be with Nick.'

I was still a few ideas behind Julia, I was still thinking about why I loved Nick. Of course I loved him, it didn't matter why or how. I was the lucky one, I was the one who had to pretend to be the perfect girlfriend, the famous Italian model and film star, the runaway bride from the Mafia. I wanted that love to stay so strong it was me would do anything to keep that illusion.

I did not want to hear this nonsense Julia was saying but she wouldn't stop. She carried on telling her what she believed and what she believed was best for me. I wasn't listening but

particular asking for things to happen is pointless because as far as God is concerned, everything has already happened.'

'But without people influencing God surely there would have been no past anyway?' I wondered.

Drinking our coffees, I said to Julia that I simply could not believe that any of our lives had been scripted.

Julia saw the opportunity: this could be my chance! Taking a big breath Julia began: 'No, no, no Pussycat, I'm not saying everything we do is already planned. We can control our lives but God can't – God just knows what will happen to us because to him it's already happened. That doesn't mean he's determining what will happen. We have choice, we are in control of our own destinies, free to choose right or wrong.'

We spoke about whether either of us really felt in control of our lives: Julia stated very categorically that she wasn't. I, of course didn't believe her; she was Julia Fairfax, she was the most together person she had ever met.

In a manner that was over-dramatic, even by her own standards, Julia began: 'This is not your life! Shake out of it Pussycat, you're just a shadow of whom you're supposed to be. Be yourself, not just a reflection of a blank page.'

Julia had waited days to tell me this, it was important. She had planned to introduce it subtlety, to drip feed a few ideas at a time but she had not accounted for her own enthusiasm.

I stared at her blankly as though she was speaking some unknown language. What she had just said hardly made any sense even to Julia so she continued slower and calmer. 'Everything, everything you believe about yourself is false. You and Nick are not in love. You just love the romantic ideal of the perfect love affair. You've convinced yourself that it's real and

'...only the music.' I said finishing off Julia's description; her private memories about the concert, her private yet my own identical memories.

I thought that in her excitement was going to crash the car on these windy roads. The 2CV wisely pulled over to the side of the road. I saw her need, so lit a calming cigarette for her and handed it to her. Julia thrust it into her mouth and sucked on like a suffocating deep sea diver who had just been handed an oxygen cylinder. Now is the perfect time to tell her, Julia thought to herself but didn't. She felt like kicking herself because of her cowardice – but it did sound utterly insane.

When we got to Liverpool Julia took me to a little flat she owned near the old docks. I loved it; my own little place. To help me settle in at Liverpool, Julia, who was staying in another flat she owned visited every day, sometimes for lunch, sometimes for dinner, sometimes for both. Each time we met, Julia tried to steer the conversation towards her theory about us sharing the same life and how it was vitally important to erase Nick from it. It was not the easiest subject to casually bring up, she knew I loved Nick.

One evening over dinner during that first week in a rather luxurious restaurant we found ourselves discussing the argument between pre-determinism and free-will. As we talked I found that I'd really missed being able to have a proper intellectual conversation. Surprising really considering that I'd been living with three university students. Nobody had a mind like Julia Fairfax.

'To God, who exists outside of time,' said Julia, 'everything has already happened. The outcome of something you pray about has already happened to him. He knows whether you win the lottery, your husband lives or dies and who won the third world war. That's why prayer or in

I had told her some horrible things about Giorgio but she recalled that when she was living with Jean-Marie she didn’t have the nicest things to say about Steve either. She resolved that she would speak to me when she picked her up to take her to Liverpool.

Following my tearful goodbye with Nick at the house, Julia drove us over the Pennines to begin that new job in Merseyside. It was so nice to be with Julia again. She seemed so together but that was before I heard about her new purpose in life. I loved talking about her and her past which Julia found both flattering but somewhat inexplicable as to how much I knew about her. She seemed to overlook that once upon a time she had been a minor celebrity with a private life trumpeted from countless gossip columns. Back in the sixties, because of her looks and especially because of her friendship with the photographer and unofficial guru of the hippies, John “Hoppy” Hopkins, it was inevitable that her face had become one of the lasting icons of that time. Even now it was still possible to find a few old books with pictures and stories about Julia Fairfax: 'the glamorous hippie’, 'the beautiful rebel,' or 'the girl who wants to cure the world.'

Julia however didn’t want to admit that I knew so much about her just from books and old magazines – that was far too prosaic. Neither had she realised that I had living in the same house as her own son for the last few weeks. The much more appealing and eventually logical explanation to Julia was that there was some sort of mystical connection. We were too similar to each other for this all this just to be coincidence. Even our love of YES was the same.

When Julia put her *Tales from Topographic Oceans* cassette on in the car, I told her how fantastic they were when I saw them last year: 'The air around me became solid with sound.'

'There was nothing: no past, no future, only the present....' Julia added with an amazed expression as she recognized her own words.

help me. Whether it was God, the stars, her destiny or something she had yet to discover, nothing was clearer to her than what she must now do.

I had not yet moved to Liverpool to start working on that independent film but Julia knew that life was going to be exciting again. Every minute she had spent with me reinforced her theory that we were leading the same life but at different times. Julia knew that it was totally preposterous but she could think of no other explanation.

It was on the night of her birthday on that ferry that she finally believed she understood. It was then that she realized what was happening and what she had to do. In her mind, my life was heading down the same disastrous path as hers and she could stop it. Julia believed she was able to change my future and deflect me from the misery that would engulf me if she did nothing.

Julia had no idea why this was happening, no idea why I was re-living her old life or why she had been chosen to save me but did know one thing. There was no doubt in Julia's mind, in just a few years' time my life will be ruined and I will not want to be alive anymore. Julia had to save me from the tragedies she herself had suffered.

Julia knew she had to tell her but could not think of a way to do this without sounding like the raving lunatic. When she thought about it herself, she had to admit is sounded more than crazy. She practised a few times in front of the mirror but it was impossible for her not to burst out laughing.

'I've got to do this.' she told herself, 'If Giuliana stays with Nick her life will be ruined; I've got to make her go back to her husband in Italy.'

....Part Two

CHAPTER FIFTEEN

May 1985

When Julia came to pick me up a few weeks after her birthday party, she looked different, happier. Since then each morning she had woken up alone and smiling. There were no sordid memories from the night before that she needed to try to forget. Her head felt fresh, her eyes were shining and her breath did not taste of stale alcohol. There was not the usual forgotten watch, cufflink or loud tie abandoned on her floor attempting but failing to remind her of the face of its owner last night. Her bed felt clean. For the first time in years Julia, alone with just her own company was happy.

Something had happened to her, one Sunday woke with a new purpose; she was going to do something good. All her life she had tried to do good, it's what drover her. She had tried to change the world, to stop wars, to end poverty. The world however was still not a good place: thousands were starving to death in East Africa, thousands of South Africans were officially third-class citizens in their own country, thousands of people were killing each other in the middle east, thousands of people had just been killed by another tropical storm in Bangladesh and worst of all, Ronald Reagan had just been re-elected president and was likely to kill millions of people in world war three. By the time she reached forty she started to accept that maybe she couldn't fix the whole world but today she knew she could do one thing, she knew she could

End of Part One....

The passenger in the next seat getting off interrupted my thoughts. Looking out of the window, I noticed some familiar sights, at last we were almost in Liverpool and I would be with her soon. When she phoned me last night, all she seemed to talk about was Julia. She told me some nonsense which sounded like Julia speaking about being able to remember Julia's trip on through the underground sewers of Paris. It was as if Julia was still writing her novels and was turning my Giuliana into one of her characters. I couldn't let that happen, I had to get my Giuliana back to be my Giuliana.

Eventually the train I was on arrived in Liverpool, and found her new flat. I was surprised because although she knew I was coming she was out. After knocking for quite a few minutes, banging louder and louder it was Julia opened the door. Julia was the last person I had expected to see there.

'Giuliana has just gone to the shops, she'll be back soon. You better come in.'

I walked in without saying a word. In an instant all my concerns, the worries that had kept me awake for the past few nights about what this woman was doing to Giuliana vanished. They were replaced once again with the embarrassment of what happened that night on that ferry.

She knew what I was thinking, she could tell. 'Don't worry about it Nick. You were drunk, I was drunk. We all act a bit silly when we're a little tiddled.'

I allowed myself a small smile but noticed that she didn't.

'It really doesn't matter Pussycat because it's not your story now. You're not the narrator of this little tragedy anymore.'

Nick walked over to the window. He looked outside waiting for Giuliana to come back and wondered what might happen to him next.

and whether the Catholic Church was good or bad. I didn't really have an opinion; I just wanted to believe what she believed. For me and for her new fan club, she could say no wrong.

The coach slowly pulled into the University car park at about eight o'clock. She had drunk the little bottle of Vodka that she bought for the journey which helped her sleep through the last hour. I squeezed her hand to wake her up as the coach stopped. As he helped her off Mr West asked if he could lend a hand.

'No, just piss off.' she answered. Mr West had not expected that of this polite and intelligent beauty. He was for once completely lost for words.

Giuliana was glad she was drunk. Telling my tutor to piss off was the highlight of her day. She couldn't stand another lecherous fan thinking she was something she wasn't. She couldn't be that perfect image on the magazines, or TV screens, that Christian or committed socialist. I had no idea then but she couldn't cope with being the perfect girlfriend either.

Apparently vodka was the only thing that could make 'new Coke' palatable so she had a few glasses when we got home then had an early night. She didn't get undressed, she was tired and fell fast asleep. The streetlight outside our bedroom was just bright enough for me to see her face. In that half light with her make-up slightly smudged she looked like a painting by Renoir. She was so beautiful. I had the urge to kiss her but didn't want to wake her. I was the luckiest person in the world. I was lying next to this gorgeous girl, this sex symbol who was madly in love with me. I could not imagine anyone more wonderful or anyone making me as happy. Our love was so special it could withstand anything.

I could not resist, I woke her up to tell her something, I told her that I loved her.

'How can you love someone who doesn't even love themselves?' she replied before turning over and going back to sleep.

proclaimed Mr Cool, who was especially pleased to have a beautiful Italian model along for the ride. I don't think I would have gone if she hadn't have come too.

When we arrived at Ely, Mr West stopped his leering at Giuliana and did his introduction to the cathedral over the coach's microphone. It was his opportunity to do his Radio 1 DJ voice; nobody was impressed. Giuliana laughed, she thought he was funny. She was keener than most of us to learn about English history. Coming from a Catholic country she was quite shocked when confronted with the results of Henry VIII's brutal vandalism on the statues, the images of the Virgin Mary and all traces of the old church. Mr West explained to her that Archbishop Cranmer personally ordered that all the heads of the statues, Catholic idolatry as he saw it, to be smashed.

Mr West was of the opinion that Henry VIII truly believed that he was doing God's work by removing what he saw as the Catholic church's suppression of Christianity. His temporary Italian student disagreed; he enjoyed her considered argument. He wished all his students were like her; she would be his perfect student.

'Henry,' Mr West said, 'believed in Luther's priesthood of all men; that everyone could commune with God. He hated the Vatican because the church of Rome was keeping God to itself.'

I knew this is was exactly what Julia Giuliana believed as well – I squeezed her hand and remembered the first time I met her in the Vatican. She looked at me and whispered, 'I love you.'

I held her hand most of the way home. When not being chatted up by Mr West who eventually began to annoy her, she talked to me and a few other salivating boys about God, Jesus

The day arrived and as the witching hour approached I felt the need to be somewhere else but I could not leave, this was to be the last time I would see my beautiful Giuliana for five days. The whine of a 2CV had never sounded so ominous as I heard her pull up outside our house. She breezed in and kissed us all even Keith, who made her a cup of coffee. There she was, standing incongruously in my living room like a lost film star who had wandered into our life from another age. I wished it was a film but unfortunately it was not watching I was watching, I was in it. Being in the same room as her after what had happened a week ago was more awkward than I could ever have dreamt.

Julia acted as though nothing had happened, as though she hadn't tried to kill herself, as though she hadn't caught me staring lustfully at her, as though that thing when I was holding her hadn't happened. A twisting knot inside me grew tighter as Julia spoke and laughed and pretended that everything was normal. It had been such a lovely few days before Julia came and ruined it. I looked at this manipulative woman laughing, drinking coffee and pretending she was one of the gang in our living room and hated her. Was she going to say anything, was she going to tell Dylan or even tell Giuliana? I knew she would tell her once she had taken her away. She had a whole week to herself to turn her against me.

All the joy that had filled me during that beautiful week before she left was suddenly missing. In its place was a frightening emptiness.

That week before she came and took my Giuliana away, Giuliana invited herself to come with us on my course field trip to Ely Cathedral. It wasn't really allowed but she had a gift of being able to talk people into doing what she wanted. None of my classmates minded this non-student freeloading on their trip, especially the male students. Mr West, our department's self-

if to avoid running over the man with the red flag in front. It was definitely getting slower and slower as we approached Liverpool; I stood up and started to pace up and down the corridor but that did not make us go any faster. Swearing under my breath every time we slowed down for every pointless, deserted station did not help although it did result in the person sitting opposite me vacating his seat. I needed to be with Giuliana. She needed to be with me, not with Dylan's mother.

After Julia's party on the Royal Iris, Giuliana and I only had a week together before she left for that job in Liverpool. That was one week ago. We managed to pack so much into that one week, it was possibly the best week of my life and I know Giuliana felt the same. This last week however has been horrible without her. We spoke on the phone every night but over the last two nights I have sensed something not quite right. It has got to be something to do with Julia, Dylan's mother. For some reason I don't know, she has been seeing that woman most evenings. I was sure she was trying to turn her against me.

It must be because of what happened on that ferry. When she calmly stated that she had watched me lusting after her it was like suddenly being thrown off a comfy sofa and finding myself standing in the middle of a motorway. When I recall what happened as I tried to comfort her I still get a feeling in my stomach as though I had swallowed a massive vat of concrete which was setting and hardening inside me. I tried so hard to expel that unthinkable memory of getting that erection and pressing it against her but failed. That memory hurt me but I thought about it constantly. My perfect week with Giuliana was so magical that I thought Julia would not enter my thoughts but at the back of my mind I knew that she was coming to our house any day now because she was coming to our house to pick Giuliana up and take her to Liverpool.

CHAPTER FOURTEEN

April 1985

‘You’re not supposed to be here.’

I put my book down and looked up at the sombre faced conductor to whom he had just shown his ticket. He said it again, a little louder this time.

‘You’re not supposed to be here.’

He waited for me to say something. ‘What, this seat? Is it reserved?’

‘No, this train. Your ticket is for tomorrow. You do not have a valid ticket to travel on this train.’

After initially informing me that I would have to get off the train at the next station, have the ticket refunded then buy another, the conductor told me with quite the most unnerving smile I’d ever seen that today was my lucky day. He was going to allow me to stay on, because of the sunshine he was in a good mood today. I thanked him profusely for allowing me to continue the journey that I’d just paid for and shook his hand. I don’t think my sarcasm quite registered with him. I hoped that as the conductor had said; today would indeed be my lucky day.

I needed to be with her. I didn’t have time to be stuck on this train yawning slowly between every railway station from Sheffield to Liverpool which seemed to be going so slow as

Julia had found a way to escape from her despair and was now a million miles from the miserable reality that had just invaded her life. She was exploding with excitement. ‘What if it is still 1973 and I’m just imagining all this, imagining you, imagining what Dylan will be like when he’s no longer ten years old and what the mid-eighties will be like. Do you think you’re real or do you think you’re just some sexual plaything I’m imagining?’

Sexual plaything! I could not face her. I could not face her ever again! Please stop talking. Let this not be happening.

‘The thing is,' she said, oblivious to the fact that I was doing my best not to listen to her. 'I don’t think it matters whether this is real or not. It doesn’t matter about all the terrible things I’ve done. Tonight, my darling everything is focussing on you and me and Giuliana. To be quite honest, I have no idea what it all means but there is something truly incredible, something magical about to happen. There's something we are all going to have to do. Something you have to do.'

since it only just happened? That was frightening but not as frightening as reliving Steve's murder. Why now? Why both things now? Even the way you were staring at me before?'

To my relief she pulled away from me and screamed at the water, she was Julia again: 'You undiscovered country from whose bourn no traveller returns, tonight I shall not be yours! Let my grief convert to anger; blunt not my heart but enrage it and spur me on to the discovery of what secrets you hide from me. No, you soft luscious sea, your route is too easy. I am not going to die, this is the beginning.'

'Tonight Nick, I think something special is happening. This very moment in time, what is happening right now to me and to Giuliana and to you is something I don't understand. It must represent something pivotal in my life or in all our lives. That's if what is happening now really is happening and it's not just another premonition I am having.'

I couldn't believe it. I couldn't believe that her pouring out her inner most secrets to me I was doing this, I was still staring at her breasts through her dress. She noticed and folded her arms to hinder my view. Suicidal or not I had to get away. I began to walk off but she shouted to me.

'Wait Nick. Wait. You know it's not just those two things that have happened tonight: vividly recalling Steve's murder and seeing my memory happen years after I first had it. I know why this is happening and I know why you were looking at me the way you did, the way you still are and why what just happened to you has. Don't you see?'

I was too embarrassed for my brain to function. I didn't want to hear what she was saying. I looked hard at the water below wanting this moment to end, wanting to leave and never, ever see her again.

embarrassed in my life. I felt like I had betrayed her, disappointed her, used her. I could almost have thrown myself into the water, I had never felt so awful.

My arms which had been tightly around her fell instantly to my sides but she still didn't let go of me. She was distraught and needed to finish, she needed to expel all these deeply buried corrosive emotions. Whether she pretended that she hadn't noticed or as I hoped hadn't actually noticed at all, she continued, 'Of course I'd never kill myself, I was just wondering what it would be like to simply jump in and drown.'

'Please,' she asked with fresh tears streaming down her cheeks, 'hold me, I need someone to hug me.'

Feeling as sad for her as I was disgusted with myself, I pulled this terribly unhappy lady close. I wanted so much to make her feel better. I didn't want my body to be doing what it was doing.

'Oh dear,' she then said, 'you've got an erection, I thought I could feel something.'

I needed to release her, I needed to step away but she was still holding me tight. This was all wrong. I still had my arms around her and I could still sense her nipples against me.

I wanted her to slap me in the face but I wasn't actually important to her at the moment. She needed to finish unburdening her heart: 'When sorrows come, they come not single spies, but in battalions. Fuck, I hate this fucking life. I really can't fucking stand it!'

I didn't want her to be like this. This wasn't Julia. This wasn't the incredible woman with the perfect life.

With her face resting on my cheek, she continued. 'I cannot express the avalanche of terror that engulfed me when Giuliana acted out that memory of mine. She was word perfect – exactly as I remembered it but how could I have been tormented by that memory for so long

I did not want to be hearing this. I did not want to see this side of her. This was what best friends say to each other, I hardly knew her, this was just my friend's mother; someone I had just been ogling. She squeezed me tighter, I could feel her breasts against me, it was wrong.

'That was until tonight,' she continued. 'As soon as I heard it tonight it was as though it was 1973 again. Sergeant Wilson, yes, I know, Dad's Army - Sergeant Wilson had just told me my husband had been brutally murdered, horribly brutally murdered just feet from where I had been sitting. And do you know who did it? Do you know who smashed his skull in with an iron bar?'

I couldn't believe she was saying this to me. It was as though all the sadness she had been hiding away for the last ten years was now pouring out. This was horrible! I had never felt such pain from anyone else before but then something worse happened. She was literally pouring out her innermost secrets and pain to me and all I was thinking about was that I could feel her nipples pressing onto me. Then it got worse, I hoped it wasn't happening but there was no denying it. I felt myself getting excited. The more I tried not to stop it happening the more obvious my arousal was.

Unaware of the effect she was having on my, Julia continued her story. 'I was Jean-Marie, the boy I loved, the boy I had just had an affair with. He killed Steve, he murdered him a few feet away from where I was sitting listening to this record. Everything was my fault. My wonderful Steve is dead because of me, Jean-Marie is dead or insane because of me, Dylan has no father because of me. I have successfully managed not just to fuck up my own life but it seems everybody I've ever loved.'

Something stopped her instantly in her tracks. She had just felt something pressing into her and she realized it was me. Her look changed to one of shock and surprise. I had never felt so

wrists. The pounding of my heart was drowning out the noise of the party then suddenly silence. She climbed back off the rail and threw her arms around me.

'Thank you.' she whispered into my ear inexplicably. She was not going to die tonight but with her arms around me and mascara stained tears running down her cheeks I still wasn't sure whether I was able to breath or not. I felt I should put my arms around her, she needed comforting, she was desperate for a hug. I wish I hadn't been ogling her, ogling my best friend's mother because how could I then put my arms around her? I felt her tears on my own cheeks. I put my arms around her.

'Do you know what track that was?' She asked me as though what had just happened never had. It was something by Yes but of course I had no idea what it was.

'*Tales from Topographic Oceans* part four.'

I wondered why she was telling me this. I asked her. The bow of the Royal Iris was turning the calm blackness into bubbling white froth. She looked at the dark churning water for a moment, thinking to herself then answered me.

'I had been waiting for months to get that record, to take it home and play it. I had everything planned down to the smallest detail.' Julia began again after a few minutes. 'I must have listened to that piece more times than the band have, I absolutely adore it. I've never allowed myself to associate it with what every cell of my being tells me I should associate it with: the murder of Steve, Dylan's dad. You know Dylan's dad is dead don't you? He was murdered on my drive at the very moment I was inside my house listening to that exact piece of music. I should have been reduced to a gibbering wreck of a woman every time I heard it but no, I've not. Somehow I've simply ignored the fact that the most horrific incident in my life inexorably linked to my first hearing this amazing album. '

The red and orange lights on the giant cranes and gantries in the empty docks and derelict shipbuilding yards reflected off the river and shimmered across Julia's exquisite silky dress.

It must have been because I was drunk because I didn't disguise the fact that I was staring at her. Without disguising the fact, I just stood behind her letting my eyes absorb the image. I could not have cared if she turned around and saw me. I could not have cared if Dylan or even Giuliana saw me. I was drunk and didn't care. I was staring at this beautiful woman in a sexy silk dress and I didn't care. The breeze off the river was forcing her dress to cling tightly to every curve and contour of her body. I was not going to stop looking.

I wasn't sure whether my eyes were playing tricks on me. No, they weren't. Julia was sitting on the railing, her feet were dangling over the edge of the boat. She just needed to nudge herself forward one inch and she would be gone, she would be under the black, churning water. Suddenly I wasn't drunk anymore. I was more sober than I had ever been before looking at my best friend's mother about to throw herself into the river. How could I have not noticed? I had been staring at her for ages and I hadn't noticed, what the hell was wrong with me?

I had to act. Do something! I didn't know what to do. This can't be happening! I was frozen. She was going to kill herself and I was going to watch. I was not going to save her. I was just going to let it happen. I was going to hate myself. I wanted to know what to do but I couldn't move.

It felt like this moment was lasting forever. Still the muffled music was drifting out of from downstairs in waves getting louder and quieter. Still I could hear people down there enjoying themselves; talking, laughing and singing. Still I just looked at her doing nothing. I don't know how but eventually I found that I had run over to her and was tightly gripping her

earthquake or floods rather than something so mind bogglingly unimportant as the name of some band that nobody has ever heard of. In other words, no mate.'

Penny, the medical student tried to explain to us that deja vu can be explained psychologically by the brain's system for short term memory becoming embedded in the system for long term memory but none of us were listening.

Across on the dance floor Julia was not finding it easy to walk. I watched her stagger towards the disco lights the DJ had set up around one of Lisa's giant Roger Dean mushrooms. They were whizzing around in front of her eyes, even though it was her beloved YES, the booming sound didn't sound like anything to her, she felt that she was going to pass out. She bumped into the light stack. She grabbed onto something that was hot. It was burning her hand but she didn't care, it kept her upright. She was going to stand there a while until she knew where she was. Neither Dylan or Lisa seemed to be too concerned, I think they was used to this type of thing.

After some monotonous YES song that seemed to last for hours the DJ put that stupid song on with the equally stupid dance. As annoying as it was, me and Dylan couldn't resist the urge to get up and dance and embarrass Penny and Giuliana. We didn't disappoint and it was nice to see Giuliana smile again. I noticed that I couldn't see Julia anymore, she must have found someone to talk to.

The next life draining YES dirge the DJ put on gave me no choice. I either find the nearest yard arm to hang myself from or get away from the disco whilst it played. I found myself out on deck, the fresh air felt good. I noticed that the ferry was turning around heading back to the Pier Head. I was kneeling down behind a bench out of the wind trying to light my cigarette and after at least twenty attempts I finally got it lit and stood up and saw Julia just ahead of me.

'Far out!' Mr Spitfire commented which for once I considered was actually appropriate response.

'Giuliana,' Julia gasped bewildered, 'what does this mean? Who are you?'

Giuliana didn't answer, she was frightened, Julia was scaring her. Julia was scaring us all.

'Answer me someone!' screamed Julia.

None of us knew what to say but we didn't need to because Julia jumped up from her chair knocking it flying onto the dance floor in panic.

'Though this be madness, yet there is method in it ' she said quoting Hamlet then draping her long flowing sleeve across her face she fled into the main lounge.

'Don't worry,' giggled Lisa, breaking the silence with a measure of normality, 'she's been doing this since she was fifteen. Last year she thought she was Judas. Not like Judas or even a reincarnation but the real guy who was going to kill Jesus. You've just got to love that crazy girl! Let's get another round of drinks shall we before she comes back?'

Giuliana was still really scared, she was confused, she was vulnerable. She didn't want to be there anymore, she didn't want to be wearing her revealing outfit anymore and slipped her coat back on unaware of how hot it was. She was crying, I put my arms around her and was angry with Julia for doing this to her. Dylan apologized on her behalf, he told Giuliana how much his mother liked her and that she didn't mean to upset her. I asked whether he thought his mother was really serious.

'What that she has some supernatural power that she can receive messages from the future like some Old Testament prophet?' Dylan replied. 'I'm sure Moses and that lot used foresee momentous or earth shattering events like the end of the world or warnings about

about that inexplicable conversation but every time Lisa had refused to recall it ever happening. Tonight was to be no exception but tonight was different because tonight Giuliana was listening.

Giuliana had never heard of the band but had heard about the May Blitz. 'May Blitz?' she butted in, 'I never thought of that until you say that. They named a band after something as horrible as bombing of Liverpool! Bloody hell, that is really bad taste.'

'Giuliana!' shouted Julia, 'I said that then! Those were the very words I remembered saying. The exact same words! Fuck! Did you hear what she said Lisa?'

Julia shouting, 'Lisa, seriously fucked up. Did you hear what she just said?' Lisa was still slouched in the chair taking in the last vapours from the soon to be expired joint.

Julia, whose excitement had turned to sheer panic carried on. 'We were on the steps of St Luke's. Lisa. Remember I said that I could see myself saying that about May Blitz but I was someone else but somehow it was still me?'

Lisa shrugged her especially padded shoulders. She had no recollection of this conversation and thought that maybe after twenty years of telling her friend this, Julia might have realized that by now.

But Julia knew she was right: 'Don't you see, I was telling you something twenty-two years ago that was a memory of now, of what's just happened. Giuliana just said now what I told you twenty-two fucking years ago! You must remember. I said I was someone else but I was there – well, I was her, Giuliana!'

'Listen to me Lisa,' she demanded at the top of her voice to Lisa's complete bemusement, 'What is happening now, right now, right at this very moment with us all sitting around this table must is something I've remembered happening before it ever happened. Oh my God Giuliana, it was your memory I remembered.'

'Yes, I am from a traditional Italian family. My father in law is what you would call the Godfather. I ran away to be with Nick. My Father in law will be having hit men looking for us now but I know I am safe here. Julia is hiding me!' She kissed Julia on the forehead.

'Well,' laughed Lisa, not even sure whether that was even an Italian accent, 'with what you are wearing, you've not quite got the hang of being inconspicuous, have you?'

I liked Lisa, I had never met her before she was one of those people that one feels one has always known. Like Julia, Lisa did not look her age, she gave off a glow of slightly tongue in cheek glamour. She was much more grounded than her old friend but just as full of energy.

'Well does this live up to expectations?' Lisa asked, referring to the fact that she had organized this extravaganza.

'It's perfect Darling, just like you said it would be when we sat on those frozen steps the day I went to London. Remember how you promised to throw a massive party for me each decade? My twentieth was to be at a club in London, my thirtieth in a palace, and my fortieth – yes darling, my fortieth on an ocean Liner sailing to New York.'

'Well,' said Lisa, 'it's pretty close and I thought you'd appreciate the cheesiness.'

Julia remembered that snowy day in 1963 really well: the big freeze of '63. She remembered the cold, hugging Lisa, even what they had spoken about: getting married to Steve, being pregnant, whether she would still have a social life. She remembered speaking about how that church got bombed and telling Lisa about a Band called 'May Blitz' and how she considered the name inappropriate considering it was named after something so hideous.

She especially remembered that conversation because that band would not exist for another six years but somehow, she remembered them. Ever since May Blitz eventually came into existence and long after they disappeared into obscurity, Julia had been reminding Lisa

inflicted sufferings. Julia’s fictional soldier knew that leaving his wife for his French tart was stupid, pointless and would ruin his life but that was the challenge he needed.’

‘I was obviously stoned out of my head when he gave me his philosophy because its complete bollocks but most things were in 1970 so it fitted in nicely to my plot.’ Julia joked to Giuliana.

‘Bollocks Pussycat?’ Mr Spitfire interrupted, ‘No, in vino veritas. Allow me to explain, everything was so great in the sixties that we had to invent things to worry about. Just like after the war, we had to find things to make us suffer. We made up things to worry about: other people’s wars, other people’s suffering, imaginary bombs that nobody was ever going to use, even sex, and of course filthy books written by sex-crazed hippies.’

‘Sex-crazed, drugged-up purveyors of filth. Must remember that for my tombstone.’ Julia laughed.

Giuliana was entranced with Mr Spitfire’s silky upper class English accent but was not sure she agreed with him. ‘Me and Nick are in love, we have everything we could ask for and life couldn’t be better.’ she said. ‘I’m not looking for something dangerous or something to make me suffer. Maybe your theory was only true after the war when people had become used to suffering.’

Eventually myself, Dylan, Penny and then Julia's friend Lisa joined them.

'This is Giuliana.' Julia told her old friend, 'She's the runaway wife of an Italian gangster on the run from the Mafia.'

Rather than laughing this introduction off like I would have expected, Giuliana took up the baton and embellished the story even more.

‘Our friend here was quite infamous about fifteen years ago.’ the old gentleman explained. ‘Purveyor of filth, I think one particularly un-erudite newspaper reviewer called you didn’t he?’

‘Drugged-up purveyor of filth.’ Julia corrected him.

‘And I was her inspiration.’ he laughed.

Julia felt her old friend’s comment needed further clarification. She told Giuliana how she had written a novel about a soldier who was in love with his wife but left her for a peasant girl he met whilst fighting in France. Why did he sacrifice his loving relationship for what was essentially lust? Would someone who was part of the 1940s leave his 1940s wife and his 1940s life simply for lust? He would if the girl in France was so exceptionally sexy, so lewd and filthy that he wouldn’t be able to resist; that was her premise. But she felt it wasn’t enough; it wouldn’t happen, he needed a better motivation.

‘When I was struggling for a reason back in 1970, Mr Spitfire gave me the answer.’

‘The answer was the danger: man’s addiction to danger. During the war,’ the old gentleman said, ‘for many people just waking up to discover they were still alive was a reason to celebrate. Can you imagine the joy of waking up and saying to yourself: I’m still alive and being amazed? Probably not.’

Mr Spitfire, taking on a school-masterly persona continued. ‘After 1945, after the war had ended people then just woke to their safe and ultimately mundane 1940s lives. After war it was unbearable for people who had lived every minute of the lives on the edge. Without life or death struggles, mankind finds other ways to challenge itself. When there is no challenge, subconsciously people make themselves suffer to see if they could escape from their self-in Texas. Mr Spitfire, never one to dress conventionally had not mellowed with age. Complimenting his long white hair, he wore a white suit and a multi-coloured psychedelic t-shirt.

'It's my mature Miami Vice look.' he said.

'Days of future passed!' exclaimed Giuliana realising what the swirling colourful pattern on his t-shirt was and wishing that he would call her Pussycat as well.

'My goodness, I didn't think someone of your age would recognise a Moody Blues album cover.'

'I must be older than I look. Una capellone!' she laughed. 'I know this one. There are hidden pictures and shapes you can only see when viewed from certain angles.'

Julia looked closely at her old friend's t-shirt: 'Giulia darling, look at that shape from this side. From this angle it's a naked girl, just like you tonight!'

Subconsciously covering herself up by folding her arms she laughed. 'And from this side it's a skull, e magnifico.'

'Bloody hell baby,' the old man said to Julia, 'Looking for hidden pictures in psychedelic album covers; it's like the sixties never went away.'

Mr Spitfire took out and lit a pre-prepared joint that he shared with his two companions. 'Giuliana,' he said, 'you remind me so much of this old tart about twenty years ago.'

'That's so right Mr Spitfire,' laughed Julia. 'I used to be Italian?'

'So my dear,' asked Mr Spitfire, 'have you read any of this beautiful lady's books?'

Giuliana admitted that not only had she read her books but she was a bit of a fan. She told the old man how amazed she was when she discovered that her boyfriend's best friend's mother was one of her heroes. It was fate.

'The decoration is wonderful.' Giuliana said to Julia when she met her again, 'I feel like I am inside *Tales from Topographic Oceans*.'

'Brilliant isn't it. You wouldn't remember but when YES toured in the 70s their sets were just like this.'

When we all walked back into the baking hot party lounge the DJ put '*Birthday*' by the Beatles on and called Julia to the front. Her friend Lisa dashed up as well and presented her with the massive card. Julia then grabbed the microphone and got everyone to stand up, grab each other and do a conga around the boat. I have no idea who grabbed me but before I had time to say hello, I was being whisked around the boat by a particularly massive German lady. Penny was behind her and Dylan behind her. It was the most uncool activity any of could imagine but it was brilliant fun. Every one of us, especially Penny, who had forgotten she was meant to be hating this, was having a fantastic time.

Dancing past the lounge on the lower deck, Julia who was at the head of the Conga with Giulianna behind her looked in and gave a scream of excitement. She pulled Giuliana purposefully from the conga-chain and dragged her in to meet someone.

'Mr Spitfire! My darling, how absolutely fantastic to see you.'

This old man with unfashionably long white hair looked equally as thrilled to see Julia. Despite his age, he sprang up from the chair like a teenager to greet his old friend.

'Pussycat - I wouldn't miss one of your parties for the world. And who is your beautiful young friend?'

Giuliana blushed at the old man's flattery and introduced herself. Julia explained who the old gentleman was: a dear old friend whom she had known for years and despite his homelessness appearance he actually owned a computer business and had homes both here and

‘Gosh my dear, that’s really impressive, it really is.’ she commented before switching the conversation back to herself. ‘Do you know that when I did my parade through Paris – and I am actually a little embarrassed about telling you this, someone decided to paint my “you know what” green, you know. like a real bush. But all we could find was green emulsion paint.’

‘For God’s sake Mother!’ Dylan exclaimed, ‘Too much information.’ The rest of us were in absolute fits of laughter as Dylan tried to crawl under the floorboards.

‘I told you I could be more embarrassing!’

‘And the next day,’ laughed Julia, ‘when that stupid green paint had dried it was like a prickly hedgehog stuck to me!”

‘Yes,’ Giuliana screamed with tears streaming down her face, ‘remember the faces of those shocked Japanese tourists in front of the Sacre Cour. The ones you didn’t notice until you were upside down doing your handstand?’

'Oh my God yes - but how do you know that? I’d forgotten about those poor innocent Japanese. Even I had forgotten that.' Julia said. Giuliana could not answer; she must have read about this. Julia was amazed and slightly shocked and wondered how Giuliana could possibly managed to share a secret memory. For just a second, Julia’s stopped laughing.

The Royal Iris started the river cruise with a blast of its tinny horn. As the floor began to rattle and shake, Giuliana grabbed my arm and we dashed up on deck to watch the city glide slowly away from us. From this distance with its lights twinkling and reflecting on the water, Liverpool was surprisingly beautiful. Although this was such a perfect romantic setting every so often, we both burst out laughing when we remembered Julia’s story. After a while we wandered back downstairs to the party.

I also felt that I was going to explode. Opposite me sat my, up to girlfriend practically topless in the company of my friends and all these respectable people most of whom were old enough to be her parents. I wanted to stare but couldn't; I didn't want Dylan's mother to notice.

'I bet you wish she was your girlfriend don't you Darling?' Julia whispered to son but not quietly enough to stop the rest of us including Penny to hear her. Julia laughed inwardly; she liked to tease people. Brushing her comment aside, Dylan purposely kissed Penny on the cheek. Giuliana was pleased for the attention to be switched from what had just happened.

'I've not seen body-paint for years.' Julia said. 'God, how can that be so many years ago? It seems like only the other day when I went parading through Paris stark naked except for body paint.'

'Thanks for embarrassing me Julia.' Dylan said.

She continued: 'I was painted as the French flag; red, white and blue. I made quite a scene as I walked down the middle of the Champs Elysée as naked as the day I was born.'

'Except for the beret.' Giuliana blurted out.

'Yes, that's right; I'd forgotten about that. I had a black beret didn't I.'

Cringing, Dylan put his head in his hands. 'Actually, this woman is a complete stranger. I was mistaken when I said she was my mother. My real mother is actually upstairs driving this boat – you'll meet her soon. Please ignore this person and anything she says.'

'I assure you Darling, I could be far more embarrassing if I wanted.'

'Giulia,' said Penny excitedly, 'show Julia your back.' She obliged.

'Look, I've even done a label and a catch!' Penny added proudly but trying not to sound like she was trying to impress her boyfriend's mother,

see-through white blouse delicately floating above a black lacy bra. On closer inspection however it was apparent that this was not actually a bra, it was body paint. It was Penny's idea. They were both going to do it together originally but she chickened out when they got to Liverpool. Apparently Penny had tried this before at the Medsoc ball to great effect and had convinced Giuliana what a laugh it would be.

It took a few seconds for everyone else to realise what they were seeing. Julia was first to notice, ‘Oh my God darling, that truly is quite a work of art!’ she gushed.

Dylan had been wondering all evening what we were up to but had never guessed this, he was impressed and not a little excited. Penny was jumping up and down with excitement.

He was impressed: ‘You know what is brilliant about this?’ Dylan laughed, staring at Giuliana’s breasts. ‘I can actually stare at your tits and you won’t slap me.’

‘But I will.’ His mother said, hitting him with another French stick.

‘This is so good,’ Dylan’s mother said as she ever so gently lifted one of Giuliana’s breasts, ‘you’ve even done the pattern here underneath.’

A tingle of excitement shot through Giuliana’s whole body like an electric shock as she felt the fingers of her idol, Julia Fairfax on her. Julia could tell it was appreciated, she could feel her new friend’s heat beating faster. Giuliana wanted to say something but she had temporarily forgotten lost the ability to speak. Getting ready earlier she had expected her exhibitionism to be both shocking and hilarious. She hadn’t expected this. Gazing with unhidden delight into Julia’s mischievous eyes, she felt her fingers tenderly lift her breast and tenderly stroke her skin before letting go. She felt suddenly naked and dreadfully self-aware. Although more uncomfortable than she could ever remember feeling before it was strangely exhilarating.

guessed that she probably did know these. By now both Penny and I were really looking forward to seeing the fruits of our efforts in getting Giuliana ready.

The upper lounge of the Royal Iris had been decorated with massive shell-like, multi-coloured inflatable decorations to give it an undersea feel. One of Dylan's mother's friends thought himself to be another Roger Dean so had done his best to make the ferry look like a YES album. To compliment the pseudo-YES artwork, the music pumping from the inside of the boat was YES. Dear God, why!

On board there was an incongruous mix of genteel English sophistication blended uneasily with middle aged people trying to be teenagers. Middle-aged people dressed as hippies annoyed me as much as middle-aged people pretending to be students. Middle aged people pretending to be hippie students was more than intolerable. I braced myself because I could sense what was coming, I knew one of them was going to say 'groovy' any moment.

'Darling!' a voice called from behind a pulsating giant pink and green bubble. It was Dylan's mother tonight looking more like Joan Collins from Dynasty than Joan Collins herself.

'Happy birthday Mother!' He gave her a massive hug. 'So how's middle age then?'

Julia thought for a few seconds which witty retort to use but then opted for a more suitable response. She picked up a French stick and broke it over his head.

'Glad you could make it.' she said to Penny. 'I'm Julia, that arsehole's mother. I am forty years old and I'm pissed already.'

Laughing as though she had just witnessed the funniest thing in her life Giuliana removed her coat and placed it on a vacant chair next to Julia. Shaking crumbs out of his hair Dylan now understood why Giuliana had taken so long getting ready. Complementing an elegant long black skirt giving her that inevitable air of elegance that so characterized her she was wearing a semi

woken up ready for yet another day struggling just to survive then just looked at itself in the mirror, sighed and gave up. The city had just given up. No hope, no future.

She told me to cheer her up and make her smile. She did not want to feel sad because tonight she was going to meet Julia, her hero again, she couldn't be unhappy tonight.

The taxi trip into town did not really help lighten our mood. Even though it passed through the city centre, what we saw seemed to get worse if anything. Shabby and neglected houses nestled with the ubiquitous boarded up shops and seedy clubs. Tacky fast-food shops and empty restaurants shone their gaudy neon lights into unkempt streets strewn with litter; nothing looked like it was ever clean. The pubs however were heaving with people, the majority of them looked surprisingly stylish. Smart, well-dressed people looked out of place here and yet nearly everyone seemed to have made an effort.

Penny noticed this too: 'Considering they're not supposed to have any jobs or any money, how come they can all afford these clothes?'

'They nick them!' Dylan replied without thinking. When his brain reminded him that he was being driven by a Liverpudlian taxi driver, he wished he hadn't tried to be funny, especially as he hadn't been.

Giuliana gave him a stern look and corrected him. 'When times are bad, people will still cling on to their dignity. It's called having pride. When all hope is gone, pride is all they have left.'

Our taxi dropped us off at the Pier Head and we joined the crowds of people queuing to get on to the Royal Iris. I wondered whether Dylan's mother knew all of these people. Some were in evening dress but quite a few were dressed in a ridiculously pretentiously manner so I

windows boarded up and covered with graffiti. The windows above had been smashed. The houses seemed to be derelict but obviously they could not all be empty. It was hard to tell which were lived in and which were abandoned. It was the sort of decay that made it difficult to determine whether there was life there or not. Countless rows and rows of identical miserable streets stretched out for miles and miles. Further down this road I could see that the rows of terraced red brick houses just suddenly stopped giving way to what could only be described as wasteland. It was horrible.

I thought I'd seen what life was like in the north by going to University in Yorkshire at a time when all the heavy industry was dying and the coal mines were closing. Looking around this place I knew he hadn't. This was unlike anything I was prepared for. It didn't even feel like being in England, everything was old, broken and decaying. How could a city in England still have bomb sites in it from World War II? Even the tarmac in the roads was cracked and broken; weeds were everywhere. In a normal city, cars and lorries would have flattened and killed them but these roads were virtually devoid of vehicles. I said to Dylan that I just couldn't understand why this town was so depressed.

'My mother would probably blame Thatcher but I can always remember Liverpool being like this, possibly even worse. Maybe it's capitalism; there's always got to be rich and poor? Oh I don't know, it's just the way it is mate.'

After our cigarettes we went back across the empty street into the house. I cheered myself up by helping Giuliana get ready and Dylan cheered himself up by having sex with Penny.

Once upon a time I would have been like Dylan, just accepting that shit happened but Giuliana's compassion was infectious. Even after I had added the finishing touches to Giuliana's outfit, I still felt quite down. She said to me that it was as if one day the whole of the city had

could visit the Liver Buildings, see the historic seafront, take in the famous Georgian and Victorian architecture, go and see what was inside that building that looked like the Parthenon of Athens. He could have a look in that futuristic Catholic cathedral or the huge Anglican one that was the biggest cathedral in the country. He could even go up that weird tower that was on the opening titles of Brookside. He liked Liverpool; England's second city, his mother's home town. She had brought him here as a little boy, he remembered being taken on the ferry across the Mersey.

He walked to the bus stop and waited a couple of minutes but no bus came. He began to doubt whether it was still in use or whether buses still came along this road so walked back. Opposite the house were a couple of swings. These were apparently designed for children who might appreciate the excitement of not knowing which component would break first before thrusting them into the blistered concrete strewn with broken glass and abandoned needled. It was a difficult judgement to make as to whether it would be the rusty chains attached to the cracked frame or the rotten wooden seats.

I had just popped out for a smoke and noticed Dylan was still there so went over and sat on the less lethal looking of the two swings.

Coupled with the smell of urine coming from somewhere close by it did not make for the most salubrious of surroundings but it was somewhere to sit.

'Couldn't be arsed going into town.' Dylan said joining me on the other swing.

With a horrible creaking sound, he gently started to swing trying not to get rust stains on himself. I elected to keep the swing stationary, it was quieter and undoubtedly safer. Looking around me, unlike Dylan, I had no compunction to explore the rest of the city if this was an indication of what Liverpool was like. Opposite me was a row of shops with their bottom

‘No,’ I pointed out, a little more forceful this time, ‘this bloke I knew was quite a sparky guy.’

Dylan’s friend wasn’t having any of it, it just spurred him on. ‘They don’t have a buffet up here, they have a buff-it. If you say buffet they literally piss themselves, they think you’re queer. Ooh, ooh, you can pronounce a French word, that's conclusive proof that you're homosexual, let’s beat you up. Tossers the lot of them! Ooh, ooh, ooh you’ve read a book, you must be a queer, let’s beat you up.’

I could tell Dylan was a little embarrassed about his friend but he was too much of a people pleaser to say anything so he just laughed and patted him on his back.

Somehow this actually encouraged him: 'And they think they're so bloody fantastic too! Just because one reasonable pop band came from here years ago they think they're God's gift to music. And they're the only ones with a sense of humour. And if the rest of the country doesn't agree then they just think that everyone has got it in for them. Self-righteous, lazy bastards who think they deserve some God given right to get fucking everything for doing fuck all, that's what Scousers are. God I hate them.'

Secretly I thought he was quite funny but to Giuliana’s relief he didn’t stay around; he went out to be angry somewhere else leaving us to get ready for Julia's party. Penny and I had a brilliant idea but it was going to take a little while to prepare. We could hear Dylan outside our room trying to figure out why we were giggling. Dylan tapped on our door, ‘I fancy having a look around the city, anyone fancy coming with me?’ He was desperate to find out what was amusing us but we weren't going to tell him.

Spurned by me and Penny, Dylan thought he’d go and explore by himself. It was only a ten minute bus ride back into the City Centre and there was a bus stop at the end of the road. He

here is there.' A few tears began to trickle down her cheeks. It didn't take much to make Giuliana cry, I thought it was a very endearing part of her.

Arriving at our temporary home for the night we discovered that Dylan's friend in whose house we were staying was a southerner who had no time for the locals.

'Miserable bastards, the lot of them.' was his reply to Giuliana's genuine enquiry about how he felt the population had coped with the terrible levels of unemployment. He was a sociology student so she had expected a slightly more erudite answer.

He continued, 'The trouble with these lot is they think the world owes them a favour; they've all got massive chips on their shoulders and they think everyone hates them. They're not paranoid though, everyone actually does hate them; the whinging, thieving gits. They're all such bloody martyrs wallowing in this derelict arsehole of the country: "Oh, oh, oh, life's so shit for us it must be everybody else's fault; it couldn't be our fault because we're bloody Scousers and we're so bloody perfect." Bastards!'

Giuliana was really glad she didn't know this particular friend of Dylan.

'I worked with a Scouser when I did a summer job last year.' I mentioned recalling a summer job I did a few years ago at B&Q: 'He wasn't too bad actually.'

'No, you're wrong.' said the Scousophobe rebuking this interruption firmly before carrying on. 'I'll give you an example. Up here, they use the word "student" as an insult. Are you a student, they say and if you say yes they say: you must be a poof then and start laughing. I kid you not. They seem to equate education with homosexuality. If you don't like football then they think you're a queer. If you don't go to the match then it's obvious to them that you're a poof. They're all bloody retards, the whole lot of them.'

CHAPTER THIRTEEN

March 1985

It was quite a short train journey over the Pennines to Liverpool but it felt like we had travelled to a different country. Everything; the light, the sights and smells were different. It was as though someone had been playing with the controls on the TV; the contrast wasn't quite as sharp; the colour and brightness were dim and the sound was muffled. Walking out into Lime Street the very atmosphere felt heavy, it was still, subdued and dejected. The city gave the impression of being in a state of mourning, mourning the loss of its own life.

Whether true or not, for years the city itself had felt it was being crushed by a vindictive Government hundreds of miles away in London. Continuously battered into submission, disliked or worse, laughed at by the rest of the country, its fight had gone. The character of this city was now gloomy resignation. Those archetypal chirpy Scousers with their famous sense of humour were conspicuous by the absence. There was nothing to joke about anymore.

As soon as our bus left the busy centre of the city, the landscape changed. The grandiose classical architecture made way for shabby run down streets. There were hardly any people outside and those that were looked like a defeated army walking back from a battle. Giuliana was shocked and upset as she looked out of the top window of the bus onto derelict housing, closed down businesses, boarded up shops and unemployed men huddled together, unsure of what to do with their newly imposed free time. Voicing her thoughts she said: 'There is no hope

The arm of the record player eventually pulled up. Julia carefully placed the shiny black vinyl disc record back into the cover. 'That was fantastic.' she said to the inspector whose name she hadn't caught. 'It was worth the wait.'

Carefully placing her new LP on the shelf, she sat down, folded her arms and smiled at Sergeant Wilson. 'So, what happens now?' she asked.

Somehow a year later that once charismatic and attractive young man had managed to organize himself to get to England to find Julia. Filthy, stinking and virtually insane he had located his one true love and crunched up her path.

It was there that he met the other poor man whose life Julia had accidentally destroyed. Realizing that this was the man who had taken Julia from him he had no other option other than to kill him, to squash him, to make him go away.

'You haven't introduced yourself.' Julia said to the sergeant.

'Sergeant Wilson.' he replied.

Julia laughed. 'Like in Dad's Army!'

Sgt. Wilson was used to unusual reactions but Julia's was more unusual than most.

'Sergeant Wilson,' Julia said very calmly, *'Tales from Topographic Oceans* was supposed to be released a month ago. I have been waiting to hear what is possibly Yes' best album ever and this morning was the time I was going to listen to it.'

The sergeant listened to Julia's composed description of the album's content, the themes it explored and how she still had ten minutes left and how nothing was going to stop her listening to it. In the most bizarre conditions he could imagine, now with his inspector present, the sergeant and four other police officers stood silently in a row in the front room as Julia turned the record player back on and sat down to listen to the music. Less than an hour ago her former lover smashed Steve's skull to pieces outside the door which was now open. Police in white overalls were still picking pieces of her dead husband out of the gravel. Some of them looked in through the door wondering what the noise was. They saw their Inspector and their colleagues standing still in a row next to the wife of the murdered man who sat down listening and clearly enjoying a record whilst following the words on the gatefold sleeve.

revolting act of inhumanity the police had ever seen, it was certain that Jean-Marie would not be going anywhere.

'We have apprehended your husband's assailant. He appears to be a young French vagrant.' the sergeant said.

Julia knew immediately that it was Jean-Marie. She knew immediately what had happened to him after she had left him. In the way novels say that one's life passes through the mind at the moment of death she saw what had happened to Jean-Marie. He was not like her, not like Steve and not like Mr Spitfire. He was 1969, that was his time. After Julia left him the sixties ended and so did his life. He didn't want the seventies, he didn't want that lonely dismal decade without Julia. He could not live without her but neither could he end his life in case one day he won her back. His escape was heroin. The drug allowed him to escape reality, to remain in 1969 waiting for the day Julia would come back to him. It was a surprise that he stayed alive; he rarely ate, he slept on the streets but by surviving on an income gained from thieving and a few menial and usually illegal jobs to keep him supplied with heroin.

Although no longer a celebrity, his former lover was still occasionally in the newspapers and magazines, even in France. The cuttings he took were his only possessions but they were all he needed. It was these tattered faded newspaper cuttings and the absurd hope that she would be his again that kept him alive. When, out of desperation he somehow managed to compose a letter to her a year ago the last thing he expected was to get a reply from her. She knew she should have thrown it straight into the bin. She knew that replying to him was the most stupid thing she could possibly do. Nevertheless she did reply to him.

driveway. People in white overalls were laying a big green sheet over part of her path, the path she had just excitedly ran up an hour ago. The gravel beneath the big green sheet was stained red, it looked like blood.

Steve had gone out without his key again, he did this a lot these days. He had heard music coming from the house so knew Julia was in so had been knocking on the door but she hadn't heard him. He decided to wait, these days he did a lot of waiting, he was patient. He would wait for hours if he needed to, he didn't mind.

He didn't recognize the person who walked up the path to him but being polite he introduced himself. The stranger picked up the metal bar from the floor and smashed it into his face. Steve fell to the floor. The stranger continued to smash the metal bar into Steve's head until it broke, until it was no longer head shaped, until it turned into a pile of red and grey mush.

The stranger then walked back down the path to a Citroën 2CV which was unlocked and sat inside and waited for the police to come. He knew the police would come because he knew that people had watched him break Steve's head. Some people had come out when they heard the noise. He knew the Citroën 2CV was Julia's because she used to say to him that she always wanted one. Jean-Marie could remember everything Julia had ever said to him. Jean-Marie remembered everything she had ever said to him all the time, he remembered very little else.

When the police dragged him from the car and threw him to the ground he could not remember smashing Julia's husband's head to a pulp or why he was covered in blood and brains. Years of pumping heroin into his veins did this to him.

Terrified by the strange uniformed men dragging him and kicking him he became a savage clawing at them and biting them in attempt to escape. Sickened and horrified by the most

'Mrs Fairfax,' the sergeant said firmly, unable to comprehend being treated like this.

Like a naughty child, Julia turned away from him and stared intently at the opposite wall.

'Mrs Fairfax, this is important. Please listen to me.' the sergeant said. Still she ignored him making him as annoyed as she was. She stood up and tried to turn the record player back on but the other policeman stopped her.

'Mrs Fairfax!' the sergeant shouted at the top of his voice. 'Your husband is dead! He has been killed.'

He realized what he had just said. His years of training on how to be sensitive in these situations had flown out of the window. Julia stopped wresting with the constable and looked at the sergeant with sheer bemusement.

'Sit down Mrs Fairfax.'

She did what he said.

'I am very, very sorry to tell you that we believe your husband, Stephen Fairfax has been killed.'

Some things cannot immediately be heard and certainly not understood and this was one of them. Julia was still furious with these policemen for ruining something that she had been looking forward to but knew that something important, something bad had just happened.

'Would you like a cup of tea?' she asked rather unexpectedly.

They didn't want one but said those same meaningless words again about Steve. They elaborated, Steve had been killed. He had been killed very recently, if fact he had just been killed. Julia looked out of her window. There were blue flashing lights everywhere. There seemed to be dozens of policemen dashing around. There were dozens of people outside staring at her garden being pushed away by more policemen. An ambulance was at the bottom of her

Besides the petrol rationing, television closing down at ten o'clock and power cuts during the day at weekends, December 1973 did offer Julia one thing to look forward to. Having seen YES live four times a few weeks earlier performing their new album, *'Tales from Topographic Oceans,'* the record was finally released and Julia had made sure that she was at the record shop at nine o'clock in the morning to be able to be the first person in London to buy it.

She had even made provision for Dylan and Bruce to get to school without her that day because that morning was assigned completely to the uninterrupted playing of the new album. Four sides comprising just one ninety minute piece based on the search for the inner eye; what could be better!

Leaping up and down like the most excited child who had just found in the most exciting toy shop ever, Julia jumped out of her car and ran up the crunchy gravel path to her house. Opening her front door, her other hand was caressing the elaborately designed album with exciting anticipation. She had already opened the lid of the record player in readiness before she left that morning so she just slipped side one on to the turntable then sat down to enjoy.

After about an hour, she had about ten minutes left of the last side to listen to when she heard banging on the door. She ignored it but the banging carried on. She turned the volume up but the banging got louder.

'No!' she could not believe it. Months she had been waiting for this and someone was intent on ruining the moment. Furious, she marched to the door and opened it as the record reached its dramatic and emotional climax. Two stone faced policemen were shouting at her but she wasn't listening. She strode back into the living room and there herself back into the chair intent on listening to the end of the record. When one of the policemen turned the record player off Julia felt like screaming.

to him a few years ago she kept thinking that maybe he was improving but he never did. She now did not find it strange that he had become this other person.

To Julia, what had happened to Steve summed up the change from the sixties to the seventies. The dreams, the hope, the love and above all, the certainty of the sixties had surreptitiously died. She couldn't remember when it had happened but the way things were now felt like the way things had always been. 1973 was not just a miserable year for Julia. The IRA were planting bombs in London, the Arabs were cutting off the oil so the world was running out of money and nobody could afford anything and because of the Ted Heath's battle with the miners, the country didn't have enough coal to run the power stations. As a result there were electricity saving power cuts every day. The only slight consolation for her was that it proved she was right about the Conservatives not having a clue about how to govern the country. In the old days she would have moaned to Steve about the state of the world and how terrible the Conservatives were but she couldn't anymore. It was horrible not to have the real Steve with her.

Steve didn't really get any better, without his keen mind he could not get a proper job again and without a proper job he became more and more depressed. He grew totally dependent on Julia for everything but Julia didn't mind looking after him; it wasn't because of the guilt she still felt, it was because she loved him with all her heart. She didn't really have a husband anymore, there was no more Steve and Julia, now there was just Julia.

She stopped writing and to Bruce's horror, became a part-tile art teacher at his school. With nothing else to get passionate about she became an even more obsessive fan of YES, going to virtually every concert they did, running a fan club and even getting on speaking terms with a few of them. She thought she was happy.

CHAPTER TWELVE

December 1973

When Julia first moved to London in the mid sixties something she found really difficult to accept was that just twenty years earlier the second world war was still happening. The war was history, it was black and white documentaries, a completely different world to now but incredibly it was just twenty years earlier. Twenty years was nothing; her parents' pet cat lived longer than twenty years! But just twenty years earlier London, England wasn't just a completely different place, the people who inhabited it were so different that they could hardly be recognized as belonging to the same species. It was not their appearance it was their way of life. Everyone back then knew their place, they never strayed out of their paths that their class had set out for them and people like Julia would never have associated with people like Steve, let alone marry him.

What really intrigued Julia was her friend Mr Spitfire. He had epitomised the swinging sixties but this same man had been a war hero. How could that kaftan wearing, long haired, peace-loving nutter who loved everyone have been a very senior RAF officer? Until recently she couldn't understand this but that was before she saw this exact same thing happen to Steve. In the last three years she had simply got used to the way Steve was now. The clever, witty, fun-loving man that she had married less than a decade ago was just a memory. Since she came back

She lit a third joint and began to consider whether the Devil was planning to take over the world using her as his weapon. She then forgot how she got on to this train of thought. She heard a splash. The pipe was still splashing into the overflowing trifle bowl that was now doubling up as a flower vase.

‘Which am I?’ she said to her reflection in the window. ‘Am I the water in the falling droplet or the water already in the bowl?’

live her own life was the right one. It was if this longing to be back with Jean-Marie was being planted in her brain by some external power. Steve used to have some peculiar friends who believed that the CIA was experimenting with mind control. She thought for a moment that maybe this wasn't as insane as she knew it was.

She went back into the front room and put her arms around her husband. This felt good. She was happy but there was no denying it; she felt drawn to Jean-Marie however hard she denied it. These were wrong feelings, she couldn't explain why she couldn't rid him from her mind. Steve was everything to her. She convinced herself that these feelings could not be her own. It was absurd but she wanted to believe it. Was she just thinking up a crazy excuse for a deep and hidden desire to go back to Paris? She didn't like this confusion, it made her angry. Since Steve was keeping an eye on the boys and the Wicked Witch of the West was not coming around today she could be allowed a joint. This would help her think.

She was going to find out where these insidious desires were coming from and stop them. It was as though someone was writing her. It was like she just someone in a story? Some parts of her life felt just too clichéd. She felt she was a character in a book that someone was altering the personality of. She wouldn't let herself be just a character in someone's novel: she was herself and would find out who this interfering writer was and stop him or her messing with her life.

After her second joint burned out in her fingers she wondered whether this author could be God. Memories of that old debate between determinism and free will wafted through her mind. Maybe we're all just mindless pawns in his grand plan. Maybe everything we do; all our actions are predetermined by him and sometimes just for a laugh he changes the plot.

Julia certainly had new hope. She now had the expectation of happiness. As 1969 fizzled out in Paris she had experienced instant gratification, love on tap, unquestioning adoration. That intense white heat of emotion had exploded into their lives without warning and without them having to actually do anything whatsoever. It had been the most wonderful few months she could ever imagine but it could never have gone on forever. It was like a firework; dazzling and burning with all the colours of the rainbow filling every cell of her body every second of the day but it had to go out.

Now in 1970 she had something different: anticipation of what would happen next. Her new book would be a success and she would have an exciting career ahead. Her two boys were fabulous and she couldn't wait to see them growing up. Her social life was as wild as ever and showed no signs of slowing down but best of all was Steve. It was obvious now that they didn't just love each other, they were in love with each other. Each day there were little signs that he was recovering and each day she sensed that they were growing closer. That's what was different now: their love was growing. The expectation of things to come was a hundred times better than just having it.

'I'm off to Decca now to record some silly arse who is insisting on doing his guitar solos in a tent he's put up inside the studio. Au revior.' said Mr Spitfire as he waved goodbye. That was the first time anyone had spoken French to her since she fled her other life at Christmas. She allowed herself to think about Jean-Marie but then tried not to. She did not want to think about him, she didn't need to think about him but it wasn't easy. She didn't want Jean-Marie in her mind, not anymore.

Julia couldn't understand why she still had a longing for that young French student. There was no question in either her head or her heart that the decision to come back to Steve, to

Steve. The boys were painting their walls, the carpet and themselves black when he knocked. Julia opened the door and handed him the flowers, she kissed him on his cheek.

'Thank you Mr Spitfire.'

'What are these for?' he asked

'Inspiration.'

He commented that they looked like they needed water so she looked for a vase but the closest appropriate thing she could find was the trifle bowl that had seemed so amazing last night still standing on the draining board.

'How is Steve?' he asked.

'Much better. He can have a proper conversation now. We can argue about music and films and even whether Star Trek is American imperialism as he contends it is.'

'What about your sex life?'

Julia was used to Mr Spitfire's directness so answered as she would a best friend: getting there.

Steve came in to the room having just checked that the boys were o.k. and hadn't fallen off the ladder. Without acknowledging their guest, he walked silently towards the TV set, switched it on then sat down to watch it.

'Good afternoon Steve.' Mr Spitfire said.

Steve looked but didn't speak.

'Steve!' shouted Julia.

'Oh sorry man,' Steve said coyly, 'I sometimes forget how rude I can be these days. I'm sorry, my brain's still screwed but they say I should be better soon. I hope so.'

'New decade, new hopes Old Boy!' exclaimed the ex-RAF man.

simply wasn't British. The majority of working people in Great Britain lived in what were almost third world conditions for decades after the war but he didn't see this, he wasn't meant to know about this so he didn't.

In the 1950s and the beginning of the 1960s, Britain was still Great Britain; it was the greatest country in the world, that was an unassailable truth. Sometime during the mid sixties he was involved in a project for the Ministry of Defence that required him to visit an up to date recording studio. The people there were not like him, they were not the English he knew. Whilst there he discovered that these young people and musicians were not the dregs of a decadent and morally corrupt society intent on destroying everything he held dear. One night he had to stay very late to complete some work but found it impossible because of the noise outside the office he had seconded. He went out to complain to the main culprit who appeared to be undisciplined, scruffily dressed but well-spoken girl under the influence of narcotics. Her disrespectful attitude and behaviour outraged him so much that he considered calling the police.

However as the straight laced servant of Her Majesty spoke to this girl he found her neither to be a crazed drug addict about to set fire to the studio nor a communist planning to overturn the state. He was first shocked by the fact that she seemed to be very intelligent. He was further shocked to discover just how charming she was. When the staff started to arrive for their next day at work he realized that he had been speaking to her all night. The girl was Julia and that day in 1966 Mr Spitfire was born.

Julia had not just changed his life, she had created it and he would be forever grateful. He would forever be her friend and was always welcome in her house. One that bitterly cold January morning he was on his way to Decca when he decided to call in on Julia, he was worried about

Today, it was like the sixties never happened. People with angry faces were rushing around, forcing their way aggressively through the unsmiling crowds of business people. Tourists were blindly taking photographs of everything trying to capture an image of a time that had now vanished. Where had the music gone? Where were the flowers? Why were all the young people so old?

Although he was fifty years old, the late sixties were his years. So many people of his age harked back to the forties and the fifties: there was no crime then, the youth respected their elders, there was deference for authority. Others talked about how society used to be so much better: there used to be a real sense of community back then and of course there was the spirit of the blitz. The youth of today wouldn't be able to cope with what we did during the war was their cry. He knew that was complete nonsense. Was he the only person of his age that knew this?

In 1966 he resigned from the MoD and lived his youth that the war had stolen from him. He resented all those years when he had to conform to the expectations of a bygone age. A time when men were men and women were the good little housewife at home. Of course it wasn't anything like as bad as Nazi Germany but it was still a time when everyone was controlled by the state. English oppression was more subtle he realized but nevertheless people were not free to think for themselves. It was a time when housewives even obeyed a cartoon potato. The ministry of food's absurd Potato Pete and the bespectacled carrot, Dr Carrot told then what to eat. The carrot knew better than they did what their husbands would like for tea. He remembered joking with his friends at the time that if carrots were so good for your eyes, why did Dr Carrot wear glasses.

Mr Spitfire had never questioned the way everything was. It was not the decent thing to question what he was told by politicians, his superiors in the service or in the newspapers. That

their friends from doing what they wanted to do. Their mum was different; she was their friend as well. Today they were in a hurry to rush home because they were going to paint their bedroom. It was Dylan's idea to make the room look like outer space. Steve had already painted the ceiling black; today the boys were going to paint the walls. When this was done they were going to paint white starts on the ceiling in the patterns of the constellations. Dylan had already planned this out; astronomy was his hobby. On clear nights he would point out the plough or the great bear and explain how the ancient Greeks had assigned mystical attributes to them.

As promised when they got home, the furniture had been moved from the bedroom and there were two tins of black emulsion along with brushes and a step ladder. Bruce was only four so wasn't allowed to go up the ladder but Julia figured that since Dylan was two years older he would be alright.

On her way back from the publishers, Julia noticed a little flower stall she had not seen before. She guessed Mr Spitfire might be calling around later so bought him a bunch of flowers as a little thank you present. At that particular moment Mr Spitfire was walking down the Kings Road; what a difference a few years makes he thought to himself. Where had the sixties gone? Standing in front of a boutique he recalled that a couple of years ago he sat down on the floor in front of the shop with a group of hippies he had never met before. They made music; some of them had guitars, others tambourines, or bells or just sticks. More and more people came and just sat until there must have been about a hundred of them just sitting and not thinking about the time or what they should be doing. Nobody tried to move them on, nobody thought it was wrong. Car drivers simply slowed down and drove around them; nobody got annoyed, no one beeped their horn.

Barret. He could only think about one thing at a time. In the month that Julia had been back, his illness had improved a little. He was still far from well, but he seemed to be getting there.

Julia was the one person whom Steve was most himself with. After his breakdown the doctors had given up on him. His mother's attempts to help only made him worse. Her bitterness and hatred for the wife he still worshipped only made him withdraw deeper into himself. It was the loss of his wife's love, the love that had been and still was the centre of his life that broke Steve. It could only be Julia and her love that could put him back together again. Dylan and Bruce knew their dad wasn't well and although young in age they seemed to understand that their father's distance from them was because he was sick. They knew he would get better and be their dad again.

It was always Julia that made Steve who he was. He was totally dependent on her; he needed her. Without Julia he would slip back into the dark distant netherworld where she wasn't present. Julia knew this and to feel such need, such total reliance, such gave her a very rewarding sense of being someone that mattered. She really loved him, she had always loved him even during her drugged up months in Paris with Jean-Marie. Her time with Jean-Marie was love, true-love but selfish love. Jean-Marie had adored her; she had stopped sensing that Steve felt anything for her. Jean-Marie couldn't live without her love, now it was Steve who couldn't live without her.

This was a different kind of love, something new and excitingly uncertain. That it was she alone, not his friends, not the boys or his cantankerous bitch of a mother was able to bring him back to reality proved how special she was to him.

When the boys saw her at the school gate they ran to her for the big hugs they knew they would get. They had the best mum in the world. Other mums shouted, moaned and stopped

The song was called “*Secret*” and he was trying to convince Steve that “*Octopus*” on Syd Barrett’s new album was a rip-off of that song.

After a long silence during which Julia was still standing in the doorway like an actor waiting for the next line, Steve spoke but not to her. ‘Man, there’s no similarities whatsoever.’ he began arguing quite passionately.

‘It’s the same chords, the same plodding melody, the same stream of consciousness thing, almost the same monotone voice.’

‘Syd’s lost his mind though. He’s no longer the piper at the gates of dawn. I’ve heard that Barrett’s been put into a mental asylum.’

‘You can lose your mind and find it again.’

‘Yes, sorry man. I wasn’t thinking.’ his friend said contritely when he realized what he had touched on such a sensitive subject.

‘Syd Barrett’s in a mental asylum?’ asked Julia concluding that the only way to get Steve to acknowledge her was to join in this conversation. She could be frank with him, he expected nothing less from her. ‘Has he had a mental breakdown like you had?’

‘Might be,’ Steve answered, ‘although some say it was just too much drugs. They say they’ve fried his brain. Apparently he bit someone in the studio a couple of months ago.’

‘No, that’s so sad.’ she said, genuinely upset. She knew that this person was Steve’s hero and also she had quite fancied him herself.

‘Guess what.’ she said, looking straight into his eyes. ‘I’ve finished my book!’

‘That’s fantastic.’ he replied. He was pleased for her. He stood up and forgetting that the boys needed picking up from school, he suggested that they went out to celebrate. He now completely forgot the fact that his friend was still there and abandoned his thoughts about Syd

needed a good reason to explain why a loyal soldier would disobey direct orders and behave so completely out of character and return to France. For weeks she had been trying to think of a reason why her hero would do this and tonight Mr Spitfire without prompting told her why and exactly how he himself disobeyed a direct order and returned to France. Brilliant; she would finish it in the morning.

So, the next day, just before she needed to go to school to collect Dylan and Bruce, her second novel was finally written. She proudly slapped the last page onto the pile of papers and slid the pack into a brown envelope onto which she wrote: chapter twenty. Grinning like a little girl Julia dashed into the front room to tell Steve. He was in there having a heated discussion about Syd Barrett's new album with a friend. These two Pink Floyd obsessives had always felt that certain records necessitated being listened to in the dark and this was one of them; they had the curtains drawn. Julia stood in the doorway looking like the Angel Gabriel with the light from behind her flooding in over her silhouette.

She raised her arms and announced, 'It is finished!'

Taken completely by surprise Steve's friend spun around. Eventually realising who she was and giving her a thumbs up gesture he said, 'Yeah, nice one man.' This friend of Steve did not want to say anything else to her. He did not want to talk to someone who did what she did to Steve. He couldn't understand why she was still living there but thought that Steve would throw her out as soon as he was better, as soon as his mind was o.k. again.

The friend turned back to Steve who did not seem to have noticed Julia. He was still deep in thought about what his friend had said about one of the songs on the record. He had brought around a fairly obscure record from a couple of years ago by the band, Virgin Sleep.

the wall that disappeared up into a hole in the ceiling above the sink was still dripping. Directly underneath it was a trifle bowl Steve's mother must have washed up earlier. It was full of water now. She took the torch out of the drawer and placing it behind the bowl she shone it through the water. She wanted to watch the next droplet of water fall into the bowl. The silence was broken as the next droplet of water fell through the darkness and splashed into the illuminated water. As the droplet pierced the surface it sent an explosion of ripples outward across the surface that sparkled in the eerie torchlight.

The next drip took longer to come but Julia steadfastly waited gripping the torch tightly against the glass in anticipation. It was like waiting for one of the German doodlebugs she had been writing about when it plummeted in silence onto its unsuspecting target below. She must have waited in the darkness and solitude of the kitchen for another ten minutes for the next drip to come. Her patience was finally rewarded as a splash sent the ripples bursting from the epicentre once again. Within a couple of seconds the water was still again. The droplet that for a few seconds had had such a dramatic effect had now completely vanished. The effect had gone. The cause of the effect had gone; it had merged with the rest of the water in the bowl. It was as if it had always been in the bowl. It looked like nothing had ever happened. Julia put her finger in the water and thought to herself that without those tiny drips there would be no water in this bowl. At that particular moment, this seemed to be something extremely profound.

She realized that she had been crouched at the sink holding her torch for about an hour. Suddenly she felt incredibly tired; too much dope often had this effect on her, so she just left the torch where it was, dropped her coat on the floor where she stood and went straight to bed.

Lying next to her husband her mind replayed the events of that evening. Her long talk with Mr Spitfire was such a brilliant piece of luck. Her novel was all but complete, she just

CHAPTER ELEVEN

January 1970

Julia had a sudden desire for a glass of milk as she tiptoed in through the front door at 3am. Before even switching the light on or taking her coat off she grabbed a glass from the draining board and poured out the contents of the last bottle in the fridge. She hoisted herself up onto the draining board knocking a saucepan lid crashing and clattering on to the tiles. Anxiously putting her finger to her lips she gestured to it to shush as it continued its spinning dance on the floor. The lid ignored her so she drank her milk: it was quite again.

The house was dead still, dark and completely silent. Steve and the boys would have been asleep for hours. She hoped his mother hadn't decided to stay over: she could do without one of her 'and what time did you crawl home last night' looks in the morning. She tried to be extra quiet, just in case she was listening upstairs. She sat perfectly still for a few minutes before ever so delicately placing the glass down beside her.

Behind her she heard a noise like a stone dropping into a pond. Startled, she looked around wondering what it was; there was nothing. Then she heard it again: there was just enough light in the kitchen for her to see what it was. The plumber to whom she had paid a small fortune last week should have fixed this. The pipe coming out of the top of the boiler on

'Julia Fairfax.' Giuliana simply sighed. 'I've been such a fan of hers for years, I adore her.'

None of us had realized that Giuliana had even known who about Julia never mind been a fan of hers. Dylan didn't even realize that his mother actually had fans! It was all quite strange but then again, everything was a little strange these days.

'Yes, I meant to mention this a few days ago. You guys can make it can't you? I've said you will.'

‘Yes, not just me. We all are; well except Keith.’ he added. I just smiled not quite taking it in.

Sensing I had no idea what he was saying, Dylan explained, ‘Yes, sorry, forgot to mention that didn’t I. We’re invited to my mother’s fortieth birthday bash in Liverpool next Saturday. She’s having a party on one of the ferry boats. I’ve got a mate at Liverpool Uni’ and he’s alright with us crashing at his place.’

‘A fortieth birthday party!’ repeated Penny with some disdain. ‘Seriously, have I really got to go to your mother’s birthday party? A middle aged woman’s birthday party; in bloody Liverpool. Bloody hell.’

‘No, you’ve met her, you like her. She’s great.’ I answered for my friend. ‘Dylan’s mum is great isn't she Giulia? Really great isn’t she? She’s a good laugh. She’s just brilliant.’ I continued making it seem that the adulation was coming from Giuliana rather than from myself.

Giuliana also rose to Julia’s defence. ‘Julia Fairfax! You must have heard of Julia Fairfax. It was Julia who told me about Judas. You’ll love her. She was really famous; she WAS the swinging sixties. She was the goddess of the sixties. You must have seen photographs of her? She was so beautiful. I couldn’t believe it when I discovered that the mother of my boyfriend’s best friend was Julia Fairfax. Just amazing - she was so beautiful.’

‘She still is beautiful.’ I added quietly.

Dylan was too relaxed to feel embarrassed about his friends' praise for his mother. He added, ‘Well, I wouldn’t say she was actually famous but she did get her picture taken a lot. And yes, she is great; she’s a real laugh, she’d do anything for anyone. I’m lucky to have a mum like that.’

then, praying that God would turn his father back into his father again. Dylan could never hide behind his mask of bravado around Giuliana. Somehow he just had to be himself with her.

He didn't voice his thoughts. Instead he said, 'My mother once said to me that you shouldn't pray to God to ask him to do stuff. You should ask him to give you the strength to do the stuff yourself.'

'Didn't Gandhi say something like that?' Giuliana asked.

Dylan didn't answer, he was absorbed in his thoughts. His memories of what happened to his father proved to him that there was no God. That six year old boy prayed and prayed for his father but the answer he received was so horrific that the only way to cope with what happened was to try and wipe out the entire memory of his father ever existing.

After our meal we all sat down with a few joints to watch the Wizard of Oz, a film Dylan suggested was one of the best films to get stoned to. Keith subsequently observed that as Dorothy opened the door to the Technicolor world of Oz, the colour actually came out of the screen into our living room. Penny just felt sleepy and a little envious of Keith's more interesting experience. Giuliana repeated her speech about Judas being chosen to save Jesus and being destined to kill himself but nobody was listening.

'We'll miss the old Sunday Roast next week everyone.' Dylan said to everyone. We looked slightly bemused and ignored him. Nobody took any notice, dope had the effect of making Dylan just talk complete nonsense. After Dorothy escaped from the wicked witch he said it again. This time I asked what he was talking about.

'Liverpool, mate.' as though that explained everything.

'You're going to Liverpool?' I asked.

Six: God made Judas betray Jesus and therefore must have made him feel guilty and must have made him kill himself.

Seven: And this is a question I don't know the answer to, if God is love, why did he do this to Judas? Why did he deliberately choose someone to do this terrible thing to? Why did he fill him with crushing guilt that he could no longer live with himself?

Giuliana looked to the vicar to see if he could respond. He was intrigued but starved for words. Would his God create someone just to betray somebody else and then be so tortured with remorse that they would be driven to suicide? Could his God do that? Could his God create a life with such a destiny?

'Maybe God saw that Judas was weak and so could be used in his plan?' Giuliana suggested. 'I think this is really important.' She finished.

By the time we had walked back home Dylan, with the help of Penny who had also virtually moved in, had prepared something to eat. A mouth-watering aroma met us just outside the house inviting us in. Although not the most domesticated young man in the world, Dylan cooked an excellent Sunday Roast. On Sundays, Giuliana always insisted on a traditional English roast dinner; it was part of living here and just had to be done. Today's dinner did not disappoint her, Dylan had prepared roast lamb.

Whilst eating Dylan asked how church had been that morning. Giuliana said the pastor was talking about prayer then asked Dylan about his own beliefs. Cockily he laughed that he only believed in himself.

Penny laughed then asked, 'Have you ever prayed Dylan?

For a moment he saw himself as a six year old boy. It was a horrible memory. He remembered sitting at the feet of his father shortly after his mental breakdown. He was praying

One Sunday morning just before Easter, I accompanied her to church. I wasn't sure whether all that stuff or not I believed but I felt that I should show some gratitude to God if he did exist in case he had been responsible for bringing us back together.

I wasn’t paying too much attention to the subject of the sermon but after the service Giuliana said she needed to speak to the pastor. She had something on her mind, something she told me Julia had told her.

'Assuming it was God’s plan for Jesus to be killed, you’ve got to say that Judas was doing the work of God.’ she said.

The Vicar started to laugh in anticipation of his glib brush-off. ‘No, Judas was not doing the work of God. Judas was a weak man. It can be argued that he might have thought he was doing the best for peace in Judea; you know helping the authorities get rid of a trouble maker but nobody can argue that he was doing the work of God.’

He had not accounted for someone like Giuliana. She presented the facts as she saw, or rather as Julia had seen them to the young clergyman.

'One: Jesus was sent by God to die.

Two: In dying he would take away our sins if we believed in him. I mean all the horrible things that were plaguing our minds, all the nasties in our past, the things we wish we hadn’t done. The things we wished we hadn't caused.

Three: If Judas hadn’t helped the priests catch Jesus and he’d not been killed and there would be no resurrection.

Four: Judas was vital to God's plan so without him nobody would be ‘saved.’

Five: If all this was God’s big plan, then Judas was doing God’s work.

Julia told us that some friends of hers in Liverpool were making an independent film and needed a young Italian actress so it seemed obvious that Giuliana would be perfect.

'Bullshit, absolute bullshit!' Debbie spluttered with a mixture of laughter and anger stumbling back into the room. 'Look love, we're not taking in any of this crap.'

Debbie's anger seemed totally illogical to me, Giuliana's story was heart-breaking but I knew that it was now going to have a happy ending. I was a hero from the movies, looking after a damsel in distress, a runaway heiress, a rich girl escaping her abusive mobster husband. Debbie however decided that if she wasn't a liar then she was utterly immoral. She was a spoilt silly rich girl who had fallen out with her husband then abandoned her family for a stupid schoolgirl's fantasy. Furthermore, she was foreign.

'I'm afraid I neither know who you are or indeed why you appear to be wearing a pair of comedy breasts,' Julia said very sternly, 'but you are an extremely rude and unpleasant girl. Have some respect.'

Briefly at least, that shut Debbie up.

In just a few days everything was back the way it was meant to be. Debbie was just an unpleasant fuzzy memory and Penny was back with Dylan and Giuliana was back with me. The acting job Julia had found for Giuliana wasn't to start until April so for the next few weeks Giuliana was simply the fourth member of house. It was even better than it was before Christmas because now there were no secrets between us. We didn't need to speak about what she did over that Christmas, her husband or her family again. We didn't need to - we were in love and that was all that mattered.

'For my love of God! For the love of God? For fuck's sake people, are you really listening to this?'

'As I was saying, it became worse and worse. It wasn't the violence, him hitting me or the mental abuse, it was having to play that character for him twenty-four hours a day. I began to slip back to my old circle of friends and my modelling agent found me an acting job at RAI. I never loved Giorgio but he was so insensitive that he never actually noticed. If I could have been bothered I would have pitied him because his life was just so empty but I just didn't care.

Giorgio told his father and that made my life even worse. My uncle's retribution was to punish my own father until I became the good wife I was meant to be. My father's role in the family business changed, he was doing jobs that a week earlier his underlings were carrying out. My parents' finances and status crashed and it was all my fault. I had to get away and that's when I came to England last year.

When I got back at Christmas I thought the situation would have improved but it was worse. I had to stay, I had to respect my uncle's wishes and be the daughter in law I was meant to be but I just couldn't do it.'

By now Debbie had left the room so uninterrupted by her fits of what I considered inexcusable laughter, the rest of us could all concentrate on this awful story.

'You see, I had fallen in love with you Nick and couldn't live without you. I have cried myself to sleep each night for the last two months hoping that the following day might be better but it never was. I wanted to come back but was so ashamed of what I had done, I thought you would never forgive me. That is when I met Julia.'

'I would love to say it was planned,' Julia interrupted, 'but it was just by accident. I was at RAI and literally bumped into Giulia in the lift. It was like it was meant to happen.'

bond between my father and his brother and it was good for the family business. We do not question what my uncle says – he knows what is best for the family.'

Debbie interrupted, 'Sorry love, I wasn't listening to the start of this bollocks but is this a remake of Godfather 1 or 2 you are talking about? Can I have a part in it too? Maybe I can play the cop who shoots you?'

We all ignored her, despite the fact that I could now not get the image of Marlon Brando's Godfather out of my head.

Wiping a tear from her eye and having a little more fish, Giuliana continued her story. This uncle ran a massive construction company and Giuliana's husband was a big player in his father's business empire. Giuliana's father who was also in the family business had benefited enormously financially from the wedding and so had overlooked the bruises that became more and more common on his daughter's face and body.

'Giorgio loved the fact that I was a model and loved even more that I was going to be an actress. He would to show me off to his friends and business associates and I would oblige by looking as beautiful as I could.'

At this revelation, several chips exploded from Debbie's mouth.

'Each evening I would have to look more stunning that I did at the last one, it was difficult but he was my husband it is what one has to do. I was the pretty wife and would always be there to make him look good but when I wasn't then the bruises would make me less pretty.'

'You don't need to try to look stunning Giulia,' Julia said giving her a reassuring hug, 'you always look amazing.'

'Out of respect for my parents and my love of God, I endured that lifestyle for about a year but Giorgio became worse and worse.'

meant to happen, I didn't want to fall in love because I knew I could not but I did and didn't know what to do. But Nick, I did fall in love with you and I am more in love with you than I knew it was possible to be in love. The last two months have been hell on earth. I have tried to do the right thing, tried to be a wife but it has been impossible. I have been so miserable, I cry every night thinking about what I have done to you, about what I have lost and about what a pointless life I was now going to have without you.'

She began to cry. Keith gave her a gentle nudge and told her to eat her chips before they went cold. She smiled back and ate a few before carrying on.

Debbie's face was the perfect example of what cynicism looked like whereas I on the other extreme must have looked like a love-sick puppy, lapping it all up. One thing I did notice however was Julia, when Giuliana spoke, Julia was virtually mouthing the words. Obviously they had rehearsed this speech in the car but it was strange; Giuliana was speaking, it was her story and very personal it was but it was like Julia was telling it.

Keith, who was even drunker than the rest of us, cut some of Giuliana's fish, put it on her fork and offered it to her. She took it, ate a little more then continued with her tale.

'As Fabio said, I am married but it is not the happy marriage that he described in his letter. No, not a happy marriage, not a marriage of love. Giorgio, my husband is much older than me, he is actually my cousin. My uncle is my father's eldest brother, he is the head of our family and we are a very traditional family. My uncle looks after the family first, then he looks after his friends and he looks after the community so everybody does what he wants because he knows what is best. He is a good man, a very respected man. It was my uncle who decided I should marry Giorgio his step-son. It helped Giorgio feel really part of the family, it strengthened the

here. She staggered in with a huge bag of fish and chips; Giuliana's authentic English welcome back meal. Very noisily Dylan removed some plates from the cupboard and handed them to his mother.

'Plates with fish and chips my Darling? No, no, no, we have to eat them out of the paper.'

With uncharacteristic inelegance Julia simply tossed the hot steaming greasy parcels to us where we were sitting.

'Am I the only one who can see how wrong this all is?' screeched Debbie, hands on hips.

Yes she was! To myself, Dylan and Keith, nothing could be less wrong that this. It was the best thing that could possibly have happened to me, a wonderful surprise and we all felt wonderful. Julia looked almost as happy as I did. She was such a romantic and was more than pleased with what she had managed to do. It had been many years since Julia had been a novelist but she was still writing our story. She was Shakespeare and Giuliana and I were her Romeo and Juliette waiting for the next scenes in this Italian tragedy to be written.

What Julia had done was incredible. She hardly knew me and yet she had done the best thing anyone had ever done for me. I could only express my gratitude by giving her a massive hug.

'Thank you so much.' I said still holding her and grinning from ear to ear.

She smiled then kissed me on my lips; that was unexpected. I did not want Giuliana to explain what had happened, she did not need to and it was certainly not for me to ask this of her. I was simply so grateful that she was back in my life. She did however want to explain and she did so as though she had been rehearsing her speech with Julia for hours.

'Fabio's letter must have upset you Nick. You must have hated me for deceiving you. I am a married woman and I allowed you to think I was single and make love to me. None of this was

Giuliana didn't speak, she didn't need to. Her beautiful dark brown eyes smiled at me, they were telling me she was back. I didn't want to know what had happened, what was going on or why she had ignored me for the last eight weeks. Like finding a reflection in a pool, this vision was so fragile that I hardly wanted to move or speak in case I made her disappear.

Debbie glared at Giuliana like a child killer had come into our room. Dylan had obviously filled her in on my recent history and Debbie was not impressed. She had only known me for a couple of hours but was ferociously defending me against this selfish and vindictive bitch that was using me! She was saying things like how dare she show her face here again after what she had done, leading me on then abandoning me after deceiving me about being married but I wasn't listening. This was possibly the most important day of my life and I wanted it to be special, amazing and memorable. I did not want some loud drunk northern girl to be in my memory of today.

Giuliana wasn't listening to Debbie ranting at her either, she was silently looking at me. I could hardly believe what was happening, it really was a miracle, God really had answered my prayers. This was the best day of my life.

'Julia said you were missing me.' were her first words.

With tears now gushing down my cheeks I stumbled across the room to her and hugged her and hugged her and hugged her. Everything was good.

Barely audible over Debbie's continuing tirade was another banging on the door which Dylan eventually noticed. Tearing himself reluctantly away from the ongoing melodrama and his girlfriend being remarkably arousing in his living room he answered the door.

'One would think that students would be glad of some free food but whenever I come bearing sustenance, none of you buggers ever let me in!' It was Julia; she had driven Giuliana up

exonerated him completely were not even considered by Penny, a reaction which he found totally inexplicable. His suggestion that she was over-reacting resulted in his beloved Atari game console being smashed into his face. With blood dripping then pouring from his incredulous face he managed to say, 'O.K. Penny, thanks for the explanation of over-reacting, I understand now.'

'I'm glad I haven't taken my Hippocratic Oath yet because it means I can happily watch you bleed to death.' was her retort.

Predictably by the time of Dylan's cheering up party Penny was back with him but we thought we would have the party anyway. Keith and I were convinced that some of his scars got worse after he got back with her and we noticed that he definitely was flirting less with girls he came into contact with. It was nice to have Penny back, we missed her short skirts.

St Patrick's Day 1985 presented quite a surprise. The first shock was when Keith and I returned home from Tesco carrying as much Guinness as it was physically possible for two people to hold. Dylan let us in and introducing us to a girl with spectacularly large breasts called Debbie who appeared to be wearing nothing other than his dressing gown.

Keith and I, both being fans of Penny gave each other a disapproving, 'just wait until she finds out' look but since this girl was half naked we thought we would forgive Dylan just this once. In keeping with the spirit of the day, we decided to celebrate our possible, although unproven and extremely unlikely Irish roots by determining the maximum volume of Guinness we could all consume.

There was a knock on the door heralding the second surprise. Debbie who seemed surprisingly drunk went to see who it was. She came back in the room followed by Giuliana carrying a suitcase.

Giulia does not work for RAI now. She is happy and back with her husband. Please do not write to her again because that is not a good thing to do for a married woman. This news is very sad for you but I hope it does not upset you too much. You should be glad to understand that Giuliana is now very happy and because you love her you will be pleased to know this.

I wish you success with your university progression and future career.

Kind Regards,

Fabio.

I put the letter back into the envelope, smoked another cigarette, went to my room and took out some work. My coursework had been mounting up, I needed to get on top of it; essays on Walpole didn't write themselves! It was remarkably easy to simply forget about Giulia; we'd had a good time, it was nice while it lasted but I was mistaken about how we felt about each other. Essentially it was just a holiday romance. In fact it was a relief to know the truth because I could stop wasting my time worrying about her now.

I really did find it incredible how simple it was to put it all behind me. I was still sad it had had ended of course but I wasn't upset, I wasn't angry, I wasn't worrying about her like I had been. Everything was good. Keith was right, I could get on with my life now; we all could. Giuliana probably would not have liked our house in January; it was cold. It was almost too cold to go to the pub some nights and almost too cold for the party we had arranged to cheer me and Dylan up the following week. He had been dumped again by Penny, Keith and I thought he ought to be getting used to that by now.

Dylan truly seemed utterly perplexed when Penny became furious upon discovering that he had slept with one of her friends. His protestations that it didn't mean anything, which to him

She hardly knew me but she knew the right words to say, she was such a kind woman. Not only did she care, not only did she believe me but she then offered me hope; something real and practical. Connected with her Italian art programme she was visiting Rome at the end of January. She told me that she actually had a meeting at RAI television in the first week in February and that she would do her best to see if she could find Giuliana. I smiled for the first time in weeks.

'No, I won't do my best to find her.' she continued, 'I WILL find her and speak to her.'

This was fantastic. It was my turn to give her a hug now. She kissed me on the cheek; that felt nice, maybe a little too nice.

I continued writing letters to anyone in Italy I thought might know how I could get in touch with her although when February came I slowed down and stopped panicking because I believed that Dylan's mother really would be able to find her. I came back from college one day and Keith called me over. 'You've got a letter from Italy, mate.'

At first I pretended I couldn't see it, I didn't want it anymore. I knew it would say something awful. I tried to smoke a cigarette first but Keith took it out of my mouth and told me to stop being a twat and just open it. He left me alone to read it by myself. It was from Fabio, the *Wuthering Heights* director.

Caro Nick,

I hope you are well. I have received your letter asking about Giuliana. She is well.

We have no more having the finance for our movie so cannot make it finished. The English man who was to pay for it no more does not want to pay. We are all very sad. This is why we have not contacted you more quickly.

By now I had convinced myself that I really had seen my letter from that restaurant in Rome in Inspector Whitman's briefcase. There was so much to worry about. I was not sleeping well. When I got back to frozen Sheffield Dylan and Keith tried to convince me just to forget her. They both assured me that girls were like this: one minute they tell you they love you, the next minute they've forgotten about you.

'Face it Nick,' Keith said, thinking he was being helpful. 'She's probably with some new Latin lover now. You didn't really know her and you don't know what's going on her life.'

I knew she wasn't with someone else but he was right, I didn't know what was going on in her life. This was exactly why I needed to go over to Rome and find out. Like an explosion it suddenly hit me in the face that it had been over a month since we kissed each other goodbye and I had done absolutely nothing to find her or help her. She needed me. I was going to get a flight to Rome the following weekend, I was going to get her back. I could not believe I had waited so long. If I had gone as soon as I realized something was wrong I might have been able to help her. I prayed to God that I was not too late to save her and cursed Dylan and Keith for slowing me down with their stupid platitudes.

So much had happened in 1984 that it seemed hard to believe that it was only one year ago when I first encountered Julia conducting the *1812 symphony* in our living room. She was there again a few days after we all got back with what looked like bags of clothes from a charity shop for Dylan. With his new image, his sense of style was vanishing by the hour.

'My poor, poor darling.' she wailed as I walked in the room and gave me a massive hug. 'I know how you must be feeling. She was very special and unlike my cynical son I can't believe that she's just forgotten about you. She will be missing you like crazy, I know that. We've got to go and get her. Follow your heart, as the songs say.'

happy anyway. He put his mother on the line to say hello. She sounded as drunk as her son was, they had friends and family around and everyone there seemed to be having a really good traditional Christmas. She said that she was flying off to Nicaragua in a couple of days to help the victims of the civil war. I had no idea what she meant but had a fleeting image of her in army combats and a big pink floppy hat stomping through the rain forest.

My father was moaning about Africans not being able to look after themselves and that all this could have been avoided if they had stayed in the British Empire. My mother was sitting by herself in the kitchen listening to sugary music on the radio as if to avoid having to have an opinion on anything. I hated being jealous of Dylan and felt guilty about that. It was nice of him to call, he genuinely wanted to cheer me up but it actually made me feel worse. He made me realize what dull, lifeless parents I had to put up with; they probably didn't even know where Nicaragua was.

I needed to stop moping about them and start moping about Giuliana. Why had I not been able to contact her? I had tried everything: the TV station, people from the production crew, the Rome phone book (which I stole from the public library) and even that restaurant by the Spanish Steps again. With all the letters and phone messages I was sending she must have received at least one but still I heard nothing from her. Maybe something terrible had happened to her. I didn't even know whether she got home alright. Maybe that Red Bow-tie man was right and her family were mixed up with crime and Giuliana had been killed? The one thing I knew with every fibre of my being was that she was not simply ignoring me. That would be more than out of character; that would be impossible. Maybe she was lying in hospital, maybe she was dead?

CHAPTER TEN

February 1985

The Christmas number one was Band Aid's "*Don't they know it's Christmas*." Ethiopia was no longer just a faraway place, it was now at the forefront of everyone's minds and the usual warm and fluffy Christmas day television fare was peppered with images of starving African children, mothers carrying their dead babies and men with sunken lifeless eyes without any hope. I was glad this was being shown, I wanted everyone to feel as horrible as I did.

Every morning at my parents' over the holidays, I had been racing the dog to the front door checking the post just in case a letter arrived there. She hadn't phoned like she promised when she got to London, she hadn't phoned from the airport, she hadn't phoned from Italy. It did not make sense. Giuliana loved me and there was nothing of earth could stop her from phoning me but she did not call. Something must have happened, something bad. I had called British Rail but there hadn't been any train crash and I'd phoned Alitalia but there hadn't been a plane crash; something must have happened. I was worried, helpless and hundreds of miles away from her.

Dylan phoned me over the Christmas to see how I was doing. I tried not to sound miserable, the last thing I wanted was to dampen his Christmas spirits but he sounded annoyingly

She looked back at Steve; he was looking at the set but wasn't actually looking at the pictures. What was wrong with him? He couldn't see what she was seeing. He couldn't see her.

'What the hell have you done to him?' Julia yelled at his mother.

'Me! What have I done to him! You did this to him you stupid bitch. You evil, evil, evil bitch. You might as well have killed him.'

Although she screamed louder and faster, none of what his mother was saying made any sense to her. Why was she still screaming at her? Julia had no intention of listening to her. Steve carried on looking at the sad pictures on the TV when the people stopped standing in front of him.

About this time back in Paris, sun would be setting over the Seine. It was Christmas day and she was home now; the dream was over.

At the railway station, Julia got out of the last train to run before Christmas day. Many hours later she nervously knocked on the door of the house. There was no answer so she knocked again, louder this time. Steve's mother opened the door; she didn't say anything she just stood there, in the doorway. Julia pushed past her into her house.

Steve was watching television but he didn't even look at her, didn't he care? Upstairs she could hear her children. She shouted up to them that she was back but neither of them came down. Didn't they want to know her either? That evil old witch has poisoned their minds she thought.

She switched the TV set off and stood in front of it waiting to Steve to speak, waiting for him to say how pleased he was that she was back or even to scream at her for leaving him. But something was horribly wrong with him. He didn't react at all. He was staring at the blank television as though it was a fairground hypnotist. She spoke to him, he briefly looked up but didn't seem to see her, he carried on gazing at the blank screen. She tried to speak but he simply wasn't hearing her. Behind her, his mother was screaming and ranting at the top of her voice. Julia turned to her as if to ask why she was making such a noise. She wasn't listening to the old bitch so why was she carrying on?

Steve's mother turned the television back on screaming that Steve was watching it. Julia stood in front of it, blocking his view. He craned his neck and continued to stare impassively at the screen. She turned around to see what he was looking at. It was a report on the tragic and horrific events in Africa where the hundreds of thousands of Africans starving to death in Biafra. For a few seconds the sights of the starving children made her freeze. She hadn't been following the news recently, she had never seen anything so awful.

On the day before Christmas Julia told him she still had a few things to do in Paris before she went so she would meet up with him later. She was going to catch the seven o'clock train and he would be waiting to meet her at the picturesque village station at about eight.

Arriving in the morning at his parents' home in the country his father looked shocked at Jean-Marie's scruffy appearance. 'You look like a bloody hippie.' he commented.

'I am a bloody hippie.' he replied to his father before being hugged by him. His mother was more reluctant to get too close to him. She kissed him but held him at arm's length in case there was anything she could catch from his clothes. She wondered what a lack of personal hygiene had to do with peace and love, it all seemed silly to her and she hoped this silly fad of his would pass soon. To placate them both and because it was Christmas, the first thing he did was to have a shower and change into 'respectable' clothes. His parents wondered what sort of vagrant this girl that they were expecting was who could find their son's unkempt and filthy appearance and smell anything other than repulsive

As he was getting dressed the smell of freshly baked bread flooded the house. It was the smell he had grown up with, he was glad to be home. He hurried downstairs and during lunch told his parents about Julia. They were his parents so he didn't tell them much, but enough for them to realize that she was something very special to their son. His father was intrigued to meet her. The old man couldn't imagine what she was like but was intrigued to hear how much she loved all things French. His mother had bought a duck from the market for that evening's meal. She was worrying now because she wasn't sure whether English people ate duck. She had to create a good impression and wondered whether there may be anyone still at the market with maybe some beef.

mattered, he couldn't be bothered to get out of bed, to eat, to drink, to wash himself or even to find out what was happening. His mother was taking care of him, she was taking care of everything.

His mother was with him constantly helping him take care of himself and also taking care of his two sons in addition to looking after her own house which she hadn't seen for weeks. The doctors told his mother that he might snap out of it one day; there was nothing they could do. The boys couldn't understand what had happened. All of a sudden, their mother had vanished and their dad had turned into someone else who acted like he didn't know them. Maybe it wasn't really him, he didn't even look the same. Their gran was now in charge and they hated her: she shouted at their dad and had shouted at their mum, maybe that's why she went away. They were scared and confused.

Back in Paris Julia thought about phoning again later: why was that old witch in her house? No, it will keep. After all her walking she was really tired and just wanted to sleep. Jean-Marie was given a quick goodnight kiss and she went to bed. She knew what she had to tell him but was scared to face it that evening.

Jean-Marie's Christmas was going to be extra special that year; Julia had agreed weeks ago to go with him to his parents' house in the countryside tomorrow. Jean-Marie had suggested that Dylan and Bruce might want like to come over as well. She had said no. They were part of Julia's old life, as much as she loved them, if she saw them again they might shatter her fragile wonderful world she wanted to remain in. She was not being selfish. Julia loved this life too much to give it up. Anyone would be mad to give it up.

light escaping through gaps in curtains soaked up by the fog appeared to be miles away. Julia felt alone. There were probably others in the street going home but she could see nobody else. She could hear nobody else, all she could hear were her own footsteps on the cobbles. She walked faster, almost running.

Jean-Marie was a welcoming sight when he opened the door for her. She surprised herself by giving him a very passionate kiss but whilst he was out of earshot cooking dinner for her, she plucked up the courage to phone Steve back in London. It seemed to ring for ages. She wanted Steve to pick it up before Jean-Marie came back in then it stopped, someone picked it up.

'Who is it?' a voice demanded. It wasn't Steve. Julia wasn't expecting anyone else.

'Julia. Who is this? Where is Steve?'

Only silence followed and Julia thought that she must have phoned the wrong number. She asked if there was anyone there.

After a few seconds there was a reply. 'How dare you! How dare you bloody well phone this house!'

The phone was slammed down. It was Steve's mother.

'Who was on the phone' Steve asked quietly back in London.

'The slut junkie. Thought we had seen the last of her.'

Steve didn't react. He hadn't reacted for weeks. Since he had lost his job, since his wife had left him his mother had been looking after him. For a few weeks a couple of months ago he didn't even know who he was. He didn't know anything, he had just stared into the steely grey sky as though looking for some long forgotten something. Gradually, he had started to speak again. He could now just about ask and answer questions, he seemed to know who he was or rather who he used to be. He didn't care who he was now, it didn't matter to him. Nothing

'Don't say that.' she replied angrily walking away from him. She could still sense his intense stare burning into her. Maybe he would kill for her but it was irrelevant, she would never leave him. She would certainly never leave him for her boring husband.

Julia needed to think. She put on her big coat, her long knitted scarf and just walked. She didn't know where she was going, she didn't have a plan. She was just drifting through the snowy Paris streets. She didn't notice the cold, she didn't know how long she had been walking or where she had been but eventually she arrived at Notre Dame Cathedral. She would climb the tower and look out at the city for one last time. During her walk she had decided it was time to go.

None of this was real; it was fantastic, it was beautiful but it wasn't real. Life in the real world might not be constant fun but maybe the challenge might be more rewarding. Her life in Paris she thought was not that different from that of Marie Antoinette, she did not want to escape reality.

At the top of the tower she started to say goodbye to her imaginary world. It was the time to go, now before the perfection started to fade. She was going to go out on a high. She took out a joint but hesitated before lighting it; was it right to smoke pot on top of a cathedral. She put it back in her bag and watched the Seine become blurred as tears filled her eyes.

When she emerged from the metro station to take the short walk home she found that the night had come into Paris. Along with the darkness, fog had sneaked surreptitiously into the city on its coat tails. It had oozed between the buildings and filled the streets and passageways. It had stolen the light from the moon, from the street-lamps and from the shop signs giving it a pale lifeless grey glow. What was once light from people's windows was now just faint glimmers indicating signs of life. The fog took away all perception of distance. Neon signs and muffled

Julia rolled herself a joint and smoked it staring out at the steely grey sky. She never knew what mood dope would put her into, that was part of the excitement about it. This morning it made her quite pensive. As the freezing cold city beneath her began to thaw from its sleep, she felt as though she also was waking up for the first time in since she had been in Paris, maybe for longer. Was her perfect life any better than her life back home? She was happier; no question about it but is happiness enough? Shouldn't there be something else in life? Was there anything in London? Her friends were there, Lisa, the scene - she missed that. She missed having to think of what she wanted to do and who she wanted to see. There was bringing up the boys; she kind of liked that, she did love their kids after all. And then there was Steve: despite everything, she still loved him. Her student lover worshiped her but the question was how long could he keep worshiping her. Could she live on adoration alone?

Julia wondered whether Jean Marie had guessed that she had started to think about Steve again because her. He said something the night before that she found slightly disturbing.

'If you ever left me for your husband, you know I could not live.' he told her. 'I would have to kill myself but before I did that I would have to kill your husband. I could not allow anyone else to have you.'

She was not sure whether he was exaggerating as he was often prone to do. There was something about him that suggested he was in love with her more and more each day. She could not put her finger on it but she also thought he had become more possessive every day. He was changing or was it her?

'You couldn't kill anyone.' she laughed.

'I would kill for you.'

because he wanted a peaceful evening that was sometimes difficult to find elsewhere in Liverpool city centre back then. That was Steve and this was their first meeting.

Looking out at the snow that was just starting to fall through the window in Jean-Marie's flat, Julia remembered how besotted she was with Steve when they first met. She remembered how they felt when they first met and how their feelings changed over the years, how they cooled as they grew older. They just got used to being together. She wished that their feelings for each other had stayed the same as they were at the moment they met. She had given up hoping ever to recapture that intensity of love until now. The love she felt for Jean-Marie was young and alive, she would not let it change, it would stay like this forever.

It was a morning just before Christmas and it was snowing. For the first time in a while she thought about her characters in her novel. She had not given up writing, she had just put her career on hold for a while. What better spiritual and inspirational refreshment could there possibly be than living here. Would her characters have stood together at a window like this looking down on the loud hustle and bustle of the XVIIIe arrondissement? Yes – everyone should, was her answer.

The snow masked the traits of the modern age. It hid the gaudy shop signs, it made people dress in the thick long garments they had worn in this weather for decades. Dozens of cars were parked below but they too were covered in a blanket of snow which obscured their modern 1960s shapes and designs. Everything outside was virginal white, it had not been coloured in yet. It could be any decade, any century down in the street below. She felt that where she was hadn't changed since the beginning of the century if not much longer. The characters in her novel would certainly feel at home here, they would maybe be feeling what she was feeling too. Plus ça change, plus c'est la même chose.

It went like clockwork, despite the cool and sophisticated air of nonchalance they both liked to bask in, when they saw each other they both jumped up and down like a couple of excited puppies. By the time the song finished both their lips were sore from kissing. The next track on the White Album that came after this was '*I Will.*' This was the nearest thing that she and Steve had to 'their tune.' She didn't want to stop kissing Jean-Marie when this song came on, she didn't want to think about her boring husband but she did. She and Steve had both loved that song from the moment they heard it last year.

The Beatles had a special place in their relationship. When Julia was a young art student in Liverpool in the early sixties, like many beatniks and arty types, she and her friends used to frequent some of the city's rare and secret gay pubs such as the Bears Paw and the Magic Clock. The latter was famous or infamous depending on what circles one moved in for its barmaids. The bar was run by two men who were unashamedly in drag. They were called Sadie and Denise. Whereas some pubs in the city could get quite rough as closing time approached, the gay pubs were always quiet and Julia and her young female friends felt safe there. There was never any trouble there and as long as Sadie and Denise stopped being Sadie and Denise the moment they stepped out of their sanctuary, they were also perfectly safe too.

Once Julia was in the Magic Clock with Lisa, her best friend. They were having a quiet drink when a very well dressed young man dashed in enthusiastically waving a poster around shouting that everyone had to come and see the latest event he was putting on. She and Lisa asked a gorgeous young student sat on the table next to them who this man was. He said it was the owner of NEMS Records who was promoting a new band of his called the Beatles. Both girls were big music fans and they got talking to the student. They were pleased to discover that despite his good looks and where he was he was not a homosexual. Like them he was only there

what was going to happen next was missing. This time there was no doubt; there was no question about whether he loved her but did she miss the thrill of being uncertain? No, she thought that it was a stupid even to ask that; nobody likes never being sure. Maybe that's what was wrong with living with Steve; it was predictable.

For just a split second an unwelcome question intruded into her mind: was this life with Jean-Marie as predictable? Was the unconditional, unfailing, unchanging adoration actually not exciting? Of course not, that thought melted away like a snowflake before it had time to settle.

None of her adolescent relationships were as fulfilling, as true and loving as this; this was unique. None of those could ever have lasted for ever like she knew this one would. She thought about that again: this will last forever. It will never change and I'll always feel like this: 'I really am a lucky bitch!'

It was dark when she got back to the flat. The naked Dutch girl was still naked and painting a picture of the sun on the back wall of their apartment block. Julia smiled to herself when she thought about what less trusting partners would think if they found a naked girl in their boyfriend's flat. 'Jean-Marie has been worried about you.' the Dutch girl said.

Jean-Marie had waited up for her. He had been looking out of the window for the last couple of hours. He wasn't getting annoyed that she had just gone out unexpectedly without letting him know where she had gone. He was getting more and more excited as the hours drifted by to the time when he would see her again. A smile shot across his face as he finally spotted her walking towards the house. He leapt into action, he had been planning this for the last couple of hours. As he heard her outside coming up the stairs he put the Beatles track '*Julia*' on the record player to welcome her home as she walked in the door.

feel the way she and Jean-Marie felt about each other. She knew that they were born to be with each other. It didn't matter why, she didn't need to know. She was just lucky, their life was so perfect. She was desperate to see him again, she wished the train would go faster.

The two passengers sitting in front of her were discussing the new Beatles LP, Abbey Road that she had bought herself a few days ago. They were talking about the quality of the production; about how different the new eight-track recording system made it sound. This was the kind of conversation she would have had with Steve. She knew all about the 8-track Studer tape machine, solid state sound boards and even knew Geoff Emerick. She was tempted join in their conversation but resisted, that would be what the old Julia would have done.

The boy reminded her of someone she used to know. She couldn't recall who it was, someone from long forgotten yesterdays. She thought about when she was as a teenager herself, pretending not to be bothered, pretending not to care about relationships, pretending to her parents that she wasn't secretly seeing boys. She remembered how she used to get so excited with anticipation, how she would never know how things would turn out. It was the uncertainty that was exciting, it was thrilling, it allowed her to hope. Not knowing what the future would bring, not knowing whether John, Jean or Giancarlo was really, truly one hundred percent in love with her was exciting.

Love then meant worrying every minute she was out of her boyfriend's sight about what he was thinking, whether he was going cold on her, whether he had found someone else. The fear kept her on her toes.

Most of the time she found out that he never did love her as much as she loved him or they were only interested in her because mummy and daddy were rich. They were all pigs anyhow but this time it was different. This time it was really different, that feeling of wondering

part of the gardens and started to cry. She knew this was stupid getting emotional over a complete stranger especially as the starving peasants outside of Versailles obviously had had a much worse time. Jean-Marie would be utterly appalled if he knew his girlfriend was crying over the fate of the Queen of France.

Today however at the palace of the Sun King, Julia was herself and it did not matter to her what Jean-Marie felt. What was wrong with being a little in love with Marie Antoinette. What was wrong with sitting on a bench and sobbing about the how sad someone's life who died two hundred years ago was? Maybe it was because people were a little wary of hippies but although Julia sat on her own crying for over half an hour only one person went over to her and asked if she was alright. It was an old man who looked almost old enough to have known Marie Antoinette personally. A stranger's concern meant a lot to her and she smiled at him through the tears. He even asked if she would like a drink of coffee; a very nice man.

She stayed at Versailles all day and as dusk began to fall she eventually had to catch the train back to Paris. As the shabby train slashed its way through the drab suburbs back to the reality of Paris she gazed impassively out of the window. She wanted to be home now. She didn't want to be on that train. Now she hated being apart from Jean-Marie and wished the journey away just so she could be back with him. She wanted to tell him all about her day, about Versailles. He was bound to know everything there was to know about it. He is so clever Julia thought to herself.

Sitting opposite her on the train was a young couple sitting who were obviously in love. They were kissing. She liked to see people happy. They reminded her of Jean-Marie and herself, they couldn't keep their hands off each other either. This couple couldn't be as much in love as she was, nobody could; she knew that. It was impossible for anyone else in the world to

was simply incredible and she found it difficult to tear herself away from it. Versailles was the most beautiful place Julia had ever been. She could not stop smiling, she was like a little girl opening her presents on Christmas morning.

It was the first day she had chosen to be somewhere on her own since moving to Paris. She stayed there all day not particularly looking at anything but feeling that she was looking for something. She looked out of place compared with the hordes of respectable middle aged tourists quietly flowing in an orderly fashion from point a, to point b, to point c. Today Julia was the hippiest of hippies. With her strings of beads and floaty clothes she was wandering erratically around the house and gardens randomly touching the walls and sitting on ancient chairs with signs saying 'keep off' as if trying to get them to reveal to her their secrets.

Inevitably she thought about Marie Antoinette. After visiting her private garden, her own chalet and her bedroom in the main palace she imagined how horrible it must have been to be her. How terrible that one minute she was the queen, part of this opulence isolated in blissful ignorance of what was happening in the real world then everything she had, everything she believed in just vanished. How unimaginable must it have been for her to suddenly realize that millions of people hated her and she would have had no idea why. None of the court knew any better, it was not their fault; they were trapped, living an illusion of life in this massive stone and gold bubble millions of miles away from France. They were as much victims of that joke of circumstance as the starving citizens of Paris.

Standing there where Marie Antoinette herself had stood she felt she could empathise with her. Julia felt so sorry for that poor foreign princess who thought she was loved and adored but then discovered that everything she had ever known was wrong. She felt so sad for her and wondered why she was feeling so much for someone she had never known. She found a quiet

air around them become filled with different sounds that were so solid she could actually feel them. She was transported out of the concert hall to somewhere without bricks and mortar. She was totally absorbed by the symphony of sound and light, she was part of the music. All her senses were tuned to the songs; there was nothing else, not even an awareness of herself. She had lost all sense of time; this was neither the start, middle of end of the show. She couldn't actually sense where she was. She didn't know whether she was in the middle of a crowd or sitting alone. There not past or future, only the present. She didn't care what town she was in or who she was with; nothing mattered other than the music.

The day after the concert Julia woke up smiling still high on the concert. She closed her eyes and tried to re-live the experience. It was the best concert she had ever been to and she wondered if anything could ever be better.

Suddenly she had an unexpected fancy that she would like to see the Palace of Versailles. Jean-Marie had been there several times so she didn't expect he'd want to go.

'I cannot stand that stinking place because of what it represents!'

She didn't mind going alone; it made a nice change to be just by herself. What struck her first was how bright the golden gates were, they seemed more golden than gold should be so much so that they did not look real. Once inside there was more gold, it was everywhere: golden railings, golden roofs, golden window frames. She could see why Jean-Marie didn't like this place, it really was opulence gone mad but nevertheless it was like being in a fairytale castle.

Inside she was again immersed by her surroundings. Maybe it was because she was by herself but she found it was easier to take in the beauty, the magnificence and history of the immense palace. She was awe struck from the moment she was inside. Some places she had visited had never lived up to their reputations but Versailles more than did. The Hall of Mirrors

she had no feelings towards him, he was irrelevant now. Her life in London had been good but that was over now. Nobody at home would miss her; Steve would be fine, Dylan and Bruce would be fine and maybe she could invite them over one day. She didn't want to think about her sons too much.

The two of them were both very high by the time Pink Floyd leapt on stage amidst the twirling, swirling, mingling lights and ethereal dry ice but they could still appreciate the music. There was nobody as psychedelic as Pink Floyd and it was a fantastic night. Afterwards Jean-Marie and Julia asked each other whether there had been someone on stage wearing a gorilla suit or whether it was the drugs messing with their minds? Since they both remembered this they were reasonably confident that this had actually happened.

Jean-Marie had seen his favourite band but the following week Julia learned that YES, her favourite band were playing in Paris. She must have mentioned this to Jean-Marie because he subsequently surprised her with a couple of tickets on her breakfast plate underneath her croissants. He was overjoyed to see the look on her face when she opened the envelope. Her radiant smile was priceless to him.

The night of the concert was the perfect romantic Parisian evening. As night fell they went to the very top of the Eiffel tower where they both watched the lights of Paris sing. By the time they arrived the gig had already started, the band was halfway through a cover of a Beatles song but that didn't matter. Beginnings, middles, ends: why did everything have to be so regimented?

The dazzling lights, the swirling colours and the hypnotic music were as hallucinogenic as any drug for her. YES took her somewhere she had never been before. The music painted a picture before her eyes; it filled every space around her, it coloured every moment. Julia felt the

beliefs and yet they would only have these beliefs because of where they were born. That's the insanity of it.'

As he spoke he became even angrier. Julia wondered how he could just get so angry at the drop of a hat without any provocation. She liked the way he could do this; it was so very French she thought. His rant became directed towards the Catholic Church. Suddenly the Pope was the most despicable tyrant on the planet.

Jean-Marie seemed really upset, she felt sorry for him and taking out a couple more cigarettes she lit them and gave him one. When they had finished, Julia felt it was down to her to snap them both out of this darkness. She had the flash of inspiration that only Julia Fairfax could have. She flung off her coat and did a naked handstand in front of him - and the handful of early rising sightseers she only noticed when she was upside down.

It did the trick; he smiled. It certainly changed her mood too, she actually surprised herself. The Japanese tourists were glad they had remembered their cameras, they had no idea that things like this happened in the West!

In her other life she would be meeting with short-haired accountants and publishers in suits talking about revenue and deadlines. But this was Paris. She thought to herself that Dickens got it wrong about the time in A Tale of Two Cities; this time, this 1969 was now the best of times. This was the age of wisdom and this age of wisdom was also the age the foolishness. It was the season of light, it was the spring of hope and yet it was winter but it was simply wonderful.

A couple of days later they went to see the Pink Floyd who were playing at the Paris Festival. Besides being Jean-Marie's favourite band, she could not help remembering that they were also Steve's favourite band too. Briefly she thought about him. He belonged in the past,

something of what she felt. Jean-Marie did not want to go into Sacre Cour; it was a matter of principle with him.

'Why won't you come in with me?' Julia asked doe-eyed and pouting.

He was not going to change his mind: 'All churches are temples to the thought tyranny of religion, to the death of the human spirit but that place is even worse!'

Jean-Marie hated the place with a passion. Julia asked him to explain. He told her how his great, great grandfather was slaughtered along with thousands of other communards in back in the 1870s by government troops. Julia listened intently to this rare insight into his life. He told her that to atone for the alleged sins of the communards, the government built this monstrosity. To slaughter thousands of Parisians and then to commemorate that by building this pretend church made him sick. He spat towards the building; she lit him a cigarette to calm himself down but to no avail.

Julia knew it was a terrible history Jean-Marie had torturing him deep within his veins and yet she was fascinated by it in an almost voyeuristic way. She knew it was wrong but she thought it quite romantic. She wanted to know more about his ancestors but Jean-Marie changed subject to his general pet hate of religion.

'You know what annoys me about religion,' he began. 'That each of them are so mutually exclusive. Christians have to believe not just that they're right but that Muslims are wrong. Muslims have to believe that they are right and that all the others are wrong. And yet what faith you have depends solely on where you're born. A baby born here in France will believe Christ is its salvation and Mohamed was wrong but a baby born in Saudi Arabia will believe Mohamed is its salvation and Christ was wrong. Both could fight and die for their

'Non!' he protested extremely vehemently. He was adamant that he would never go in that building because of what it stood for.

Julia didn't know about the history of what looked like a fairy tale castle to her. She just thought he was demonstrating his usual anti-religious tendencies. His parents had brought him up to be an unquestioning Catholic just like they themselves were. In their version of Christianity, God made the world and controlled everything in it. Everything good that happened showed the glory of God but every bad thing that happened such as an earthquake killing thousands, a volcano killing hundreds or a maniac with a gun in New York shooting a busload of children was ignored.

Jean-Marie was never meant to ask why if God was in charge of everything, why He should be praised for a particularly good wheat harvest in France but not be condemned for letting thousands of people starve in the famine in East Africa. It was impossible for Jean-Marie to believe in a God like this so he didn't.

'Religion is the cradle of despotism.' He was fond of saying, quoting the Marquis de Sade.

This was not Julia's God. Her God was not the master puppeteer sitting in the clouds making the wind blow, the snows fall and the earth tremble. For Julia, Jesus offered her warmth and companionship, peace and an assurance that there was something more than she could see. Julia was happy to have Jesus in her life but didn't really know why. She didn't have a strong faith and certainly not a conventional one but hoped that Jean-Marie might become a Christian too. She wanted him to feel what she felt but she wasn't going to actually do anything about it. Naively she thought that if he went into Sacre Cour that morning maybe he might sense

Drivers looked on in disbelief at the multi-coloured hippie dodging the traffic making her way to the Arc de Triomphe; the world has gone insane most of them thought. A few drivers started to beep their horns in admiration and then more and more joined in. People came out of their shops and homes to see what the noise was. It was quite spectacular.

To some people it was art, to some it was youthful spirits, to most it was bloody hippies stoned out of their heads trying to get themselves run over. Julia was the centre of attraction, she was the centre of France.

Julia wasn't sure how she got there but as the following dawn broke she found herself with Jean-Marie on the grass at the side of the steps leading to the Basilica de Sacre Cour. He had been a true gentleman and wrapped her in his long, heavy overcoat. She was just about to return it to him when she realized she didn't have any clothes on underneath; not even shoes. She stared in disbelief at herself. There were still patches of the body paint on her suggestive of some tropical skin infection. An old paintbrush with dried green paint also appeared to be attached to her. This brought the events of the previous evening flooding back to her. She woke Jean-Marie up and quickly opened her coat to him. After the initial shock, they both fell into fits of laughter.

Whether it was the after-effects of the previous night's LSD she wasn't sure but the whiteness of the Sacre Cour looked exceptionally bright and radiant in the sparkling morning sunshine. Julia said to Jean-Marie that the beauty of the building was speaking directly to her. She wanted to go in; she had never been inside before. She wrapped the coat tightly around herself and started to drag Jean-Marie up but he wasn't budging. It was the first time he had disagreed with her. Jean-Marie did not go into churches but this was something more.

The enigmatic paper burner looked over to her and shouted that she was the new Marianne. Julia thought that was a fantastic thing to say and rushed over to whoever he was and kissed him on his lips leaving his face smudged with blue paint. It was decided by all that the world must be allowed to see this symbol of their new Republic, this embodiment of beauty, love, youth and France.

Beardy physics bloke owned a battered old Citroën 2CV and he suggested he take them to the heart of the city, to the Champs d'Elysée. Julia found herself in the uncharacteristic position of being the sensible one. 'I can't get into someone's car like this. This paint's still wet; it'll go all over your seats. Look!' she said wiping her hand over the paint that was still dripping wet. She held up her bright green hand up to show them.

Everyone suddenly froze as if they were playing the game statues and the music had stopped. Even in this rather laissez-fair household, the sight of a tricoloured naked English girl with bright green pubic hair dripping on to the carpet was unusual. Everyone, including Julia suddenly realized how completely surreal this situation had become. Julia also became aware of how unexpectedly erotic this was; it was never meant to be, maybe that was why it made it even more fun.

The 2CV owner said he didn't mind and when the others saw the dilapidated state of it they understood why. Leaving the person still tearing up his pieces of paper behind, the others pushed eagerly to get inside the car. Five people managed to squeeze themselves into the back of the tiny car, Jean-Marie sat in the front with his girlfriend perched on his knee and they set off through the streets of Paris to the Champs d'Elysée. When they got there, flanked by her hippy entourage and making sure her beret was at the right angle, she marched proudly down the middle of the carriageway.

‘Have you ever thought that you might already be dead,’ said Jean-Marie, ‘and we’re just memories of someone else? That guy over there might actually be eighty years old, dying on his hospital bed and just remembering this moment and we are just characters in his memory.’

‘What guy?’

‘That long hairy, beardy physics bloke over there stroking that Dutch girl’s tits.’

‘Wow,’ said Julia sarcastically, ‘if that’s true then hairy, beardy physic bloke over there must either be God or you’re talking bollocks.’

Beardy physics bloke took up Jean-Marie’s point. ‘That’s a really wild thought man; we could all have died fifty years ago and some really old guy who knew us years ago could be lying in his hospital bed is thinking about us right now. We’re not real, we're not here. We are just thoughts and memories in that guy's head. We just think we are real because we’re how he is remembering us.’

The naked Dutch girl added, ‘Hey, we might have been completely different when we were real and alive. We might not have been anything like this when we were alive. Shit man, we might have been bastards or fascists. Oh shit, shit!’

The bearded one tried to calm her down but then realized: ‘You’re right, everyone here, even you Julia are just memories happening in an old guys mind in the future. We may not have even known each other, we may not have even lived in Paris!’

Julia had stopped paying attention, she had got bored and was marching around the room saluting her friends boisterously singing to the chorus of La Marseillaise. ‘*Aux armes, citoyens, Formez vos bataillons, Marchons, marchons! Qu'un sang impur; Abreuve nos sillons*!’ There was something about this song that always brought tears to her eyes: it was the passion and emotion, it epitomized the France she loved, the France of her dreams.

One of his more outré friends however seemed completely oblivious to the painted girl. He had been sat in the middle of the room slowly and carefully tearing a piece of paper into small pieces all this time. He then set each of them alight with his lighter and held the pieces until the flame started to burn his fingers. Nobody noticed how long he had been doing this although each time the ashen remains fell to the floor he loudly proclaimed how many times he had done this. Nobody cared.

'This is the tenth piece I turn to dust.' he said. The next time he did it he said, 'This is the thirty-sixth piece I turn to dust.'

Julia asked him what he was doing but he was in his own world. He just smiled at the naked red, green and blue English girl and said, 'Je vous aime tous.'

Next to him was another girl whom Julia was sure had been lying on the floor on a pile of blankets for about two days and hadn't spoken before she recently came to life. She also was completely naked and Julia was pretty sure she had always been naked. From her accent she seemed to be Dutch and although Jean-Marie had no idea who she was or how long she had been there he floated over to her and gave her a massive hug.

As if she was carrying on some conversation, the Dutch girl asked nobody in particular if anyone had ever wondered what it would be like if one day they woke up not just to find out that they were the only person left alive in the whole world but that they had always been the only person alive and that all her friends and family had just existed in their imagination.

A particularly bearded student – almost definitely physics or maths, called her over to him. She tip-toed across the room and sat on his lap. The bearded one asked the question, could this person survive alone or die of loneliness. Nobody was sure but it didn't stop them talking about it.

One dreamy evening, he gave Julia a present. It was a beret and he told her that she was now a real French girl. To celebrate her re-birth, she decided she to make a statement. One of the group who was interning at one of the theatres had copious amounts of grease paint and this gave Julia an inspirational idea. She stood naked, Christ-like with her arms outstretched in the middle of the room whilst Jean=Marie and several of his friends painted her body. They painted one side of her red and the other side blue leaving her face and an uncoloured strip down the middle. She was the French flag.

'What would your readers think if they could see you now?' asked Jean-Marie.

'Je nous suis pas un écrivain, Je suis français.' she exclaimed.

She stood in front of a full-length mirror and laughed along with everyone else. She stopped and turned to the others in the room who were laughing hysterically. Aware that Julia wanted to say something they tried their best to stop giggling but it was difficult after so much marijuana. Eventually they managed it and Julia looked quizzically at them: 'My bush: should I cover it?'

'No!' protested Jean-Marie just managing to find his voice. He then had what he considered at that particular moment to be the most imaginative, clever and symbolic idea that anyone in the whole of France had ever had. 'Paint it green, make it like a real bush!'

They didn't have any green body paint but one of his friends found a tin of green emulsion in the kitchen. The finder of the paint was rewarded with the task of completing this piece of rather unusual art. When it was complete, she topped the whole effect off with her new black beret. She stood in front of the mirror and admired herself. Jean-Marie admired her too. He could have spent the rest of his life just looking at her.

Something so easy to get now, something that even the poorest beggar out on the streets could find in a skip would have been out of the reach for so many people?'

Julia was moved. She knew all about poverty in the last century but Jean-Marie's words coupled with actually living in the middle of what used to be one of the most deprived areas of the world made her cry. She turned away from the window and looked at the pile of rugs scattered on their floor and thought how much they took for granted now. Everything was so easy to get hold of now, it was almost unimaginable to think that something as commonplace as a blanket would be unobtainable for so many people. They quite literally never knew where their next meal would come from. She could almost feel the presence of the hundreds of starving souls who lived in this very building. It made her shiver, but she was glad she could feel it.

She wished she didn't have such a macabre fascination with that unhappy age. When Jean-Marie explained that his family had lived here in such circumstances in the last century she felt even guiltier. Poverty, disease and misery were not something for the voyeur.

She had never heard Jean-Marie talk about his past or indeed his heritage before. That he was directly connected to this fascinating period in history, to the characters in a Zola novel made him even more romantic, more French. She held his hand and squeezed it tight. He was right, they were the luckiest people alive.

He was not always so deep. For a lot of the time he was smiling and joking. For a lot of the time he was making love to Julia. For all of the time, as Julia observed he was always the suave sophisticated French intellectual. He used to say that love was a pretence, a fabrication forced upon people to make them conform but he had completely altered his opinion when he met Julia. He loved her totally, he worshipped her. This suave, sophisticated young Frenchman knew that without her he would be a gibbering wreck of a man.

‘I stand next to you, I look down into that old street and I realize just how lucky I am.’ He replied quietly. ‘I have everything I want.’

Before Julia had time to blush, he explained that it wasn’t just because he had met the loveliest girl in the world he felt so blessed. It was being alive at this time. Jean-Marie sighed as he reflected on how his life would have been if he had been born a hundred years earlier. ‘These very apartment blocks would have housed thousands of people all with just one purpose: to stay alive. In a time celebrated for its splendour and wealth, the golden age of France, the life expectancy here where we are now was thirty-five years. Only one in four babies would survive until their first birthday. The dead were probably the lucky ones. Those that survived would be born into a life of utter poverty, it would be a challenge just to survive to see the sun rise the following morning.

There could be no escape. People born in poverty would stay there, they had no choice. If they were born starving in these slums they would live the same way, starving in the slums, there was no question that it could be any other way.’

He paused to light another Gitane. ‘The people who lived here would never know what it was like not to be hungry. They would never know what it was to be happy. They would not even know the concept of happiness. They would never know what free time was. To them misery, starvation and deprivation were normal, they would not know of any other world so could never dream of escaping. For the slum dwellers of the Goutte D’Or, to dream of living a better life would be as absurd as a dog thinking it could lead the life of its master.’

Julia went over to the window where he was standing and looked out with him.

He carried on. ‘Summers would be unbearably hot and winters would be a time when they knew they could freeze to death. A blanket would be a luxury. Can you imagine that?

It was a community of love. One of these friends who called himself Windmill had discovered he could interpret dreams. Some evenings they would sit on the floor in a circle.

'In this circle we are all without corners. Nobody is on the outside. Our spirits are all as one.' Jean-Marie told us.

They would close the curtains so the only light would be from the ends of joints that everyone was smoking. Windmill would move from person to person hugging each in turn and would see their dreams. He was always completely accurate, even when Julia didn't know that she had dreamt something, Windmill would remind her, he told her what they meant. She thought that he was amazing. All of Windmill's interpretations proved how much they all loved each other and how they would always be together.

LSD made days and nights blur together, people and places merged into one mass of love, warmth and happiness. The one thing she knew throughout was that Jean-Marie loved her more than anything and she loved him exactly as much. Their love was perfectly equal, balanced and more beautiful than she ever thought could exist.

Sometimes Julia and Jean-Marie would go out by themselves maybe to one of the city's premier restaurants for a romantic dinner or just a walk by the river in the moonlight. Sometimes the whole commune would go out and hit the clubs or just fool about like the time they went out in their pyjamas and played a game of seeing who could stick the most clothes pegs to strangers. Sometimes they would stay in and Jean-Marie would just stare out of the window for hours without moving. Julia loved to watch him. She wanted to paint her eyes with him, she thought him so beautiful to behold. Sometimes she wondered what he was thinking, other times, the mystery seemed more intriguing. 'What are you thinking about?' she asked him once.

neither of them could resist each other. They found themselves making love on the heavy wooden floor between the desks.

'If I knew our tutorial room was as much fun as this, I would have attended more diligently.' Jean-Marie said afterwards holding Julia tightly in his arms. Julia laughed but didn't reply. La Sorbonne was now even more special.

After this unexpected pleasure they strolled into the heart of the Latin Quarter. They would always meet someone they knew. Jean-Marie seemed to know everyone and although Julia had only been there a few weeks, she had become both well-known and well liked. Students smoking at tables in the bars, quiet intellectuals reading at pavement cafes and groups of hippies sitting together on the Quai de la Tournelle would all say hello to her as she walked by. Paris was her city.

Where she lived was more like a community than a home. She loved the constant flow of new faces coming and going, some of them staying for just a few minutes some of them staying for weeks. She was sharing her life with all of them, they were her extended family. She kept no secretes from them and she knew they kept no secrets from her. Even a few years ago in her hippiest of hippy days in London she could never have dreamt that she would be in a room sharing a meal with her boy friend whilst in that same room a boy and a girl were naked, making love and a young school teacher was marking his class's homework at the table. Now this seemed normal, everyone was totally comfortable with each other, people were beautiful and everything was just groovy.

Since moving to Paris, her life had suddenly become enriched with warmth, understanding and the sincerest, truest friendship possible from all of their friends and visitors.

‘Rousseau’s idea that our true spirits are pure and that evil is only bleeding to us by the world is such nonsense.’ She casually said to a complete stranger whilst wandering around the university.

‘Oui Mademoiselle,’ her fellow student replied. ‘Je suis d’accord – you are English – I agree - as de Sade said, we cannot know what our true natures are unless we follow our desires to the absolute limit no matter how appalling the disclosures might be.’

Where else in the world could she strike up such a conversation? She loved it there. La Sorbonne became her intellectual home. It was a gorgeous building in a gorgeous part of a gorgeous city and she adored wandering around, mingling with the real students, even attending the occasional lecture. Jean-Marie joked that she probably went to more lectures than he did. The university was everything Julia had imagined it would be. She was walking in the footsteps of Thomas Aquinas, John Calvin, Dante but above all she was in the cauldron where last year’s student revolts were born. Jean-Marie was there then, he was even photographed throwing a petrol bomb at the fascist police on the Boulevard Saint Germain.

One Friday afternoon Jean-Marie showed her around his department. The place was, as she had always suspected, was virtually deserted. Every wall, every window sill, every door handle breathed the university’s illustrious history. The whole faculty was alive with the past. Jean-Marie showed her where he usually sat; next to the window. She sat in his place and imagined the great philosophical arguments that must have happened in that very room. The view out of the window was everything Paris should be. She soaked up the sights, his sights of the Pantheon, the Latin Quarter, his life. Jean-Marie put his arm around her. She looked up at him and smiled. Neither of them had planned what happened next, neither of them felt entirely comfortable with it afterwards but just at that moment, everything was so perfect, so magical that

The recent departure of Charles de Gaulle had put Paris in a party mood. Everything was spontaneous, wild things just happened. Music seemed to be everywhere and everyone seemed to be in a band. Paris was now a young person's city. The Paris of 1969 that Julia found was even more far out than London and she threw every fibre of her being into it. This was her city, it was where she belonged, it was where the man she loved more than anything lived. It did not matter that she knew nothing about the man she was sharing her life with, all that mattered was that he was her soul mate and he made her happy.

She told him that once: 'It's not who you are that is important to me; it is how you make me feel. That's why I love you.'

Jean-Marie was studying philosophy so what would have been a succinct clever remark to most people escalated into an hour long conversation about the meaning of love with him. This was what Julia loved about him, the way he spoke and the way he thought. Some people would have called him pretentious but she saw him a true intellectual destined to follow in the footsteps of Sartre or Jack Kerouac or even the Marquis de Sade whom she discovered he had quite a following amongst the young intellectuals of Paris.

Julia knew he must actually go to university sometimes because he often had work to do but she never noticed him attending any lectures. She thought that his faculty must be deserted most of the time because nearly everyone from his course seemed at some time to be in their apartment. She had no idea who most of the people who floated around with her were but the constant supply drugs made their identities somewhat trivial. There were none of them that she didn't think were utterly wonderful. She felt as though she too was actually part of the University: Julia Fairfax, reading philosophy at Paris.

we the audience are dreaming when we watch it. When we, who are actually dreaming actually experience a dream then that dream is itself reality.'

'I think it is simpler than that.' a long-haired girl said as she finished off her glass of wine. 'What we are seeing is not the story of a group of people. We are seeing the experience, or rather the memory of the hotel itself. It exists out of time; out of the constraints of consequence. We don't need to ask whether the Delphine Seyrig character has been there before, whether she ever met the stranger a year ago; that is irrelevant. It is the house's reality.'

Julia chipped in; 'Everyone can exist in their own reality. Our existences don't always run at the same speed as everyone else's. Sometimes our orbits of existence coincide; they meet and then we exist in the orbits of those we meet. That's when we are real and when we are real we affect these other orbits, we change others' lives.'

Julia passed her joint to the long-haired girl who carried on. 'If we only exist in the orbits of other people, we would be different people to those who perceive us. That could explain why the man knew so much about the Seyrig's past and she didn't. Both were true and both were false.'

Julia interrupted excitedly: 'Marien bad but Jean-Mari-en good.' She thought this was absolutely hilarious, none of the others did. She stopped the discussion dead with an outburst of laughter both at her own comment and the confused faces of her friends. The others thought she was so sweet; so English. They ended their evening playing the 'un-winnable game' with the matches that was in the film. Other people wandered over to their table to watch. As each game ran inevitably to the same result, onlookers offered their opinions on reality, the futility of hope and whether time progressed in a linear fashion or not. Julia could not imagine an evening more French, more left-bank. She was in existential heaven!

was covered with table cloths. Paris was everything she imagined it would be; she was living in a black and white new-wave French film. She could not imagine how life could be better or how she or anyone could be happier. Everything was perfect.

Their evenings were sometimes spent with Jean-Marie's student friends in the more traditional settings of the Left Bank area. They would drink, smoke, discuss philosophy, argue about the existence of God and worship Julia. Julia was a breath of fresh air to Jean-Marie's sometimes rather too serious crowd. She was different: so English and yet more French than they were. She was slightly older and wiser but more youthful and eager to experience life. This was the eve of the modern age, when women would not viewed just as sex objects like Brigitte Bardot, women were men's intellectual equals.

Although Julia bore a striking resemblance to Brigitte Bardot and some people thought she must consciously model herself on her, she considered herself the antithesis of France's favourite sex kitten. It infuriated Julia that Brigitte Bardot had become the most famous woman in France not because of any particular talent but simply because she was born with those incredible good looks. One evening, in one of the bars Julia and Jean-Marie regularly frequented, some of the young men who hung around with them ended up arguing about who was the more attractive: Julia or Brigitte. The shallowness and whole concept of this discussion annoyed Julia to the core but it did not annoy her as much as when every one of them decided that Brigitte was the most attractive.

After watching the film, *'L'annee Derniere a Marienbad'* at one of Paris' many obscure little cinemas, Julia and Jean-Marie's friends sat in a café discussing passionately the meaning of the film until the small hours. Jean-Marie was confident he had solved the riddle of the film. 'It's not a dream,' he explained with utter conviction, 'it is reality but we have to understand that

Julia was no longer a middle class Londoner, no longer a writer, no longer a wife or a mother. Since she had gone to Paris she had become re-born. She had not phoned anyone back in England because that would break the spell. She never thought about Steve, Dylan or Bruce, not even Lisa or any of her friends. It was as though she was in a dream and if there were any signs of the real world she might wake up. Hidden in a locked cupboard at the back of her mind she knew that Steve would manage without her and the boys would not miss her. She wasn't born for that life, she was born to find love and she had found it.

One of Julia's favourite books was Zola's *L'Assommoir*, about a young woman's awful life in the squalor and poverty in the slums of nineteenth century Paris. When she read how Gervaise's life reached its terrible yet inevitable denouement, Julia was in tears. She had grown to know her, grown to love her and was devastated as though she had lost a real friend. In the novel, Gervaise lived in the ramshackle Rue de la Goutte D'Or area. When she had read this book she imagined what that place must have been like and now to her and delight she was living there. It was a hundred years later but she was there nevertheless: she was in a story. Even more amazingly, she discovered that Jean-Marie had actually chosen to live here because he too was in love with that novel. Another of his favourite books was her book, the one she wrote last year: it was almost too good to be true.

It was September but still summer in Paris. The high tenements of the narrow streets of La Chapelle trapped the heat like a great stone cooking pot. The air was dusty and stale as though it could have been breathed by Gervaise herself. The sun never shone through the narrow window of their apartment: somehow this added to the romantic realism of Julia's new life. This part of Paris was a lifetime away from swinging London, it was of a different time. Just five minutes' walk from their flat however they were back in the sixties, albeit that the Formica there

lives together. We had been holding each other through the train door window until the train started to move. With a jerk it pulled away and she slipped out of my arms.

I walked back though town unashamed about the tears streaming down my face. It was cold, I felt sick but I didn't take the bus, I wanted to walk, I didn't want anything to be easy. Back at the house, Keith brought a fried egg sandwich up to my room after I had been back a while. He didn't say anything, there was nothing to be said.

CHAPTER NINE

September 1969

me that a waterfall of swirling colours of lights and images flooded her senses. There was nothing else except the music. Nothing else was there at all, not even an awareness of herself.

She said she had lost all sense of time; this was neither the start, middle of end of the show. She had no sense of being in a concert hall. She didn't know whether she was in the middle of a crowd or sitting alone. She didn't even know whether I was there or not. There was only the music, the sound, the atmosphere. There no past or future, there had only been the 'now.' It wasn't that she couldn't sense anything else; there simply was no need in knowing anything else. There was only the music.... I loved her passion.

The day after the concert was the saddest day of my life, it was Giuliana's last day in England. Giuliana seemed to be on a permanent high because of last night's show which felt so wrong. I was devastated yet she was ebulliently recalling moments from that bloody concert. I wanted her to be crying. I had been expecting her to be sobbing on the floor clinging to my trouser legs but she wasn't - she was talking about how great bloody YES had been. It was as though nothing was happening, it was as though she didn't care.

Tomorrow came and she was gone and I was alone. It was more horrible than I could ever have thought. It was nothing like one of our normal goodbyes. We could no longer look forward to meeting again in a few days' time. This wasn't just going to London, this was going to a different country. She was going to call me as soon as she got to London, then when she got to the airport and then when she got home in Rome.

At the railway station we finally accepted that this was really happening. We made a thousand plans of how we were going to meet up soon, what I was going to see in Rome, how she could stay at my mum and dad's and of course how we were going to live the rest of our

She was like a little puppy on the bus as we chugged along to the concert venue. Grinning from ear to ear with excitement, she was as unlike the angry young Italian from that night before at the Cuttlers' Hall as was possible. I could understand why she had got so cross with that rich idiot but what I could not figure out was what she ever saw in him in the first place other than he was English and I knew she had a thing about us English. He was however very English, the sort of countryman who makes one ashamed to be English. I never spoke about what he had said. I didn't need to because it was all drunken nonsense.

At the theatre, we bumped into a couple of girls from my course. I joked that they were not the type of people I thought would go to a YES gig - they were girls! Giuliana gave me a stare, there were clearly things that were not to be joked about, YES being one of them.

The girls from my course figured that their Smiths t-shirts made it acceptable for them to be there as some sort of post-ironic statement. Stepping outside with them for a deep and meaningful chat about The Smiths, we all shared a couple of joints. They were quite strong, finishing the last drag Giuliana then said that she wished I hadn't smoked them because she really wanted me to be one hundred percent alert for the show. The dope did however relax me enough to take away the 'going to the dentist look' from my face.

She knew since she got the tickets that she would love this show. The band did not disappoint her and I did not find it too terrible. Although I was with her and endured the whole three long hours of it, on the way home she told me all about it again. She effused that she was transported back to the band's prog rock hey-day of the early seventies by the fusion of psychedelia, poetry and professionalism. How she was encased inside the soaring almost solid sounds that filled every space around her. How she was completely immersed by the symphony of sound and light. The nonsensical pseudo-poetic lyrics must have infected her because she told

news. The death of their principal financier was having an immediate effect on the funding of the production. RAI had told them that they would no longer be paying for the actors' flat from next month they were going to finish the filming and post-production in Rome. This was more than devastating, it put into the shade the visit from the police, whether or not the police had a copy of that letter and what Red Bow Tie had said about her. All of those things I was going to ignore, I was going to bury those thoughts deep at the back of my mind.

The move back to Italy was too difficult to believe so we both resolved to pretend it wasn't happening. We would not accept that this crazy bubble of happiness we had stolen from someone much more deserving was going to burst. It sounds both idiotic and impossible to ignore something so life changing but it was all we could do.

There was now however something else to take Giuliana's mind off her forthcoming repatriation. She had learned that YES were touring. She managed to get a couple of seats almost on the front row; the perks of working in the entertainment industry. When she surprised me with the tickets on the day of the concert she couldn't understand why I wasn't excited. It was my last night with her and I was having to spend it watching those dinosaurs of pretentious progressive rock.

'You do like YES don't you?' she asked gazing out of the window across the steely grey sky that morning. I could see that she didn't expect an answer; it was obvious to her that everyone should like YES.

Pretentious, pompous shite where the songs go on and on and on with that ageing hippy with the stupid girly voice thinking he's reciting great masterpieces of poetry and having a unique insight into the meaning of life. I would rather stick my head in the vacuum cleaner for four hours....'Of course I like YES. What a lovely surprise.'

screaming at her. A few minutes later the wife emerged with blood dripping from her nose. Giuliana stormed towards me and told me she was going to bed. I didn't see her again that night. I did not tell the Inspector about this but somehow she already knew that Giuliana had assaulted this idiot's wife.

Red-Bow tie was glaring at me – I needed to leave straight away. I caught the bus back home getting back before midnight.

Dylan confirmed that I was definitely back before midnight and as the police inspector finished her cup of tea and she informed me that she was grateful for my help. She let us know that I was back home several hours before Red-Bow tie was killed. I had nothing to worry about, she assured me, 'just getting a bit of background Mr Knight.'

'Sorry about Nick, Dylan repeated, 'he's never had a girlfriend before.'

Inspector Whitman slipped her notebook back into her briefcase and went.

'Well, that was odd wasn't it!' was all Dylan said to me before getting back to his film.

I was too shocked to talk to him anyway although there was something which I thought I saw that I wanted to ask him about. I wasn't sure whether I saw it or not but in the inspector's briefcase I thought I saw that letter, or at least a copy of that letter which the owner of that restaurant in Rome wrote back to me. That wonderful letter which started my new life, my life with Giuliana. I must have imagined it, why would the British police possibly be interested in that?

##

I was not looking forward to speaking to Giuliana about the visit from the police but the next time I saw her, the opportunity just didn't happen. Circumstances took over. There was something wrong when I met up with her, a couple of the Italian guys were with her. She had bad

'But that mad bitch,' he continued, 'talk about clingy! There's got to be a medical term for whatever she's got; obsessive love syndrome, behavioural addiction or something but I'd just call her a crazy bitch. He paused to light another cigarette. 'Sorry old boy, you don't actually like her do you. I mean she may look like a princess but she's just a mad whore. As crazy as fuck, if you'll forgive my French. Wouldn't be surprised if she ended up in jail for murder. Do yourself a favour sonny, run as fast as you can away from her.'

##

My recollections of Red Bow Tie to Inspector Whitham seemed to grab her attention. Her ears pricked up when I mentioned what he had said. Why the hell did I tell her he said: '*Wouldn't be surprised if she ended up in jail for murder'* but I stressed to her that this man was horribly drunk, he was a horrible man and someone who was clearly still bitter about being dumped by the most beautiful girl in the world.

I didn't tell the Inspector what he shouted after me as I walked away from him that evening: 'Don't be surprised if you wake up one morning with a bullet in your head old boy!'

I asked Giuliana who he was. She didn't want to speak about him. I knew he was a drunk idiot.

Red Bow-Tie was dragged away to a table by a woman with far too much make-up on whom I assumed to be his wife. I turned around to find that Giuliana had also walked away. Giuliana was restless when I found her. She was glaring at Red Bow-Tie and the wife was obviously whispering about us. Giuliana was getting agitated, I felt I should do something but Giuliana beat me to it. More upset than I'd ever seen her before, she stormed over to them screaming in Italian, telling them to stop being so nasty. I wasn't used to seeing Giulia like this, I found it strangely exciting. The wife went to the toilets and Giuliana followed her, still

‘You are joking! I’m having a great time. It’s worth it just to see you in that dress.’

It was a simple yet exquisitely styled dress made of glistening silk. The colour matched her dark green, sparkling eyes. Only she could get away with it: it was gossamer thin, almost transparent as if painted onto her yet breathtakingly elegant. To me she looked like a goddess. The other mere mortals present were awe-stuck. Her hair, her skin, the way she moved across the room was simply perfect.

She was just about to kiss me when she saw who I was standing next to. Nothing was said but as soon as she saw him she turned around and walked away.

'Mad bitch.' Red Bow-Tie slurred.

'What?' He couldn't be talking about Giuliana could he?

'I said, mad bitch. Surely you and Giuliana Moltisani are not an item are you?'

I wanted to smack him in the face but I also wanted to hear what he wanted to say. It consisted mainly of calling her a mad bitch.

Why was he saying this? 'You know Giuliana do you?'

'Know her, fucked her, dumped her, stalked by her.'

This took the air from my lungs. Who the hell was this person?

'By your expression I infer that she hasn't mentioned me to you. Never mentioned that I stayed in her disgustingly vulgar villa with her in Wop-land for a few weeks until I realized that she was clinically insane. Inherited of course from her psycho father or rather wannabe Godfather, Vito Corleone, and the rest of those criminals she called her family. Bunch of throwbacks from the middle-ages. Christ, living there was like being in some bad film – not as monumentally bad as this Wuthering Heights bollocks of course.'

He dropped his cigarette into my glass. I looked at it fizzing getting angrier.

with. I was however never one for knowing my place so went over to Claudio and said hello - he clearly had no idea who I was.

A young man wearing a red bow-tie noticed I was smoking so asked for a light.

'Are you with us or them?' Red bow-tie enquired in an unexpectedly polished voice.

'I'm a friend of one of the cast, so I'm not really anyone.'

'If you're a nobody then you must be one of the producers of this abhorrent vat of arse gravy.'

Red Bow Tie clearly had a very low regard for this modern take on one his beloved classics. I don't know how long he had been there but he was already very drunk. He was not a happy drunk.

'See that self-indulgent pretentious tenth rate Bertolucci over there?' He looked towards Fabio the director. 'Couldn't direct his own fart into the lavatory.'

'I watched some filming the other day, I thought he seemed really professional.'

'Professional my hairy arse! Shoot upwards with lots of sky for a happy mood, shoot down with lots of floor for a sad mood. That's his only two techniques – very bloody art school. Thieving twat!'

I asked him what his connection was to this film and he told me he was the financier. It was his money that had paid for the whole thing, including bringing Giuliana over to England! I seemed to owe him a more than he could ever realize.

Red bow-tie took a long thoughtful drag on his cigarette, 'I'd sue the buggers if I could. Bloody Italians, served me right.'

At that moment Giuliana walked in to the room. Sorry Darling, are you angry that I made you come?'

During the next days, the snow changed everything; it made the world completely silent. The usual traffic noises, distant voices and even birdsong vanished. Everything was silent; it was as though the snow had absorbed the city's voice. There was no sound, no colour, there wasn't even any smell. There was just snow; clean pure white snow hiding everything, changing everything; wiping everything clean.

After looking increasingly frustrated and almost contracting diabetes from my sugary recollections of my last few months, Inspector Whitman became interested when I finally began talking about the wrap party. That was when I met the dead man. It was a couple of days after that snowfall when all that was left of the snowman was a lump of ice at the end of the path. Giuliana kicked it to pieces next time she walked past it. It was snowing again at the end of the week which was when the wrap party was held at the Cutlers' Hall.

I had never been to a posh party before and was a little nervous. I needed a few pints for courage before arriving. I was glad of them because this was very different from a miners' benefit at the Student Union! This was the sort of function the likes of Penny or Dylan or even Keith, if he admitted it, would be so at home at but I felt very self-conscious there. A few hours later however I was amongst chandeliers and evening gowns. I was on board the Queen Mary in the 1930s. It was sublime, this was where I saw myself in a few years from now.

The thick heat of the room hit me like a croquet mallet in the face as I walked alone into the grand hall. I wanted to find this opulence distasteful, I wanted to think that all this money should be spent on the poor but I was seduced. Pretty waitresses were handing out free glasses of Champagne, I availed myself freely. The important people were easy to identify and there was an invisible yet obvious barrier between them and the people I suppose I was meant to associate

Edgar a young well-meaning but misguided Tory MP. It was a surreal experience watching them film half an hour of action over four hours, time was slowed down, I thought it quite relaxing. Giuliana was right about Claudio though, he did tend to shout a lot.

Lunch was called which offered a welcome break from all the sitting around. This was the first chance we had to spend some time with each other so we wandered up to Cathy and Heathcliffe's 'castle' out of sight from the rest of the crew and could not resist the unique opportunity of making love in the snow. It was painfully cold but absolutely fantastic. We laughed at the hollow in the snow we had made afterwards. Giuliana thought we should kick snow into the hole to hide it.

The snow made for an excellent morning's filming but as the weather deteriorated, rather than be stranded in a blizzard, Claudio decided to call it a day and we went back to the city. Snow was not common in Rome so this was a novelty to Giuliana. This was just how England should be. Back at the house she was like a little child in the back garden. She stretched her arms out and watched them get covered in snow. After a few more hours, the snow had become almost knee deep; Giuliana was in fairy-tale land. She did something she felt she had missed out on as a child. She made a snowman, a huge snowman.

News reports on the radio were saying that dozens of people were stranded in their cars on the roads going over the Pennines, Giuliana was glad they finished early today or she could have been one of them. The snow had made darkness fall quite early that afternoon. It was a unique sort of opaque darkness that Giuliana found fascinating. The milky sky reflected the lights of the city like a giant dust encrusted mirror; it gave her snowman a strange ethereal orange glow.

Giuliana thought Penny was cruel and heartless sometimes but I wasn't sure. Penny was a kind person in her own way, it was just that she was very analytical and thought that sentimentality was a weakness, maybe that's why she was suited to a career in medicine.

Towards the end of filming, Giuliana persuaded Claudio to let me come and watch some shooting on the moors. We left before dawn in order to do a few scenes at daybreak as the sun rose above the craggy moorland. The outline of the hills against the anthracite sky could be made out as the coach drove us out of the city. We arrived at the location and all stared out of the window trying to determine any features. We didn't seem to be anywhere but the director, who was far too awake for this time of day eagerly ushered everyone off our nice warm coach.

The Italians were the first to complain about the cold. The novelty of being able to see their breath was no compensation for that of hearing their teeth chattering. The sky looked solid, it had been painted above the feathery landscape using a coarse brush. Fabio, the director could not have dreamed a more dramatic backdrop for his shoot. The technicians started setting up the necessary equipment whilst the actors crept back on the warm coach.

Within a few minutes the first echoes of the sun started to glimmer in the darkness behind the mountains. Then dawn arrived. Fingers of sunlight trickled over the hills and valleys colouring in the world. Not even the freezing cold could keep the actors inside when they saw that sunrise. It was a stunning view and none of us had any regrets about having to get up so early. To the director's delight it started to snow. As the sun lit the world up the snow began turning the fields that just an hour ago had been black, from green to white. As it settled on the trees, the bare branches look like bolts of lightning against the heavy grey sky.

I had been led to believe that filming was a really dull and uneventful process but I thought it was exciting. Giuliana was playing Isabella Linton, who in this version was the sister

eliminated the impossible, whatever remains, however improbable, must be the truth. Improbable as is certainly was, the presence of Jesus seemed to be the most logical explanation.

The filming switched to location in Yorkshire which enabled us to spend more time together during the week. At that time we watched some terrible reports on TV about thousands of people starving in Ethiopia. I had to switch it off, it was too upsetting and there was nothing we could do about it. Giuliana on the other hand was obsessed with the crisis over there. She couldn't sleep worrying what could be done about it. She told me that she wished she was more like me, able to switch off. She liked the way I didn't become furious at the treatment of the blacks in South Africa or worried about Ronald Regan blowing the world up with his nuclear bombs. I just couldn't see the point in worrying. I said that the problems of the world were too big for anyone to do anything about so it wasn't worth losing sleep over. Giuliana tried her best to ignore the suffering and horrors of the world but could never quite do it, she knew something had to be done and she had to do it but didn't know what. I wanted to be like her, I wanted to be upset and moved by these tragedies.

It was one of Penny's hobby-horses that we shouldn't get emotional about these catastrophes or no sensible solution will be drawn up. Her summing up of the Ethiopian situation was that Europe should neither help nor get involved because European interference is what caused it in the first place. Because of globalization, we have thrust a backward continent into our world where it cannot cope. Black people, she said were different to us and should be allowed to evolve on their own. When they try and be like us, who have had thousands of years to practice of getting it right, they just can't cope.

'Christians,' he mused. 'They bury their dead outside the church and bury the living inside.' He was quite pleased with himself with that and looked at me as if expecting applause.

'Don't think I'm turning into a Bible basher or anything but it wasn't as bad as you would imagine you know.' It was a little odd to hear myself condoning religion or rather Christianity; I appreciated the difference now. I would have been embarrassed about even mentioning Jesus a few days ago but because of Giuliana, I was comfortable about this now. When I noticed that there was a meeting that night I said that if I had someone to go with, I would quite like to go again. I knew it was a safe thing to say because apart from Giuliana, I didn't like any of the Christians I knew.

'My mate Stevie, you know, guitarist in that band Sparkling Steel, we saw a few months ago yes? He plays guitar in there. If you fancy going, I'll come with you. Wouldn't mind catching up with Stevie anyway.'

Keith could be a good friend at times. It was a lovely gesture and we both had a good time. He enjoyed seeing his friend and talking about NAD amplifiers whilst ensuring that everyone he spoke to were made aware that he was not there because he could not cope with life but he was simply there to 'hold my hand.'

I couldn't wait to call Giuliana and tell her where I'd been. I knew she would love to hear it and I was right. I didn't know whether I went there just to be able to tell her that I had gone or whether I really wanted to go for myself. If I did become a Christian it would make Giuliana so happy. The following Wednesday I found myself going again, this time on my own although when I was there I didn't feel alone. It wasn't just the friendliness of the other people there either. Maybe Giuliana was right, maybe Jesus was trying to speak to me. I did feel something, it wasn't just forced emotion, happy songs and hand clapping. As Sherlock Holmes said, *when you have*

any emotion whatsoever. After all I was British and this American style born again stuff was not what we did over here! Maybe it was because of her Latin roots but Giuliana was loving it.

I had to confess that after the initial shock I honestly did enjoy myself. Leaving the church, I found myself grinning and I didn't know why. I turned to her and asked her why I felt so great.

'Because you have been with God.' she answered hoping not to sound too intense.

'Behave!' I laughed.

I could not admit even to myself that I had experienced something in that strange little church. It wasn't God or Jesus, it was just a lot of excited young people focussing their emotions onto this vision they had of God which made them even more excited. It certainly made them, and me, if I am honest, happy. Maybe that's what God is, just us finding a way to feel happy and loved? It was too much for me to think about then and Giuliana could tell so didn't mention it anymore. In her mind something had been planted in me that could grow, it just needed a little help from her. She wanted me to enjoy that feeling of everlasting love that she craved.

Our Monday separations had become easier, we were both busy during the week and this time rather optimistically, Giuliana also seemed excited about the possibility that I might become a Christian. She was so happy, it was wonderful to see that joy in her face, I almost wanted to become a Christian just to make her happier.

To get a bit of exercise, Keith and I decided to walk back from university on Wednesday. It was quite an orange evening, the sky, the ever-present Yorkshire mist, the buildings even the smell of the night seemed slightly orange. We came to that little Christian Fellowship that Giuliana and I visited on Sunday, I pointed it out to Keith.

We both woke up late that Sunday. I jumped out of bed and forgetting the inevitable hangover I shuffled downstairs to see if it really was as late as I thought.

It was; Giuliana would be annoyed when I told her: 'It's ten o'clock, we've missed the service at the Cathedral.'

'What about that place just down the road, I've seen people going in there at about eleven o'clock I think.' she replied. O.K. I thought, if Giulia wants to go to a church then of course I'll go with her but I resolved not to sing. I would always associate hymns with school and I hated school.

As we approached the rather plain little building that had the look of a municipal library I felt rather uneasy. Was this some of cult? It certainly did not resemble a church. Out of breath, we nervously poked our heads through the door. It was very full and most of the people looked like students. About five people dashed over to us as though we had just completed the London marathon and welcomed us like old friends. The vicar didn't call himself a vicar and didn't wear the costumes that I assumed they all wore. We did the Holy Communion thing, something I'd come across before and said some prayers I vaguely knew so I was assured that this was indeed a proper church not a weird cult where they were going to brainwash us, feed us gruel and make us give them all our money.

There was no church organ pumping out Victorian hymns that I was expecting. Instead: electric guitars, modern songs and people our age. When they all started to sing was the time I decided I either wanted to leave or crawl under a chair because they started lifting their hands in the air and clapping. I wasn't sure what to think when Giuliana also started waving her arms in the air too so I just quietly stared forwards at the OHP and spoke the words without expressing

When we woke up the following morning all five of us had the worst hangovers north of equator. Giuliana and I knew that we would only have this weekend together before she had to go back to London so we decided we had to make the most of every second of it. We forced ourselves to recover, we could not waste any moments by just lying in bed. We didn't get very far though. We lost count of the number of times we made love that wonderful morning. Again, every single minute together was perfect. We both knew that nothing could ever be better than this. The pyjama jump certainly made this weekend memorable but it was just being back together that they made it so special.

Another sad Monday morning came, another frustrating lonely week followed but then it was the weekend again. As soon as her train got in that next Saturday I thought I would treat her to a good old-fashioned Saturday night English treat – the Kebab. It would be a completely new experience for her, I knew she would love it.

'I have never put a more utterly disgusting thing into my mouth before.' were the words she inexplicably spat out along with the contents of her mouth. Consequently, I ended up eating two kebabs which did not result in me feeling especially energetic. We were near the Cathedral so we went into the grounds and sat on a bench like a couple of pensioners, I needed to rest after my mammoth intake of grease. Giuliana as always looked irresistible but weighed down by several litres of lamb fat I had to content myself with just sitting next to her. She held my hand in the moonlit shadow of the great church and it was really quite lovely just sitting there. The comforting silhouette of the massive Cathedral somehow reassured us both that everything was going to be alright. Sometimes, there were things that were so much nicer than sex.

Before we moved off, still holding my hand, she looked at the towering Cathedral for a moment then turned to me saying, 'On Sunday we will come to this Duomo for mass.'

perplexed was an understatement. She was however relieved to see that there were hundreds of other people all dressed the same. I explained that it was pyjama jump night. It was the last day of Twikker week, or rag week when all the male students hit the town dressed in nighties and all the girls go out in men's pyjama tops.

Giuliana felt decidedly over-dressed in the bustling city centre. Young men and women who earlier that afternoon could have discussing Nietzsche or observing cardio-thoracic surgery were now inexplicably drunk in the middle of the afternoon looking like they had just walked out of a rather risqué magazine. I thought that Giuliana might be too reserved to join in but I was so wrong. She couldn't wait to get home and change into something so vulgar it would make the prostitutes of the Spital Hill blush. She didn't like to ask why Keith had a spare pair of fishnet stockings that he found for her but we all agreed that she looked better in them than he did.

We played a game that Penny invented called the clothes peg game. We had to attach pegs onto strangers' clothes without them noticing. When they noticed one of us fiddling with their scanty clothing there was a variety of responses depending on their state of our drunkenness. Being caught with her hand apparently poised to dive into a gentleman's underpants Penny answered with, 'It's perfectly alright, I'm a trainee doctor. Just doing a bit of coursework here, carry on sir.'

Giuliana joked that she hoped we wouldn't bump into Claudio dressed like that or he'd have her staring in films of a very different nature! It was a fantastic night and what made it even better was how much my Giuliana enjoyed herself. She said that she had never had such a crazy night before. By the end of that night Giuliana was as much a Sheffield student as any of us were.

age and it made her skin tingle. She was so excited to be going to London but, not wanting to hurt my feelings, she tried to hide that from me.'

The police inspector smiled when I told her this. Maybe she did have a heart; I didn't care I just wanted to tell her how much I loved Giuliana. I wanted to everyone how much I loved Giuliana.

As Dylan made the police officer a cup of tea and babbled on about Greta Garbo again, I remembered that first time Giuliana had to go down to London to start filming. It was a cold morning that Monday as we stood in each other's arms on the London platform with tears trickling down our cheeks. We were secretly praying that the train didn't come and then tried to pretend that we hadn't heard the announcement of its imminent arrival over the Tannoy. We held each other even tighter. When the train arrived beside us we closed our eyes in an attempt to make it go away but it didn't. She had to go.

'I am phoning you as soon as I am getting to the studio.' Giuliana sobbed as the train pulled away.

For the next few hours I sat at home next to the phone waiting for it to ring. At lunchtime it rang, she had arrived safely at London. I was so elated to have heard her voice that I actually went to lectures.

That following week was the longest week of my life. We spoke to each other a couple of times each night but when we put the phone down it made our separation even worse. Giuliana confessed to me that she cried herself to sleep that first Monday night.

When she came back from London the following Friday I met her at Sheffield station dressed in a 1970s style frilly nightie and particularly grotesque make-up. I suppose I should have warned her but I wanted to her how surprised she would be. To say she was a little

imagined myself growing old in a cold jail cell, protecting the girl I loved. But this was stupid – as if Giuliana could have anything to do with this man's death!

Saying that I couldn't really remember, Inspector Whitman knew I was lying; I was a terrible liar. Yet again, she insisted that I told her exactly what had happened. She asked me to describe my relationship with Giuliana. What had really happened had been the most wonderful couple of months of my life.

I was more than happy to tell her about my relationship with Giuliana. 'From the moment I met Giuliana at the airport to the moment I said goodbye to her on the train the other day feels like what I had been born for.'

'Sorry about my friend – he's never had a girlfriend before.' Dylan said.

After correcting him on that fact and pointing out that I wasn't a tart like he was, I carried on recalling to the Inspector about these last few months. When I spoke about Giuliana it was always difficult to stop but I knew I ought to be extra careful with this woman and not say anything that could incriminate her. I was going to protect my girlfriend, it felt good protecting her.

'After that first week we had together it was time for her to start working, working in London. I had only known her a week but already Giuliana's happiness was the most important thing for me. I didn't want her to go to London, I wanted to be with her every minute of every day but what would keep me happy would be the knowledge that she was doing something she had always wanted to do.

For Giuliana, London was the most wonderful city on the earth. Carnaby Street and the swinging sixties were long gone but if she closed her eyes she could still feel the shadow of that

discern what that expression on her face was, it made me nervous. I didn't think I had done anything but I must have done something. Why else was she here? She was not just any old police officer, she was an inspector!

As she continued to ignore me my mind began to hurt. Why was she here? It can't be that someone's been hurt or killed, she would have told me that straight away. Was it drugs? Was this a drugs raid? Was it something to do with Dylan – she did seem to be speaking with him? Maybe it was his mother, Dylan had said that she had been in trouble with the police before; some political protesting – I couldn't remember. It couldn't be Giuliana – maybe there had been something wrong with her work visa? Why didn't Dylan shut up?

Finally she turned to me and opened her brief case. She showed me a photograph of a man. I recognized him immediately. He was that unpleasant rich drunk from the wrap-party I went to with Giuliana. She asked me if I knew him, tentatively I told her that I did. She asked me what we had spoken about, she wanted to know exactly what we had said. I still didn't know why she was asking me this, I had only met him for about five minutes.

It seemed that he was dead, he had been murdered. He was murdered just after I met him, immediately after I had met him. Was I a suspect? I didn't like that guy after what he had said, I wanted to hit him. I was so drunk that night I can't remember everything... no of course I didn't kill him, I remember leaving the party and he was still there. Giuliana had attacked his wife; no of course she wouldn't have killed him. What if she had? No, I had to stop thinking this nonsense, it was ridiculous.

Inspector Whitmam asked me to tell her everything, everything we had said. I was not going to tell her; what he said about Giuliana was just nasty, complete drunken nonsense. I was not going to repeat anything he said about her. I would rather go to jail myself. For a moment I

CHAPTER EIGHT

November 1984

It was obvious that the woman who knocked on our door that windy winter evening was a police officer. She strode and shook my hand purposely: 'Nicolas Knight? Inspector Whitman, South Yorkshire Constabulary – do you mind if I come in?'

I could not think of what I could possibly have done but I immediately felt guilty. She knew my name, it was me she came to see, I must have done something.

'Good evening,' she said to Dylan who was engrossed in a silent Greta Garbo film. 'What are you watching?'

'*Flesh and the Devil*. Greta Garbo, 1927.' he replied without really looking up. His attitude perplexed me – there was a policeman in our house; why wasn't he concerned?

'Ah yes, John Gilbert. They reckon they fell in love on the set of this very film.' she said.

That got his attention, he was impressed. They began to talk about John Gilbert and his fall from stardom. I couldn't believe this: a police inspector had just come into my house to speak to me, to question me but Dylan was talking to her about dead film stars. Having a visit from the police was not normal, I was desperate to know what it was all about. Why was he doing this? She carried on talking to him about this nonsense occasionally glancing towards me. I couldn't

Giuliana was silent, holding on to the window frame and staring out across the city. I wasn't sure how she looked, for a moment I thought she might be upset, even shocked. Seconds later she looked at me, smiled and threw her arms around me.

Walking back to our house afterwards she told me that something strange did happen to her up to her there. After we made love, she said she felt dizzy and the view across the city towards the mountains became fuzzy. She felt faint as if she was going to collapse.

'Ho sentito molto strano. Sorry - I felt very strange,' she told me. 'Not just the emotion after such wonderful love making, no Nick, this was different. Do you know, just for a few seconds I was looking at Paris not Sheffield. I was looking at Paris and I felt really sad. It was just like when I remembered the trip under the streets of Paris – it was somebody else's memory.'

waiting for the wind to blow the girls' skirts up. She playfully slapped my bottom for being naughty.

We went inside then up and down the tower on our lift that was best described as stepping into rows of shallow shoe boxes all connected, one on top of the other. One side was going up and one side was going down. There were no doors but it moved really slowly. I had been at Sheffield for two years but I constantly found our Paternoster lift the source of endless amusement. I was like a little boy with his favourite toy, going up one side and coming down the other. I took her right to the top and our compartment then went sideways then down the other side. Inexplicably to me Giuliana did not realize that this was the most amazing thing in the entire world. We got out and I took her over the top again to prove how much fun it was. She was still unimpressed! About half the way down we stepped off and I showed her my tutorial room. The view from up there was exceptional, we could see for miles.

There was something so special about being there with her. It was like sharing a new part of my life with her. At that precise moment I felt closer to her than ever before. I know I had only been with her for less than a week but I knew her completely, I knew her more than anyone else I had ever known.

I don't know how it happened but before we knew it our passions had possessed us and we were making love on the floor. Described that way it sounds rather sordid but nothing could be further from the truth. It was not tawdry and dirty, it was absolutely magical. It was unlike any other time before or after. It was absolutely magical.

'If I knew our tutorial room was as much fun as this, I would have attended more diligently.' I said getting my breath back.

‘What signposts?’ I asked somewhat confused.

She wasn't able to answer. She didn’t know why she had said that, there were no signposts. She was thinking about somewhere else, somewhere similar but she couldn’t remember where and apologised. She asked where was it that you can go on a boat ride along big sewers like underground canals under a city where the sewers are exactly in the same place as the roads above them.

‘That’s Paris.’ Dylan answered, showing off. ‘The sewers were deigned at the time of the Third Republic and they’re an exact copy of Hausmann's city streets above them and yes, they do have the same street names. They used to have underground boat trips. My mum told me she had done this.’

Keith interrupted. ’Are you bloody serious? Boat trips along shitty sewers ploughing through hundreds of tonnes of garlic flavoured turds? Stuck in a tunnel without any fresh air; that must be romantic. I must get down to the travel agents first thing in the morning.’

Dylan ignored Keith's ridiculing and asked Giuliana when she went there because he thought they had stopped doing those trips about ten years ago. Again, she couldn’t answer because she had never even been to Paris so how could she remember this? It must have been on television and being on that little boat reminded her of it. We all dismissed this but she told me later that it was really odd, it was like remembering somebody else’s memory.

The last place I took her before she had to go to London was closer to home. She had asked to see my university so I took her after lectures were over. At the bottom of our very tall arts tower building it was really windy. I explained that it was always windy there, something to do with the its design. Me and my friends used to have a great time sitting on the benches there

the Spotted Cow. She actually loved it; a real authentic English pub, she called it. She was so funny about English things. The next day we went somewhere much more picturesque, after just a short bus ride we were no longer in the city centre but in the middle of the beautiful Derbyshire countryside. It reminded her of Tuscany but with rain. She said it was so much prettier than Tuscany and couldn't understand why English tourists went to Italy when their own country was so much prettier.

The place we went had deep caves and water filled caverns. When the tour guide found out Giuliana was Italian we were given star treatment. We sat at the front of the little boat that took us along the underground caves beneath the massive green and grey sparkling stalactites. It was so romantic.

Dylan told us when we got back that he had been there with Penny last term. 'Did the lights go off and the guide pretended to start panicking shouting: 'Oh no, we've had a power cut how will we ever find our way out?' Dylan laughed.

'Yes.' Giuliana laughed, 'I bet they always do that.'

'No Sweetheart, it's the ghost of Blue John himself who was tricked by Italian ice cream manufacturers one hundred years ago into buying a dodgy franchise so now hides in the darkness waiting for innocent Italians. When he sniffs them out – you'll have to do something about all the garlic you're eating love - he lures them into the dark tunnels by singing the Cornetto song where they're lost forever, damned to wander the dark tunnels until the end of time.'

Giuliana did not quite understand Dylan's humour but laughed politely. She then said something about the boat ride: 'Incredible how the segnaletica, sorry the name plates that say what the streets are called are the same as they are above ground.'

'You mean signposts?' Keith said.

Dylan went back to bed and I sat alone wondering what had just happened. The room I occupied was the largest and most pleasant in our house. I had a large easy chair near the window from which the city skyline provided a constant picture postcard. By day the city filled every space, it was solid, strong and loud. By night, this night, it seemed a million miles away, I was completely isolated. For hours, I gazed with glazed eyes the life outside and soaked it up. I could feel the clouds of lazy smoke coming from the few factories still working in the east of the city, I could smell it, I could taste it. The hazy red glow of a city at night used to give me a reassuring warmth but this night nothing was reassuring, nothing was right.

I looked to my bed and noticed a hair on my pillow, was it hers? I picked it up, twirled it in my fingers and dropped it on the floor. Dylan tapped on my door came in, sat down and lit a cigarette.

‘Fancy a king size?’ he asked.

‘Already got one of them mate but I will have a cigarette.’ I answered briefly slipping back in to character.

'Two things to say mate,’ Dylan began. 'Firstly, what the hell did you say to Giuliana to make her run off and secondly, fucking hell mate, she was stark-fucking-naked in my bedroom!'

I told him what I had said. Told him she was going on about religion or something, about wanting to be perfect and how I told her that she was already. Even I winced when I recollected saying: 'no guy could wish for anything more gorgeous.' Yes, that was more than stupid.

After a few more cigarettes Dylan gave me a hug and said, ‘Don't worry mate, she's either crazy or crazy about you and whichever is which she'll be back tomorrow.'

He was nearly right. It wasn't tomorrow but the day after she called around to see me. We didn't speak about our row, we just carried on as if the whole thing never happened. We went to

My favourite band then was Yes, and they still are. They epitomised England: clever and sophisticated yet fun and quirky. I really wished I had been born earlier and could have been a flower child and lived in London in the late sixties. Think how amazing it would have been to have witnessed the birth of bands like these, watched them play at hippy festivals, smoked dope, worn flowers in my hair and shopped in Carnaby Street. Think how amazing it would have been to have been part of a generation that actually did something.

It's so sad that there is nothing about this decade. It's just bland and filled with blank pages like me wanting everything but with nothing to contribute.'

As I lay beside her simply being astonished by how beautiful she was her words sounded ridiculous. Why would someone as amazing as this want to be different, something other than what she already was. Giuliana was talking nonsense and I told her so

'No Giulia, you are perfect.'

'Perfect! How dare you. Are you saying that I should be like this for ever and never change?' She wrestled free of my arms and got out of bed.

I did not understand what was happening - she was perfect. We were perfect and I couldn't believe we were arguing. It all happened so quickly.

'But Giulia, you are perfect. Look at you, you're the most gorgeous girl I've ever seen. No guy could ever want anything more.'

'Vaffanculo! Vaffanculo! Have you not listened to a word I have been saying? You do not know me. You do not who I am or anything about me. Vaffanculo!'

She stormed out of my room and marched into Dylan's. Completely stark naked with her hands aggressively on her hips she demanded Dylan called her a taxi. Dylan certainly could not say no to a naked girl especially one shouting at him so did it immediately.

wanted God to stop her doing what she was doing and to make her into the girl she knew she should be but nothing happened. She just carried on praying wondering if anyone was listening.

'Well, just goes to show that God's cool about sex then.' I said, not really grasping what she was trying to say.

'No, I wanted a thunderbolt,'

I let her carry on uninterrupted. She said she felt unable to live up to the near perfect image she was portraying. She was living a lie.

'About that time I made some real deep friendships; people who are still my best friends. They had more in common with me than just being a disappointment to Jesus, they were really interested in music and radical politics. Back then I wasn't sure what socialism was but I was a hundred percent sure that I was a socialist.

To us Italians back then, politics was black or white. We were all idealists, we thought we could see what was wrong and what needed to be done but we were so arrogant and probably very annoying. It was so exciting to know with such certainty that we could change the world. I felt like I was champagne after the cork had just been shot off. I was suddenly full of energy and ideas and ambition. For me however there was so much else I was discovering too, things that were fun. We all had the same taste in music and I gradually started to become more of a fan of the bands we liked more than the politics.

My friends were really in to English Progressive Rock, which was something I had never heard of before but I just loved it. It opened a whole new world to me. I think this is where my love of England came from. I would sit in their houses listening to Genesis, Van der Graaf Generator, Pink Floyd and Yes for hours on end analysing every word and change in tempo to discover the real meaning of the songs.

respectable, very proper and strict upbringing. She was clever, she enjoyed school and learning, she could play music and was kind and polite. She didn't disappoint them except when she decided that she wasn't a Catholic.

Initially they were embarrassed about her denial of the 'true faith.' Then, justified by the belief that eventually she would see the error of her ways and return to their church they forgave her. That was not going to happen; Giuliana had discovered Jesus and she tried to explain to me that he was as real to her as any of her family were. He wasn't just in church, she didn't need a priest to speak to him, she didn't need to use special words; he was everywhere and anywhere.

I was extremely surprised to hear that she was religious, I would never have guessed. Religion was something I associated with old ladies in hats not sexy young Italian girls, especially one lying next to me in bed naked.

She told me how she loved her new church and they loved her but had started to wonder whether she had disappointed. She didn't think she could ever live up to their ideals, she could never be as good a Christian as most of them were. I did not understand what she was saying but she seemed genuinely upset about not being able to be what she thought was expected of her. She tried so hard to be as committed but said that it was just hopeless. Her pastor told her that that Jesus loved her anyway and it didn't matter how hard she tried as long as she tried. Apparently that wasn't good enough for her, Giuliana wanted to be devoted and committed and the more she tried the more she realized she couldn't do it.

When she was about fifteen and very miserable she was with some Christian friends sitting in a circle praying to help their non-Christian friends resist the temptation of sex. Jesus obviously knew she was lying, he knew that she was already having sex but nothing happened, no thunderbolt from the sky came crashing in on her. She wanted something to happen, she

Dylan apologised and offered her my beer which I hadn't started yet.

His mother knew that Giuliana would be there. 'La bella Giuliana, pleased to finally meet the girl who has swept young Nick here off his feet.' She said kissing her hand theatrically.

Julia was in a hurry to get to another party somewhere but she and her 'new best friend from Italy' somehow managed to squeeze an hour's worth of conversation into half an hour; I don't know which of them could talk the most! In just thirty minutes I don't think either of them stopped for breath.

When our rather rushed Chinese banquet drew to a close Julia kissed both her son and Giuliana goodbye and drove off in her little French car which Giuliana thought was such a funny vehicle. She didn't hug me this time which I was glad of but wondered why. After Julia had left, we no longer needed to be polite to each other so the true silliness of Dylan's bizarre new hair style became apparent. Me and Keith were in fits of laughter. Gone was the Freddie Mercury look and in was the 'just been electrocuted' look.

'So, what the hell are you meant to be this term?' Keith asked.

'You've got to move with the times man.' replied the stranger with the gelled jet-black hair. He said that had decided that his taste in music needed bringing into the 1980s so had thrown himself feet first into new alternative bands such as The Cure, The Sisters of Mercy and The Cult. He explained that some friends in Liverpool had dragged him to see the Cure a few days ago and as a result he decided he needed to renew himself.

Giuliana thought he was betraying his musical identity but in a way, knew what he was talking about. After we had gone to bed she told me all about how her adolescence he had completely changed who she was. When she was younger she was never really anything other than her parents' perfect little girl. They were respectable people and Giuliana was given a

when he burst in. He ran at Guiliana, grabbed her like a bear and spun her around in the air before giving her a kiss.

I didn't go in for such displays of emotion simply said: Good to see you Dylan. Dylan knew me well enough to realize how really glad I was to see him. He thrust one of his many plastic carrier bags onto the kitchen table sending papers, books and unopened letters flying across the room.

'Look what I've bought for us.' he grinned. 'Chinese take-away. You do like Chinese don't you? Yes, of course you do, who doesn't? Come on Giuliana, get the plates warmed up. Nick, a couple of our finest beers if we've got any I think.'

Dylan was so full of energy and his almost electrical presence was quite a shock to our relaxed evening. Without hesitation, Giuliana took three plates out of the cupboard and I dutifully opened a couple of bottles of Italian beer. As we did this Dylan leapt onto a chair and began to Sellotape a poster of scantily clad Lesley Ann Downe onto our kitchen wall: 'Gentlemen,' he said, 'I give you the world's most beautiful woman.'

'Present company excluded.' I said. Giuliana gave me a quick kiss for that. Taking the lids off the foil containers of the mysterious brown and red gooey substances, the names of which she had no ideas, she was startled by a banging on the window.

'Bloody well let me in!' someone demanded banging even louder on the door.

Quickly trying to swallow a mouthful of prawn crackers, Dylan dashed to the door: 'Shit, I forgot my mother was here!' He opened the door and allowed her to drag his own suitcase in.

'Tell you what Darling,' his mother said, 'I'll drive you all the way down here, and bring all your luggage out from the car by myself whilst you eat the Chinese that I have just paid for shall I?'

We made the most of our time together before Giuliana had to travel down to London to start filming. One afternoon I took her to the dullest industrial museum in England but we loved it. I tried to explain how the molten iron used to run out of these kilns in little streams similar to a pig suckling her young which was why this type of iron was called pig iron.

‘A crying bloody shame.’ said an old man said in a thick northern accent. Giuliana was startled and grabbed my hand tightly; it felt nice. He went on, ‘British Industry under Thatcher: turned into bloody museums.’

Her grasp of English was not good then so she could not really understand what he was saying but she enjoyed his subsequent frustrated struggles to explain. She really had no idea what he was talking about so just stood amongst those middle aged men in fits of uncontrollable laughter. Even at this shabby industrial museum we were having one of the best days of our lives.

‘You used to work here?’ she asked.

I winced; I knew that we were now going to get about half an hour’s lecture on the destruction of British Industry by Thatcher. Giuliana surprised me with how much she knew about our country’s economy. She had always been interested in British politics and quite the expert on the devastating effects on our economy Margaret Thatcher was having. She knew all about the dozens of factories closing down, the strikes, the riots, Scargill and the miners’ strike, how unemployment had doubled to two million under her reign and in parts of Liverpool unemployment was at sixty percent. I was impressed, I wanted to be interested.

Dylan had been staying at his mother's flat for a few days so missed Giuliana's arrival. She was home when Dylan came back. Apart from his new hairstyle, he was just like she remembered him from Rome with just as much gusto. He almost knocked the door off its hinges

on and whether she saw me scanning every coach on the motorway was not really important; we knew we saw each other.

Giuliana enjoyed the journey, even if they wouldn't let me go with her. She loved driving through London and seeing the sites and couldn't wait to get back and explore. She loved seeing just how different England was; it was even better and more English than she imagined. She loved reading the road signs, the shop signs, she loved everything. English words had fascinated her for as long as she could remember. She thought they were just so crazy and used to laugh at them with me.

'I love the way you don't seem to have rules about spelling; like why isn't 'one' spelt 'won'? Why isn't 'own' spelt 'one' like in 'phone,' it's the same sound just without the 'f' at the beginning. And why isn't phone spelt with an 'f'? Foam isn't phoam but then that's got an 'a' in it for no reason whatsoever.'

I loved the way she loved everything.

I knew that she would need to settle in to her flat so would not want me calling on her straight away but I could not keep away. She seemed however to be expecting me. It wasn't planned, or maybe it was, I don't know, but I stayed with her that night. Without any question, it was the most fantastic night both of us had ever had in our lives. It was just so right, so absolutely perfect in every way. Like most people who have been excited about the thought and the expectation of making love I would imagine how brilliant it would be but then find it never was quite as perfect as hoped for. I had learned to lower my expectations then if it was good; great but if it was a bit rubbish, then I would not be disappointed. With Giuliana however I knew immediately that it was going to be the most romantic and passionate night of my life. This time we both knew we were not going to be disappointed and we were not.

film, but she was coming to see someone who she had only met for a few hours but who she knew she wanted to spend the rest of her life with. It was just too mind blowing to realize that she was looking forward to seeing me as I was about seeing her.

She was so nervous and unsure that I was actually real that she couldn't tell her friends that she actually had met this perfect boy. Sitting there on the plane getting slightly drunk with her friends from Rome she didn't quite believe it could be true; it was so insane. She had only met me for a few hours! She needed to see me, to see if I really did feel the same way about her before telling everyone that I was the one. When she stumbled off the plane she hoped she wasn't too drunk; the last thing she wanted was for me to see her drunk.

Claudio, their producer got one of his assistants to retrieve all their baggage from the carrousel. Whilst he was waiting for Giuliana's suitcase to come through she ran, she really did. She ran through the arrivals gate into the lounge. I was there, waiting. Her recollection about that moment was a fuzzy as mine. She didn't remember saying anything or even how she got to my side of the barrier all she could remember was being in my arms. I picked her off the floor, hugged her and spun her around and around. It was the cliched final scene from the old film where the hero is re-united with his true love.

When she arrived she didn't realize how far away from London Sheffield was; it took five hours. Claudio had bought some wine so the party mood that began on the plane carried on but now uninhibited by the sour expressions of those stewards. Neither of us actually expected that we would go up to Sheffield together since we had to admit that didn't actually know each other yet. But like me, she wished I could have gone up with her in the coach but Claudio said I wasn't allowed. We both remembered one romantic point when the motorway and the railway line ran alongside each other and her train went past my coach. Whether I saw the actual train she was

glasses, tossed her hair back and ran into my arms. Without any words we embraced, gazed into each other's eyes and kissed. Somewhere nearby, the theme from Tchaikovsky's Romeo and Juliette started to play.

The next few months we were in a fairy story romance. For Giuliana and me it was love at first, second, third and fourth sight. Neither of us could keep our eyes of each other, neither of us could look at the other without feeling weak at the knees. We were inseparable, although Keith describe us as insufferable. What was so amazing was that although I didn't think anyone could love anyone as much as I loved Giuliana was that Giuliana loved me the same.

She told me how terrified she had been whether I would feel the same way about her as she flew over. She could hardly believe that it was only a couple of months ago when she boarded that flight from Rome and sipped vodka and tonic beyond the clouds. She could not have hoped in her wildest dreams that her life could have turned out so ridiculously amazing.

There was something she couldn't quite put her finger on about Alitalia stewards that was insidiously intimidating. They looked like disapproving fathers to her who had just seen their daughter smoke a cigarette for the first time. For some reason she and her friends just couldn't stop giggling that morning. For Giuliana it was nerves about seeing me mixed with the flying and the excitement about going to England. The more disapproving and stern the stewards glared at them, the more giggly they became.

The stewards were used to theatrical types; they tolerated them. There were about twenty of them going to London to start filming a modern dress version of *Wuthering Heights*. Heathcliffe was a homeless Italian immigrant and Cathy was the daughter of a prominent Yorkshire businessman. Giuliana became more and more excited with each passing minute of the flight. Not only was she going to England, not only did she have a role in an international TV

could actually believe she was actually coming or whether they thought it was amazing or not. The day of her arrival eventually came, it was the day I was going to meet her in London.

I left so early I didn't have any breakfast so was very hungry by the time I arrived in London. The first thing upon arriving at Kings Cross was to buy a Big Mac. After one bite I knew it was a mistake: onions, my breath would stink. I scraped the onions off but then thought that even the de-onioned burger might make my breath smell. Everything had to be perfect so the whole thing went in the bin. Still hungry I found a corner shop and bought a small loaf of sliced white bread; just plain bread would fill me up whilst being completely odour-free. I felt somewhat conspicuous walking along the Euston Road gnawing at a dry loaf of bread but then again, this was London and nobody knew me here.

What drink would leave my breath the freshest: Coke, lemonade, certainly not blackcurrant, coffee or those strangely solid milk shakes from the burger bars? After much deliberation I opted for an odourless diet Coke. It was then a short walk back to the underground to wait for the tube to Heathrow where I had time for a couple of cigarettes.

Heathrow was bustling, people off all colours, languages and styles of dress tossed together into a snapshot of the modern world. It was the first time I had been there but nevertheless I knew exactly where to go. All my senses were on overdrive to ensure everything went perfectly. I was at the arrivals gate for the Alitalia flight from Rome before anyone else.

It was just like a film. She was the first to come through the door and she looked even more beautiful than I had remembered. She was every inch the film star. She was wearing a long silky white dress that conjured up its own breeze to flutter in. The lights of the arrivals lounge seemed to focus on her like spotlights; colours sparkled, reflected off her long flowing hair. She saw me standing by the barrier and smiled a smile of such joy. She took off her sun

At first I could not believe that it was not actually bad news. It was difficult for me to accept that it was in fact the best news in the whole world. The most I had secretly been hoping might happen was that someone would know what her full name was or where she might be contacted. What I was holding in my hands was simply too fantastic to be real. I read the letter again, then again. Without exaggerating, it was a miracle. After the fourth or fifth time it eventually sunk in what I had. She had replied herself. Giuliana had actually written this letter that I was holding. She had folded this very piece of paper with her own hands and licked this envelope with her own tongue and now it was in my own hands.

I had to sit down. It was the letter that I wrote to the restaurant in Rome that had done this magic. As I had hoped, the owner did know her and passed it on to her. I kept reading it, wondering whether I was understanding it properly. A sudden panic; was I sleeping, was all this a dream? I went to the front door to get some air; I was definitely awake. I was awake and I had a letter from Guiliana! I couldn't help doing a little dance around the living room. There was no other explanation; what I was reading was a letter from Giuliana. She was coming to England in a few days' time, not just for a couple of days, she would be here for months, she would be living in Sheffield. 'What an incredible coincidence!' she wrote. It could not just be coincidence.

Giuliana had got a role in a new BBC-RAI joint project being made in England, she would be working both in London and Yorkshire. She told me what flight she was arriving on. After calmly placing the letter back in the envelope, subsequently leaping around the room laughing, screaming and punching the air I dashed up to Dylan's room to tell him.

The days that followed were the slowest I had ever experienced, for Dylan and Keith, they were the most annoying. They lost count the number of times I asked them if they actually examined the letter and then as guardians of our nation's security slowly looked me up and down. 'Well, with all that's going on it's a very irresponsible for them to call themselves that.' she said as she dropped it in the international box.

The IRA bombing was old news by the next day. Everyone at lectures when I got in was talking about the assassination of Indira Gandhi. With the Alarm concert and my letter writing, I clearly missed that on the news last night. Some friends were saying that this could be the start of the third world war off. Maybe Keith was right after all. It wasn't Chernenko who was going to press the nuclear button, it would be India or Pakistan then everyone would join in. Nobody seemed remotely interested in my story about the suspicious woman at the post office.

I know I should have been thinking about the possible slaughter and suffering of millions, my family and friends being turned to nuclear dust but what concerned me right then was that with the prospect of World War III starting, was would the Italian Prime Minister now have time to reply to my letter? Even if there isn't a war, would my get put the bottom of the pile underneath a mountain of diplomatic correspondences about India? Would war mean no flights between Italy and England?

#

It lay there on the floor like an unexploded bomb. It had been a couple of weeks since I had sent those letters to Italy and now in front of my feet was a reply complete with a stylish Italian stamp in the corner. What if it was just a 'sorry, can't help you'? I hadn't slept properly for the last fortnight worrying about this exact moment and now it was here. My default setting kicked in, I knew it was going to tell me to stop wasting my time. Preparing for the worst I ripped the letter open.

that ever came to anything so it was all a complete waste of time. There were less jobs, less places to work, less money to go around; what good would moaning about it do?

There was a collection bucket for the striking miners' families on the way in to the Leadmill. It made me feel better to throw a few pence in, I was supporting them so that was my conscious clear!

The Alarm were excellent and we didn't get back home until after one in the morning. Despite the lateness of the hour I determined that now was the time to set about my mission to find Giuliana. With my ears still ringing after the concert, the first thing I did was to write a letter to RAI, the Italian broadcasting company in Rome asking if they could put me in touch with their new star. That done I wrote a letter to the Italian Prime Minister; if anyone could help find her, then surely their Prime Minister could. I was just about to get into bed and had one more idea: the manager of the restaurant we met in Rome. He seemed to know her; she might be a regular. Excellent, I still had the receipt from our meal with the address on it.

Before going into college the next morning I called in at the post office to buy some stamps for Italy. The lady on the counter looked very suspicious when she was given a letter addressed to RAI.

'What's this all about then?' she asked, taking her glasses off to look more serious. I looked puzzled.

'IRA?' she said accusingly.

'No, it's RAI: the Italian television company. It's not IRA, I'm not writing a letter to the IRA. I wouldn't put IRA on a letter would I!'

The woman took a loud intake of breath as if to reprimand me for suggesting that her assumption that I was a terrorist was mistaken. She summoned her colleague over who

that he liked the fact that it was a student-free zone. In reality it was a Mecca for students pretending that they weren't students where they would meet other students pretending there weren't students. Furthermore, students and the unemployed could get in to this club for half price and since there was no work anymore most people were students or unemployed nobody ever paid full price. Keith re-defined the half price entrance criteria as 'unemployed or those training to be unemployed.'

Keith wasn't in the best of moods that night. He had made the mistake of thinking about what he was going to go after he got his degree. Keith of all people should have known better than to do that. Graduation was something akin to lemmings reaching the edge of the cliff. It was definitely not something to think about, more than just figuratively, it really was the end of the road. Businesses, factories, even whole industries were closing down every week. Rises in the unemployment figures were becoming so commonplace that they were the dullest thing on the news and nobody took any notice these days.

We were supposed to be desperately worried about what Thatcher was doing to the country. We were supposed to be concerned about South Africa, Nelson Mandela, Northern Ireland even Nicaragua if that's where the Sandinista was, whatever that was? Nobody was, except Keith. Occasionally some of us would wear a discrete 'support the miners' badge but that was about as active as protests were this sterile age of the new order. It wasn't 1969 anymore. I wondered what Dylan's mother made of our student apathy after all the efforts her generation made.

Except when Penny's legs were involved of course, I could never understand why Keith used to get so agitated about politics, it was just the way things were. There was nothing that anyone could do so what was the point? Students tried all that back in Julia's time but none of

She turned back as said to me, ‘Someone once told me, “We cannot know what our true natures are unless we follow our desires to the absolute limit no matter how appalling the disclosures might be.” And that Darling was probably the worst advice I was ever given but advice I’d still follow today.’

I watched her get into her 2CV which like everything else she did was executed with sublime elegance.

Annoyed with myself for thinking stupid thoughts I went back inside. Ambulance crews were bringing Norman Tebbitt out of the burning hotel on a stretcher, he seemed o.k. so I turned the TV off. Keith had phoned me the day before to let me know that he was going to The Leadmill that night. After unpacking a little, I caught the bus back into town and hoped I could find him. Standing at the bar, someone slapped me on the back and said in a deep drawn-out growling voice, ‘Beer Good!’ Keith’s broad Manchester accent could not be disguised by his impression of Boris Karloff’s monster in the *Bride of Frankenstein*. Since we saw that film, that silly line had become our catchphrase every time they were buying each other drinks. It got us talking about Penny. Keith told me that she and Dylan had had a massive row because he found out she had been sleeping with someone else. Ironically she had also found out that at the same time he had been sleeping with someone else too.

‘They're a match made in heaven then?’ I suggested.

'Clearly,' he carried on, 'because they're back together again; can’t imagine anyone else putting up with his weird taste in films can you?’

A band Keith liked: The Alarm was playing there at The Leadmill that night. Keith liked that club and was turning into quite a regular there. He liked the basic, no-nonsense approach, the concrete floors and the original turnstiles from when the place was a flour mill. He told me just to be so constantly entertaining was unique. She asked me what I had done about contacting her. I felt quite embarrassed to tell her that I had done nothing.

‘My God boy, why not?’ she exclaimed throwing her arms into the air as if in despair. ‘You only get once chance at life, once chance at being young. Follow your heart – always follow your heart. Love is what life if meant for, live to love. She had only spoken to me for a couple of minutes but I knew that I would remember every word she said to me for years to come. She was so fascinating, so utterly different from my mother. I only wished I had got back sooner because she was already preparing to leave when I arrived.

'Nick,' she asked. 'Do you have any cigarettes?'

Having just bought some one the way, I offered her the pack. I thought she was going to take one but Julia being Julia simply took the whole packet. She was brilliant! With my new packet of cigarettes secreted in her bag she stood up and gave Dylan a hug then approached me. She was going to hug me too. Having just spent two weeks at the emotionally starved touch-free zone of my parents' house I started to panic, what was I meant to do? Should I put my arms around her too? Did I know her well enough to actually embrace her? Will she think I am fondling her? Dylan will be watching and what would he think after what I said about his mother when we were in Rome? If I just leave my arms dangling she will think I am simple or something. What if I accidentally touch her breasts! It could easily happen, I could brush against them and then what would she think? I wished she didn’t look like that. I wished she didn’t dress like that. What if I just brushed against her breast on purpose? No, why did I even think that? I didn't have time to mither about this any longer because as my mind and my stomach did somersaults she had already given me a friendly little hug and was walking towards her car.

Predictably that dull boy had not done anything about finding the girl from Rome and when I got back to Sheffield I was furious with myself that I had wasted weeks doing nothing about it.

The house seemed unusually clean when I walked in on my first day back for the new term. An unfamiliar smell of freshness had trespassed into the house as though the whole building was refreshed having taken a holiday itself. Dylan and his mother were already there. They were watching television. Something had happened because the news was on both channels. Was that right? Thatcher had been killed? The IRA had blown her up on holiday at Brighton.

'Oh my God,' Julia gasped before saying hello to me. 'She's really dead. I should be pleased but of course I am not. This is really absolutely horrible.'

We watched a bit longer and found that that Mrs Thatcher was not one of the fatalities nor was she even injured. As soon as Julia knew Mrs Thatcher was alive and well she felt comfortable to again wish that she was dead.

Dylan had clearly been telling his mother about Giuliana. 'I hear that you have been struck by Cupid's arrow.' was her first words to me as we watched Brighton's Grand Hotel burning on the TV.

It was the first time since leaving Dylan at the airport those few weeks ago that I had the chance of speaking about her. Obviously, I would not have spoken to my parents or my sister about her but it felt so easy to tell Julia all about that mysterious girl and how I felt about her. It also felt good to say her name: Giuliana.

'Who ever loved that loved not at first sight?' she said quoting Shakespeare. It didn't take her long to have that effect on me again. I was so jealous of Dylan; I wished Julia was my mother. Her ability to always find an appropriate quotation or to come back with a witty retort or

CHAPTER SEVEN

October 1984

The time I had to spend at my parents' house over the summer was thankfully brief. As always, I watched a lot of TV, caught up with a few old friends with whom I had nothing in common anymore but did nothing in particular. For those few of weeks I reverted back into the character who lived there. That rather dull boy who didn't really do anything and whose role there was simply to offer contrast with my perfect sister - to show how well she was doing at the Midland Bank, how funny and clever she was, what a fun filled social life she had and how successful she was. What I hated most about being home was that I could not be bothered to actually hate being there even though I knew I should. I was not the same person I was in Sheffield and that person just didn't care.

I was dragged down into my mum and dad's pessimistic routine of predictability which when I was at home which always seemed absolutely natural. Everything was the way it had been since I could remember and no one, including me, or rather the me that lived there, wanted this to change. Nobody was expected to show any enthusiasm or spark of spontaneity except of course for my perfect sister. She, unlike me, was not a disappointment to my parents.

the bathroom was soaking wet. She could hear a tap running. She nudged the door open and looked inside. Sitting in the bath, staring at the wall just as he had been all night was her son, still fully clothed.

moment that he needed to do anything to keep their marriage healthy. He had just assumed everything would be groovy. Everything was not groovy.

Had he actually realized that Julia seemed to have gone a couple of days ago but was ignoring it? Was he pretending he was too busy at work to notice? He marvelled at his own stupidity. Finding an empty bus shelter he sat down and cried. He thought more about how his life had turned out and found himself screaming at the pavement. He didn't care if anyone was watching.

He walked for a long time so consequently he arrived home quite late. His mother was in her usual stinking mood. As she had been doing for the last few days, she had got up at five in the morning and caught two buses to get to her son's house before he left for work. Julia had been away somewhere for a few days now so yet again she had been there all day. Dylan and Bruce had been playing up in the afternoon; they weren't her kids so why was she having to look after them all the time? She had had enough of that tart's little brats. When was that slut-junkie of a wife of his coming home? Why was her son letting her do what she liked? He was pathetic.

As soon as he walked in the door he was hit by his mother's full-scale verbal onslaught. He was a disappointment of a son, a useless husband and useless father. She was embarrassed to consider him her own flesh and blood. It was a good job his father was dead because he would be ashamed of him. He was married to a whore who was probably out whoring now. Why wasn't he a real man?

His mother slept in the spare room and had calmed down by the following morning. She dragged herself downstairs and had some corn flakes before having to face yet another day. Steve wasn't up, the lazy sod, she thought. Annoyed, as she always was, his mother stormed up the stairs to get him to actually do something. He wasn't in his room. She noticed that the carpet outside

remembered that experience confirming his belief that love was all that was needed. Today however, he had been proven to be wrong.

He wasn't even sure what he would say to his wife, he wasn't even sure he wanted to speak to her now. Would she care? He didn't excite her anymore, he didn't make her a social life buzz. She seemed to be living a non-stop party without his help these days. Maybe if he didn't have the hassle of having to go to work he could fit in better? His train of thought juddered to a violent halt. Why would a gorgeous successful writer want anything to do with an unemployed would-be hippie? It had been bad enough before but at least he was a 'somebody' not a 'nobody.'

He loved her so much but convinced himself that she couldn't love him. Why would she? What was he there for? She never said anything but she must think he is a waste of space, especially now. All he had was his stupid job and now he'd found out he was a failure at that. He decided not to make a snap decision on his future so walked home trying to grasp what had just happened.

He was scared. He was scared of what Julia would think of him. He had never felt like this before. He had always exuded confidence but he had never realized how close he was to losing something so precious, Julia. He hoped she would be in tonight, he needed to see her. He could not remember if she had been at home this morning, he couldn't remember if she was home last night. He had been so wrapped up with work that he hadn't noticed. It frightened him when he realized that he really did not know when he last saw her. What sort of husband does not even know when their wife is in the same house? When did he last speak to her? When did he last kiss her? When did he last tell her that he loved her? Julia was everything to him, he knew he loved her and couldn't survive without her but had never thought for one fraction of a

Steve was asked to stay late that evening for a meeting with his boss. The meeting was short with just one piece of information to convey. Steve was demoted with immediate effect: he was no longer to be the departmental head. The technician whom he had protected was to take charge, to become his boss. He was to vacate his office by the end of the week. He went and sat in the self-service canteen with a cup of coffee before he went home. He literally had come down in the world, or at least in the BBC.

He couldn't believe it; he had been a brilliant boss and had done a brilliant job hadn't he? Studios six and eight were now kitted out for colour transmissions, people were rushing to Radio Rentals getting more and more colour sets: would any of this would happened if it hadn't been for him. Man, it's my department, he thought, I can't work for somebody else in my own department. He sipped his coffee, it tasted bitter. He considered whether he should walk back into the divisional head's office and resign. He could survive without the money; Julia's parents were probably the wealthiest people he knew. Probably even wealthier than Kenneth bloody Williams sat up there he thought. Look at that smug git eating his posh food, smiling down on us: still thinks he's Julius Bloody Caesar.

As he sat alone with his cold coffee Steve started to wonder what was the point of him existing. No job, no career: so clearly his six years at the BBC had been completely pointless and had served no purpose. That's how he felt: he had no purpose. He wasn't even a good husband or father because of that stupid job! He knew he was hardly ever at home because of that pointless job.

The world was a very different place to how it was this morning when he breezed into his office. Everything had gone suddenly dark and everything he had believed now seemed wrong. Just a couple of years earlier he and Julia were at the Fourteen Hour Technicolor Dream and he

He bumped in to Kenneth Williams again. He said hello to him but Mr Williams was not disposed to speaking to strangers, even if they were in the executive restaurant. Steve though it might be because he asked for his autograph the other day, was that a bit pathetic? He didn't need it anyway, he had one much more unique. He had got a rare autograph from little Carol Hersee, the girl off the test card as her father, who designed it had a few spare cards which Steve acquired. He was quite proud of his signed test card, better than one from Kenneth bloody Williams, that's for sure.

After lunch today was an important meeting with his divisional head: two more colour transmitters were to be brought on line. Steve learnt that his team should have completed the strategy review two weeks ago. He knew who was to blame but decided, as departmental head he should accept responsibility for this. He didn't want to get anyone into trouble. He felt his team was a family, everyone as important as each other and there were no bosses. It was his little socialist Utopia secretly existing inside the establishment. It was a seed that would eventually grow and flower changing the whole organisation.

Unfortunately, the 'Bringing Colour to Britain' agenda was the commissioners' top priority and had to be absolutely hitch-free and perfect. The eyes of the world were watching our television, as they were prone to saying. There could be no mistakes. Schedules had to be kept; ITV were apparently on schedule so the BBC had to guarantee that would be ready for the big switch over on the 15th November. Steve's little department might be one of the happiest, most chilled team in the corporation but Steve was starting to think right now that maybe he should not have let his technician put off doing the report because, 'his mind was not in the right place yet.'

She sped along the Rue du Faubourg St Denis passing businessmen sitting at tables outside of cafes drinking red wine. Then turning left off the Rue de la Chapelle the pavement cafes were replaced by stalls selling bright coloured vegetables, fresh meat and cheese. She rolled down the window of the Citroën so that she could fully appreciate the smells of these wonderful streets.

In just a few minutes, her driver pulled up outside a tall apartment building which like all the other buildings seemed to be overhanging the street below. The driver pointed at the reading on his metre. Julia was quite disappointed as she realized that he figured out she wasn't French after all and that the only reason he wasn't speaking English to her was that he either didn't know how to or simply couldn't be bothered. It didn't matter; it was a fantastic drive through the city and now she was standing outside *his* apartment.

At the side of the large door were a series of buzzers. She pressed button number 403 and waited biting her bottom lip. She heard the sound of equally excited footsteps running down stairs then he opened the door. It was as magic as she could have possibly imagined. He looked just like she remembered him. He didn't say a word; he didn't need to. He smiled, opened his arms and they embraced. This was love.

#

Steve didn't care that most of his colleagues in his department wore a suit to work, he liked his old yellow trousers: they went well his paisley shirts. Julia liked the way he dressed. Having lunch in the 'waitress service' restaurant he could look down on the self-service canteen on the floor below; he used to have to eat there a couple of years ago. He didn't 'dig' of the us and them divisions at the corporation but he had to admit that the food was nicer on the upper floor and furthermore, up here he could mingle with the stars.

grinning from ear to ear constantly giggling with excitement. She didn't succeed but she didn't care.

As she walked off the platform onto the station concourse she felt as though she had entered a Jean Luc Goddard film. Everything was French, very French. No garish BBC2 colour here, everyone was in classic black and white. She glided gracefully through the beautifully lit backdrop of this turn of the century station. Poets, writers and musicians were brushing past her. Workers, revolutionaries and artisans breezed past smoking Gitanes just like she did. Like an excited puppy she dashed out of the station through the Grandes Lignes exit onto the Place Napoléon III and realized she was really there. She was really here, she was really in Paris!

Everything looked French, everything looked wonderful. The people were so sophisticated, the buildings so elegant, the cars so different. Even reading the signposts in the road sent a quiver of excitement through her. To her side was a massive cast iron lamppost elaborately decorated in the art deco style. She could not resist putting her arms around it and hugging it. She walked on. She was not acting quite as cool as she had planned.

Just like a Parisian girl, she hailed a taxi. Without taking the drooping cigarette from his mouth, the driver shouted something to her in French. Excellent, she thought, he thinks I'm French. She gave him the address and he hurled his taxi headlong into the mass of moving metal that was Paris' traffic. With just one hand he wove his taxi like an insect through what appeared to be cars, lorries, buses and bikes randomly driving at each other but never quite managing to make contact. She loved the way they ignored red lights and stop signs, she loved the way that there didn't appear to be any rules or if there were they didn't care; it was her sort of system. Julia even fell in love with the city's traffic jams.

No, she had been home last night he remembered giving her the letter from France. A letter from France: his mind raced, he knew something had happened to her when she went away with Lisa in the spring. He wondered was anything wrong. It was impossible for him to entertain even the possibility that she kept any secrets from hi - they weren't like that.

For now, he had more immediate concerns. He had to get the boys up, take Steve to school and then see if his mother could look after Bruce again. He would be late for work but he didn't care too much considering the extra hours he had been putting in recently. Never one to rush or to panic, Steve strolled leisurely up the stairs and gently woke his sons up then poured some porridge in to a saucepan.

Julia arrived at the Garre de Nord just as the late summer sun was going down. Until the train had stopped, everything had felt as though she were reading some great adventure book or watching a film. It wasn't until the train stopped that she fully appreciated what she had actually done. It was too late to think about it now, there was going back. She didn't do 'going back,' she was Julia.

She opened the door and was blasted by the noise of reality. A panorama of sound shook her as she savoured her first lungful of Parisian air. Oblivious to the queue of people behind her trying to get off the train, she stood momentarily in the doorway of the carriage. She bathed in the noise of thousands of people, the clatter of trains and traffic outside and the whimsical fanfare heralding the announcements over the station Tannoy. This was the sound of Paris.

She had to restrain herself from skipping along the platform, some semblance of decorum had to be maintained. She was in Paris, the capital of style. Walking through the ticket barrier she tried to look French, nonchalant, moody and above all someone who was not wide-eyed and

noticed her, now he was staring at her with a curious grin wondering who it was from. She had to open it.

He had got her address from a friend of a friend who worked at her publishers Paris office. He wanted to see her again. He wanted her to come to see him in France. It all sounded so insane but it also sounded like a fairy-tale and Julia so wanted to believe.

Something inside her was telling her that she was meant to be with him, nothing had ever been as certain. As for who he was, all she knew about him was he was a student, she didn't need to know anything else. She looked at the letter to see what his name was: Jean-Marie, she liked the sound of that; so French.

Steve doted on Dylan and Bruce, he was a great dad and the boys got on so much better with their dad than with their mum. Steve and Bruce would have a great time on their own with Steve for a few days she convinced herself. The boys would only get upset if their mum told them she was going on holiday again for a while and leaving them behind. She figured that the kindest thing to do was just to sneak out in the morning before either Dylan, Bruce or their dad were awake.

By ten o'clock in the morning she was already at Dover waiting to board the next ferry to Fairyland. Back at the house, Steve had woken up with a vague recollection of his wife getting up in the middle of the night and kissing him. She wasn't in the house and as his brain slowly started to fire up, he wondered whether she had actually been home last night. He was used to her staggering in at about six or seven in the morning straight from whichever club she had been to, collapsing on the sofa for an hour then waking up to take the boys to school looking unfeasibly immaculate again.

eye. In Steve's opinion however, just because they've been to university doesn't make wearing a wig clever.

Julia was looking at her husband. She wondered how long it would be before he looked over to her and smiled. It must have been a quarter of an hour and he never glanced at her once. She went and sat next to him on the sofa. He gave her a smile but then turned back to the TV. Would he put his arms around her? Would he give her a cuddle and ask how her day had been? Would he tell her that he loved her? She knew he loved her but she knew he would never do any of these things tonight. He didn't do things like that anymore. She loved him as much as she did when they first met: why didn't he? Why didn't her love her as much as the soldier in her story loved the French waitress? Why didn't he love her as much as the French student she met?

'Fantastic colour!' he said when the credits for Monty Python rolled up.
Was that it? Was that all he could think of she thought: his bloody job. At the BBC Steve was one of the bearded boffins responsible for turning television from black and white in to colour. Julia thought that colour TV was absolutely amazing and she knew Steve was very good at what he did but she didn't want to know about electronics, valves and transistors. She wanted him to tell her that he loved her but he didn't.

'Sorry baby, I picked up some post of ours on my way out to work this morning.' Steve said handing his wife a letter. 'What are you doing getting French letters?'

Her heart jumped when she saw the French postage stamp of the letter. She knew instantly that it was from him, her stranger, her lover. A letter written by her lover was in the hand of her husband. She could hardly take it from him; not too fast, that would look suspicious, she mustn't look too excited. Casually she took it from his hand. All night he hadn't even

saw on the black and white television. They didn't really believe that hippies were real, they were just some weirdoes in San Francisco. Steve might as well have stood amongst these dockers in his underpants considering the reaction he elicited.

Despite the Beatles, who now lived in London anyway, the hippie movement was no more significant in Liverpool as was China's Cultural Revolution. Those brave enough to speak to him however found that despite his appearance he was almost one of them. He wasn't one of the bosses, he wasn't a junkie, he wasn't a queer. He was a southerner but he was a socialist so he wasn't all bad.

It did him good to get out of London for those few days to see the real world. When he got back he was even more committed to changing the world. He suggested to Julia that they needed to get out of London more often: they were too sheltered here, their life was too comfortable, they needed to appreciate how terrible other parts of the country really were. She looked at him as if he had gone mad, she liked being happy.

On night when Steve was working late again, Lisa called Julia to tell her about a new show on BBC2 called 'Monty Python's Flying Circus.' It had some of the comics from the David Frost's 1948 show along with Michael Palin who they both thought was rather sexy. Steve was planning to work late but when he heard that this new show was supposed to be quite anarchic he decided to go home and watch it. Anarchy from within the hallowed halls of his BBC itself appealed to him.

He arrived home from work in time for it to start, eagerly anticipating something as good as people had said. He couldn't see what all the fuss was about; flying sheep, silly voices: surely this was a kids' programme. Julia enjoyed it, the silliness appealed to what she called her child's

Shortly after Paris, Steve was asked to go to Liverpool for a week to work on Ken Loach's play, 'The Big Flame.' He grumbled but Julia knew he would go.
As much as he hated the BBC for what it stood for he also loved it with equal passion, interestingly for what it stood for. Although to Steve it may have been the authoritarian voice of the establishment, it was also a greenhouse of individualism and free expression. For all the faults with England, he couldn't imagine any other country allowing its main TV station to broadcast Ken Loach's overtly Marxist call for revolution. That the BBC was making this and he was part of it made him feel he was doing his bit for the revolution. It was these rare starbursts of expression and hope at the corporation that made him love his job. He couldn't imagine working anywhere else.

Working on that drama allowed him a rare visit back to his old University city. He had forgotten just how grey and depressing it was up there. The play was set in the docks, a place where every morning sixty thousand dockers would traipse down the Dock Road hoping that they would be picked for one of the twenty thousand jobs that would be available that day. Sixty thousand people and just twenty thousand jobs.

It made Steve even more determined that a revolution was needed. Forty thousand men would have no work to do that day and would get no pay. But just as their fathers had done, they would get up the following day before dawn and go down to the docks again hoping that that day they would be able to earn a wage. It was this desperate necessity to be competitive, to shout louder and that appreciation that life wasn't fair that moulded the Liverpool character.

Steve with his long hair, ribbons and beads, dressed in his caftan looked like he had come from another planet rather from another city. Liverpool was a different world to not just to London but to anywhere else in the country. Flower power was just something that people there knew. People just wanted to be with her, be her friend or go to her parties, the whole of the city wanted her to be around and usually was. She was as much a part of London as Big Ben or rather the Marquee club was. Some of her friends that lived out of town really envied her because she was living in the heart of swinging London. Even Steve envied the way she could throw herself in to the scene so much easier than he could. She didn't seem to have to try. She was not just into the scene, she was part of it. This was who Julia was but as she walked through those happy bustling streets that night she reflected that during those brief hours in Paris a few months ago she would willingly have given all this up. This thought stopped her in her tracks. She took off her floppy hat and looked almost reverentially at the stars shining in the neon black sky. These were the same stars she looked at in Paris.

Steve and Julia enjoyed the rest of the summer of '69 even though they were both somewhat annoyed about missing the Woodstock festival in America. Neither of them could have gone anyway; Steve would have had difficulty taking time off work and the boys, as always would have needed looking after. Dylan and Bruce spent the majority of the summer holiday with their grandparents. This suited everyone; it gave the boys a holiday and gave Steve and Julia time off from being parents, Julia was too young to be tied down to motherhood when there was so much else to do.

As the nights began to gradually draw in, Steve found it happening more and more that he had to work late. He started to look very tired and seemed slower, less fun. Sometimes he would come home so late he would just eat his dinner and then go straight to bed. Julia hated being alone. The boys were there of course but she missed her husband. Even when he was home she missed him.

Spitfire, not just because he was the grooviest fifty year old, not just because he was one of the most caring and kindest people in music but because he was acknowledged as one of the true geniuses in the recording industry. He adored Julia, he saw some of himself in her, another free spirit who refused to grow up.

When he saw Julia come in to the studio, he leapt up from the desk and threw his arms around her. 'Julia baby, how's your new book going?'

'Not too good Mr Spitfire, I need inspiration.'

'Don't look to me then.'

She reflected for a moment whether Mr Spitfire could be her inspiration; he was in the war. This was difficult; she couldn't equate who she was looking at now with somebody from the second world-war. How could this middle aged man dressed in a multi-coloured kaftan and loon pants with long white hair and a prolific bald patch be the RAF's young whiz kid in the black and white days of 1944? Mr Spitfire had changed along with the world. Julia knew that her world was a tiny bubble within the real world. Virtually everybody else in London still lived as they did in 1944 but Mr Spitfire was proud not to be one of them. He wasn't going to be her inspiration tonight.

'No man, you're all wrong!' she eventually said, shaking her finger at him.

Mr Spitfire was used to Julia not making any sense; she was generally stoned at the times when they met. His engineer was saying something in his headphones; he was just about to apologise to Julia for having to speak to him when he noticed that she had gone. Mr Spitfire smiled, even just a few seconds with Julia made him smile.

Julia never needed to make the effort to find people when she was out, they just appeared. Minutes after leaving Mr Spitfire she was in the street chatting and laughing with people she

Steve viewed recording sessions as other people's work. He would not expect a gang of hippies, stoned out their minds to barge into his office when he was at work and have a party so didn't feel comfortable about doing this to others. Much to the envy of his wife however, he did manage once to crash his way into a session of his all-time favourite band, Pink Floyd and have a chat with George Harrison who was also there a few months ago. Steve thought it was hilarious to mention this as many times as possible especially after Julia had moaned to him that once again EMI wouldn't let her barge in last night. However hard she had she begged, pleaded and even tried to bribe with drugs, Abbey Road wouldn't let her in.

A few nights ago she gate-crashed an all-night session at Advision Studios. She recalled that it had been a really beautiful night although she couldn't remember much about it: was the band Quintessence? She fancied doing the same again tonight so started wandering towards Advision from Soho with some fellow night people she had met. Steve was good friends with an engineer who worked at Trident studios on the way, just at the top end of Soho. He would always let her in; maybe she'd bump into Steve there? She had a feeling Spooky Tooth might be in there tonight but wasn't sure. It didn't really didn't matter, it was always a fantastic night.

Soho at midnight, summer 1969, so alive with people, colour, music and love. Everyone they met seemed to be smoking a joint, the police didn't mind back then. For Julia and her friends it was like the 1950s smogs had never gone away since they saw the whole outside world through a permanent haze of marijuana smoke that followed them around. It was a real community, it was her family; it was where she felt at home.

If this was her family, Mr Spitfire was her uncle. He wasn't really called Mr Spitfire, he was an engineer in the RAF during the war so Mr Spitfire seemed appropriate. Although he was now about fifty he was at home with the bright young things and the hippies. They all loved Mr

needed, the wife who cooked and cleaned and waited patiently for her husband to get home from work was no longer that woman. He could never return to his former life, to who he used to be. Like everyone else returning from the war, he had to start his life again, be someone different.'

She stopped for a smoke and decided something wasn't working about the story. Was it too bleak? Her friends commented that they couldn't figure out works of un-mitigating misery could come from the mind of someone like her who was always so positive and optimistic. The plot was going to change a bit. The soldier would come home but he would secretly long to be back in France, yes back in France even with the bombs and bullets. The risk would be worth it. His wife would sense that something was wrong although he wouldn't be able to see it himself. Somehow, she would have to get her hero back to France to the mysterious waitress or whatever she was.

Why would a soldier leave his wife to go back to occupied France in 1945? How would they meet again? She didn't know yet, the answer would come to her sometime but probably not at a quarter to midnight. She wondered where Steve was; he couldn't still be at work. She wondered if he had mentioned something about having to attend some function the BBC were holding to do with the Moon landing tonight?

She couldn't write this evening, she needed inspiration so she grabbed her latest floppy hat and wandered into town. There were usually a few bands cutting albums at this time of night when recording time was cheaper. She had started making a habit recently of hanging out in recording studios in the early hours of the morning. It was one of the real happening places to be where the cool cats went. The studios didn't seem to mind except for Norman Smith who had Pink Floyd at EMI over in Abbey Road.

most conducive way of expunging her own guilty thoughts about her French lover she decided. Nevertheless, she forced herself to type a few lines.

'It was colour that was missing, that's what he noticed more than anything. Everything was either brown or grey and washed out. Like food or clothes or petrol, colour now seemed to be rationed since he was last here four years earlier. He strolled along the street to his house. The flagstones were cracked but he seemed to think that they had always been this way. The street was different. Where once stood houses, there were now gaps. To the boys kicking a ball about, these were convenient knock-about areas. To the silent ghost-like women trying to find food for their families, these were short-cuts to the shops. He wondered how they could just walk through these bomb sites without screaming. 'How can they accept this as normality?'

It wasn't just the street that had gaps in it, his life had gaps. That was the real difference. He was a father but there were whole pieces about his son he knew nothing about. He was a husband but he hadn't even talked to his wife in years. He was a man, a working man of the 1930s where did he fit now? Where was his gap?

The other thing that was different was the quietness. The street was virtually deserted, nobody had anywhere to go. The soldier did have somewhere to go, that was home but after that he had no idea. He couldn't go back to work; his job was a soldier but there was no war anymore. He was now part of the army of nobodies. Back in the thirties who a man was defined by what he did and in the last five years like every other man his purpose was to defeat the enemy. Now there was no enemy, nobody could be who there were anymore.

England was victorious but the price of victory was that it was a nation without a purpose. The job the soldier did no longer existed, the business that he worked in was no longer

she met at a café near Notre Dame Cathedral. She couldn't remember actually meeting him, she couldn't remember saying goodbye to him; time seemed jumbled up. She could just remember the breath-taking intense sense of utter joy and the feeling of being totally adored. He had no reason to love her but he did, it was instant. When he looked at her she knew instantly that he could see nothing else in the whole world other than herself. Had the great cathedral come crashing down or the waters of the Seine completely flooded the city, she knew he would be totally unaware of it. The only thing that existed in his world at that moment was Julia. His dark, deep and intense eyes held her rigid. It was the most mystical thing that had ever happened to her. She knew it was her destiny.

Lisa knew her friend well enough to know she hadn't gone off by herself just to do some sightseeing that second evening in Paris. Lisa was a little worried because the last saw her friend she was pretty stoned. In the early hours of the following morning she was woken up by Julia stumbling into their room rambling about her destiny and meeting the man of her dreams. Even though it was 3am, Lisa didn't mind too much, at least she seemed alright. After a good night's sleep Julia had woken up to another lovely Parisian morning had tried to shrug off what had happened. She had been high most of the previous day and put those insane feelings down to the drugs. It couldn't have been as she remembered it could it? That just wasn't the way things happened. After all she was a happily married young woman: a happily married young mother with a successful writing career. She loved Steve so much but that night in Paris she would not have even known his name.

Now, months later, staring at that blank page she could still feel those beautiful eyes of that stranger looking back. Writing a book about a passionate love affair in France was not the

remembered were all destroyed by the war. Destroyed not by Hitler's bombs but destroyed just the same. Those women sat at home wishing for their men to be back were real enough but those women waiting for them were no longer just wives. Men were meant to look after their wives, to provide and care for them, to make the right choices for them; what were men to do now?

Women had tasted freedom but it was like having eaten the forbidden fruit. It felt wrong so they would try to conceal it from their men. They would pretend nothing was different for the sake of their marriage. They would try but they would know that this dishonesty was just as wrong. Men sensed that they were no longer essential but had to pretend they were. They pretended it was still 1939 and nothing had changed. The whole of society, family life and relationships were rooted in deceit and pretence. For these reunited families there was no script of what to do next. Yes, Julia thought, there were some ideas here but still why did the soldier go back to France?

Jane Birkin and Serge Gainsbourg's number one, '*Je T'Aime ... Moi non plus*' was playing on Radio Caroline. If ever a song was appropriate to her, this one was. She had been back from her short stay in Paris for over two months now. Nothing was different; her life was just as it had been before she left as it had been for years now. Her unfinished novel was still an unfinished novel. Her friends were the same, her routine was still the same, even the Formica was still the same. Steve, her husband still loved her and she still loved him but there was something different now. Whatever it was would never be the same again.

It wasn't just the borrowing of another life for a few weeks that she missed. What she missed was something much more intense, something secret, something that changed her life. She was not even completely sure it happened the way she remembered it did, it all happened so fast but it was so wonderful. She couldn't even remember the name of that wonderful stranger

CHAPTER SIX

August 1969

Julia sat alone looking through the net curtains of the bay window into the night. Her typewriter was silent as it had been for most of the day. The page was blank, her mind was blank. Could she really be bothered with the love life of her imaginary lovers during the Second World War? Was she bothered whether or not the soldier ever got back from France or whether he stayed with the mysterious girl he met there? This novel, her second had just become too similar to her own life.

The only difference was she both of the characters. She was the soldier discovering there's more to love than just being in love but also the wife comfortably drifting through life. She didn't need to stir her imagination too hard for the character of the wife. She was a woman longing for the return of her husband but also knowing that she would be disappointed when he finally did walk through the door. He would just slop into his chair, maybe give his wife a smile and then watch the television; or in the case of her soldier, read the paper.

Come on think, she told herself. Think about the war: war changed everything. Wives had to learn how to live for themselves and more importantly, how to enjoy themselves without their husbands. Husbands longed to return home but the homes they left and the families they

I have no idea what we talked about, I have no idea what we ate, I have no idea when she and Alessia left the restaurant to go back to their hotel. My last memory was saying goodnight to her with a long, long hug at the top of the Spanish Steps. I wanted Dylan to be quite that night, I just wanted to close my eyes and remember her.

By the time the bright Mediterranean sun was starting to rise the next morning Dylan and I were already in the taxi on our way to the airport. Driving out of Rome the taxi stopped at traffic lights and I looked across to an empty square with an empty restaurant in the corner not unlike the one we were at just a few hours earlier. If I closed my eyes I could see her face, I couldn't help grinning. Dylan told me it was too early in the morning to be smiling but I couldn't help myself. I didn't want to stop grinning either. To hell with being cool and moody – I wanted to open the window of the taxi and shout out that I was in love. I had met the loveliest girl in the world and we were in love. Dylan thought I'd get over it. He knew the feeling; he'd been madly in love with loads of girls. I'd forget about her as soon as we got back to Sheffield.

He asked if I had the girl's phone number: no, I didn't. Her address: no. Her full name: no. Laughing at my incompetence he wondered whether I going to try and get in touch with her. Dylan wasn't used to being surprised by me but I think I managed it this time. Yes, I told him. I also told him without any doubt or insincerity that I was going marry her. That was an answer my friend was not expecting. It did however not surprise him as much as it surprised me hearing myself say it. It surprised me was because I knew it was the truth. I was going to spend the rest of my life with her. It was wonderful to know something with such absolute certainty. I felt on top of the world.

two very attractive young women. Even stranger, to his annoyance the prettiest one appeared to be chatting me up.

The two girls were in Rome to celebrate the news that they had got jobs on a new daytime soap about to start on RAI1. They only had small parts but that didn't matter, they could now justifiably call themselves television actresses instead of models. When Dylan picked up on the words attrice meaning actress and televisione he thought that this whole thing could be a stunt for Italian television: 'Stupid English students think they're being picked up by sexy celebrities show.' For a moment he actually considered that he might look good on television. He quickly dismissed this; the girls seemed too genuine and it was not in his nature to accept that anybody would take him for a ride.

The girl from the Vatican introduced herself as being called Giuliana. Her friend was called Alessia. They were from the same town, they were best friends and had been since school and had until about three hours ago they were models. All my Christmases had come at once! I sat gazing into her big brown eyes without any fear of embarrassment. I was having dinner with a real life Italian model and TV star. Giuliana could not stop smiling either.

This was the strangest evening Dylan had ever spent. Had he been diabetic he would be dead now; his blood having adsorbed the vast tonnages of sugar and sweetness that was turning the air around me and Giuliana into sickly syrup. He tried to have a conversation with Giuliana's friend but her English was only marginally better than his non-existent Italian. Their bemused expressions trying to comprehend the utter strangeness of what was happening between their respective friends seemed to compensate for their inability to communicate. I didn't even notice them and to my utter delight neither did Giuliana.

Eventually we found an open-air restaurant not too far from the Spanish Steps and had drunk just enough to ward off any embarrassment we should have had about sharing a candle-lit table; we hoped we wouldn't get serenaded. After a few minutes, a waiter with dandruff on his polished black shoulders squeezed a table between us and our view. It didn't bother me but Dylan thought this was rather bad form and since we hadn't actually ordered anything yet considered walking out. Then another waiter or possibly the manager led two young ladies to that table.

'Hello again,' the girl from the Vatican said to me as she sat down next to me. I think I stopped breathing again, this was incredible. Was I dreaming? Was it really the same girl? Had a genie granted me a wish? Back in the other-worldliness atmosphere of Saint Peter's it was acceptable to stare. Now with the sun setting over the terracotta roof-tops of the city that defined romance, it was not but it was impossible not to. Whoever this girl was, she really was the most stunning, almost unbelievable beautiful person I could believe could exist. Her face was perfect, her hair, her complexion, those lovely brown eyes, that incredible body; everything was simply perfect.

'Are you remember me da San Pietro?' she asked smiling.

'I do.' I beamed, still I think without breathing. 'Why don't you join us? If we put our tables together we'll all have more room.'

I had no idea where this uncharacteristic confidence came from. It wasn't from the normal me that lived in the normal world. Dylan thought he had slipped into a parallel universe. He knew I did not do things like this. Ten minutes ago, he was sat with his best mate having a beer chatting about nothing of consequence and now because of me of all people, he was sat with

'Of course she's not.' he snapped back. 'I've told you before, it's all an act.'

This was getting too personal, I really didn't want another conversation about his mother.

'Come on then gay-boy, let's go and find a couple of Italian super-models.' I joked.

Unlike Dylan's Freddie Mercury impression, there was no sexual ambiguity with my look. I had recently grown my hair big-style and thought I looked a little like George Michael from Wham; I even had the Choose Life t-shirt which looked good with my new stonewashed jeans. George Michael was one of the biggest sex symbols around, girls loved him ipso facto, girls would love me. It was simple logic but it was good enough for me.

'You know my mother knew her when she was at art college in London.' said Dylan pointing at my chest.

'Who?'

'Katherine Hamnet.'

'Who?'

'She designed the t shirt you've got on.'

'What,' I asked feigning bemusement, 'are you telling me that an actual fashion designer was paid money for getting a white t shirt and writing two words from a Wham song on the front if it in black ink?'

'Yep, Katherine Hamnet she's called; you must have heard of her, she's dead famous. She did the Frankie goes to Hollywood one too.'

I gave him my cynical sneer. 'How can you be famous for something like that?'

'Look, you just can, right. It's art man!'

'No,' I said looking at the amazing view of the city: 'that's art.'

‘So, as a red blooded male, when did you first fancy someone?’ I asked.

‘Easy.’ he answered. ‘1975: Lesley Anne Down in Upstairs Downstairs. ITV every Sunday night when I was living at my gran’s. It was the highlight of my week when I was twelve. I think you agree with me on this one mate, there’s never been anyone else on telly, in films or in music as utterly gorgeous as Lesley Anne Down and there never will be. Sexier than anyone: and I’m including Debbie Harry.’

‘Yes - and Sally James.’ I added then mentioned that Lesley Ann Down was also Esmeralda in that new *Hunchback of Notre Dame* film that was on the TV last year. Dylan, her number one fan of course replied that despite it being a dreadful version – he then rambled on about the merits of the 1939 version and the silent 1922 version - he had the new video.

‘I’ve got it too.’ I laughed, ‘and I do agree with you there mate; Lesley Anne Down, fittest woman of all time.’ ....I said that because I still wasn’t too sure if that girl I had seen earlier in the Vatican had been real or not. He mentioned that he lived with his gran so I asked him why.

‘About ten years ago some real shit hit my mother’s life. She was seriously screwed up. You don’t want to know all the details but it was as bad as it could be. It really messed her. Before all that happened she was so much fun. She was a brilliant mother. But after what happened and then my little brother Bruce died which everybody said was her fault because she took us off to Bangladesh, I ended up living at my gran’s for a few years until she had sorted herself out.’

Until then I didn’t even know he had had a little brother. It felt nice to be confided in but also a little awkward - we were best friends but we didn’t really have these types of personal conversations.

‘Well she seems fine now.’ I said which was probably the crassest thing I could have said.

drink it all in. I held my breath, I couldn't exhale in fear of losing the fragrant sweet scent. The whole incident took less than half a minute but it was the most intense moment of my life.

'Are we done then mate?' asked Dylan finding me looking like I had just had a religious experience.

'Did you see her? Did you see that incredible girl?' I asked excitedly. He hadn't - I don't understand how he missed her but he said he didn't even notice her. She was my secret discovery, my private memory to take home with me so I decided to say no more. I just followed him silently around the Vatican museum and then headed back into the city. Back in the sunlight I wondered whether she really was that beautiful. In my mind she always would be but I guessed that I would never know. I bought a bottle of water and gulped it down. I was definitely not feeling myself, must be dehydrated after queuing in the sun for an hour and a half.

Dylan was someone who was always being bubbly so it was difficult to tell if there was ever anything wrong but I sensed a certain discomfort; probably because of what I said last night. I tried to ignore it, after all that evening was to be our last night in Rome. After we had showered and shaved we hit the town for one last time.

'He's definitely giving us a funny look.' said Dylan referring to the man on the reception desk when we walked out of the hotel. 'I'm sure he thinks we're gay.' After a couple of days of funny looks, like myself he was no longer seeing the funny side. 'I don't look like a queer do I?' he asked.

I assured him that he didn't even though Dylan's idol at that moment was Queen's Freddie Mercury and he had cultivated the look right down to the tight t-shirt, biker jacket and little moustache. We must have been more sheltered than we thought because Freddie Mercury and that look didn't actually seem in any way gay to us.

For over an hour we stood under the Mediterranean sun in the queue that slowly trickled around Saint Peter's Square then passed through the doors in to cool basilica. Dylan found the cameras of the tourists both annoying and disrespectful. The more he dwelled on them they more they wound him up: surely someone should stop them using flashes. Dylan was not enjoying Saint Peter's. I on the other hand was feeling something entirely new. Amongst the ostentatious gold, the hordes of tourists mindlessly flashing their mindless cameras, security guards and neon-lit book stalls, I walked in reverential silence, with no other people around me towards the altar. Sitting down I wondered what this strange sensation was. I couldn't be feeling the presence of God? Of course not: I didn't do God. It must be the architecture, the sheer beauty of the place: it was truly breath taking.

Feeling somewhat unnerved I looked across the aisle and sitting opposite me was a long-haired, very Italian looking girl. She wasn't just beautiful, she was very beautiful. The light was poor so I couldn't see her properly but I could just tell that she would be the most beautiful girl that I had ever seen in my life. I tried blinking to make my eyes adjust quicker to the light to see her better. She really was as beautiful as I first thought. Saint Peter's had been built just for this moment, it was her perfect backdrop. It wasn't wrong to stare; it was no different to the way one stares at any other great masterpiece of art because she was without doubt the most beautiful thing I had ever seen, she was God's masterpiece. She noticed me looking at her and she stood up. That suddenly snapped me out of my trance. She was walking towards me, what she was going to say? 'Buongiorno.' she said as she passed me.

'Buongiorno.' I replied smiling back. Then she carried on walking, I followed her with my eyes, I don't think I could move. I could still smell the delicate perfume she wore and tried to

‘Your mother,’ I began, knowing that I really should shut up but was unable to stop these words coming out of my mouth, ‘I think she’s wonderful.’ I definitely knew I didn’t want to say that. It was the clearest most lucid message my mind had ever screamed at me: ‘do not say this!’

Why am I still speaking? Shut up: ‘I think your mother is really, really, really sexy.’

‘No, Jesus Christ! No!’ Dylan didn’t want to hear this,’ No, mate, don’t tell me you fancy my mother; that’s just wrong, really fucking wrong!’

The previous night including the vivid recollection of that conversation sadly still existed when I woke the next following morning. Dylan was already dressed and smoking a cigarette out of the window.

‘I’m going to get up and get dressed now.’ I announced. Dylan quickly threw his cigarette down into the street and left the room to allow me to get ready in privacy. We had over-slept and missed breakfast so bought some cakes in the little supermarket next door that we ate on the way to the underground station. The train journey to the Vatican was longer than yesterday’s: this one took two cigarettes. Neither of us spoke much. He didn’t mention what I said last night about his mother – maybe it didn’t happen.

The area around the Ottaviano San Pietro train station was not like the Rome on the other side of the river. This part of town was ordinary to the point of drabness. The excited snakes of tourists looked so out of context as they traipsed, detached from their surroundings past the furniture shops, DIY stores and derelict sweet shops. The few token souvenir shops amongst this mundanity looked as out of place as the tourists. Then suddenly and without warning we were in another world; one where the grey concrete was replaced with white shining marble. The sterile lacklustre of suburbia gave way to the magnificent medieval glory of Vatican City.

There were several inviting bars around the square in front of the Pantheon and since we had missed lunch we decided it was time to sample una birra locale. Walking past the floodlit Trevi Fountain we both suddenly realized that it had become dark and we were not drunk yet. By midnight this had been rectified and we staggered back to the hotel. Dylan appeared to know all about the fountain and Nicola Salvi, its designer and decided for some reason that I also needed to know everything about them. Then he insisted that we threw coins into the fountain over our left shoulders.

'I thought this was Benini's fountain.' I said.

'Oh no, no, no, no. If you'd been brought up by my mother mate, I promise you, you would be an expert on this place and every sculpture, piece of art and every sodding statue.'

Forgetting how we got our free holiday and that she was some sort of TV art critic I asked why she would know this. Dylan reminded me about her new career.

'But she's still runs that charity? I asked, a little confused.

He told me that she did.

'So she's not a writer anymore?'

'How many times do I have to tell you, you drunken sod; she was a writer but that was ages ago. Then she tried to change the world with her charity shops and now, God knows how she's an art critic on the telly.' he begrudgingly explained, 'Oh and she's also involved in that homeless charity in London. You wouldn't believe it mate but she spends every other Saturday night with tramps, junkies and drop-outs. They take the piss out of her posh accent but they seem to like her.'

'Your mother is wonderful.' I heard myself slurring.

'What?'

As it began to cool down a little we left the un-shaded Forum and wandered back into the modern city. In the Piazza Venezia Dylan spotted a gellateria which he ran over to. A minute later he strolled back eating an enormous multi-layered gellato.

'You selfish git!' I said, staggered that he hadn't bothered to get me one. A couple of minutes ago I had just been telling him that my mouth felt like the Sahara desert. I felt like slapping the stupid ice cream out of his hands. Dylan then acted completely out of character and offered to go back to the gellateria and get me another. I stood outside waiting, stood there for ages so went inside to investigate what was keeping him. The reason for Dylan's surprising act of generosity then became apparent. Dylan had taken a fancy to the girl serving and was now, despite the language barrier doing his best to chat her up. He was leaning over the counter being fed by the girl with a spoon when I walked in.

'What flavour mate?' Dylan asked remembering why he was there. The green one looked good. We left and strolled in the direction, we hoped was towards the river. Around each corner from each amazing square there was always something even more amazing. There was a bank next door to a medieval church, a Roman temple partly converted into a snack bar yet none of the locals seemed to appreciate the amazingness of what they had. Compared with the greyness of England with Thatcher, unemployment, and riots, Rome was a fantasy land.

We found the Pantheon, the famous domed temple with the oculus in the centre of the roof. Dylan translated the Latin inscription on the front of the building: Marcus Agrippa, third consul, built this.

'He didn't actually,' I said, 'The original Pantheon was destroyed in a fire. This is a re-built one commissioned by Hadrian a hundred and fifty years later.'

'Smart arse.' said Dylan.

No, this was not at all acceptable. I was going to speak to reception and get another room. I started towards the door.

'Chill out man; we'll be so drunk we won't notice.' Dylan replied, not squeezing into the wardrobe so that I couldn't get past him. 'Come on Darling, let's get some sightseeing done.'

Maybe he was right. 'Absolutely ducky, the sooner we've done the culture stuff we can get pissed.'

From the free map in our room it looked like the Coliseum was the thing furthest away so we would get the underground there then work our way back. The centre of the coliseum at midday was hottest place in Italy. We were ants being burnt by the sun under a massive Roman magnifying glass. We certainly didn't feel like a three-mile sight-seeing walk back through this heat but the allure of the city was far stronger than either of us expected. Even the extortionate cost of bottled water and the psychotic Roman traffic did not deter us from three hours baking in the Roman Forum.

According to Dylan, the Hollywood guru, they build an exact replica of this forum in California for the silent version of Ben Hur. For once, his film trivia seemed quite interesting. Although we were both history students, we had always considered ancient Rome a little too obvious, a bit primary school curriculum but despite our best intentions to avoid the tourist trail we both became instantly infatuated with the eternal city. Every trace of cynicism left us as we drank in the living history that was around us. We abandoned our intentions to simply blend in with the locals, to avoid the tourist trail and remain cool and nonchalant. I am sure we would have bought candyfloss, kiss me quick hats and gone on donkey rides on the beach if they had had them. We absolutely loved it there.

CHAPTER FIVE

July 1984

When we got to Rome I was relieved to find that I had stopped thinking about my best friend's mother; that had been so totally wrong. I had also stopped thinking about my best friend's girlfriend too. Obviously that had been less uncomfortable, after all she was lovely but she was Dylan's girlfriend. When we arrived in Rome Dylan also seemed to have forgotten about Penny. He informed me that tonight we were going out on the pull. In some ways I was glad about that but I was really disappointed with his lack of loyalty. Penny was a lovely girl and she deserved better. I didn't think Dylan was like that.

The Roman tourist board described our hotel as bijou, we would have called it very small. I didn't like the way the man on the reception desk was smirking at us as we checked in. I certainly didn't appreciate his comedy wink as he emphasised one *single* room. Dylan winked back – that was not the best response. We squeezed into the smallest lift in Italy then found our home for the next couple of nights.

'He thinks we're a couple of queers.' I said trying to un-jam the key from the door.

'I reckon we're going to have to be mate: look at that.' laughed Dylan pointing at our one double-bed.

Wondering whether it would be possible for this investment to be included in the previous tax year Julia obliged Gavin with a few obligatory sighs and unconvincing moans. Despite Gavin's noisy activities and the copious amounts of alcohol she had consumed Julia tried to remember whether her accountant had said the tax year started in April or May. Gavin was making it difficult for her to concentrate, she hated men like this. One day she would try and find out why she kept doing this but for now she would just put up with it. After every time this happened she would resolve not to let it happen again but because it was horrible. She didn't enjoy it, she hated the sort of coke-fuelled yuppies she seemed to attract these days, it was just a bad habit. She noticed he had finished and hoped he wasn't going to stay the night. It seemed a little impolite to ask him if he needed a taxi.

'Oh My God! Oh My God! That really was the most amazing sex wasn't it?' he gasped.

The compliment was nice to hear but she attributed his low pleasure threshold to the coke. He went to the bathroom to clean himself up and asked if she would be offended if he left; his wife would be expecting him.

'Keep in touch.' she said kissing him goodnight knowing that he would not.

'My God Julia, you are so beautiful.' he whispered as he left the room with her still lying on the bed. Being beautiful was neither how she felt nor wanted to feel. His sticky perspiration coated her like a film of dirt and her bed was damp and ugly. She did not want to clean herself up, she took a Gitane from her packet and lit it and looked at the ceiling.

very emotional; she had to pull herself together. Twelve years ago Julia found and rescued Shobna, a little girl in Bangladesh who was starving to death. The little girl was so sick that she had not realized that the rest of her family had already died. Shobna was one of the first children Julia saved from the famines and poverty of Bangladesh was presenting a thank you gift to Julia and her organization. She was no longer a twelve year old girl but a qualified doctor still living in her old village, helping her own community. Julia had been out to Bangladesh to see her a few times before but this was the first time she had come to England. Julia was so proud.

She did not have much time. It was time for a quick shower then an intensive make-up session before dashing out. If she was late then they would just have to wait for her; she couldn't possibly see anyone looking less than perfect.

Hours later Julia was still thinking about how wonderful little Shobna had turned out. The evening's event had also been very profitable, a lot of necessary work could now be done. In bed she was considering the most effective way her organization could invest the five thousand pounds she had secured earlier that evening. Banking offshore in the Isle of Man because of the tax advantage might be sensible. Why should the Tories earn twenty percent of the money? A thousand pounds would go a long way in Bangladesh. Gavin, who appeared to be sweating more than anyone else at the party earlier was now dripping like a freshly caught salmon as he progressed from foreplay to intercourse.

Julia ascribed this to him just having snorted a line of cocaine before joining her in bed. From her experience of the numerous nameless men who ended up in her bed these days, she found that coke made them sweat. She could feel Gavin's heart pounding through his clammy skin as he began thrusting himself in and out of her.

After negotiating the London traffic Julia did not arrive back to her flat until about the same time as we got to Rome. Her flat that had previously seemed so sophisticated was now a vast gleaming white Antarctic expanse. The afternoon sunlight poured in onto Julia trough the huge windows. She drew the curtains. Having been up since dawn and exhausted after the long drive she was tired and thought about catching up on some sleep. Instead she found herself sitting in the dark empty room just crying. She must have been crying for at least an hour. When and more importantly why she started, she didn't know. She felt so stupid but couldn't help it. There was no logical reason; it was ridiculous, it really annoyed her.

When she managed to stop herself she stood in front of one of her many full length mirrors and yelled: 'Stupid bitch' at her reflection. The combination of tears, mascara and eye liner made her reflection look like a watercolour that had been left standing in the rain. For a moment she didn't recognise herself, for a moment she was looking at a stranger. It was a stranger she had seen before, a stranger who was always hiding behind her reflection.

She didn't know why she saw that sad pathetic woman. That woman could not have been more different from who she really was. The first time she saw her was with Lisa in the university library all those years ago. It had frightened her then but now it just confused her. That time-ravaged woman in the mirror then went but Julia could still feel the woman's glassy eyes cold against her skin. Screaming at her she threw a heavy crystal ash tray into the glass. The image shattered and the shards embedded themselves into the soft white carpet. Carefully she stepped backwards so as not to cut her feet.

Lighting up a calming Gitane she scribbled a note for her cleaner to be careful with the broken glass then realised that she had to hurry up. She had arranged a fund-raising event for her charity that evening. Tonight was going to be a very momentous event. It was also going to be

out in the cut glass ash tray as if nothing had happened. This woman was like no one else I'd ever met.

The situation became more surreal when Dylan walked back in from the kitchen smoking a joint. He took a long drag, walked over to his mother and passed it to her. This was not normal so I was glad she offered me some too, I needed something to calm me down.

When we had finished our coffee, Julia said it was time to go. After the joint, I didn't feel like going just yet but she reminded us that we had a plane to catch. She got her keys and hurried us downstairs to her little car. I had never been in a 2CV before and maybe it was the marijuana but the car felt extremely unsteady, it was like being in a boat. I was convinced it would fall over if she turned a corner to fast so clung onto the back of the seat. At least this impending disaster almost took my mind off thinking about Julia's lack of underwear. But not quite, it was impossible to think of anything except Dylan's mother sitting in front of me driving this car through London with nothing on whatsoever beneath that little thin dress.

I couldn't take my eyes off her and placed my hands on the back of her seat ostensibly for stability but really so that I could feel her skin against my fingers when she leaned to the side. I was trying not to look at her face in the mirror; if I can see her eyes can she see me? Will one of those shoulder straps on her dress slip down? Does she know how naughty she is?

We arrived at the airport in plenty of time. Julia stopped to let us out on the double yellow lines directly in front of the terminal entrance. She was just about get out of the car and have a cigarette with us but noticed an angry faced traffic warden approaching so thought she had better not. I didn't care whether she got a parking ticket I wanted to see her standing in the sunlight and the breeze in just that thin little dress again but it was not to be. She wished us both, 'Bon vacance' and sped off. It was stupid but I felt sad after she had gone.

the place but that I went there with my parents. I tried to focus, tried to say something intelligent. 'Fascinating really to think that until a few years ago it was still a Fascist country run by a Franco who was one of Hitler's allies isn't it?'

My comment silenced her; she looked like she had stopped breathing. Had I said something wrong? Instantly her face then changed to reflect such sadness. Within seconds tears were gushing down her cheeks.

'I cry for Spain and I cry for what that man did to all those poor innocent people; poor innocent and forgotten people. Tissue, tissue! Hand me a tissue my Darling.' With one trembling hand over her eyes, she held out her other one for me to but I couldn't see any tissues handy. She began to sob louder and louder bemoaning the fate of the oppressed masses. Real genuine tears of sadness, of compassion and concern were streaming from her eyes. She was incredible! At that very moment Dylan came bouncing in to the room and threw himself down next to me.

'Stop showing off Julia and for fuck's sake cover yourself up.' he said. 'Nick doesn't want to see your wrinkled up old fanny when he's drinking his coffee. Can't you afford knickers these days?'

She stopped crying as quickly as she had started and lowered her legs in mock petulance as if to show it was just a gesture to please her disapproving prudish son.

'I humbly apologise and crave your forgiveness your holiness!' she laughed.

I couldn't believe Dylan had just said that to his mother. I looked at my friend with utter incredulity and then looked at his mother. She had not even reacted. I didn't know what shocked me more: the fact that Dylan spoke to her like that or that his mother just laughed it off. She didn't seem remotely taken aback either by what her son had said or embarrassed that she had been exposing herself to her son's best mate. Julia simply finished her cigarette and stubbed it

she would know I had been looking. I didn't know who would be more embarrassed. Ignored it, I just carried on smoking one of her cigarettes.

'Spain, Granada, the Alhambra, Seville, the Giralda, the Alcazar, Cordova. What vitality! So old and majestic yet so youthful and vibrant! And of course Toledo.' She seemed to be just saying random Spanish words but with such feeling it was like poetry. 'Oh and Madrid; I was there a couple of months ago. Not a city, more a pulsating affirmation of being alive. Everyone should be made to visit Madrid just once in their lives...

Doesn't it make you sick that the Brits go all the way to Spain just sit sweating for hours on end on some vile beach covered in slime turning themselves into pieces of bacon on legs? What fun can that possibly be?'

She enjoyed having me as her audience. I wondered was she like this when she was by herself. She continued extolling the virtues and beauties of Spain with even more fervour waving her arms around like she was dancing Carmen. As much as I didn't want to, I was finding it impossible not to look up her dress. I felt my face growing as red and as hot as if I actually was in one of those Spanish cities she was describing. Any moment now she would realize and it was going to be a horrible situation.

I really honestly didn't want her to be sexy, I liked Dylan's mother but I didn't want the reason I liked her to be because she was sexy. She was funny, enchanting, intriguing and above all, charming. She was so different to anyone else I knew. Dylan's mother was so entertaining to be with and I loved how genuinely passionate about her beliefs she was. These were the reasons I liked her and those reasons should be good enough.

Oblivious to my increasing uneasiness, she asked about the time I went to Spain. I just about managed to say enough words to convey the facts that I couldn't remember the name of

I replied that I hadn't been to Italy. 'The closest I've ever been to Italy was Spain a couple of years ago.'

'Oh Spain! I adore Spain, the land of fire and passion! Flamenco, Flamenco, Fla-men-co! That says it all doesn't it: just the word evokes the all-consuming flames of intense emotions: despair, love and anguish.' She began to click imaginary castanets together over her head.

I wasn't sure whether I was expected to reply: was she asking a question? I simply smiled. She put her coffee down on glass table, it was a little too hot to drink at the moment. She reached into her bag and pulled out a pack of Gitanes. She sensed me eyeing the packet like only a smoker who hasn't had a smoke for hours can. I had never smoked one of those vile French things before but to impress Julia I tried my best to neither cough or be sick. Why was I trying to impress my friend's mother? I knew what I was doing and it was ridiculous.

With passion and eloquence, she began to compare her own nature, her inner spirit with that of Spain. Laughing at her from the kitchen, Dylan shouted in, 'Sorry about my mother, I don't think you'll ever meet anyone as self-obsessed.'

'In my case, self-absorption is completely justified. I have never discovered any other subject quite so worthy of my attention.' she snapped back.

She let out a quiet but satisfied sigh of relief as she pulled her shoes off. She snuggled her knees up to her chin and rubbed her tired feet. I was now desperately not trying to stare but the temptation was too strong. My best friend's mother was a few feet away from me and I could see up her dress. I didn't know what to do, it would be too obvious to avert my eyes and I was not sure that I would actually be able to do that. Obviously I could not say anything because

Dylan was used to his mother's outbursts: 'Don't worry mate,' he said to me, 'she'll calm down in a minute.'

I sat down on one of the massive white sofas. Subconsciously tidying, I picked up Dylan's discarded Kit Kat wrapper and put it surreptitiously into my pocket. Julia had been driving since just before six in the morning to get to London on time, she looked quite tired. Noticing her yawning, Dylan asked her if she would like him to make some coffee. 'Oh my Darling, that would be simply divine!' she exclaimed. 'That drive has drained me – frailty, thy name is woman.'

With the panache of a 1940s film star she flung herself onto the other sofa opposite me. I felt like I was in a film. The sofas, I discovered were much too large to sit on normally so I found myself sitting somewhat inelegantly with my legs sticking horizontally out like a little boy on a really big chair. Dylan's mother however looked like she was posing for the front cover of Vogue. She lay down upon the expanse of white fur and mountainous cushions resting her head on her hand. She asked me if he had been to Rome before. Reclining across the giant cushions she reminded me of one of the ladies of ancient Rome pictured in one of the famous mosaics that we would probably be looking at tomorrow.

I didn't answer straight away, I was distracted by her legs. She was not showing an excessive amount of bare flesh so I don't know why I couldn't help staring. I tried to stop. I told her that I hadn't been there and was really grateful for this and wondered whether the hem of her dress would rise up anymore. She asked if I had ever been to Italy as Dylan handed her a coffee. Taking the cup, I was relieved when she pushed her dress back over her legs. Considering her age, she did have exceptionally nice legs.

out of place. Her voice was not quite as polished as I recalled, she still however spoke like nobody else I knew. She glided up the steps like Audrey Hepburn and kissed her son with exclamations of 'Darling Boy' and apologised for making us wait.

From the outside, the flat looked like any other London flat but inside it was far from ordinary. It was like nothing I had ever seen before except on television. Everything was white, very white and very minimalist, obscure pieces of art and strange objects appeared to be floating mysteriously in the air. Even the air smelled stylish. As apartments go, this was quite breath-taking. Dylan however did not seem at all impressed; for him it was just his mother's London flat. He wandered nonchalantly into the kitchen on the off-chance that there might be something to eat.

He grabbed a Kit Kat and tossed the wrapper onto the sofa. Had this been my mother she would have yelled but his didn't seem to notice. She was ranting to herself about something Mrs Thatcher had just been saying on the radio on her drive down. Speaking about the miners' strike, Thatcher had described the miners as 'the enemy within.'

Julia was furious: 'What gives her the right to say that the vast majority of the population are behind her vindictive little war? I'll tell you what gives her the right: the bloody media. The state controlled mouthpiece of the Conservative party is broadcasting directly into everybody's minds every day polluting their brainwaves with their nasty perverted version of the truth. People are starting to believe it! There's going to be families soon with fathers who won't have been able to find work for years, mothers who can't afford to feed their kids, thrown out of their council houses with no benefits, no hopes and no futures but they'll say, 'Thatcher – oh she's doing great things for us, God bless her.' She's got every bloody newspaper by the balls now – even the Mirror. Bastard woman!'

Naturally she thought about taking Lisa but found that Lisa was running a summer school for exchange students that weekend. As soon as Lisa said that, she remembered that she too had arranged to do something with under-privileged kids in Manchester that weekend so she couldn't go either. Begrudgingly, she called Dylan and asked if he would like a free trip to Rome during the summer break. Dylan and Penny's relationship seemed to consist of a week together, a week where she had left him, another week together followed by a week when he had left her. This cycle had been going on since Christmas and this particular week was a 'I will never even speak to that bitch again' week. Consequently, Dylan's mother she suggested that he should ask me if I would like the other ticket. How could I possibly refuse!

On the morning of the trip Dylan and I met at his mother's flat in London. I had not seen his mother since that first time when she deafened me with Tchaikovsky and was quite looking forward to meeting her again. I was probably looking forward to that a little too much. I got to the flat at the same time as Dylan, his mother had not arrived yet so we waited in the hallway. I had made a bit of an effort with my appearance but Dylan looked like he had just been working on a building site.

'I see you've made the effort.' I commented sarcastically.

'I'll still pull before you though mate.' Dylan laughed.

After a few minutes we heard the unmistakable whine of a Citroën 2CV pulling up outside. Dylan's mother was exactly how I remembered her from the time he met her before. Just as bubbly and as enthusiastic about absolutely everything. This morning she was dressed like she was about to go to a garden party at a country house. Everything about her said subtle sophistication. She was wearing a short red dress which fitted her perfectly; her make-up was exquisite and somehow, even after driving an open-topped car, not a single hair appeared to be

CHAPTER FOUR

July 1984

Nothing much happened to the three of us during the first half of 1984. Dylan was happier than usual because after six months Penny was miraculously still his girlfriend. She was at our house every other night which Keith and I were also happy about this because as the months grew warmer Penny's skits became increasingly shorter. During the summer Keith also became convinced that there was a really high chance that there was going to be a nuclear war. He had read somewhere that one in three people would die as a result of it and wondered which one of us would be the unlucky one. He was wrong about the cause but regarding my future he was correct about the statistics.

The Galleria Nazionale d'Arte Antica in Rome's Palazzo Barberini was a place Julia was as familiar with as she was with the moons of Saturn. However, with her new burgeoning TV career of bringing art to the masses raising her to minor celebrity status she was invited to help with a production Channel Four were making about Italian art. She was flattered and approached this project with her typical evangelistic fervour. She was not surprised in the slightest about how extremely well her contribution was appreciated. As part of the gallery's own thank you, they offered to her and a friend an all expenses weekend break to Rome.

Keith was not joining in. Even after sharing the couple of joints we had just smoked he still thought this was a load of old crap: classic cinema my arse. He just contented himself with just looking at Penny's legs instead. Noticing, she smiled an innocent smile back to him. Keith could take no more of the film or the commentary so dragged me away into the kitchen to help him make us all some fried egg sandwiches.

Keith set about heating up the frying pan that still had some fat in it from a few days ago. With the aroma of Thursday's bacon beginning to fill the dank air of the kitchen, Keith cracked three eggs in to the frying pan which sizzled and spat. When I began to drift back in the front room Keith called me back into the kitchen. He knew I had forgotten that I was watching the film and was just trying to look up Penny's skirt and he objected to me doing this without him. He flicked some hot fat on to the tops of the eggs which bubbled instantly making them white. Before the eggs became too well done, he slipped them on to the slices of bread that I had already placed out.

'Even a couple of seconds too long in the pan can completely ruin the runniness of the yolk.' the great craftsman explained.

Finally I added a dollop of brown sauce onto each egg and placed another piece of bread on top. We took them in and eagerly grabbed them. In unison the four of us all gave our sandwiches a gentle squeeze to burst the yolks. The warm thick yellow liquid, mixed with the brown sauce infused itself thoroughly in to the bread. The taste when we bit through the bread into the warm and spicy egg was possibly the most wonderful thing any of us had ever experienced; we were simple souls.

She came back with us that evening bragging all the way about being the only one who could ice skate. After I had hobbled up the stairs to bed I could hear everyone downstairs enjoying themselves watching television so I stumbled back down. One of Penny's all-time favourite films was on: *Bride of Frankenstein.* Keith had never seen this before and learned that evening that he was glad he hadn't; he couldn't believe this was supposed to be a classic, he thought it was total tripe and voiced his opinion at regular intervals. The only part he laughed at was when the monster met the blind man who taught him: 'drink – good', a phrase that he thought would be useful henceforth in the Union bar.

'You know this isn't about monsters.' Dylan said during a slow bit, 'It's about the unobtainable.' I looked at Penny and remembered the party. He went on, 'The monster represents man, the monster's mate represents what we want but know we can't have. The more we know we can't have it, or realize it doesn't exist we think we can make it.'

Penny added, 'When we do make it, it isn't real and it destroys us. It is a fact that if you want something you can't have you make it yourself and what you've made isn't really what you wanted. You see it's the "being wanted" that you want.'

'What you make isn't real because if it is real then it's not what you wanted.' Dylan added smugly, as if he'd just discovered the meaning of life.

I then felt the need to join in: 'Looking at this from the Bride's point of view; does she really know that she is only what someone wanted, a physical manifestation of someone else's desire? A dream-girl?'

'Yes!' shouted Penny extremely loudly. 'She's just his dream girl. That's exactly why she kills him in the end.'

Now I just had to prove to her how much better I was so jettisoned myself out into the middle of the ice and promptly fell over. Undeterred by this or the ensuing pain I resolved to have another go and fell over again.

‘Do you want a hand?’

I looked up to see who was talking.

‘You look stuck.’ said a girl. 'Do you want a hand?'

‘I wouldn’t mind.’ I answered, not really noticing her. I was just being grateful for being rescued. The girl spun in front of me, gripped my wrists and started moving backwards pulling me behind her. I closed my eyes.

‘Nick, it's me.' she said when we finally reached the barrier.

It was Penny. My best friend's girlfriend had just dragged me across the ice and I hadn't realized. Partly with relief at reaching solid ground but mostly with amazement at seeing her I started to laugh. I couldn’t think of anything to say but I had to say something. Out of nervousness the only thing I could say was that I had fallen over and hurt my leg.

‘Just because I’m a medical student doesn’t mean you can take your trousers off in front of me.’ she laughed.

Since our party, Dylan and Penny had become an item and I think that Dylan might actually have loved her. He thought it particularly amazing to find someone who shared his enthusiasm for old and silent films especially someone who was a girl. She may have been what his mother would have called a shallow rich bitch with the social conscious of Genghis Kahn but she did wear ridiculously short mini-skirts which compensated for all possible failings known to mankind.

People like this didn’t seem to annoy anyone else as much as they annoyed me. The sight of a caftan or a string of beads made me want to scream at them: 'Stop pretending you're someone you're not and stop getting your facts from the Ladybird book of made up identities.' Dylan asked me why I was cringing. When I told him he could not understand why she irritated me so much. He said he was used to all that nonsense with his mother. He'd said it before but I didn't believe him then either: don't be fooled by that exuberant persona she does, it's all an act.

‘Simon’s been to Morocco before,’ the girl continued. ‘He tells me that when you come back you’re like really spiritually renewed, at one with nature. You dig what I mean? Oh man, I can’t wait, it’s just going to be so... far-out.’

Dylan stopped this horror by interrupting her performance with the suggestion of going ice skating instead. None of us had ever done this and the prospect of sliding across a sheet of ice with knives strapped to our feet was not that attractive but it would be different. Generally when Dylan suggested something we all ended up doing it.

Queuing up outside that evening, I was surprised how popular ice skating was. Inside when we saw everyone racing around and not falling over we all wished we had braved the rain and gone to the pub instead. I decided I hated ice skating. I couldn’t do it and even if I could, it was stupid. The P.A. system was playing a typically depressing Smiths song, not especially conducive to boosting my confidence. There was one thing however which lightened my mood. The girl who thought it was 1967 skated straight into the barrier then fell over right in front of me. Looking around I noticed that I was the closest to her. I felt obliged to help her to her feet and tried not to laugh.

‘Coming here was a bloody stupid idea of yours.’ she complained without a trace of peace or love in her voice.

‘As senile as ever.’ answered one of the girls before burning her mouth with her drink. After swearing at the offending coffee she asked ‘We’re planning some sort of piss-up tonight. Do you fancy coming?’

‘Not in this rain.’

‘Don’t be a tart.’ Dylan said, ‘It’s only April showers.’

‘No, it’s pissing down, it’s cold and it’s windy.’

Dylan had to concede this and added: ‘The rain battering the windows looks like a scene from “*The Wind*.” You know that one; made in 1928, one of MGM’s last silents, the last proper film Lillian Gish ever made. She kills her rapist then buries him in the sand? You must have seen it.’

‘Hey, hey, hey!’ butted in one of the girls ignoring him, ‘I haven’t told you guys yet where Simon’s taking me this summer, have I? This is so far-out, you’ll never guess. He’s like... taking me to, like, Morocco, man. Is that like cool or what!’

Any second now I just knew she was going to say ‘groovy’. I braced myself for it - she did. She was one of those irritating people who had decided to pretend it was the sixties. Along with knowing that all Americans are stupid and fat, all French are rude and smell, all Scots are drunk and violent and that all Scandinavians are obsessed with sex, she also knew that every single person in the sixties were long haired hippies waving their arms in the air saying ‘groovy man’ every ten minutes. She used her groovy sixties expressions at every available opportunity to prove just how cool and happening she was. Of course, if she saw the CND symbol she would think it was a pie chart representing the equity dividends of financial investment comparing return with revenue against labour costs in outsourced manufacturing industries.

CHAPTER THREE

April 1984

Watching the rain thrash relentlessly against the massive windows of the sixth floor common room the following Thursday, I waited for Dylan to emerge from his tutorial so we could grab a burger in Bonny's. Sheffield was completely grey today. The rain had drained the colour from the city making everything sodden and limp. These windows usually afforded quite a pleasant view across the city to the Pennines beyond but today all that could be seen was wet greyness.

I found 10p in my pocket. I considered putting it in the vending machine in exchange for a plastic cup of the yet to be identified brown liquid that seemingly could only exist at temperatures in excess of 180°C. I was diverted from this masochistic ritual by seeing Dylan and some others from his course walking in. They didn't notice me pondering at the coffee machine and sat with some other people. I had to go over and join them.

'So how was Dr Morris this morning?' I asked doodling on the steamed up glass.

It was two weeks that changed Julia's life forever and indeed the lives of nearly all of us who came into contact with her. She came back a different person, a lonelier person but one with hope. Hope that there could be something better than the comfortable life she that was starting to think was normal. She loved Steve just the same, he loved her just as much but it was no longer good enough. Nothing was different between them; that was the problem. Everything was the same: her life was the same, Steve was the same, their love for each other was the same, even the Formica was the same.

She had had a brief taste of freedom and wanted more, she wanted to know what came next. Unfortunately for Steve and Julia there wasn't anything next. She knew that Steve was a wonderful father and would do anything for her and the boys but had forgotten that he loved her. Steve had certainly not forgotten this but he had not told her in ages. Julia needed him to be like he used to be; fun, romantic and spontaneous – she could not understand why he could not be the person she wanted him to be anymore.

Nothing was wrong but nothing was right. Everything was just nice; nice and comfortable: Julia knew that this wasn't who she was. Before Paris, she could cope with the compromise but Paris showed her that she didn't need to.

She therefore knew Steve would agree with her in the end so just let him carry on ranting as she finished off smoking and thought about what clothes to wear. When Saturday came, Lisa appeared in her hand painted pink mini and they were gone. It took them hours to get to Dover and when they arrived because they had not booked a crossing, they had to wait until the next day before getting onto a ferry. It felt kind of cool sleeping on the floor in the ferry terminal especially as there was a couple of German students with guitars there too so they hung out with them creating a miniature hippie campsite but sheltered by the terminal building and with proper bathrooms. Neither Lisa or Julia could speak German and the Germans could not speak English however the Germans were really into The Doors and knew a load of English songs fluently so they all had fun although nobody else who was in earshot of them had a peaceful night. After they'd played their guitars out Lisa read aloud, very loud from her copy of Castenata's Don Juan. Julia told her that she was being pretentious.

'You of all the people in the world cannot call anyone pretentious!' laughed Lisa, an observation that Julia had to agree with.

By Sunday lunchtime they had reached their halfway point, Paris. They felt like they had come home. Unlike London, which was always changing, always rushing to become something it wasn't, apart from the ubiquitous Formica, Paris seemed just happy to be the same as it ever was. Paris knew that there was more to life than just increasing its speed, it knew how to have fun.

They had missed the student uprisings by a few months but could still smell a certain buzz in the air. Rome would have to wait. They managed to find some old friends and stayed with them until they realized they were expensive house guests. They ate their food, drank their wine, smoked their dope and borrowed their lives for a couple of weeks.

She could not understand how selfish he was: ‘But Steve, it’s a once in a lifetime trip. I’ve always wanted to climb the coliseum.’

‘Baby, you can’t just leave our sons and go gallivanting across Europe. You’ve got responsibilities Julia. I can’t simply not turn up for work for however long you’re gone. I’m so busy at the moment baby, the whole of the corporation is in the middle of a re-organisation so I need to show the bosses that I’m useful. We’re getting new offices once the new bit of television centre is finished.’

He carried on explaining the reasons why it was impossible; she thought he was starting to sound like his mother. She lit another joint and let him carry on. She was so disappointed with him: where was that groovy, reckless and spontaneous boy she married six years ago?

‘They reckon that half the guys the BBC are taking on to cover the moon landing will be got rid of as soon as that’s over; I need to be seen to be keen. I can’t be seen leaving early to look after kids. I know it’s wrong but there’s a lot of old squares there who think that looking after kids is still a woman’s job.’

‘But Steve, Dylan and Bruce will be at school. You won’t need to take any time off.’

‘Baby, the kids are only five and six – how are they going to get there? Who’ll pick them up and bring them home?’

After meeting Julia just for that first hour at our house in Sheffield that day of the party after the Christmas break I knew that she was the type of person who always gets their own way. People like Julia do not need to force their opinions on people or even need to argue and argue their points over and over again. People like Julia get their way because people simply want to do what she wants, they want to please her. It somehow felt natural for us all to please her. It felt good to do what she wanted.

like her, it's normal; you have to love her. If you don't love the Queen you're not patriotic. Why do we all have to be the same? Why does everything need to look the same? And why is everything covered in Formica? What is the point of Formica? Why is it normal for it to be everything? Formica tables, Formica chairs Formica walls: even the backs of bus seats are covered in the fucking stuff. She looked at her scribbling: she thought ought to try it again without the swearing.

The phone rang on the Formica table. It was her friend Lisa. She loved hearing Lisa's voice, it usually meant fun. Since they first met at Art College in Liverpool she had always loved Lisa; Lisa exuded a joy that was infectious. She overflowed with that innocent nursery freshness that can only exist in good people. Lisa also believed that she looked like Julie Christie but Julia could never see that. With Lisa Julia could pretend she wasn't married, she could pretend she wasn't a mother and that she was just Julia.

Lisa had called with an idea so completely irresponsible and unplanned that it appealed immediately to Julia. Inspired by the film, 'The Italian Job' she had decided she was going to drive her pink mini to Rome. She wanted Julia to go with her. Julia didn't need to think about that; of course, she was going.

About five minutes later she phoned back to check whether Julia had a passport. There didn't seem anything to stop them. She never thought about paying for the ferry, whether she should take any money, how long they would be gone for, where they were going to sleep, what they would do when they got there and they certainly didn't wonder whether anyone would miss them whilst they were away. Julia assumed that their dad would look after the boys but when Steve got back from work at the Ministry of Truth he didn't quite see it her way.

department. She finished her cup of tea and left. It was a very cordial visit. She was under no illusions that the report he was scribbling down during their meeting would be tossed into the waste paper bin even before she had left the building but at least she had made herself known.

When she arrived home Steve was out, he always seemed to be at work these days. She was annoyed, she wanted to go out and celebrate. Instead she thought she could do her new part time job. As one of the 'faces of 1969,' she had recently been asked to write a regular column in the Evening Standard. She lit a joint, put the radio on and contemplated what to write about this week. She knew today's adventure in the American Embassy would be too sensitive for Fleet Street so tried to think of something else. She realised that she was listening to Radio One. The traitor Johnnie Walker was on, she could never forgive him for jumping ship from Radio Caroline to the BBC.

That would do: her thoughts on the evils of Radio One, that it was all part of an insidious government plot to brainwash everyone: The BBC played stuff to make us conform - to quell our rebellion. If they played something enough times to enough people then the people would believe it was what they were supposed to like. Everyone else would think they liked it too and because of crowd mentality the taste of the nation could be controlled. That was the whole point of the charts: just another way to control our minds. We'd be told that some mind numbing happy nonsense sung by some grinning pretty boys this is this week's number one and that you will buy it, you will like it because everybody else has. You will like it because everybody else does. The prime function of the BBC or the Ministry of Truth as it should be known is thought control, suppressing free will in an attempt to preserve their moribund society.

Her article began to take shape: It's the same with television: this is popular, you will like it, you will become fans, you'll never want to miss it. Even people: here is the Queen, you will

made aware of an extraordinarily disturbing incident connected with your policing action in Vietnam earlier today. My husband and I were discussing this beastly business over lunch and unless a satisfactory response is received from Mr Bruce, then his grace may have to withdraw his support for the American overseas intervention.'

Still the American said nothing. His demeanour suggested he was losing patience with the girl but had to be one hundred percent convinced she was an imposter before throwing her out. English eccentrics had fooled him before and he did not want the embarrassment of being named as the official responsible for forcibly ejecting a Duchess from the US Embassy.

'His grace knew Mr Bruce's predecessor, Winthrop Aldrich. He used to play golf with him.' she added because she remembered his unusual name from one of the portraits downstairs. 'Mr Aldrich was ambassador her in the early fifties ma'am. You don't look old enough to have known him, if you'll permit me saying so.'

'Not at all my good fellow. His grace, the Duke is a few years older than me.' She had managed to engage with him, she knew she didn't have to add anything else but she just couldn't rest it. 'He has just enjoyed his seventieth birthday.' The American tried to hide his shock.

'The first Duchess sadly died some months ago leaving him without an heir but we are so absolutely delighted that in just six months' time he will be a father. I do apologise but it is such absolutely thrilling news, I'm afraid I cannot stop telling almost everyone I meet.' The American stopped hiding the revulsion he was feeling.

Whether he was gullible enough to believe this pretence or entertained her simply for her audacity, he did grant her ten minutes in which she fully expressed her outrage at the report in the newspaper and demanded that whoever was in charge of that operation should be brought to trial. She was assured that her concerns would be brought to the attention of the appropriate

indignation and suggested that if her husband, the Duke were here then Mr Bruce would no doubt make the time to see him. After a short time, Julia was escorted to an ante-room on the first floor. She half suspected that she had been rumbled and was shortly going to find herself being handcuffed and taken to one of the CIA's underground dungeons to be tortured. The risk was worth it though, she was having too much fun to stop and run away now, besides which, it was important that she made her point.

She noticed that a door to the main office had been nudged open very slightly. She could see shadows moving inside. She sat down and crossed her long legs for whoever was watching. It did the trick. Within a few moments she was invited in by a junior official of the Public Affairs Section who was either very sceptical about her Aristocratic credentials or just very rude.

'I am not familiar with the Duke of Waterloo. Isn't Waterloo in Belgium Ma'am?' the American said somewhat smugly.

She was surprised at his knowledge of European geography. 'Yes, but there is also a Waterloo in Liverpool of course; part of Crosby. You must be familiar with the song by the Kinks called "Waterloo Sunset"?' she asked. 'It's a gibe at The Beatles because Ray Davies considers that the Liverpool music scene has had its day. He wrote it looking at the Mersey from Waterloo. You know, dirty old river, must you keep flowing. He changed some of the words just before they recorded it to make it a London song, reference to underground stations and such...'

The American neither answered nor showed any expression in his face. What the bloody hell am I going on about! She thought to herself. I'm sounding more like Tony Blackburn that a Duchess...or did I say I was a Baroness. She tried something different. 'My husband knows your superior very well. His grace has always been a supporter of your government's international policies in the House of Lords but I fear he may be unable to continue. We were

apparent reason. A few days after the event at Alexandra Palace the dream seemed dead. Julia came storming into the house, threw her bag across the room and stomped upstairs. Concerned, Steve dashed up after her: 'What's up baby?'

'Bastard Americans!' she screamed pushing The Daily Mirror in front of her husband's face. 'They're killing kids now. Kids no older than Dylan and Bruce. We've got to do something.'

Steve took a moment and then snatched the paper from her in disbelief. 'Evil murderous bastards.' he mouthed, hardly believing what he was reading. His mother sighed in desperation about her son and daughter-in-law's ridiculous attitude.

Within the hour she was in the foyer of the American Embassy in Grosvenor Square. Most anti-war protesters would not even have been allowed near the Embassy never mind allowed inside but Julia was different. She neither spoke like nor when required, dressed like the typical angry hippy. Correctly calculating that the young American soldiers on the door would not be able to refuse entry to someone introducing herself as the Baroness of Waterloo wearing an ostentatiously expensive but also outrageously short mini dress she now waited in an opulent reception chamber. She felt quite the part flouncing around the sculptures and portraits of American presidents smoking a cigarette in her genuine 1930s cigarette holder. A clean cut American boy swamped under a neatly pressed uniform handed her an ash tray. She thanked him. 'A pleasure ma'am.' he barked back.

'The Baroness of Waterloo.' she explained. 'I wish to see David Bruce, the Ambassador to the Court of St James. I am a personal friend.'

Very courteously, she was informed that Mr Bruce was otherwise engaged attending to the situation brewing up in Egypt. Might anyone else be of help, she was asked. She feigned

Nothing of what she said made any sense to Steve's mother; if anything, their conversations served to only to inflame the situations. Nothing she could say to her mother in law would ever be of value. Eventually Julia gave up and decided that in the future not even to try, it was a waste of time. She didn't need to convince people like her that she was a good person, she didn't matter.

In the spring of '67 Julia and Steve were amongst the ten thousand hippies who were at the Fourteen Hour Technicolor Dream at Alexandra Palace. This concert was in aid of the 'International Times,' the newspaper of choice of Steve, Julia and all like-minded spirits. Yoko Ono opened the event at ten in the morning performing her poetry in action although even Steve had no idea what she was doing. In the centre of the hall next to the helter skelter there was a giant igloo giving out banana skin joints. Since most people were so stoned on normal joints, nobody could tell whether smoking a banana had any effect, this was not important, it was all about the experience.

After a whole day of love, art and music, as sun was starting to rise, Steve's heroes, The Pink Floyd came on stage. Rays of the morning sun like bright shining diagonals burst through the giant windows and painted the smoky atmosphere inside the hall with clear sparkling lines. With awe at the beauty and majesty of nature everyone held hands and stood still as Pink Floyd began to play. The world had changed; with so many people believing that this is the way to live, how could it not? How could there possibly be more war? How could there be intolerance, poverty and injustice? Love was all that was needed. Steve and Julia had no doubt that their generation had saved mankind.

In the real world however, love was not all you need. It was ironic that in the middle of the summer of love the horror of Vietnam was happening on the other side of the world for no

Like most people in the late sixties, Steve's mother only ever heard about hippies by reading about them or by seeing programmes on the television about them. Depending on the programme, they were youths who didn't wash, didn't cut their hair who were either childishly naive or joke figures in appalling comedies. Normal 'respectable' people like her who had ordinary lives did not come into contact with hippies. That her son had married one and was now becoming one himself was a living nightmare.

Not only was she was frightened for him, she was frightened for her grandchildren. It was obvious to her that this self-centred little tart couldn't look after them; they could burn to death and she would be too stoned to notice. But Steve's mother was wrong, Julia absolutely adored her sons, she made them happy and they loved her totally. She didn't want her sons to have the same cold austere upbringing that she had had. She saw herself as a very modern mother, as much a friend as a parent. She was determined to allow her sons the freedom to be who they wanted to be. Of course to Steve's mother, Julia had it all wrong; the boys needed guidance, they needed discipline, they needed to have rules. She felt she had to stay around, they needed somebody that they could rely on; they needed someone who could remember to come home and remember to feed them.

Once Steve's mother made up her mind not to get to know her the arguments stopped. It was easier that way. She didn't need to get to know her, she knew she would never understand her. Likewise, Julia didn't understand her mother-in-law and truly had no idea why she didn't like her. Everyone Julia associated with liked her so why didn't her mother-in-law? At the beginning Julia tried to be friends with her, she tried to explain why she believed in love, why she was a good mother and a good wife and even why she wore the clothes she did.

This woman whom Julia thought bore a remarkable resemblance to Mary Whitehouse found it appropriate one day to leave a copy of the Daily Mirror open on the breakfast table. It featured an article written by the evangelist Billy Graham: 'Mini Skirts mean Mini Morals.' The paper was subsequently flung against the wall. This enraged Julia; just because her morals were different to her mother in law's did not mean she didn't have any. She would protect her children with her life, she loved her husband with all her heart but where she felt superior to her mother-in-law was that she knew that the most important things in the whole universe were peace and love.

How dare this so-called Christian leader, this member of the establishment, an establishment that was waging war on innocent Vietnamese civilians accuse her of poor morals. Wasn't peace and love meant to be something to do with their religion? How dare he suggest that she was a less worthy person to her because she wore a short skirt. To Steve's mother, her little temper tantrum at the table again showed how unable to control her emotions this little slut was.

Despite Julia's belief that this was a time of cultural revolution, a time of self-expression and an age of love nothing was further from the truth. For nearly everyone in England, life in 1968 was not much different to how it had been in 1958. England was a country where husbands worked, wives cooked, middle-class houses had privet hedges that were shaped and trimmed every Sunday. In a different part of town, working-class houses had spotlessly clean front steps that were scrubbed every day where wives cooked and husbands worked. Like most people, Steve's mother would have been just as at home in 1958 as in 1968. Everything in her life was normal, the way it should be, the way it had always been. The one thing that did not fit into her world was Julia.

Never one to waste an opportunity, she used that LSD experience to write a novel. It was no surprise to Julia whatsoever that this, her first novel became an enormous success. The thought that she would not be hugely successful never entered her head once – of course not, she was Julia and could do anything. The book was not just popular with the Oz readers and hippies, it was critically acclaimed by the serious literary press too. The only person who was not impressed was Steve's mother.

Steve's mother could not understand how someone like that could possibly have talent to write a best seller. That her son had not just married a girl like that but stayed with her despite what she called her sickening adultery was even more difficult for her to digest. She loathed Julia passionately; she represented everything she hated about the way the world was heading. She hated her because she had turned her son into a spineless little puppy dragged around on a lead who allowed her to do what she wanted with whoever she wanted. The woman did not know what to do; it was like discovering that one and one were no longer two. She had told her son about his wife sleeping around but he said it was fine. He seemed to have no sense of reason.

Julia got off on the wrong foot almost straight away with his mother. It was an annual ritual of the widow to visit her husband's grave once a year on the anniversary of his death. Shortly after Steve and Julia were married, she took Julia with her. As the widow tidied the grave, cleaned the headstone and planted a few discrete bedding plants she chatted to him about what she had been doing, about her plans, about what she was going to have for tea that evening.

Kneeling down had given Julia pins and needles in her legs. Leaping up from the grave Julia began to jump up and down shaking her limbs in an attempt to get the feeling back. The sight of her daughter in law effectively dancing on her dead husband's grave was not especially endearing.

thirty become middle aged overnight. She had already taken on that characterless appearance that she would have for the rest of her life. There was something about the woman's lifeless face that Julia found disturbing. Julia wanted a closer look but in doing so knocked a stack of books over.

'This is a library, a place of learning, have some respect and be quite please.' the woman whispered.

'Haven't we met before?' Julia demanded.

At first she didn't answer. She seemed scared of Julia's aggressive tone and started shuffling her papers around of the desk and pretending to look in her voluminous bag wishing that she hadn't started this uncomfortable confrontation. These types of mousy women had always really irritated Julia, they were wasting the gift of life.

Julia asked again who she was, this time even more forcefully.

'I'm sorry miss,' she finally replied very timidly. 'You know who I am, don't you? Don't you recognize me? I am you in just a few years' time. I what you become after you kill Steve, after you kill Steve and ruin your life.'

The woman cowered and covered her face with her hands as Julia lunged towards her but when Julia got to where she was the woman had vanished. Julia's heart was pounding, she could hardly breathe. Lisa put her arm around her but she pushed her away and ran out of the library and sat on the steps outside to get her breath back. Lisa asked whether she was she having a bad trip but Julia didn't say anything. She was horrified, she couldn't speak.

'At least you've still got your shoes.' Lisa giggled wiggling her toes.

Julia was not listening. All she could hear was the thumping of her heart and the grinding sound of that vision etching itself permanently into her sub-consciousness. It felt like something much more than just a bad trip.

couple of tabs of LSD. Consequently the twinkling lights of the West End theatres began to twinkle more than usual and the red London buses became considerably more red.

The girls called into their favourite Italian Espresso bar where Lisa stared intently at the back of her hand watching the blood cells travelling though her veins. Steve had told Julia that the last time he took acid he saw a cow standing in the toilets; Julia went to the toilet to see if she could see one too. There was nothing remotely bovine in there so she tried the gents; there were none there either. Coming back from the gents she stared at some pictures of Rome, the owner had proudly placed on his walls.

As Lisa became even more completely enthralled with the back of her hand Julia became disappointed with the lack of hallucinogenic effect so took another tab. The photographs on the wall suddenly captured her attention and she found that she could not look away from a photograph of the coliseum. She began to cry because that building was now a ruin. She shouted this devastating fact to Lisa but Lisa wasn't listening, she was busy drinking her espresso. Julia found the view from the top of the coliseum across to the forum quite amazing and incredible that she could see it even though she was well aware that she was in an espresso bar in London.

'I can see from the top of the Coliseum!' she shouted excitedly to Lisa who was then inexplicably giving the café owner her shoes. Julia then led her bare-footed friend across the road into the university library that was just about to close. Inside it was dark, it was completely dark and echoed with emptiness. From behind one the imposing heavy wooden bookcases somebody gestured the girls to hush. Julia looked around to see who it was. Sitting at a reading desk lit by a very dim lamp barely bright enough to see by was a grey haired woman. She was wearing a thick grey suit, the type of clothing worn in the 1950s by sensible middle aged ladies. Everything about her was grey. This was one of those women whom upon reaching the age of

She felt blessed to have someone so perfect for her as Steve as her husband and the world they lived in for the next five years was Utopia. Neither of them could imagine anything better. Neither of them could imagine their never ending party ever ending but it would. As 1968 was coming to an end, they had quite noticed that they were starting, just very slightly to drift apart. Even so, Julia could not have imagined the tragedy that she was about to write for herself. Nobody could imagine that.

But it was still 1968 and for Julia, everything was 'groovy.' Everyone wanted to know Julia and Julia loved that. She was wealthy, she was beautiful and she was living in the most happening place in the world. Whatever she wanted she could have and whatever she wanted to do she did. Her life was an endless party filled with all the pretty young things of the age. With Steve or Lisa or her countless other friends she would go to the Roundhouse, the Marquee, the UFO and the Coliseum where new rock bands seemed to be emerging every day. The music scene became her absolute passion, she could not conceive of life without music, clubs and records. With what became an expert knowledge coupled with absolute confidence and burgeoning minor celebrity status it was not difficult for Julia to convince the music press that she was an experienced music journalist. The reviews and articles she subsequently wrote for the underground press set her on the path to her literary success.

Somehow between being a mother, an almost twenty-four hour a day social life and her part-time career in music journalism she also managed to attend University in London with Lisa. Unlike her old friend, she never managed to complete her course but that didn't matter to her. She didn't want qualifications or to be categorised and put in a box. Julia's last official day at University was as good a reason as any for her and Lisa to celebrate which they did by taking a

wrong. He discovered people with different ideas, different beliefs and values. He realized that he need not simply take on the role expected of him by his family but like these other people he now knew, he could do whatever he wanted. What he wanted was to then do something completely different. He announced one day that he had taken a University scholarship exam and had won a place at Liverpool to study Physics and Electronics.

He was so glad to get away from the East End and away from his mother. Liverpool offered and escape from the obligation of being constantly grateful to her for all the suffering and sacrifices she had made for him. He did appreciate what she had done for him, but he so wished she hadn't. As much as he tried, he couldn't make himself grateful. Steve hated the guilt so had to get away from her and everything she was doing for him but even that made him feel bad.

He resented what she had nearly turned him in to. He hated her prejudices and her dislike of anyone wealthier than herself. He didn't like her friends, her lifestyle and the East End's expectation of how he should think. Despite his mother's best efforts, he refused to become the son she wanted. Nothing was inevitable, he was not going to be forged into his father. Julia was just the person he chose to lead him into his new world.

Just like the way I first saw Dylan all those years later, Julia gave off the impression of being the typical spoilt little rich girl; selfish and pretentious and arrogant with an almost comical superiority complex. Despite outward appearances and what would then have been called, extremely 'permissive behaviour,' Julia considered herself a Christian. She believed in God, in the teachings of Jesus and that he died for her sins. Also, although she was sure that she wasn't always a nice person Julia knew that she was a good person. Those who subsequently made the effort to get to know here quickly realized that she wasn't just a good person but one of the most loving people they would ever know.

lived in was when they would pay to visit them at weekends. Steve's father died during the war just a few months after getting married so Steve never knew him. His mother never re-married; the little boy had it drummed into him that she didn't have time because looking after him was a full-time job. Through Britain's years of austerity and rationing she always made sure that Steve never went to bed hungry or to school without shoes on his feet. Her sacrifice was something she never kept secret.

He was an unusually clever boy and excelled at school especially in art. Like other working-class boys in the late fifties who could not afford to go to University so he went to Art College. These places were a melting pot for the whole of society. Up until that moment in Steve's life, the rigid social order had ensured that he would never come into contact with anyone, at least socially, from another class. Boys like Steve only really met girls like Julia when they were delivering groceries or fixing the plumbing. At art colleges there were people from all backgrounds, from all cultures and classes. There were the gifted working-class rebels, forging out revolutionary chunks of metal to smash the state with and there were young ladies whose parents had sent them there as an alternative to a finishing school in Switzerland.

A few of his contemporaries used to laugh at the posh accents of the posh girls in their posh frocks. A few of the posh girls would in turn laugh at the common boys with ideas above their stations. Nearly all the students however realized what a fabulously unique experience this was in 1957. They were breaking through the class system, they were smashing the system. Although nobody could have been prepared for the human whirlwind that was Julia either in 1984 or back in 1963 Steve's experience at Art College at least gave him helped him a little.

Steve discovered people with ambitions beyond what the East End of London could ever offer. He discovered that his in-bred prejudices against anyone not from his class were all

was involved in she would always be in love with him. He was the ideal husband for Julia; his view on life, his dry sense of humour, his taste in music and his need to have fun were so similar to hers.

He could not have wished for anyone better. She was unlike anyone he had ever met before. She was everything his mother wasn't. He adored her complete disregard for the consequences of anything she ever did. He loved her sublime ignorance of any of the polite social niceties his mother aspired to. His mother said she had obviously been spoilt disgustingly as a child but Steve loved her naive sense of entitlement. He thought it was wonderful the way she never saw the need to say please and how she just assumed that if there was something she liked then she could have it. She didn't care what she did or what she said. If she decided to take a friend's car without asking or even sleep with a friend's boyfriend it was somehow endearing.

Since meeting Steve that evening a couple of years earlier in Liverpool's notorious Magic Clock pub, Julia knew he was special. She knew straight away that she wanted him to be part of her life but she had never planned to marry him. Her parents however had other plans; a daughter of theirs could not be an unmarried mother. Julia and Steve did not have a choice. Fortunately, Julia's parents were not just wealthy, they were exceptionally wealthy. To Steve's complete amazement they were real actual members of the landed gentry. Her parents happened to own a spare house near the centre of London which they gave to their little girl and Steve as a wedding present. Her father also happened to know someone at the BBC with whom he had a quiet word. That resulted in Steve being offered the job at Broadcasting House.

Steve was not used to strings being pulled for him. His background was very different from his new wife. The only time his parents would see houses like those that Julia's parents

Steve's mother was then almost permanently in their house looking after the baby. Teaching her son and daughter-in-law to be proper parents, the way she had been, was a futile struggle. 'Completely bloody useless, the pair of them' was muttered on her lips at least every hour. Steve and Julia could not understand why this woman was constantly so frustrated with them but on the other hand, Steve's mother relished proving how invaluable she was and how this proved that her son should never have married that ridiculous girl. His mother ended up doing almost everything for baby Dylan. Of course she complained about this but what option did she have? She could not trust her son and certainly could not trust that stupid over privileged tart to be able to look after the baby on their own. To Julia, who had a nanny when she was little, this seemed perfectly natural so wasn't going to object - too much.

When summer arrived so did Lisa. The two friends began where they left off in Liverpool six months earlier; it was party time. The smoky clubs and student parties in Liverpool had just been a rehearsal for London, this was the real thing. As the swinging sixties slowly unfolded in London they threw themselves head first into it. Julia, Lisa and Steve knew that they had been born exactly at the right time, this was what they were made for. Although technically Julia was a married mother, when night came, she and Lisa were young, free and single. Steve had no objections whatsoever in Julia's wild abandon of her responsibilities, it was part of her, it was what he loved about her. Julia was an untamed spirit, a wild unpredictable force of nature painting the town red then burning it down.

Steve relished with quiet amusement receiving the looks of pity and outrage from friends and neighbours who had about the latest scandal his wife was mixed up with. They simply didn't understand. Whatever she did just made him realize just how exciting she was. He never had to worry about their marriage because he knew, as did Julia that whatever indiscretion she

able to see Lisa behind her but with the icy cold wind biting into the back of her neck she didn't really want to look around. Quickly turning her face into the wind with her eyes clenched she scanned the scene behind her. All she could see was the cold grey city, even with a covering of snow nothing looked clean, nothing looked bright. Grime and soot encrusted every brick, every stone and most noticeably of all, every pane of glass. The snow just made the grey seem colder.

The few buses that had dared to venture out were chugging through the black sludge climbing the hill heading for the suburbs. There were a few cold grey people scurrying around but none of them was Lisa, she had gone. She was missing her already. She wished she hadn't wasted her last conversation with her going on about one of her stupid dreams but Lisa was used to her doing that.

Cutting through Great Charlotte Street, Julia found herself passing by the imposing Blacklers department store. For a brief respite from the cold she went inside. She had always thought the ladies who worked there with identical beehive hairdos, bizarrely plucked eyebrows and scary eye make-up were a little eerie. Today however they just looked cold, even inside they needed to wear their outdoor coats. The last time she came in here was shortly after Christmas, it was busy then. She remembered the decorations; the grotto and the tree suspended above the central stairway. This enormous cavernous area with its massive art deco lanterns hanging from the ceiling seemed strangely empty now. Despite the slightly yellow toned light that flooded from these giant painted glass chambers everything still looked grey and lifeless. Julia was glad; she didn't want Liverpool to be attractive now, it would be easier to move on if it wasn't. She tossed her bright red scarf over her face and strode on to Lime Street station to meet her parents.

A few weeks later, Julia and Steve were married in a registry office. Steve started his job at the BBC the following day, and a few weeks after that my best friend, Dylan was born.

horrible happens to somewhere spiritual. God Julia, can you imagine how horrible that bombing must have been? Can you imagine being trapped inside there, surrounded by nothing but walls of fire roaring towards you? The May Blitz they called it didn't they.'

'They're a band.' Julia said somewhat flippantly.

'What?'

'May Blitz. It's the name of a band. A bit bad taste if you ask me.'

In 1963 Julia was not the oracle on rock and pop music that she later became. Back then it was Lisa who prided herself on her encyclopaedic knowledge of the music scene so it was annoying for her to have to admit to Julia that she had never heard of May Blitz. She didn't like her friend to know a band that she didn't but asked her to tell her about them anyway.

'Do you know,' said Julia looking perplexed. 'This is really weird but I honestly don't know. I was just going to say that they were a one hit wonder in 1970 but I don't know why. I remember saying to someone that it was really bad taste to name a band after something so unpleasant as that a bombing raid. Must have been a dream because I was someone else but at the same time I was definitely me. I was talking to me but I was…'

'Had you been smoking one of Steve's reefers?'

'No, listen. I was talking to this woman who was with me but she was me too and I wasn't...' she trailed off.

'You shouldn't smoke grass before going to bed love!'

The girls smoked their last cigarettes, they hugged each other and with tears freezing on their cheeks they parted. Julia began to trudge through the sludge encrusted pavements towards the railway station. Passing the faded Victorian grandeur of the Midland pub, she looked inside and saw it was virtually deserted. Sheltering in its doorway she wondered if she would still be

was to disown their children and grand-children and never welcome them back to their own homes again. Julia knew that she was one of the lucky ones. She was getting married to Steve and anyone who offered to be a husband to an unmarried mother of 1963, even one from a family like hers, offered the ultimate great escape from the Mother and Baby Home.

She took a long, thoughtful drag on the cigarette and asked Lisa when she thought she might regain her figure. Lisa thought about some sarcastic reply but today wasn't the time for that. Instead she put her arm around her, 'I'm going to miss you so much.'

Smoking their cigarettes and holding back the tears, the girls stared through the cold grey emptiness along Bold Street towards the old Lyceum club. Spilling from the windows and doorways of the few shops that had bothered to open, harsh electric light peppered the dullness. It mingled with the soot and fumes that always hung in the air these days creating a dirty yellow haze.

'I still can't believe you're going.' Lisa said. 'I can't imagine it here without you: college, going out, the clubs, the shops, everything. Even this church is going to make me think of you now.'

'What, because it's empty, hollow and derelict?' Julia laughed recalling that St Luke's was bombed during the war and left that way as a reminder.

'No, 'cos this is where we had our last ciggy together.'

'I'm not dying you know – I'm only moving to bloody London.' She took a final drag on her cigarette, stubbed it out and changed the subject. 'They say this church is haunted. I'm sure someone told me that sometimes you can hear organ music coming from inside.'

'Yes, I know that, soft-girl!' Lisa said. 'It was me who told you that! People have even seen lights inside and heard singing. They reckon it's what happens when something intensely

The icy wind was freezing her face so much that it hurt Lisa to speak. ‘I’m going to miss you so much.’ she said.

Julia squeezed her friend’s hand through thick woollen gloves. ‘You’ll be moving down in London too in a few months’ time; it’s not too long to wait.’

‘I don’t know how I’m going to manage. It’s going to be horrible.’

Taking off her gloves, Lisa clumsily shook out another couple of cigarettes from the packet, lit them and gave one to her friend. ‘Don’t be so soft. I’m so jealous of you. You look like Brigitte Bardot, marrying lovely Steve, your mum and dad give you more money than I’ve ever seen and to top it all, a house in London. You’re a really lucky bitch.’

‘Oh yeah, and a husband and a baby. What’s the point of living in London if I’ve got a bloody baby to look after?’

‘You know as much as I do that Steve’s mother will be the one looking after the baby. I can’t imagine that woman even giving you a look in. You’re going to have a real fab time.’

‘No, *we’re* going to have a real fab time.’ Julia corrected her.

As much as she protested that she would never be able to go out and enjoy herself ever again, secretly she fully expected that as soon as she had the baby her life would be back to normal. It was far from ideal but it was a million times more preferable than being forced to go into a Mother and Baby Home until the baby was born and then have it secreted away for adoption a few hours after it was born. She knew someone at her college who had become pregnant. No members of her family of course admitted it had happened; gone to stay with her aunt they said. Julia however knew she was now living in a freezing cold bare undecorated room in one of those shabby out of town buildings sharing with five other girls. These unfortunate daughters had disgraced their decent parents so much that the only Christian thing they could do

CHAPTER TWO

January 1963

On the snow covered steps of St Luke's Church on another freezing cold February afternoon two friends sat smoking. Like everybody else who had ventured out today they were wrapped up in the uniform of the winter, long thick black coats. Julia, one of these girls however had a bright red scarf around her neck; it was the only splash of colour in this whole monochrome city. Everything else, even the snow was grey. Everything and everyone else just blended into one uncoloured homogenous mass.

The big freeze, as it was called was determined as ever to deny Liverpool any respite from the blizzards and sub-zero temperatures. People had begun to forget what it was like not to be cold all the time. They had forgotten how roads, alleyways and fields looked before they were all levelled by the colourless and oppressive ice. It felt like a heavy paralysing shroud under which nothing could move and nothing could change had been dropped onto the city. People would say how the constant greyness and the never ending cold drained their energy and sapped their spirit. The vivacity however that sparkled inside both Julia and Lisa had always been too alive to be quenched by anything. Today however for the first time ever, they felt exactly like everyone else.

larger I became positive that I had made a connection with her. Me and Penny had clicked; I just knew it.

'Working class men go home to their houses, their mindless wives and their screaming brats and moan that they are bored! Why don't they change things? Why are they like this? I'll tell you why, because they are stupid. Too stupid to realize that life can be fun if you make it so. It's as though they need to be downtrodden, it's as though they feel that this is how life should be.'

Keith was not going to let her get away with this. He told her that not everyone has the opportunity to improve their lives. She disagreed. 'As Mrs Thatcher has explained, opportunity is there for everyone to take. The trouble is the working class think that it's going to be given to them whereas in reality they have to find it – it's always there you've just got to have the intelligence to recognise it.'

'Fascist.' was the best response Keith could be bothered to come up with.

I felt like speaking. Now was my chance to impress her. 'Wasn't it Confucius who said, be careful what you wish for because it might come true?'

'And what the fuck has that got what to do with what we're talking about?' quizzed Penny putting me in my place which transpired to be several feet under the carpet.

'Well, I mean that if the thing they wish for doesn't happen it will show that they can't actually wish for anything after all which will show how helpless we all are.' I mumbled.

Penny had as much idea why I said that as I did and told me so. Being admonished by a drunk, fascist version of Stevie Nicks was an unusual experience. It didn't matter too much to me that she was telling me that I was an idiot with irrelevant opinions, she was talking to me. My hopes of continuing our conversation however were dashed when Dylan decided that she could now accompany him to his bedroom. The royal couple rose and retired to the bedchamber leaving Keith and me to endure their pretentious friends. As the night drew on and I drunk more

stereotypes from bad sit-coms. They were all either horribly drunk or stoned and although having difficulty even talking one group was trying to discuss the meaning of life. They prattled on about things they knew nothing about trying to sound clever to each other. Although I disliked these people deep down I had to admit that I wanted to be like them. I didn't want to be on the outside, I wanted to be in their crowd talking pretentious crap and looking down my nose as people who hadn't managed to get into University. Of course I would never ever admit this to anyone, especially to myself.

After having drunk far too much I went into the room where Penny was. The alcoholic soaked synapses in my brain reliably informed me that it was possible that if I just sat opposite her she would fling herself at me. By now she and Dylan seemed to have been elevated to king and queen and were sat holding court. Unopposed, she was giving her audience her rather unsympathetic view that apathy was a working-class problem. Becoming quite animated she continued, 'Even Orwell had despaired of any positive or constructive action from the working class which is why he is so scathing of the proles in 1984.'

I wasn't really listening to what she was saying, I was trying to figure out who she reminded me. That was it - Stevie Nicks from Fleetwood Mac. She explained that they chose apathy because it was the easy way. She had met factory workers, she had met manual labourers and they made her sick. 'This real 1984 is going to be worse than Orwell's version. Why are these people so stupid that they spend most of their waking hours doing a job that they hate? These sorts of people live for five o'clock or whatever time they finish work. And what do they do then? Nothing, absolutely nothing.'

I could tell that Dylan wasn't really listening to what she was saying either. She was lovely. Only Keith was getting annoyed but she continued oblivious to his ever rising eyebrows.

'O.K.' I said remembering something I wasn't quite sure was true or not. 'Until the time of William of Orange, carrots used to be purple. To gather support for the new king, the horticulturalists at the time made them orange by selective breeding.'

'How do you breed a carrot?'

How should I know? What the hell was talking about carrots for? But she didn't seem to mind, she was still there. She was still smiling and she had her arm around me. It felt nice. Penny was one of those people who were naturally tactile. She would greet anyone with a hug. I didn't know too many people like that and I certainly wasn't like that myself. I was quite conscious of physical contact so tried my best to act casual about Penny having her arm around me. With inhibitions dulled by far too much alcohol I awkwardly put my arm around her too. To Penny this was nothing but to me it virtually a sexual experience.

I still had my arm around her; she hadn't pushed me away; she was still actually smiling and laughing. I was making her laugh. How brilliant was this! Her face was so close that I could feel her breath on my face. Now was the moment, now was the actual second that I should kiss her. In another second it would be too late. It had to be right now. She was still smiling, her mouth was just inches away, I had to kiss her now.

Why am I not doing anything? Why am I standing next to her like some sort of stupid dummy? I've only got to move my face a few millimetres; I've got to do it now, right now... The moment passed, Penny squeezed my arm and said, 'See you in a bit. Going inside to see who's here.'

I continued smiling, wondering how conspicuous I now looked sitting alone on the grass. I resolved to sit there until the record changed and then slip surreptitiously inside. I didn't really care what everyone else thought anyway, most of them were arseholes, they were student

'Six cans of Guinness.' I answered cautiously, not quite sure if I should know who she was. This girl with golden hair confessed to have drunk two of them and hidden the others on top of the garden shed. I followed her out in to the cool night air of our surprisingly tidy garden. The garden was full of people and bizarrely also full of cigarette smoke which clung solidly to the air. Without saying a word, she effortlessly climbed up on to the snow covered shed roof and handed me the cans.

'Well if you were as pissed as me, it would seem like a logical place to put your drink. See, nicely chilled!' she explained steadying herself by resting her warm hand on my shoulder.

I thanked her and offered her one of the cans back. I was feeling really pleased with myself. For the first time ever, I had met a girl at a party and was now was drinking with her under the stars. She was also definitely the prettiest girl at the party. This is too easy, I thought, something has got to go wrong.

'So, what do I call you then?'

'Penny.'

Something had gone wrong!

Inevitably and annoyingly we both began to relate how funny, kind, generous and caring Dylan was. We could both see Dylan through the doorway, posing, telling jokes and swaggering about but she was still talking to me; maybe she prefers my company?

'So what course are you on?' she asked.

'History.'

'Tell me something interesting about history then.'

not interested in people who did not directly affect her. She was the centre of her own sparkling universe.

It was getting close to party time and after Dylan kissed his mother goodbye she drove off to York. “Sorry about my mother – she’s been at the dressing up box again.”

I told him not to apologise adding that she was quite a character.

‘Yes, I suppose she’s pretty cool.” he conceded. ‘But don’t be fooled by all that carefree bohemian bollocks she does. It’s all a big act - she likes to give the impression that she’s always so bloody happy. I wish she’d just be herself sometimes.’

By the time Dylan’s mother had gone the pieces of the jigsaw had already been spread upon the table. Events had already begun that I was hopeless to do anything about. I was as unaware that I was part of Julia’s plan just as she was aware that she even had a plan but our futures were now inevitably tied together.

###

Just a couple of hours after deafening me with Tchaikovsky, our hi-fi was deafening the neighbours with AC/DC. It was getting smoky in that room so I went for a drink. There should have been some cans left in the fridge but no, it was devoid of anything except an old blue china cup of something so unspeakably nasty that it should never be touched except by trained Hazchem handlers. I think it was something Keith put in there last term because it was too horrible to pour down the sink. The party had only been going a couple of hours and all my drink had gone. I looked accusingly around the kitchen hoping to see one of my cans of Guinness in someone’s thieving hands.

‘Lost something?’ asked a voice from behind.

The Keith we had would look at those who called themselves rockers or had joined rocksoc or any organised clubs with total incredulity: 'Mindless sheep' he would call them. He would usually get his fix of heavy metal from rock pubs like The Wap or Rebels in the town centre. These places were a mecca for students to go and pretend to be real people.

Keith loved his music and I was actually a little jealous that. So many people I knew were obsessed with this band or that band or some singer but I just never could get that bothered. Like everyone else I watched Top of the Pops every Thursday but that was about the limit of my interest. I just could not get enthusiastic about music. Thinking about it, I could never really get enthusiastic about anything. I did however know what music I didn't like. Keith and Dylan and me hated punk. I think the thing I disliked it was that it was anti-establishment. I knew it was considered cool to be anti-establishment but I didn't care. I wanted to be part of the establishment. I wanted to work my way in to that comfortable middle-class lifestyle that both Dylan and Keith came from. Whilst some students were out marching against the system I was thinking to myself how a nice new Barrett semi-detached with a nice neat front lawn and a nice Ford Escort parked on the nice tarmac drive would be.

Dylan was talking to his mother as though he was talking to us about this girl he had met. 'Penny's really different. Cute and lovely, you know the kind? A friend of mine has been shagging her but last night he gave her the push. Crazy sod; she's absolutely gorgeous.'

As I listened to Dylan and his mother chatting away like this I realised that I was smiling at them both. This suddenly gave me an attack of self-consciousness, I looked away. I wondered what this fascinating and rather beautiful woman thought of me. Did she think I was boring? Was she thinking that I was rather a dull companion for her son? I got the feeling that she was

‘As a matter of fact,’ Dylan protested, ‘as Keith very well knows I was talking to a girl who is a friend. Well a friend of a friend or rather an ex-friend of a friend: ex of last night anyway. Poor Penny was so upset she needed a shoulder to cry on and talk to. Poor girl - so sweet. I really know what she’s going through.’

His mother suggested that he was a regular Father Tiresias.

Her comment stopped Dylan’s train of thought. He quoted what sounded like some high-brow poetry and then his mother quoted something back, equally as nebulous. Julia sensed my complete bewilderment. ‘Genesis lyrics in case you’re wondering. *Cinema Show*, from *Selling England by the Pound.* 1973’

‘Father Tiresias by the way was this guy in Greek mythology who became a woman for seven years to find out how women felt.’ added Dylan.

That Dylan liked the same music as his mother seemed strange enough in itself to me but that they were quoting lyrics at each other like a couple of mates in a sixth form common room was just weird. Keith mentioned that even though it was a Genesis album he quite liked ‘*Duke*.’ Julia glared at him like he had just bitten the ears off her cat. ‘That’s not real Genesis, that’s The Phil Collins Band.’

'Phil Collins – wanker.' was Keith's erudite comment on the debate.

Keith made me laugh but just like with Dylan, I certainly would not have gone out of my way to get to know him had he not been put into our house by the accommodation office. Everyone in 1984 knew a Keith: long hair, jeans, denim jacket and a collection of identical black t-shirts. Like all Keiths who were at Universities he was a maths student (although some Keiths, usually bearded ones studied physics). As a rule, Keiths hated being labelled. Although they all looked the same and spoke almost in unison, they weren't just rockers, they were all individuals.

'No, I never got around to it.' I lied. I couldn't think of anything I'd rather less do.

For someone who was quite obviously one of the cool guys, nobody would have guessed that he had an almost obsessive fascination with silent films. Those flickering images seemed to occupy most of his conversations with us and although we tried to ignore him, Keith and I were both sure that we could have gone on Mastermind with all that useless knowledge we had absorbed. We could have answered the most obscure questions about the life and works Irving Thalberg, defined the six key differences between Paramount's photographic style with that of RKO's and probably could name everyone who had slept with Clara Bow or Louise Brooks. We never found out where he used to get these films from but his video collection seemed to increase daily.

Dylan was evangelistic in introducing us to his creaky old films. After initial reluctance, we eventually gave up and simply accepted that we would have to endure them. Neither Keith or myself became fans, we had made up our minds long ago about that, but we both found a certain fascination in watching those young people who were now many years dead still living, laughing and loving. It was a glimpse into another age, the closest thing we had to time travel.

Since I never watched '*Birth of a Nation*' he told me he would find a copy for me later; I changed the subject hoping he would forget. Dylan's mother came back from the shop so we tossed our cigarettes into the snow and followed her back inside.

'So, how was the pub?' Julia asked her son. At the mention of the magic word 'pub' Keith re-appeared.

'Your son's a fast mover.' Keith answered nudging Dylan and laughing.

'Who have you been chatting up now?' she asked knowingly.

'Hi, mate!' exclaimed Dylan with a grin beaming from ear to ear. I could see where he had inherited his ebullient nature from. I told him I'd just met his mother.

'Yes, I've just bumped in to her on her way to the newsagent. What's she still doing here?' Dylan flicked a cigarette out of a packet in a manner just too cool to be unrehearsed and tossed the pack to over me. I tried unsuccessfully to do the same. We smoked in the doorway flicking our ash onto the virginal white snow.

Had it not been for the student accommodation office for putting us together I know that we would never have bothered to get to know each other. If I didn't know him I would have thought of him as a typical posh public school boy, one of those intimidating toffs who look down their noses at normal people like me. When Dylan appeared in *my* house last term as if he owned it I really did not like him. It only took a few days however for me to realize that he was going to be one of my closest friends.

When I was at sixth form I used to think that if I worked more I could be the clever one, if I had a bit more confidence I could be more successful with girls and if I thought a bit harder I could be the one who always had a witty thing to say. When I met Dylan however I realized that he was the naturally clever one, he was the annoyingly good-looking one the girls wanted to be with and he was the one who could always think of a witty comment for every occasion. He was the person I had always wanted to be. I had to admit to myself that I could never be like him so I gradually took on the role of his side-kick instead. Dylan was my idea of a how a real student should be. He was arty, he read poetry, he could always think of something clever and funny to say – he even wore the university scarf.

Shivering in our cold doorway as we finished our cigarettes Dylan asked me if I had watched *'Birth of a Nation'* over Christmas as I apparently told him I would.

“They say that that the Conservatives didn’t win the election; Labour lost it by virtue of their manifesto.”

“Indeed,” she elaborated, “the longest suicide note in politics.’ She emptied the bottle into her glass and continued. ‘I feel so sorry for Michael Foot having to lead our unruly rabble of back-stabbers. He’s too much of a gentleman for all that duplicity, too much of a thinker for Westminster. Poor old sod probably doesn’t even realize that he’s been so cruelly used, thrown on the scrapheap and made to look a laughing stock.’

I asked if she meant by Neil Kinnock.

‘No, of course not by Kinnock.’ she shouted back with surprising anger. In her fury at my answer her wine splattered across the table as she slammed her glass down. I sat frozen as she admonished my ignorance about the internal politics of the Labour Party and voiced her contempt for “the devious bastards of the old guard” whoever they were.

She needed more cigarettes. Getting up to get another packet from her car she tossed her empty glass through the crust of grease into the washing up bowl where last term’s dirty dishes were no doubt festering away in the murky depths of that dark uncharted water. My own mother would have done that washing up as soon as she came into the room and would then have probably have done the vacuuming. This woman was not like a mother.

'Typical, no fucking cigarettes in the car!'

No, she was definitely not like a mother. Without even pausing for breath she announced that she was going to the shop to replenish her stock.

After a few but refreshing minutes of silence I heard footsteps outside. It was either Dylan or his mother returning with her cigarettes. I was relieved that it was be Dylan.

I nodded and smiled, not quite sure who Thor-Heyerdahl was or whether I felt very comfortable with her or very uncomfortable with her. I could not decide whether she was putting on an act but couldn't imagine why she would bother simply for my benefit. Eventually I decided that I did actually feel quite uncomfortable in her presence. Being around her engendered the same sort of uncertainty and fascination of seeing how close to the edge of a cliff one can stand.

Taking her car keys from her handbag, she stared at them for a moment, she rose her game. "You know, I once gave a lift to Lady Diana once."

"You know Princess Diana?"

Her smile suggested that she got my attention. "Well, not really, a friend of a friend but a lovely girl. Such an innocent young thing." Seamlessly she then spoke about getting drunk and stoned at parties, she referred to '*The Young Ones*' wondering if our party would be like theirs. People of her age and background surely shouldn't watch '*The Young Ones*' and they certainly shouldn't like it.

Dylan's mother seemed to circulate with people I had only seen on television but she didn't like politicians or particularly the Tories with as much venom as Keith did. 'God, I can't believe that they were ever children. They're probably the result of some top-secret genetic experiment that went hideously wrong during the war. Can you imagine that bastard Tebbit as a child - the thought makes your blood run cold. How the hell did they get in again?'

'Who?' I asked very politely.

'The sodding Tories. I mean how, honestly Darling?' She felt that it was so obvious that it did not warrant a reply.

imagine living on the streets in this weather? Not just the homeless though it is, it's so sad to be old, so sad to be alone....'

I wanted to tell her about the old man on the bus. I could finally join in with her conversation. I so wanted to be able to talk mellifluously like she was but before I had the chance her face changed again and became more animated. She carried on again oblivious to me.

'Do you know that under Thatcher there are more people homeless than there were in the Great Depression of the thirties? Astonishing isn't it but with the media in her pocket we will never be able to rid ourselves of that evil bitch.' She stopped talking to take a long intense drag on her cigarette, then with her lungs re-fuelled continued. 'How the fuck did she manage to win the election?'

I was shocked. I could not really believe that she was Dylan's mother, whatever she was, she was not a mother. Mothers did not say that. They certainly didn't say it to complete strangers.

I felt I had to say something quickly, 'The Falklands War.' I answered with some uncertainty, still quite taken aback that she had used that word. She took the opportunity of me speaking to finish her cigarette. I had never seen anyone use a cigarette holder before, she certainly was different. It was as though she was from another time, a more elegant era. She changed the subject instantly: 'You said you've come far today?'

'Yes.' I replied, now managing to keep up with her although I knew she wasn't remotely interested in anything I had to say. 'I've been on the road, or rather the train since ten o'clock. It was so hot and it was one of those trains that you can't open the windows. Supposed to be air conditioned but you know, nothing works these days. That's progress for you!'

'Progress is the decay of beauty. Wasn't it Thor-Heyerdahl who said, progress is man's ability to complicate simplicity or something like that?'

I was a history student so did actually know but she didn’t give me an opportunity to show off. She carried on talking, laughing and smoking with increased gusto. I didn’t care that she was ignoring every single thing I was saying. I didn't care that ten minutes ago I was desperate for a cigarette and someone was now chain smoking next to me without even offering me one. I had never met anyone so completely self-absorbed before but so utterly enthralling to listen to. She was absolutely marvellous. She was a dazzling light, impossible to turn away from.

She spoke and I didn’t bother trying to interrupt her, I didn’t think that I wasn’t expected to. The only time I remembered answering her was when she looked at me and said, ‘You look really familiar, we’ve met before have we?’ She didn’t listen to my reply anyway but simply continued talking about something else. Her conversation flitted seamlessly between herself, Dylan, whether it was cruel to keep animals in zoos, that the song *Rule Britannia* was written as a rallying song for Prince Frederick against his father George II, whether the moon is bright enough to read by and what a bad night's sleep she had had.

‘The darkest hour is just before dawn...I adore that Mamas and Papas song don’t you and wasn’t Michelle Philips absolutely gorgeous? Her parents were Greek you know. Oh, and do you like Greek food?’ she continued without punctuation, ‘Dylan asked me to a Darling little taverna a few weeks ago. Food was divine and Dylan being Dylan charmed his way into the shell of our Aphrodite-like waitress. So slick - she gave him her phone number on the bill. I adore Greece, don’t you? And where have you come from - far? Are you sure we’ve never met before? You look so, so familiar.’

She finished off her glass of Champagne then pouring another one, in a less ebullient tone of voice carried on speaking. ‘I noticed quite a few homeless people around here. Can you

I nearly missed my cue to speak; I told her who I was: Nick and that I lived here with her son and with Keith whom she had already met. This allowed her to finish her Champagne, light a cigarette and pour herself another glass. I had just started to relate the story of my totally uneventful train journey up from Oxfordshire this morning when she interrupted me mid-sentence.

'What do you think looks best?' She presented her hands to me, in particular the two different colours of nail varnish she had on each one. 'Does bright volcano red suggest wild exuberance or is it too obvious?' She thrust her other hand towards my face, 'Too subtle? Quite insipid I think. If one's to be wild and raw then what's wrong with vulgarity? Sorry my darling what were you saying?'

I realized that what I had been saying was actually really boring so I was glad of the interruption. It didn't matter anyway because she continued to speak about her own journey that morning. What was it that I found so completely fascinating: her voice, her choice of words, her exuberance or just her other worldlines? I don't know what she looked like but one thing she didn't look like was a mother, she couldn't possibly be old enough to be Dylan's mother. Dylan was my age so surely Dylan's mother should look as old as mine did. My mother looked old enough to be her mother.

She walked back to the stereo, I hoped that she wasn't going to play *1812* again; the neighbours would call the police. She didn't, she simply picked up the record sleeve and started to read it. 'Wish I had this on cassette, I could take it with me in the car to olde Yorvik. Might keep me awake until that gorgeous vista of the Minster greets me. Were these medieval times I'd be searching the horizon for a candle in the window of a bridge house when I get there. You do know what the medieval bridge houses were don't you my darling?'

I did not dare disobey and sensed her creeping up behind me again. There was a loud pop, it was either my eardrums bursting or she had opened a bottle of Champagne. Still too confused to reason properly I continued standing perfectly still in silence as though I was in a bank hold-up.

'Champagne - well sort of.' she said handing me a glass of bubbly. 'The bubbles will burst in your mouth and transport you back from this world to that of the music. Don't speak, just do it! There are certain pieces of music after which you simply have to drink Champagne: a means of perpetuating the energy. You must agree.'

Confirming to myself eventually that yes, this was my home I smiled politely at her in a way that said, '...and you are?'

'I'm Julia: Dylan's mother by the way. I dropped Dylan off an hour or so ago but he disappeared somewhere with what is considered to be a student these days; Keith I think he called him.'

I tried to tell her who I was but Dylan's mother apparently did not need to pause for air and was carrying on speaking. 'Off to York shortly. Oh, how terribly tiresome. Not as if there's anything wrong with York or my friends there, delightful people and such a divine city, yes absolutely divine. No, it's the driving there that's so beastly. It will take me an age but then again getting anywhere in my darling 2CV takes an age these days. It's like me: seen better days. And you are?'

What I initially thought was a wand was actually something equally as bizarre, a long, polished cigarette holder. She noticed me examining it. "An antique, or so the chap who charged me £50 for it told me. One has to maintain a certain air of sophistication." She said, affecting an absurd upper-class accent which didn't actually sound that different to me to her normal voice.

that then. I assumed that it was simply someone's who had come for our party. Having a party on the first day back was a stupidly impossible event to organize but we didn't believe that anything was impossible or rather Dylan didn't believe anything was impossible, he was like that.

Someone had left our front door open. There was music playing, classical music, very loud classical music. Dumping my bag in the hallway I ventured cautiously into our front room. It actually hurt when I walked in. I had timed my entrance just as the deafening sound of cannons exploded from the speakers. Was this what it was like to be shot? It was the finale of Tchaikovsky's *1812* and she had flicked the volume up to full blast exactly at that instant. Without warning she grabbed me by my shoulders and thrust me into the middle of the room. I couldn't see her face but the music was too loud to think about anything else such as, 'who is this woman?'

'Stand exactly here, precisely half way between both speakers.' she demanded at the top of her voice.

I had no idea who this person was and why she was in my house and definitely no idea that my stereo could be that loud. What was happening? I just did what this mysterious voice ordered and stood there waiting for my ears to begin bleeding. Whoever she was, she started dashing around the room conducting the music with what looked like a wand.

She carried on waving her arms dementedly at the speakers. 'Victory! Victory! Victory!' she screamed as the piece reached its climax. 'The Bells! The Bells!' she continued as the music finally came to an end.

'No don't move! Absorb what you have just heard. Let it live inside you a little longer. Allow yourself to float as though angels are lifting you up from the carpet but a fraction of an inch. Don't move. Can you feel yourself floating?'

downwards, it attacked sideways and like guides missiles, it knew how to fly around corners to catch those who thought it safe to hide in doorways or bus shelters.

I had to brave it; with the snow biting into my face I dashed over to the bus station where the number 12 was nearly ready to leave. The bus was full downstairs but that was fine, I preferred it upstairs; I could see where I was going and of course could smoke. With all the vents closed to keep the fresh air out, that damp, smoky mist that only exists on the upper floor of buses in winter shrouded me as I found an empty seat. The windows were steamed up and as was wiping mine with the sleeve of my coat an old man flopped down next to me. His long overcoat was covered in snow which he did not seem to care was splashing over me. Snow on his leathery face was thawing and water dripped from the end of his nose. Little droplets had also formed on the ends of his bushy eyebrows, they looked like Christmas decorations.

Glancing at him I thought his eyes looked devoid of life, there was just watery, empty nothingness. He was even more anonymous than me, just one of the thousands of unnoticed forgotten shadows that used to be somebody once upon a time. He would have fought in the war, possibly even the First World War; could have been a hero, could have been in all the papers, might have really been somebody once. I wondered how people get like this – how they can just give up on being who they are, give up on life? To me it did not really seem that difficult to become like this and it scared me.

Eventually it was my stop, I stood up. Without moving his head, without showing any signs of life he swivelled his knees in to the aisle then took an extra long drag on his cigarette as though he feared I was going to run off with it. Dragging my oversized bag, I jumped off and was back in the cold. Over the road in front of the familiar telephone box was number 163, our house. There was a red Citroën 2CV parked outside; it was hers but I had no way of knowing

Looking back, it is so obvious that she would end that life and yet despite knowing this, if I was given the chance again I know that I would do absolutely anything to be part of that story again.

That moment when I first met Julia was the first day back after the Christmas break, the day before the new term was about to start. Like always, I came back by train and everything seemed completely normal when I got to the station. There were no ominous black crows silhouetted against a blood red sunset, no thunder and lightning, no sinister organ music or chilly winds other than what would be expected at a Yorkshire railway station in January. It was just another normal day.

I was glad to be back home. Where I had just spent Christmas was my parents' home, not mine. I don't know how or when it happened but I didn't feel I belonged there now. Home was Sheffield, this was I belonged. Here were my friends and this was where my house which I shared with two other students called Dylan and Keith was. I was looking forward to seeing them again, especially as tonight we were having a late New Year's party at our house.

Eagerly I rushed through the station's enormous polished glass doors to again become a part of the city, part of my city. It was a busy evening and the road outside the station was bustling with people. The familiar rush hour traffic jams, the cacophony of beeping horns, the drone of the traffic and thousands of people all trying to get home made it loud, hectic and alive. Despite the freezing temperature I could feel the city's warm embrace as I merged into the crowd to become just a faceless part of the background. It was comfortable, it was anonymous.

It had been really cold back in Oxford when I had left that morning but this was authentic Yorkshire coldness. The snow here did not just flutter down gently, here it bludgeoned its way into the streets with purpose and determination. There was no hiding from it; it didn't just dive

CHAPTER ONE

January 1984

Looking back, it is now obvious to me that from that very first moment when I met Julia she would change my life. I don't think it was because I wanted my life to change, I just didn't have a choice. I know it was all because of her, my old and very normal life became something unreal and she made that unreality normal. I don't know how or when it happened but I began to feel like I was trapped on a magical mystery tour not knowing where I was heading but not caring in the slightest. Julia was a writer, she created characters, she invented lives, she gave them hope and love and she gave them despair and death. Julia, I came to realise was writing my life and being part of her story was the most addictive drug in the world. I knew, we all knew, that this story was not going to have a happy ending but none of us could ever think of getting off our personal tumbrels careering past those wonderful, blinding bright lights into the inevitable darkness.

Looking back, I don't think that it was just me who was one of her characters. Everything I knew, everyone I knew including Julia herself had to be part of her story as well. It made no sense to for Julia to be one her own inventions but it perhaps explained who she was.

"THE GIRL WHO CHANGED THE TIME"

A novel by Mark Bowman